USA TODAY bestselling author **Barb Han** lives in north Texas with her very own hero-worthy husband, three beautiful children, a spunky golden retriever/standard poodle mix and too many books in her to-read pile.

In her downtime, she plays video games and spends much of her time on or around a basketball court. She loves interacting with readers and is grateful for their support. You can reach her at barbhan.com

Nicole Helm grew up with her nose in a book and the dream of one day becoming a writer. Luckily, after a few failed career choices, she gets to follow that dream—writing down-to-earth contemporary romance and romantic suspense. From farmers to cowboys, Midwest to *the* West, Nicole writes stories about people finding themselves and finding love in the process. She lives in Missouri with her husband a̶n̶d̶ ̶t̶w̶o̶ sons and dreams of someday own̶i̶n̶

Also by Barb Han

Cornered at Christmas
Ransom at Christmas
Ambushed at Christmas
What She Did
Sudden Setup
Endangered Heiress
Texas Grit
Kidnapped at Christmas
Murder and Mistletoe
Bulletproof Christmas

Also by Nicole Helm

South Dakota Showdown
Covert Complication
Wyoming Cowboy Marine
Wyoming Cowboy Sniper
Wyoming Cowboy Ranger
Wyoming Cowboy Bodyguard
Wyoming Cowboy Justice
Wyoming Cowboy Protection
Wyoming Christmas Ransom
Stone Cold Texas Ranger

Discover more at millsandboon.co.uk

WHAT SHE KNEW

BARB HAN

BACKCOUNTRY ESCAPE

NICOLE HELM

MILLS & BOON

First Published in Great Britain 2020
by Mills & Boon, an imprint of HarperCollins*Publishers*
1 London Bridge Street, London, SE1 9GF

What She Knew © 2020 Barb Han
Backcountry Escape © 2020 Nicole Helm

ISBN: 978-0-263-28030-2

0520

MIX
Paper from
responsible sources
FSC™ C007454

This book is produced from independently certified FSC™ paper to ensure responsible forest management.

For more information visit: www.harpercollins.co.uk/green

Printed and bound in Spain
by CPI, Barcelona

WHAT SHE KNEW

BARB HAN

All my love to Brandon, Jacob and Tori, the three great loves of my life.

To Babe, my hero, for being my greatest love and my place to call home.

Chapter One

Amber Kent didn't normally pick up calls from numbers she didn't recognize on her personal cell. She tapped her toe on the floorboard while waiting for Harvey Baily to finish loading hay bales onto her truck. He'd insisted she stay in the cab in order to keep warm.

The temperature hovered just above forty degrees. The sun was covered by thick gray clouds. She stared at her buzzing phone. The call could be coming from a distant relative. She'd had a few of those since losing her parents a few years ago. It was past the holidays.

Glancing in the rearview mirror, she noticed that Harvey wasn't even close to being done loading. She had a couple of minutes to spare.

"Hello," she said. The silence on the other end had her thinking answering was a bad idea.

"Amber, this is Rylan Anderson..." The familiar voice came through the line clearly. He didn't need to say his name for her to know that voice. It was deeper now, but that unmistakable timbre goose bumped her arms. Talk about a blast from the past. How long had it been? Eight years? Nine?

"I heard you moved back to town, but I thought people were pulling my leg." After nearly a decade of being gone, she was surprised he'd come back to Jacobstown, Texas.

"Yeah, sorry I didn't get in touch." That was an odd thing to say. Had he planned on seeing her at some point?

"It's fine," she said quickly. Too quickly?

"I know it's been a long time but I need a favor." At least he didn't pretend this was a social call. So why did disappointment wrap around her? A little piece of her wished he was calling to see how she was, or if she wanted to meet up for coffee. Hearing from him after all these years was a shock to the system.

"What can I do for you?" she asked, suppressing a small sigh.

She heard something *or someone* in the background. Then again, it could be a TV. She couldn't make out the noise clearly.

"I didn't have anyone else to call who could handle…" His voice trailed off, and that really got her curiosity going. He didn't sound like himself. Although, what did she expect? He'd gone dim on social media after leaving Jacobstown to join the military. Platforms had changed, phone numbers had changed and she didn't keep up with him.

"What is it?" she asked. Curiosity was getting the best of her. What on earth could make him call after all this time?

"It's hard to explain. Can you stop by my house?"

"Um, sure." She didn't have a clue about why. "Are you in some kind of trouble?"

"Yeah. Kind of," he hedged. "I don't know—"

"The bank's closed if you need mon—"

"It's not like that." There was a hint of defensiveness in his voice that she hadn't meant to put there. "You know what? Never mind. This is a mistake."

"Hold on, Rylan—"

It was too late. He'd ended the call.

Amber wasn't letting him get away with that. She called him back.

He picked up on the first ring. The noise in the background confused her. "Where are you? What's going on?"

He issued a sharp sigh.

"Rylan, I can drop by. Don't be a mule," she said.

There was a long pause. "I'd really appreciate it."

He sounded like someone with a migraine coming on, and for a split second she wondered if he needed medical attention.

"You're okay, right? I mean, you're not injured," she said, and she didn't bother hiding the worry in her tone.

"It's not like that." At least she'd ruled out a trip to the ER.

"Text your address and I'll stop by on my way home." She should probably turn and drive in the opposite direction from her brother's former best friend. The trouble was that she'd counted Rylan as a friend once, too. Plus, it was just beyond the holiday season. Rumors that he'd moved back to town were true. And he shouldn't be on his own. How could she refuse his plea for help? The text came through immediately after the call ended. She knew exactly where that was. Mrs. Parker used to live there, and Amber had stopped by many times to drop off a meal before the widow moved away.

Harvey tapped on Amber's truck bed as he closed the tailgate. He waved. His job was done. She rolled down the driver's side window and shouted a thank-you through the howling wind. A chill settled over her, and she realized the temperature had dropped another ten degrees. It was going to be a cold night if the rest of that front moved through town.

Jacobstown was an hour's drive south of Fort Worth. It was considered a bedroom community that had been a safe haven until recent weeks when some twisted individual started mutilating the left hooves of animals. The perp had started with small animals and then worked his way up to heifers. Several had been found on the Kent Ranch, a place she owned with five brothers.

Amber navigated onto Main Street and across town to Mrs. Parker's old house. It was Saturday, and there weren't many vehicles on the roads. She imagined grocery stores were probably busy with everyone anticipating the weather. She tapped her right thumb against the steering wheel. There was something about the tone of Rylan's voice that wasn't sitting right. Her first thought was that she should've asked him to come to the ranch. But she was close enough to stop by his house on her way home from the feed store, and she figured part of the reason he hadn't contacted her yet was because of the blowout he'd had with her brother Will. Eight years was a long time to hold on to a grudge. It wasn't like Will to do that, either.

Whatever had transpired between the two of them was kept quiet, no small feat for a town that seemed to know everyone's business in real time. People weren't nosy. They cared. Ranch families had a long history of looking out for one another.

Fifteen minutes later Amber pulled up in front of Rylan's bungalow-style house and parked. At least the place wasn't on fire. She'd worried his emergency was something like that based on the urgency in his voice, but she also realized he'd be calling the fire department and not her.

Her curiosity had her mind running through half a dozen wild scenarios before she'd arrived. Last she'd heard, Rylan was a Navy SEAL. There probably wasn't much that he couldn't handle on his own. Needing her made even less sense as she rolled over possible problems in her head.

By most accounts Rylan had been in Jacobstown for two weeks already, and she had yet to see him. He'd basically pushed her out of his life before he'd signed up with the military eight years ago. He'd walked away without looking back not long after the one kiss they'd shared, but this wasn't the time to rehash that memory. Besides, he probably didn't even remember it.

Amber hopped out of the truck, took a deep breath and moved to the front door. There were ten-gallon buckets of paint littering the covered porch. Paint chipped off the outside of the building. She stepped over a ladder in order to get to the front door.

Rylan didn't seem to expect any visitors. She knocked, and it felt like it took forever for him to answer. It didn't. She had a case of nerves. She'd tried to shake them off before seeing him again and clearly hadn't.

"Thanks for coming, Amber." Rylan opened the door

for a peek, blocking her view into his home. He looked a little too good in what she could see of his jeans and long-sleeve T-shirt. Her heart performed an inappropriate little flip-flop routine at seeing him again. She didn't want to have those feelings for him, like the childhood crush she'd had. She was an adult now, and there was no room in her life for childish pursuits.

Rylan's dark curls had been clipped off, but that did nothing to take away from his good looks. The military had filled him out even more, and she had to force her eyes away from his chest, which had always been at eye level.

"You're welcome." She tried to look past him and see what he was blocking. "What's going on, Rylan? I don't hear from you in eight or nine—"

"Eight," he interjected.

"Fine, eight years it's been, and now I get an emergency call from you out of the blue? I don't see your house burning down, and you're not letting me inside. I'm a little confused as to why I'm here."

"Damn." He muttered something else under his breath that she couldn't make out. "This is harder than I thought."

"What is it, Rylan? Why did you call me?" Impatience had her tapping the toe of her boot on his concrete porch.

"Did you buy this place?" She hoped Mrs. Parker was okay. She'd moved six months ago to be closer to her daughter in San Antonio.

"I'm in the process," he said, and an emotion she couldn't quite pinpoint darkened his eyes.

"It's good to see you, Amber." He closed the door

a little tighter against his side. He was massive at six foot three inches. He'd always been tall, but now he was filled out, too. It made a huge difference in his size and aided his ability to completely block her view.

Amber planted a balled fist on her hip, ignoring the reaction her body was having at seeing him again. "What's so important that my hay had to wait?"

A baby let out a wail.

"Come on in and see for yourself." He looked at her with the most helpless expression.

"What have you done, Rylan Anderson?" Amber stomped through the doorway and froze. Her jaw must've dropped. Rylan stared at her, but all she could focus on was the baby on the floor, lying on a blanket with couch pillows tucked all around her. "Is this yours?"

"I don't know," he admitted.

"What do you mean by that?" Okay, she understood what he was saying, but it was more like a *seriously? How could this happen? And how could you not know if this is your child?*

"A random person showed up at my door with her." Rylan looked helplessly at the little girl who'd settled back down already. He really did sound lost and confused. His dark eyes had that lost quality, too.

"Where's her mother?" Amber scanned the place. Her blood boiled that a person could drop a baby off and run like that.

"That's a great question." His voice held a mixture of frustration and desperation.

Thankfully, the baby had gone back to sleep.

"How did this happen?" She walked over and stood

near the little pink bundle. She was young, a few months old if Amber had to guess. She'd been around her brothers' children enough to know a little bit about babies.

Looking down at that sleeping angel caused Amber's heart to squeeze. The air thinned, and it became difficult to breathe. She would never be able to look at such a young baby without remembering her loss. She reminded herself that it was a long time ago. And she still couldn't go there, couldn't allow her thoughts to run rogue without the world trying to crash down around her. She refocused on her former friend.

Rylan stood there, looking at a loss for words and staring at her like she had three foreheads.

"Okay, fine. I'm not that naive. I know *how* this happened. I'm just wondering…never mind…you got coffee?" She figured she was going to need some serious caffeine if she was going to think straight. She shook off the cold and shrugged out of her coat, which he immediately took from her and tossed onto the chair near the door.

"I put on a pot." He turned toward the kitchen. "Here, let me—"

"No, thanks. You stay in here in case she wakes up again." Amber didn't want to explain the sudden burst of emotion that made tears well in her eyes. She knew better than to let Rylan see them, or he'd have too many questions. She stalked past him and into the adjacent kitchen.

She opened a couple of cabinets before she found the right cupboard. The coffeemaker was near the sink and easy to spot. There were unpacked boxes stacked against the wall in one corner. "You want a cup?"

"Yes. Please."

Amber wiped her eyes and straightened her back before filling the mugs she'd taken from the cupboard and returning to the living room with two steaming coffees.

"Here you go." She handed one to him and then took a sip of hers, enjoying the burn. She needed to clear a few cobwebs in order to think clearly. She plopped down on the floor, near the baby.

"Come join me, Rylan," she said.

He did.

"You've been in some messes before, Rylan Anderson, but I can't even begin with this one." She took another sip and lowered her voice. "You don't know if you're the father?"

"This is the first time I've set eyes on her," he admitted. "I had no clue that she existed until someone knocked on my door looking panicked, asked me to hold her and then ran. She was crying, and I had no idea what to do. The person said her mother asked him to drop the child off. He also said I'm her father, apologized and was gone before I could stop him."

Amber looked down at the sleeping baby. She had Rylan's dark curls, which didn't exactly mean she belonged to him. She just looked like she *could* be his daughter. The thought of Rylan being a daddy hit her hard in the chest.

"Okay. Here's what we'll do. You can get a DNA test down at the store. I think they're pretty easy to take. If she's yours, we'll take the next legal steps for you to claim her." Her statement didn't get the reaction she was hoping for.

"How accurate can a drugstore test be?" Rylan looked even more lost. "I need to track down her mother, and I can't do that if I don't know who she is."

"How many women have you been with?" Before he could answer, she held up a hand. "Don't answer that. It's not my business."

"This situation is complicated, Amber. But I'm not some jerk who runs around getting women pregnant and then ditching them. I just got out of the military and, yes, there've been a few women, but none who were important, and I'm *always* careful." The indignation in his voice shouldn't make her want to smile. Rylan would be considered hot by pretty much any woman with eyes. He was also smart and funny.

"I'm not trying to judge you unfairly, Rylan. I'm really not." It was a mistake to look into his dark brown eyes while sitting this close.

He looked away and took a sip of coffee. "It doesn't matter. She's here and I have no idea who she is, where she came from, or if she's mine. But I can't help wondering who would track me down and play a twisted prank like this, either."

"Did you say the stranger dropped off a diaper bag?" She was already looking around for one.

The living room had a sofa, chair and boxes. On the opposite wall was a perfectly set up and organized flat screen. There were two-by-two-inch swatches of paint colors taped to the wall that got the most natural light.

"It's over there." He pointed next to the sofa.

"Did you check it for a name?" she asked.

He shook his head.

Amber retrieved it and opened the zipper compartments one by one. She blew out a breath. "I don't see anything."

She held up the bag. A name was embroidered on the front pocket in small letters. *Brooklyn.* She showed it to Rylan. "The bag might've been borrowed, but we can call her Brooklyn for now."

"It's a start," he agreed.

"What about social media? Surely, if you spent time with someone intimately you'd be following them or the other way around." Discussing Rylan's sex life wasn't high on her list of post-holiday musts. Jealousy took another jab at her, so she straightened her shoulders. A man as hot and charming as Rylan had sex with women, probably any women he wanted. It wasn't her place to judge. She'd had sex, too. She figured the only difference was that they were presently talking about *his* sex life.

"I'm not much on that computer stuff," he said, that lost look in his eyes returning. "But, Amber, wouldn't I know if I had a child?"

Chapter Two

Rylan didn't expect seeing Amber again to hit him like a physical blow. It did. All he'd known when he'd made the SOS call was that he was in way over his head and he needed a female perspective. His mind had immediately snapped to Amber. He'd tried to tell himself the reason was that he'd dated most of the women in Jacobstown, which wasn't much once high school was over, and that he figured Amber was safe. He nearly laughed out loud. Amber Kent safe.

The knockout youngest member of the Kent family could not be more fireworks and temptation. She was beautiful as ever. No, check that, she was even more beautiful than before. And that wasn't exactly good for Rylan's heart.

Her nutmeg-colored hair was in one of those thick French braids. A few strands broke free and fell beside her heart-shaped face, framing eyes that could best be described as a warm, light brown. She was the total package, full pink lips and creamy skin. She stood at roughly five foot seven and had legs that went on for days. Her hips were curvier than he remembered, which only made her sexier. He knew better than to let those unproductive thoughts occupy his mind.

As much as he liked looking at a pretty face and a hot body, Amber was so much more. Her intelligence and sense of humor had been the first things he'd noticed about her. Well, after they'd both gotten over those awkward teen years. She'd come through it all so easily. Not him. He'd become angry and headed down a bad path with the wrong people, which had led to him shutting out his best friend. This wasn't the time to dive down that slippery slope of shame and regret.

"I'm drawing a blank on who the mother could be." Embarrassing as it was to admit, he had no clue. He had no excuses, either.

"This baby looks to be few months old. My best guess is around three," she stated.

"How do you know?" He had no clue.

"We've had a baby boom at the ranch." She shot him a look like she just realized he wasn't caught up on her family's life. "Don't ask."

He glanced at her ring finger. Relief he had no right to own washed over him when he saw no gold band. "Didn't plan to."

"Good. The mother would've been pregnant for nine months. So where were you…" She paused looking like she was making a mental calculation and counted on her fingers. "Twelve months ago, give or take?"

Rylan rubbed the scruff on his chin. He looked away from those distracting eyes. "There was a weekend that I don't remember much about. I must've had too much to drink."

"No one drinks so much that they can't remember where they were or who they were with, Rylan," she argued.

He thought back to where he might've been a year ago and drew a blank. "The thing is... I used to drink and that got me into a lot of trouble. I quit. Even when I drank, I never partied so much that I was careless enough to..." He motioned toward the baby.

"Well, that's good to know." She blew out a breath. "She's probably not even yours. This is most likely a mix-up."

Amber pulled out a piece of paper from the diaper bag. "I didn't see this before."

"What is it?"

"A note from someone. The mother?"

Guilt stabbed at Rylan. There was that one time he'd gone to a party and woke up the next day in a motel room, alone. A hazy memory said there was a woman with him that night. Everything was foggy, and it felt more like a dream than reality. He'd felt off for a few days afterward, most likely the effects of alcohol after not drinking anything stronger than a cup of coffee for years.

She skimmed the note. "It's not signed. But it's addressed to you, and the baby's name *is* Brooklyn."

Rylan thought back to that weekend. Was that twelve months ago? It seemed longer than that, which meant he couldn't be the father of the child. What would the odds be of those dates matching up? They had to be slim. "What else?"

Amber held up the piece of paper and shrugged. "That's it. At least we know her name for certain now."

Rylan studied Amber. She had that same lost look from when she first saw the baby.

"I need to call Zach." Rylan referred to the sheriff, who also happened to be Amber's cousin.

"What can he do?" she asked.

"I don't know. Call in Child Protective Services?" There was no conviction in his words. "Find this kid's mother?"

"And what if she is yours? Do you plan to ignore that fact, Rylan, because if you do I won't recognize you anymore." She was all anger and ire. Damn that she was even more beautiful when she was scolding him. He shouldn't find it amusing or cute as hell.

"I would never deny my own child." It was true. Rylan knew firsthand what it was like to have a father who couldn't be bothered with his child. When Rylan was young, his mother had told him that his father had gone camping. He later realized that she was covering for the fact that Rylan's father had walked out on them both. The man didn't look back. He just disappeared one day, leaving Rylan's mother to care for him long before Rylan had any memories of his father.

His mother had worked two, sometimes three jobs to pay the bills. He'd loved her and respected her, but he never knew her. Loralee Anderson was always gone, working, trying to make a living. When she became sick and passed away when Rylan was in high school, he had rebelled. He'd gotten out of control. And then the night he'll never forget happened. Even now, he couldn't go there mentally.

The US Navy had become his family once he decided to get his act together and join. Then, his brothers on his

SEAL team were his only family. And yet he'd never quite been able to erase Jacobstown from his mind.

Now that his time was up in the military, and he'd had no designs on a forever career, Rylan came back to the only place he'd ever known as home. Except nothing was the same anymore. Strange how moving away from the place he grew up made him think it would somehow be frozen in time when he returned. It didn't work that way. Life moved on. People grew up and grew older.

"Are you listening?" Amber interrupted his heavy thoughts. She blinked at him.

"Yes. Sorry. What were you saying again?" He took another sip of coffee to wake up his mind. He'd stayed up too late last night unpacking the kitchen, but at least the place was close to livable now. He planned to move a wall in order to open up the living area to the kitchen. There were other renovations on deck. Once the place was updated, Rylan had planned to decide if it was worth sticking around Jacobstown.

"Where's your laptop?" Amber set her coffee on the table next to the couch.

"Ah, over here." He retrieved it and sat next to her.

She opened it and asked him to log into his social media page. She looked at his story and skimmed all the people—mostly women—who followed him.

He could've sworn she'd blown out a frustrated breath.

"There are a lot of names here, Rylan." She studied the screen.

"Yeah, I know a lot of people thanks to traveling all over the world," he said.

"Thank you for your service," she said, and there was

a hint of admiration in her voice. It made him proud to hear it.

"You're welcome," he said reflexively. He'd heard it dozens of times over the years, but it sounded somehow sweeter coming from Amber. He told himself that he couldn't afford to care about what she really thought of him, even though a little voice in the back of his head called him out on the lie.

"Okay." She refocused on the screen. "Let's get to work on these names."

She pulled up picture after picture, but he didn't remember being with any of the faces. Especially not in the time frame that would be necessary for one of them to be the mother of the child.

"It's no good." He was getting frustrated.

"We'll figure it out," Amber reassured him.

It was easy for her to say. Everything in life came easy to Amber Kent. Beauty? Check. Brains? Check. Great family who loved her? Check. Money? Check.

"Everything can't be fixed by the Kent charm." He nudged her shoulder with his. A surprising amount of electricity pulsed from where they made contact. Well, that was a bad idea. One Rylan had no intention of repeating.

His attraction to Amber came roaring back, but he remembered the promise he'd made to his best friend. Will Kent knew Rylan better than anyone else, and if Will thought Rylan dating Amber was a bad idea, then it was. Period.

Besides, Rylan would never break a promise to his former best friend.

"Ha-ha. Very funny. You know, luck visits those

wearing overalls more often than someone who can't be bothered to get his hands in the dirt," she shot back.

"True." He picked up her hand and showed off her manicured nails.

"Just because I know how to clean up doesn't mean I don't put in the work, Rylan Anderson." Hearing his name roll off her tongue shouldn't sound so good. He should also ignore the electricity bouncing between them. Those were things that had gotten him into trouble before, and he'd touched the hot stove once.

Rylan liked to think that he learned from his mistakes.

The baby stirred. Rylan had never been around kids and he hoped, no prayed, the little thing wouldn't wake before someone from CPS could get here. He had no idea what to do with a baby, and was grateful that Amber had shown up before the little girl woke and started crying again. Her wails had damn near broken his heart before she tuckered herself out and fell asleep.

Rylan had never felt so useless or helpless in his life. He'd practically worn a path in the carpet making circles in the living room as he held her against his chest. It was the only position she seemed remotely soothed in.

"I know you work hard," he conceded. "I also know that you're smarter than me. So, what do I do with this?" He motioned toward the black-haired angel. "Because I'm out of my league here. I surrender."

"Like you said, we can start by calling Zach. You know my cousin will come right over. News will get out, too. News that you're possibly a daddy. News that I was here." She flashed eyes at him, and he realized she was asking if he was prepared for her brother to know she was at his place. "Are you prepared for her to be tied up in the system until the courts figure out paternity?"

He hadn't thought of it that way. He'd been too focused on trying to ensure he wasn't left alone with her for long. He didn't have the first clue how to care for a baby. But Amber made a good point, and it was something he needed to seriously consider.

"No. If she's mine, then I want her with me. I'd also like to figure out who her mother is either way. I mean, having this dropped on my doorstep has rocked my world, and I want to know if this is a babysitting detail or if some person is going to show up in six months with a court order demanding her baby back."

He didn't do the unknown real well, especially with stakes this high.

Chapter Three

Amber's cousin, Zach McWilliams, happened to be nearby when she called to explain Rylan's situation. The sheriff was on his way over. Questions were mounting, and Rylan needed answers. He could hardly imagine that a person could abandon such a sweet child. Even when Brooklyn had cried in his arms earlier she'd done it softly.

There was something delicate and tiny about the little girl that brought out Rylan's protective instincts. She had the roundest cheeks, the thickest head of curly hair and the most angelic features he'd ever seen.

Granted, Rylan hadn't been much on babies before, and had no intention of having one of his own until he had something to offer. That was one of many reasons he hoped this one had a different father. But as far as babies went, he'd be lucky to have one like her.

A soft knock sounded at the door, and Rylan immediately walked over and let Zach in.

"Thanks for coming on such short notice," Rylan said.

"Good to see you again." Zach's wary expression made sense given the circumstances. All Amber had told her cousin was that she needed to speak to him at Rylan's house, and that she'd explain everything when Zach arrived.

His gaze bounced from Amber to the sleeping baby to Rylan. Amber gave her cousin a hug. He eyed the stacks of unpacked boxes.

"I'm still getting settled," Rylan said by way of explanation.

"I heard you were back," Zach said. "Welcome home."

Rylan thanked him. He hadn't been sure of the reception he'd get from anyone connected to the Kent family. But then it wasn't like Will Kent to go spreading rumors.

Amber motioned toward the couch. "Sit down."

"I'm good." Zach stood in an athletic stance like he was preparing himself for just about anything. He looked to Rylan. "What's going on?"

"A guy shows up at my door. He's holding a baby in a carrier and has a diaper bag on his shoulder. I just moved in so I figure he has the wrong address or is looking to visit Mrs. Parker, who used to own this place."

"She moved to San Antonio to be close to her daughter," Zach confirmed. He'd pulled out a notebook and pencil. He looked up from the notes he was scribbling.

"Yeah. The place had been empty and she needed the money. I figured we'd both win if I bought it," Rylan said.

"So, you're planning on sticking around?" Zach asked.

Rylan glanced at Amber before returning his gaze

to Zach. "That's the idea for now. I figure I can always rent the place out if I decide to move to the city."

"People need affordable housing." Zach was nodding. "The guy who showed up. Had you ever seen him before that you can recall?"

"First time," Rylan said. "He shows up and asks if I'm Rylan Anderson. I tell him yes and then his cell goes off. It wakes the baby and she starts crying. He looks flustered, asks me if I can hold the baby carrier while he answers his phone. The minute I take the carrier he drops the diaper bag at my feet, tells me the kid is mine and then bolts."

"Did you chase him?" Zach asked.

"By the time I set the baby down and kicked the bag out of the way, he had too much of a head start. She was crying, sounding pitiful, so I didn't have it in my heart to leave her. I looked up, but by then the guy disappeared in between the neighbors' houses." Rylan was still annoyed that he'd been outplayed.

"What did he look like?" Zach jotted down notes.

"He was around five feet nine inches. He had blond hair and blue eyes. He was young. I'd say in his early twenties. He was slim, looked like a runner. He had thin features," Rylan stated.

"Think you could work with a sketch artist?" Zach asked.

Rylan nodded as the little girl stirred. She immediately started winding up to cry. Again, Rylan felt useless. He looked toward Amber.

"She's probably hungry," Amber said, picking the baby up like it was as natural as a Sunday walk. Bouncing the little girl kept her from wailing. "You two keep talking. I'll figure out how to make her a bottle. Do you have a microwave?"

"Yes," Rylan said. He turned his attention back to Zach as Amber disappeared.

The baby cried louder once in the kitchen, and he figured Amber had her hands full. She probably needed help.

Rylan followed the sound. "What do you want me to do?" He had to do something. He couldn't stand helplessly by and watch Amber do all the work. He wasn't a jerk.

Zach waited with the patience of a Sunday-school teacher in church.

Amber mixed a packet of formula with bottled water that she'd heated. She filled the bottle and secured the lid. The little girl latched on and then settled in Amber's arms. Rylan didn't want to notice how natural Amber looked holding a baby. *His baby?*

"I have no idea if the child is mine. There was one time I was with someone, but I'm not even sure the dates match up," Rylan admitted.

Zach asked a few routine-sounding questions that Rylan didn't know the answers to.

"What happens now, Zach?" Rylan needed to know what was going to happen to the little girl.

"This is where we call in Child Protect—"

"Let's say that wasn't an option," Rylan interrupted. "What then?"

Amber's gaze darted from the little girl in her arms to Rylan and back.

"A case could be made for her to stay with a parent," Zach informed him.

"We haven't established paternity." Rylan had no idea if he was the little girl's father, but no kid deserved to be dropped off and left behind. Being rejected by the two people who were supposed to love a kid the most made for a bad upbringing. Although Rylan was never a bad kid, per se, he'd managed his fair share of trouble over the years, especially in high school. Thinking about restitution for the trouble he'd caused the Willow family was a large part of the reason he'd moved back to town. He owed them and had every intention of making good.

"I'll make that call and see who's available at CPS," Zach said. "Before you tell me you don't have to meet the CPS worker and that you have a comfort level with the child, I'll make that call to see who's available. The other option is to let her stay here."

Rylan looked at the little girl, who seemed content to curl up in Amber's arms. "I'll meet the person you send."

Brooklyn Anderson? He did like how that sounded.

Zach excused himself to make a call. He returned a minute later. "Elise Shelton is on her way."

"What will happen to her?" Rylan motioned toward Brooklyn.

"She'll be placed in a temporary home until her identity can be established via a DNA test and her parents are located," Zach informed him.

Rylan appreciated Zach for not automatically assuming she belonged to him. If she turned out to be his daughter, he would figure out a way to make her feel at home in his house, in *their* home.

"Any chance I can keep her here until this mess is

sorted out?" Rylan didn't have a legal leg to stand on. Maybe there was a loophole? If not, he'd have to rely on Zach's good nature.

The sheriff's eyebrows shot up in surprise. "You would want to do that? Don't get me wrong, it's a noble gesture but babies need a lot of care. Do you know how to make a bottle or change a diaper?"

Rylan shrugged. "I wouldn't sign up for it voluntarily but here she is. Being dropped off here must've been traumatic for her, and the thought of sending her off to someone and changing her environment again doesn't sit right. And here's the thing, what if she *is* my child? Then what? She gets bounced back here right where we started?"

"I see your point." Zach's expression was calm, serious. "What if she's not your child? What if a mother is running away from someone? What if she picked your name off a mailbox and found a random person to tell you this story?"

"That's all the more reason for me to keep her. I can protect her." Rylan was dead serious about that. His military training made him the best qualified to handle a threat, foreign or domestic.

"Do you know how to care for a baby?" Zach asked again. "Don't take this the wrong way, but they're a handful."

Rylan needed to think long and hard about his next move.

"I'LL STICK AROUND and help with the baby until her paternity gets sorted out," Amber volunteered.

Zach's gaze flew to her. She shrugged, trying to dismiss the innuendo that she was offering for another reason, like she was attracted to Rylan.

"You sure that's such a good idea?" Zach asked.

"I'm not going to turn my back on a friend, Zach. Besides, he's never taken care of a baby before as far as I know, and you just pointed out what a handful one could be." Throwing his own words back at him usually worked in disagreements with her cousin. She knew he had her best interests at heart, but she also knew her own mind. "Do you really want this sweet little girl bounced around? And, as Rylan said, there's a chance you'll be bringing her right back here at the end of a couple of days anyway."

Zach stood there, staring at the carpet. She knew she was getting through to him.

"I doubt this will take long to decipher, and then I'll be back at the ranch doing my own thing again," she added for good measure.

"What if the DNA test reveals that Rylan is the father?" Zach was tapping his toe. "What then?"

"He'll have to figure out his next moves when that time comes," Amber admitted. "Until then, I plan to give him a hand."

Rylan would have to hire help. There were a few grandmothers in Jacobstown who had free time on their hands and who wouldn't mind a babysitting job. Amber could think of three off the top of her head, and she'd be happy to supply names. Heck, at least one of them would babysit for free just to have something to do. Granted, individually they couldn't handle Brooklyn all day by themselves, but something could be worked out.

"Your heart's in the right place, Amber. It is," Zach started. "But you have a full plate at the ranch right now."

"I can do some of the work from here. Calves aren't due for another couple of weeks, so that gives me some time," she said. Zach could only give her advice. Amber was old enough to make her own decisions, and she would. He knew it, too, based on the look in his eyes.

"If that's the decision, I'd better track down this little one's parents," he finally said.

"What about a home paternity test? Don't they sell those at the drugstore?" Amber already had her cell phone out, checking out names of tests on the internet. "Do you think those are accurate?"

"Sometimes they are. Sometimes they aren't. This is too important to leave to chance," Zach stated.

"You're right about that." Rylan folded his arms.

"The courts will want me involved to prove paternity," Zach said. "They'll want me to control the chain of evidence. We'll get Dr. Logan out here to take the sample. Let me text Elise and tell her not to come. She probably won't want to get out in this weather anyway."

The fact that Rylan could be a father slammed into Amber. She couldn't see him waking up at three thirty in the morning for feedings or diaper changes until this moment. There was something about the look in his eye that said he would do whatever he needed to in order to care for his child.

Amber's chest squeezed at thinking about the baby's mother showing up and wanting to be a family. It was silly, really. Amber and Rylan had never dated. A relationship with her older brother's friend was completely out of the question, especially considering no one would clue her in as to why they'd stopped talking. And yet an inappropriate stab of jealousy struck anyway.

Did she want another baby? Was that the reason for the strange emotions coursing through her? The one she'd lost with her ex had nearly done her in emotionally. She couldn't even talk about the baby that had been stillborn, the divorce that had followed.

When she really thought about it…no. Amber had too many responsibilities at the ranch and in town.

Thinking about babies struck her as odd. She'd never been the type to sit around and daydream about weddings and kids. She'd never really been certain that having a family of her own was the right decision for her, especially after losing her parents, her baby, and then getting divorced before she turned twenty. She'd seen a few of her brothers find happiness and settle down. Marriage had been good for them.

Amber couldn't fathom trying again. Besides, she had too much to accomplish. And she may never decide to have a family of her own. It would take a special guy in her life to make her want those things again. He would have to be someone incredibly special to make her able to face another pregnancy.

And the funny thing was that she wasn't even ready to begin looking for him.

But, sitting in Rylan's kitchen, holding what could be *his* baby, she couldn't deny a certain pull toward the child.

Then again, those big brown eyes and round cheeks had a way of casting a spell on a person. *Quit being so cute, kiddo.*

Amber refocused on the conversation going on between Zach and Rylan. It involved a doctor and the court and words she never expected to hear in a conversation about Rylan. Fatherhood. Wow. It looked like he was about to grow up if this was real. Looking at his body—a body he'd filled out during his time in the military—it looked like Rylan had already accomplished that on his own.

Her heart stuttered when he caught her gaze. He also busted her staring at his chest. Her cheeks flamed. This was turning out to be a red-letter day.

He walked close to her as Zach made a phone call, presumably to Dr. Logan.

"Thank you for offering to stay, Amber." He started to say more, but she put her hand up to stop him.

"It's nothing." Her heart argued against her offer amounting to nothing. "Don't worry about it."

How long could it take to get answers?

Chapter Four

"I'm sure I would've heard gossip if Amber Kent had had a baby. So, who does this little bean belong to?" Dr. Logan smiled at Brooklyn. She cooed. Wow, Amber thought. Five kids definitely gave him the experience edge. Thankfully, he'd been on his way home from the hospital and didn't mind diverting for a few minutes to lend a hand.

Amber and her family had known Dr. Logan since forever. His green eyes were as warm as ever even though the rest of him was aging. He was graying everywhere else. He was a gentle man, fairly tall at five feet eleven inches but much shorter than Rylan. Dr. Logan kept himself in shape by running.

The times Amber headed into town in the morning she'd see him on a run. He was an honest man who'd been married to the same woman since graduating high school. They'd had five children, and the joke had always been that they needed one more to keep up with the Kents. Mrs. Logan and Amber's mother had been close friends. Amber's heart squeezed. Even though it had been years and she should be used to it by now, she still missed her mother. She missed her father, too, of course. But after losing her child, Amber could have used her mother to help get her through. The recent holidays left her feeling blue without her parents.

"She's not mine. We're trying to figure out if she belongs to Rylan Anderson," Amber said to the doctor with a wink. She'd asked to be the one to answer the door when he knocked.

"I'd heard he was back in town. Didn't realize he brought back a family." Dr. Logan wasn't being judgmental when he said it. He glanced past Amber.

Seeing him made her miss her folks that much more, and between Brooklyn and her brothers' babies maternal feelings stirred inside Amber after shutting them off after losing her baby.

"Zach and Rylan are in the kitchen." She motioned toward the back of the house. She stopped short of walking in the next room. "Rylan had his world shaken up, Dr. Logan. He just learned about this little angel and has no idea if she's his."

"Oh. I see. Zach mentioned there was a question about the little girl. I didn't connect the dots. Forgive an old man." His smile lit up his eyes and made her think about her own pop. He would be close to the same age as Dr. Logan now. Her father's eyes had been hazel, like looking across the sea.

"Thanks for understanding." Amber's eyes started welling up. That was embarrassing. She shoved her feelings aside, wiped a rogue tear and focused on the baby in her arms.

Amber followed Dr. Logan into the kitchen. She'd believed that she'd dealt with her sense of loss with her parents a couple of years ago, but emotion brimmed just under the surface. "Thank you for coming, Dr. Logan," Zach said with an outstretched hand.

He took Zach's offering first and then Rylan's.

"How about you sit right here," Dr. Logan said to Amber, motioning toward the chair next to the kitchen table. "This won't take but a second."

He made goofy faces at Brooklyn. The baby laughed. He played peekaboo, and the little angel's laugh caused an ache in Amber's chest. Doc opened his medical bag and pulled out a swab. He used it to collect a sample from the inside of the little girl's cheek.

Rylan paced circles on the tile floor behind Amber.

She avoided eye contact with her cousin because she could already read the disapproval on his features. He wouldn't want her around Rylan any more than her brother Will would.

Rylan had made a few mistakes, she'd give Will that much. And she knew deep down her brother still cared about his former best friend even though he'd refused to talk about him the first year Rylan was gone. Anyone who mentioned Rylan's name got a dirty stare before Will excused himself and left the room. Something had happened between them, and she couldn't for the life of her figure out what it had been. And she'd tried. She'd quietly asked around, but either no one knew or no one was talking. Knowing her brother, no one knew but Will and Rylan. Will had gone quiet and Rylan signed up for the military.

Will was stubborn. Especially when he thought he was right.

The problem was that she had no idea how her brother felt about Rylan anymore. Her relationships with her siblings had changed after losing their parents. In some ways the loss had brought them all closer. In others it had taken a toll. Everyone had been busy in the last few years changing their lives in order to take over their rightful places at the ranch.

Nothing felt settled. Of course, that could just be Amber. She was the broken one.

Brooklyn cooed once more at Dr. Logan, who could win Dad of the Year based on his exchange with the baby. In fact, Amber figured she could learn a few things from the man.

Again, the thought of Rylan being a dad struck a strange chord. She needed to get a grip. They were old friends and nothing more. He needed help and had been back in town only a week or two. He'd reached out to her as a friend, and she was helping because of their past and because the recent holiday season had her feeling melancholy. That was all. Her body might have an inappropriate reaction to seeing Rylan again, but logically she knew better than to put too much stock into it.

So the military had filled him out and he looked even more gorgeous than before, if that was even possible. That wasn't all. Something was different. They were both eight years older; both had changed.

"One more sample and I'll be on my way," Dr. Logan said, looking toward Rylan.

Amber figured that Rylan would want to know immediately about the results and part of her wanted to know, too. Again, the thought of Rylan being a dad blew her away. He hardly seemed old enough, but he very much was. Several of her brothers were married and had children.

Reality was a hard smack. When had everyone gotten this old?

Okay, granted, being in their twenties and early thirties wasn't exactly *old*. She meant when had everyone matured enough to have families of their own? It felt like only a minute had passed since she'd been running in the fields with one or more of her brothers and some of their neighbors playing Keep Away or Freeze Tag.

And now?

She'd blinked and everything was different.

"Any chance you can share the results with Rylan the minute they come in?" she asked the doctor.

"I think that would be okay as long as the sheriff doesn't have a problem with it," Dr. Logan answered.

All eyes flew to Zach.

"I'm fine with it." The sheriff raked his fingers through his hair. "I'd want to know as soon as possible if this was me. Official word is for the courts."

"Thank you," Amber said, and she could see some measure of relief on Rylan's face. Otherwise, he looked pretty out of his element.

The doctor finished his tests in a matter of minutes. He handed one to Zach and placed one in his carrying case. "I won't have the results until Monday. The lab's closed for the day."

Amber figured it was going to be an uncomfortable night, but they could power through.

"Thank you." Rylan walked Dr. Logan to the front door.

Amber turned to Zach. "There's a diaper bag with a handwritten note in it."

"I'll take it into evidence." Zach excused himself and then returned a minute later with a paper bag.

"It's in there," she said.

Zach was careful to remove the note. "Maybe we'll get lucky with a fingerprint match."

"Mine will be on there. Sorry." Amber wasn't sure she wanted Brooklyn's mother to be in the criminal database. That would mean her mother had committed other crimes, which was not exactly ideal.

Amber's stomach performed that annoying flip-flop routine when Rylan came back into the kitchen.

"I better run. Let me know if Dr. Logan sends word to you, okay?" Zach held tight to the evidence bag that now had a companion.

"We will," Amber answered before Zach let himself out.

Rylan motioned toward the coffee machine on the counter. "You want another cup?"

"Yes, please." Amber didn't want to think about how right it felt to be in this man's kitchen. There was a lot she didn't know about Rylan, like what he'd been doing for the past eight years. "What did you do in the military?"

He rolled massive shoulders. "Not much. I was a diver."

She'd known a Navy SEAL once who used that line. It also meant that he wouldn't tell her much more. She glanced around the room. "You're still getting settled in?"

"Yep." He turned the tables on her when he asked, "What have you been up to for the past eight years?"

"I'm the one asking questions," she shot back.

"Why is that?" He picked up her coffee mug and walked toward the machine.

"You're the one who asked for my help, remember?" She wasn't ready to talk about her past with anyone.

"Is that how this works?"

"It is if you want me to stick around," she said playfully.

"I do. So, I guess you're in charge." He poured a cup and started the second.

"Be honest. How come you and my brother stopped talking?"

Rylan froze for a split second but then recovered quickly and went back to work. "People change."

"What's that supposed to mean?" Amber didn't see how two best friends could become so distanced in two seconds flat. She understood people growing apart or moving in different directions in life, but this had been like stepping in front of a bus.

"It's not important," he said, dismissing the conversation. He turned around with two mugs in his hands. "But she is, and that's my first priority right now." He motioned toward the baby.

He set the mugs down.

Amber bounced the little girl, who cooed. It was satisfying to be able to help with Brooklyn. Maybe Amber wasn't all thumbs at taking care of little ones after all. She was getting enough experience with her brothers recently, that was for sure.

"There's a cold front coming tonight," Rylan said.

"That does tend to happen this time of year." Christmas was a few weeks ago. It had always been Amber's favorite holiday. Except for the past few years. Since losing her parents, she hadn't found her footing. Being with her brothers and their families had been the best part about it. Amber couldn't help but notice the absence of her parents even more this time of year.

"All I have is what's in that diaper bag." He took a sip of coffee. "She'll freeze in what she's wearing."

"Don't be dramatic, Rylan. She'll be fine. You'll wrap her in extra blankets," she said.

"And what if she kicks them off? I'm a whirlwind sleeper. What if she's the same?" His look of concern was endearing. Her stomach performed another somersault routine. "Let's worry about getting some lunch first. Then we can think about sleeping arrangements later."

Rylan didn't speak for a few minutes. He looked tired and concerned.

"However this turns out will be okay, Rylan. You know that, right?" she asked.

"No, it won't."

RYLAN DIDN'T HAVE the first idea how to be a dad. He was probably going to damage the child beyond repair *if* she turned out to be his. Part of him was still holding out hope that there'd been some mistake. It wasn't Brooklyn's fault. The kid was adorable. He was the problem.

Besides, a mother would have to be desperate to leave her child with someone she hadn't seen in a year who'd never met the child. To make matters worse, he didn't even remember the child's mother. What kind of jerk did that make him?

"Tell me what you're thinking, Rylan." Amber's voice—a voice he'd thought about more than he should admit while he was overseas—cut through his heavy thoughts. Telling his best friend that he'd kissed his little sister before shipping off had been a disaster, especially after the mistakes Rylan had made. He didn't blame Will for not trusting him. Rylan hadn't deserved his friend's confidence.

Even so, Will's reaction had set Rylan off. Will had blown up. Rylan had gotten offended. He'd been so hotheaded back then. Ready to fight the world and, stupidly, his best friend when his reaction wasn't what Rylan was hoping for.

There was more to it than that. Rylan had been pushing boundaries and heading toward dangerous territory. Will had tried to intervene and talk him down from doing stupid things. What had Rylan's response been to his friend's concern? He'd told him to get a life and had gone off and messed up royally.

"I'm thinking that I'm in a whole mess of trouble." The baby was one thing. Rylan had come back to make amends for his mistakes. Now, his life had just gotten a whole lot more complicated.

"Well, it's no use feeling sorry for yourself," Amber said a bit more emphatically than he liked.

He couldn't help but smile. "That's not what I was doing."

"What do you call it then?" There was a hint of mischief in her eyes, and he didn't want to think it was sexy even though he did.

He missed talking to Amber. With her, conversation wasn't work like with most people. She had a quick wit and sharp sense of humor, but it was her intelligence that drew him in. Seeing her again was supposed to stop him from thinking about her. That, like many of his plans of late, had gone to hell in a handbasket the second he put eyes on the woman.

She was still beautiful. More so now that she had a few curves. She had big eyes, not saucers because that description would be way too plain. And they were the most beautiful shade of brown. Her nutmeg-colored hair fell past her shoulders in that braid. She'd grown it out a little more, and it looked good on her.

"Where do you think her mother could be?" Amber asked. She must've noticed that he'd been staring at her with the way her cheeks flushed.

"That's a great question," he said.

"A woman would have to be awfully desperate to convince a person to drop off an angel like this at a man's house sight unseen." Amber's brow shot up. "Why'd you really come back to Jacobstown?"

Rylan shrugged. He wasn't ready to talk about the real reasons, and there were many. He settled on, "It's where I'm from."

"I figured you'd end up in the city," she admitted.

"Fort Worth? Nah."

"No, I was thinking someplace farther than Fort Worth. Austin, maybe. San Antonio. I didn't think you'd come back here," she said.

"Austin's nice. I have work here, though," he said. What he meant to say was that he had work to do. He had retribution to pay, and would never be able to get on with life as a man if he didn't right a wrong. He didn't want to go into the details until he figured out how to go about it.

There was another reason why he'd come back to Jacobstown. He had nowhere else to go.

"You came back for a job?" she asked.

"Something like that," he said. "Why all the questions? Don't you think I should be here?"

"I never said that," she said quickly. "I'm just surprised. I figured you put this town behind you and didn't want to look back."

"I served in the military. I didn't sign up to live on Mars." A big part of him didn't want to look back at Jacobstown; facing this town again was harder than he expected. But he could never move forward until he made amends for the past. The Willow family deserved that and more.

"Why not?" she asked with a smirk.

"Mars doesn't have a Jacobstown," he quipped.

"You always said you couldn't wait to leave this town, to get out and make your mark on the world." She took a sip of coffee, which wasn't an easy feat with a baby in her lap. She managed to balance both without letting Brooklyn grab the cup.

"I was fifteen years old the last time I said that. What did I know?" He stood and walked over to the window. The wind had picked up, and he could see the oak tree in his backyard sway.

"Your head was filled with ideas about what you were going to do when you turned eighteen," she continued. She fell quiet for a few minutes, bouncing and playing with the baby on her lap. "Did you find what you were looking for out there?"

Rylan didn't answer.

Instead, he took another sip of coffee and contemplated the storm.

"It's going to get a lot worse out there. You okay with being here if it really comes down?"

Amber looked up at him and locked on to his gaze.

"A storm never stopped me, Rylan."

Chapter Five

"It's important to get the exact brand of formula or she can get an upset stomach. Think you can find everything on the list all right by yourself?" Amber asked Rylan after giving him a few items to purchase from the store for an overnight with the baby.

"Yes." The one word answer gave more of a hint that he was so far out of his element he didn't know where to begin.

Amber couldn't help but smile. Her heart pounded her ribs as she thought about spending the night alone with the former SEAL. She could admit to having had a childhood crush on her older brother's former best friend. Speaking of which, she still had a lot of questions about what had happened between the two of them. Based on the earlier conversation with Rylan, she wasn't going to get easy answers.

"What's so funny?" He stood at the front door, searching his pockets for his keys.

"Not a thing." Amber shouldn't break what little confidence he seemed to have when it came to the baby. "But when was the last time you went shopping?"

"Yesterday," he shot back.

"Your keys are on the kitchen table, by the way." She couldn't help herself from smiling again.

Frustration came off Rylan in waves. He made eye contact, which did a whole bunch of things to Amber's stomach. Unwelcome things at that.

"Thanks." He stalked into the next room, and she heard his keys jingle a moment later. "You sure you'll be okay alone with her?"

"Yes." The fact that he was worried about the little bean caused Amber's heart to squeeze. There was something incredibly sexy about a strong and outwardly tough man's vulnerability when it came to protecting a baby.

Amber reminded herself that Brooklyn had a mother out there who could walk through that door any second. The woman had obviously tracked Rylan down. She held the cards until the paternity test came back. Again, the thought of Rylan being a dad hit hard.

"Where's the list I gave you?" she asked an uncharacteristically frazzled-looking Rylan.

He glanced around and checked his pockets again. This time, he came up with a crumpled piece of paper.

"I should come with you," she said.

"No child seat in my Jeep. Remember?" For a split second she saw the relief in his eyes. It shouldn't amuse her.

"Fine. I'll take her for a walk instead. She could use some fresh air." Amber stood.

"You sure it's not too cold outside?" His concern was evident in his wrinkled brow.

"Get out of here, Rylan. We'll be fine. I'll wrap her in a blanket if I have to." She shooed him out the door and followed him onto the porch. "Call if you get stuck on something, you hear? I'll have my phone with me at all times."

He nodded and then hopped off the porch.

Amber glanced around at the land, land that was as much part of her soul as the ranch her family owned. Texas was everything to her.

Rylan stopped before climbing inside his Jeep. He looked like he wanted to say something. It took a few seconds as he seemed to be searching for the words. "I owe you one for this big time, Amber."

"Go on, Rylan," she urged. Figuring out a way to keep an emotional distance was difficult when he stood there staring at her. Her stomach decided to flip like a gymnast again, and she took a deep breath in order to calm it down. She needed to collect her thoughts and keep control of her mental game.

He smiled one of those devastating Rylan smiles before backing out of the drive.

There was a serious chill in the air. Amber decided on that blanket. She walked inside and moved into the master bedroom, ignoring the sensual shivers racing across her skin at being in Rylan's personal space.

"Where's a blanket that won't swallow you whole?" she said to the baby.

Brooklyn smiled up at Amber.

"You sure are a cutie," Amber soothed, pleased that the little girl seemed to be happy. Amber was good with her nieces and nephews, but she'd had practice with them. This baby was little, and she couldn't hold this bean without thinking of her nieces and nephews as well as the one she'd lost.

More of those adorable dimples showed. Amber wiped a rogue tear and refocused. She couldn't go there mentally with the one she'd lost. It still hurt too damn much even though it had happened years ago.

The only blanket Amber could find was on the bed. She didn't want to wrap Brooklyn in the one he used for sleep. She moved to the bathroom and opened the cupboard, looking for a good-size, thick towel. She noted the size of the bathroom was perfect for one person.

In fact, the two-bedroom house was made for a single person. The space was in disarray, which was not Rylan's fault, but it was no place for an infant. There were unpacked boxes in the bedroom, too. It looked like one of the walls had been marked for demolition. Old wallpaper hung from walls in the bathroom and bedroom. This place was a construction nightmare. Also, the carpet seemed as old as the house. It had probably been a nice color of beige at one point. Now it was stained and had ripples so big from wear a person could trip over them. There was no way a baby could safely crawl around on this germy floor.

"How long did he say he'd lived here?" Amber said to Brooklyn because the little one seemed to like the sound of Amber's voice.

She located a towel in the hall cupboard, held it to her nose and sniffed it.

"Clean," she announced to the baby. "Are you ready to go outside for a walk?"

Brooklyn stuffed her fist in her mouth. Drool dripped from her chin.

"Are you an early teether?" Amber hadn't seen any teeth so far, but that didn't mean one wasn't trying to

peek out of her gums. Three months old was early to
be getting her first tooth, but it wasn't unheard of. Six
months was the general rule of thumb, but with her
nieces and nephews Amber had learned that while there
were general guidelines, when it came down to it every
child was unique.

Without her nieces and nephews, Amber would be
lost right now. She'd never been the babysitting type
until her oldest brother Mitch and his wife, Andrea, had
had twins. Rea and Aaron were the first Kent babies and
kicked off a baby boom at the ranch that Amber wanted
no part of personally. She loved every bit of being an
aunt. But babies of her own after what had happened?
Amber didn't see herself going down that path again.

Besides, she'd always been the outdoorsy type and
loved working long hours on the ranch. A fact she
blamed on having five brothers. She was also the youngest, which probably should've made her spoiled rotten,
but she had too much of her father's hard-working at-
titude for that nonsense. She'd never been one for inside chores. The only kind of cooking she was good at
was for holidays or daily survival. The only remotely
motherly thing she ever did was cook at Christmas, and
that was because her mother had insisted. Lydia Kent
had been revolutionary for her generation. She hadn't
seen cooking as women's work, and Amber couldn't
agree more. Mother had made a point of having all
of her children pitch in for holiday meals. Everyone
had grumbled about it growing up. And now, Amber
couldn't be more grateful.

Because of her mother's ideals and stubbornness in
the face of opposition, Amber and her brothers had

been continuing the tradition of Crown Pork Roast with Cranberry Pecan Stuffing as a main course along with Make-Ahead Yeast Rolls and desserts like Apple-Bourbon Pie and Orange Bundt Cake. They baked molasses crunch cookies, staying up too late in the week leading up to Christmas after daily chores were done.

The smiles on everyone's faces once they quit grumbling about helping and started rolling up their sleeves and working easily made up for the lost sleep. Their mother would turn up the radio that was locked on to the station that played nonstop Christmas carols. She practically danced around the kitchen. She used to joke that Dad got the children most of the year after the age of five but Christmas belonged to her.

She'd blocked out holiday memories in the years after losing her mother. Her father, a devoted husband, had joined his wife a few short years after her death.

Amber's mother was the bright light, the warmth, that everyone had migrated toward.

Brooklyn stirred in Amber's arms, and she ignored the pang in her chest as she stared at the little girl happily sucking on her fist. Amber put on her coat and then wrapped the baby in the towel like a burrito. She gathered Brooklyn in her arms and headed outside for some fresh air, reminding herself that she always got a little melancholy after the holidays.

Rylan lived in town in a neighborhood with quarter- to half-acre lots. It was nice to walk around the area. Make no mistake, she loved living on the ranch but this was pleasant, too. It seemed like a change of pace, and she could see how a kid might enjoy having neighbors close by. Amber had grown up with brothers and around ranch hands. Her only respite was her cousin Amy, who was also Amber's best friend.

Speaking of which, she owed Amy a phone call. She had been the one to warn Amber that Rylan had come back to Jacobstown. Amber had been caught off guard that her cousin had felt the need to approach the subject with caution. When Amber had cornered Amy about it, she'd acted like it was no big deal. But her cousin always had a reason for her actions. She was probably warning of the fireworks to come between Rylan and Will.

She'd traveled two blocks from Rylan's house before she snapped out of her mental walk down memory lane. There was a school playground at the end of the street, so she picked up the pace.

"You'll probably like going to the playground, right?" Amber was keenly aware that she was enjoying a conversation with a little one who had no ability to talk back. She was trying to distract herself from thinking about Rylan too much. He was never far from her thoughts.

The playground could use some updating, Amber thought as she climbed the four metal stairs to the smallest slide. She held on to a rail as she positioned herself at the top and then slid down. Brooklyn laughed. The park consisted of a slide, three swings and a seesaw. The wood chips needed replacing, she thought as she made her way to the swings. She made a mental note to tour other parks and see if she could form a neighborhood beautification committee. Everyone in the community would benefit from updated playground equipment, and there'd been great strides making the features safer in the last five years. A committee could evaluate parks across Jacobstown, identify the ones in the most need of new equipment and start from there.

Amber also needed to call home and let everyone know she wouldn't be back tonight. She had a load of hay in the bed of her truck that needed to be taken home at some point. Their bulk order was delayed and this would be enough to get them by until it's delivered.

"You like the swing, don't you?" Amber asked, pleased with herself for being able to make the little girl happy. Besides, she needed to keep her mind busy because her thoughts kept wandering to Rylan, and that was as productive as milking a boar. Get close enough to one of those and she'd end up hurt, too.

She half expected to hear from Rylan at some point. That he hadn't called so far was probably good news, but also worried her. Was he *that* lost? Or *that* embarrassed to ask for help? Her brothers wouldn't stop for help unless the car was on fire.

"You ready to go again?" she asked Brooklyn, and Amber's heart melted a little more when the little girl with the big eyes smiled up at her.

If the slide was popular, the swing was like Christmas morning to Brooklyn. Amber held on to the little angel while swinging so long her arms felt like they might fall off.

"Okay, little miss. We better head home." She figured the baby would be hungry soon.

It was chilly outside so they'd had the entire park to themselves, which was good given the size. There were enough houses nearby to warrant further digging into an expansion.

Amber held Brooklyn to her chest and marveled at

the warmth from the little bundle. As she turned the corner toward Rylan's house, the hairs on the back of her neck pricked. She had a strange feeling that someone was watching her, but it was probably just her imagination. Her nerves were on edge.

Amber glanced behind her and quickened her pace. She heard a car in the distance. It was otherwise a quiet Saturday afternoon. She surveyed the sidewalk across the street, looking for movement. There were tall pines and mesquite trees lining the street. It was windy, and the temperature felt like it was dropping with every forward step she took.

Something or someone moved down the street. The person was too far away to get a good look. Amber quickened her stride, needing to get to Rylan's house as soon as possible. It felt like fire ants crept across her skin. She'd feel more comfortable behind a locked door at this point. Unfortunately, that meant moving toward the person—and she was certain the object was a him now—who'd ducked behind a tree.

Amber hugged Brooklyn tighter to her chest. The baby didn't seem to mind. She happily cooed and blew raspberries on her fist, unaware of the possible danger.

Another twenty feet and Amber would have the baby inside.

This probably wasn't the time to think about the fact that she'd left Rylan's door unlocked. Of course, she didn't have a key.

The figure moved. It was tall and broad, so her initial guess was right. He had to be male.

Brooklyn stirred and let out a sad little cry. Amber's heart battered her ribs as she soothed the baby.

She hoped that Zach could get a hit from the description Rylan gave of the man who'd dropped Brooklyn off and ran.

Who did that? Granted, people could be desperate for money. She'd been blessed to grow up in a house where she never wanted for anything. But this was a life, a child. Who could be so cold as to drop a baby and run?

Amber couldn't get inside the house fast enough. She'd lost visual contact with the male, and her nerves were pulled taut. Rylan's house was close. So, Amber broke into a run. Brooklyn fussed louder as she was bounced up and down so Amber slowed her pace to a fast walk.

"It's okay," Amber soothed.

She cut across the front lawn, praying the man was gone. She wasn't exactly fast with a baby in her arms, and Brooklyn was most likely picking up on Amber's stress. She'd read somewhere that babies could do that. They could absorb emotions and react. She willed herself to be calm and soothing.

It was too early to be relieved, but making it onto the porch felt like a win. Noise from behind startled her. She spun around to investigate.

Her back thudded against the door when she saw him. He was too close. There was no way she could get inside before he got to her.

The tall male wore a hoodie, scarf and jeans. Sunglasses shielded his eyes. Amber couldn't make out the details of his face.

"Fire," she screamed at the top of her lungs. She'd been taught by her law enforcement cousin never to yell for help in a situation such as this. He'd taught her that people reacted to hearing the news of a fire. It might be self-preservation instinct and them wanting to make sure their property wasn't about to burn, but she didn't care.

Brooklyn went into full-on crying mode, and Amber could only pray someone heard her own screams over the sound of the baby.

The male sneered at her as he closed the gap between them, his mouth and nose were the only things visible. As he neared, she smelled tobacco and figured the scent would be burned into her nostrils for the rest of her life.

"Fire," she shouted again, but feared the neighbors were too far away to hear. It was cold enough for windows and doors to be closed, and the wind howled. She had to think of something. She had to assume the man was there to take Brooklyn, and no way was she letting him walk away with the innocent child without a fight.

Running would do no good. Amber wouldn't get far while holding a baby. Besides, this guy had to have run behind the houses in order to sneak up on her like that, and he didn't seem winded. He was tall, maybe six feet, with a runner's build.

When the male was close enough to reach for the baby, Amber started memorizing details of what little she could see of his face. His skin was light, pale. His eyebrows red. He had a small mole on the left side of his nose.

"I don't have anything for you," she shouted with more authority than she owned. "Step away."

His gloved hands were reaching for the baby. No doubt he'd be stronger than her. Amber had seconds to make her move.

She let him get close, so close she could smell his awful breath. In one quick motion, she stepped into him and brought her right knee up hard into his groin. She ducked out of his grasp as he winced and coughed.

She'd barely bought a few seconds. Making a run for her truck was her best option. She'd left the keys under the mat on the driver's side and maybe could make it inside without him catching up by some miracle. Driving with a baby in her arms was not ideal.

Brooklyn was screaming at the top of her lungs as Amber hopped off the porch. She made it all of two steps when his hands gripped her arms. She struggled against his grasp, but it was like being locked in a vise-like grip.

All she could think to do was to drop down, but he stopped her. He was strong. Too strong. Brooklyn was fussing and fidgeting. It was all Amber could do to hang on to the little girl.

In the next second, Amber was being spun around and the baby pulled from her arms. She couldn't let this happen. She couldn't let this man get away with Brooklyn. And she couldn't stop him, either.

He ripped the crying baby from her arms.

It dawned on Amber that he would have the same problem she did. Trying to run with a baby was next to impossible. So, Amber grabbed onto his neck. She didn't want to risk hurting the baby, but if she let this criminal take off with Brooklyn, the child's life could be over before it got started. What kind of a person tried to steal a baby?

Amber fisted his metal frame sunglasses as she was

dragged forward a few steps. She crushed them against his face.

He ground out a few curses before giving a shake that was so hard she lost her grip. She kept repeating the word *fire* at the top of her lungs, praying someone would hear her.

Amber clawed at his right arm until she was able to get in front of him. She grabbed Brooklyn and before he could rip the baby out of her arms again, she heard the sounds of an approaching vehicle coming. She risked a glance and saw a Jeep.

The assailant must've seen it, too, because he sprinted in the opposite direction.

Amber held Brooklyn to her chest as she checked the little girl for any signs of being hurt. Tears streamed down Amber's face at the thought of what had just happened, what *could've* happened.

The Jeep came roaring up and came to an abrupt stop. In the next second, Rylan was out the driver's door and giving chase to the attacker, who'd disappeared behind the neighbor's house.

Amber wasted no time locating the keys. She wouldn't give that jerk an escape route if he doubled back.

Heart pounding, she darted toward the house and locked them both inside.

Hands shaking, she managed to calm the baby by rocking her.

Stomach lurching, she conceded to being rattled as she sat down and balanced the baby in her lap so she could call Zach.

Chapter Six

Rylan lost track of the hooded male two blocks east of the park down the street from his house. The guy was a good sprinter, and Rylan figured that he had a vehicle tucked away over there on the ready. He must've planned for the run scenario, which meant there was premeditation on his part. Any thought this could have been a spur of the moment decision, however minuscule, died.

Frustration was a gut punch. The only reason the jerk got away in the first place was because Rylan had hesitated at the get-go, wondering if he should stick with Amber and the baby in order to protect them.

The decision to run was predicated on two things. Trying to find out who that little girl was and who she belonged to. Both of those might still be a mystery, but someone seemed determined to take her from Amber.

Blood ran hot in Rylan's veins. The kid didn't need to belong to Rylan for him to want to make sure she wasn't put in harm's way.

Was this the reason the girl's mother had found him? More questions surfaced as he broke into a run back to his place. Was he even the father? Or had a desperate woman sought him out for his ability to keep her baby safe? Had this been the move of a woman who had no choices left?

Rylan of all people couldn't judge another person for those actions. He'd been in his fair share of circumstances that had caused him to act out of character. Hell, he'd taken and run with a lie and tangled his best friend in it, too. That had cost him—he'd lost someone who he'd considered to be the brother he'd never had. Will Kent wasn't a liar, but he'd lied to keep Rylan out of jail. Rylan had been young and stupid. He'd made too many mistakes thinking he wasn't worth anything. Not even his best friend could convince him otherwise.

Rylan had a stubborn streak a mile long. And just to prove his friend wrong, Rylan started drinking and hanging around with the wrong crowd in nearby Collinsville. He'd done things to be ashamed of. Yeah, he could play the abandoned kid card all day long. Down deep, he'd known better. The military had helped him get his anger out. He'd gone in looking for a fight and found one. He'd hoped that he'd come out a better man for it.

If that baby turned out to be his child, he wouldn't shy away from the responsibility. He did need to find the kid's mother and learn what the drop-and-run routine had been all about.

"Rylan, what happened? I was scared half to death. Get in here." Amber's eyes were wide as she stood in the open doorway, the baby fussing in her arms.

"I lost him." He stepped inside, chest heaving, allowing her to usher him in.

"At least he didn't get her." Amber closed and locked

the door behind him. "Zach's on his way. I called him immediately. He should be here any minute."

For the moment Rylan needed to catch his breath.

"He was wearing sunglasses, and I couldn't get a good look at his eyes. He wore a hoodie and scarf, too. His skin was pale, and his eyebrows were red. And he had a small mole on the left side of his nose." Stress lines creased her forehead. "I smashed his sunglasses into his face to stop him from running away. Maybe there's a piece out there. It might give Zach some DNA to work with. I'm pretty sure I scratched his face up, so he'd be easily identifiable if he showed up in public. Plus, there should be some of his DNA under my fingernails."

"That was smart thinking, Amber." He should have known she'd be savvy enough to leave a trail for Zach. Facial marks would be difficult to hide in a public place. If this person was part of the Jacobstown community, he wouldn't be able to walk around freely until his face healed. All law enforcement would be on the lookout.

"What about prints? It looked like you two were struggling for the baby," he said.

"Zach won't have any luck there. The guy wore gloves." She shook her head for emphasis.

"You know what?" Rylan paced. Nothing inside him wanted to say these next words. "After you give Zach your statement, I want you to go home. Brooklyn and I will make it through the night okay. We'll figure it out."

The thought of being alone with a baby for an entire night sent an icy chill up his back. He had no knowledge of babies and no particular skills with them, either. Hell, he hadn't been around any until this little one.

"Absolutely not, Rylan."

"Look. I have more supplies in the Jeep. I'll get those and take over with her." He could be stubborn when he needed to be, and this situation called for it. Putting Amber in danger was never meant to be part of this deal. Now that he realized his mistake he needed to fix it ASAP.

"Don't go out there yet," she warned. "And I'm not leaving you alone with her. Do you even know how to change her diaper?"

"How hard can it be?" he asked.

She harrumphed and her jaw set, like when she was determined about something.

"Don't go digging your heels in the sand, Amber," he warned. "When I called for help earlier, I had no idea what I was committing you to. If anything happened to you it would be my…"

The look of understanding that overtook her features stopped him dead in his tracks.

"You called me because you knew I could help. How could you have known there'd be an attempted kidnapping?" She stared at him. "I'm not leaving you stranded when you need a friend, Rylan. I'm not built that way, so it won't do any good to argue. Besides, she's taken to me and I won't abandon her until we know who this angel's mother is and why she saw fit to drop her on your doorstep. Now that that's settled—"

A knock at the door interrupted her speech.

"That's probably Zach. I got this." Rylan knew Amber well enough to know when he'd lost an argument. It might've been years, but that same stubborn streak he'd noticed when they were teens seemed to have grown.

Zach stood on the porch. Rylan opened the door and invited him inside.

"Is the baby okay?" Zach asked before crossing the threshold.

"Yes."

"And how about Amber?" Zach didn't miss a beat.

"She is."

"Make sure she stays that way." Zach's tone issued a warning.

"Hold on there, Zach." Rylan put his hand on the sheriff's shoulder. "I just spent the past five minutes trying to convince her to leave. If you think I brought her into this knowing it could turn into a cluster—"

"Don't put words in my mouth, Rylan." The welcome home tone was gone from Zach's voice now. The man's words had hit hard.

"I didn't." Rylan heard the defensiveness in his own tone—defensiveness because the conversation he needed to have with her brother Will was on Rylan's mind.

AMBER DESCRIBED THE ATTACKER the best she could as she recounted her story to Zach. Her cousin nodded and scribbled down a few notes while she spoke. She could almost see his wheels turning, and he did a heck of a job not freaking out that she'd been part of the attack.

Rylan had already warned her about sticking around. After spending a little time with Brooklyn, Amber was hooked. She couldn't step aside while that little girl's future was so uncertain. Besides, Kents weren't made to walk away from danger. Kents stuck together and Kents stuck around. Her brothers and cousin hated to admit it during times like these, but she was no different from them. Not one would turn a blind eye to someone in need or in danger. Granted, she was the baby of the family and that fact had her siblings trying to play protector from time to time. Lucky for her, she'd grown up with five brothers to ensure she could handle herself in almost any situation.

Case in point, the attempted abduction had been stressful and her nerves were still shaky, but she'd managed to ward off the attack. Brooklyn was safe because Amber had been there.

"I broke his sunglasses, and I'm hoping something is left of them in the front yard." Before she could finish, Zach was on his way to the door. His back was turned so she couldn't see the look of panic she knew would be there at the admission.

The baby had had a bottle, which seemed to be enough to keep her satisfied. She was back to sucking on her fist. So, Amber hopped up, settled Brooklyn in her arms and followed.

The sun was starting its descent. This time of year, that meant it was a little after five o'clock. The yard was visible as they searched.

"This is where it happened." She pointed to the spot, and thinking about what had happened gave her a chill. So much could've gone wrong. Brooklyn could be in the hands of that man, who couldn't want her for good reasons. An honest man with good intentions would've knocked on the door and explained the situation calmly.

Only someone with something to hide would try to rip a child out of a stranger's arms.

She knew to stay back and let Zach do his job. Trampling all over his crime scene wouldn't help. Rylan seemed to realize it, too. He stayed with her, and she could see the anger on his face. She figured the anger was for what had almost happened to Brooklyn even though a little piece of her wanted the anger to be for her, too.

It was a silly notion and one best left alone.

Amber tucked that idea away with all the other up-to-no-good thoughts racing in her head whenever he was near. He'd always had that effect on her. Well, not always. She'd thought him to be pretty darn annoying in middle school. High school had turned around her feelings toward him. But then his mother had died and he'd gone inside himself. He shut out all his old friends, and rumor had it that he'd gotten involved with a bad crowd in Collinsville.

She'd kept busy with the ranch and with school over the years. And then her mother had gotten sick. She and her brothers became orphans when her dad died a few years later. Granted, they'd been adults when that had happened. But none of them had truly ever gotten over losing their parents. Did anyone ever?

Coming from a tight-knit family had made them feel the losses that much more. And then everyone had scattered like buckshot in order to handle family business. She'd always known their family had each other's backs; that was a given. But no one ever talked about losing their parents or how that had changed everything. How that had changed the family's dynamic.

"Got something." Zach put on a pair of rubber gloves and retrieved a paper bag from his SUV. He returned to the spot he'd zeroed in on, careful as he stepped so as not to trample on evidence, and then squatted. Metal glinted in the sunlight as he picked up what looked like a piece of sunglass frame. He held it up toward the sun like he was examining a prize. "Between this and the DNA under your fingernails, we might have the break we need."

Amber had been around law enforcement long enough to realize this was too early to expect good news and that the evidence would have to be sent to a crime lab. Getting results could take weeks if not months depending on how busy the lab was.

After examining the area, Zach motioned for them to go inside. He was a few steps behind them because he put the evidence bag into his locked SUV for safe-keeping.

Zach spun around on her the minute the door was closed. His gaze flew to Rylan. "Do you mind giving us a minute to talk?"

Rylan locked gazes with Amber like he was checking to make sure that's what she wanted before he complied.

She nodded.

"I'll be in the kitchen if anyone needs me." Rylan winked and she smiled as he left the room.

"I don't like you being anywhere near this case." Zach cornered Amber. She sidestepped him and moved to the couch.

The minute she turned on him, ready to put up an argument, he brought his hand up to stop her.

"I do realize that I have no authority in which to

make that request, and I also know that you aren't the type to be told what to do under any circumstances. But hear me out because I'm only saying this because I care about you."

"Fine. What do you want to say to me, Zach?"

His gaze moved from her to the baby and back. "She hasn't left your side since the last time I was here, has she?"

"Nope." Amber had no plans to abandon this little angel, either. She also had no plans to defend herself or try to convince him this was different.

Before she could respond, Zach blew out a sharp breath.

"I figured that would be the case." He sounded resigned to that end.

"So, what's next?" There was no use going down the road of him trying to talk her out of staying.

"I'm not finished," he said.

"Really? Because you know as well as I do that I'm not leaving this house until this girl is in safe hands. She's been through a lot already, and I don't want to traumatize her further by abandoning her." Those last words nearly caught in her throat. She coughed to clear them. "I know this situation stinks and none of us realized how dangerous it was going to be, but none of this is her fault. She's taken to me, and I have no plans to leave Rylan alone overnight with a child when he has no experience caring for one."

Brooklyn had leaned into Amber, and she was rubbing the little girl's back.

"What if that guy comes back? What if he brings

others with him? We have no idea what we're dealing with here."

"All good points. I was thinking that maybe I could ask Rylan to stay over at the ranch tonight—"

"I'm not going where I'm not wanted." Rylan appeared in the doorway to the kitchen, and she'd known he was listening.

"I just invited you," she countered.

"You're not the problem." Rylan positioned his feet in an athletic stance and folded muscled arms over his broad chest.

"Then who is?" she asked.

"That's between me and your brother. Trust me when I say that door is closed." Rylan's voice was steady, even. She wondered if it took much effort to come off that way. He and her brother had been close. It made no sense that they were still at odds.

"I can speak to my brother—"

"Like I already said, not an option. Can we just leave it at that?" Rylan's granite features gave away nothing, and he was a bull when he wanted to be. "You didn't leave when I told you to. I respect that. Now, you need to return the favor."

He made a good point. One she knew better than to argue.

"It might not be safe to stay here, Rylan. Have you considered that?" Those words seemed to sink in as he nodded.

"What are we dealing with here?" he asked Zach.

"The worst-case scenario is an illegal baby adoption ring. These groups are high stakes, and there's a lot on the line since they work outside the law. People who don't want their name in the press or who can't adopt a baby by legal means turn to folks like these." Zach wasn't trying to scare them. Amber knew that. He was putting his cards on the table. "There's generally a lot of money at stake, and that tends to draw very good criminals to the business."

"One of which I was able to stop because of the training you and my brothers gave me growing up," Amber pointed out.

"Once they know who and what they're dealing with, they'll come back more prepared next time." Zach's jaw set.

"They aren't the only ones," she started to say, but her cousin interrupted with a hand in the surrender position.

"Granted, what you did a little while ago might've saved the baby's life. Hell, I'm proud of you. The problem is that we don't know who she belongs to. We haven't established paternity, and technically have no rights to keep her." Zach's words hit harder than Amber had thought possible.

Being with Brooklyn was always going to be a temporary situation. So, why was Amber letting herself get so attached to the little bean?

She decided it was nothing more than protective instincts kicking in. Who wouldn't want to ensure this kid was okay? And maybe there was something motherly inside Amber after all. She'd doubted it after losing her own child within hours of his birth. Prior to getting pregnant, she'd never considered herself the marriage and kids type. But, hey, there was nothing wrong with being a fabulous aunt. Those were in short supply from what she'd heard.

And she loved the land, working on the ranch, being part of something bigger than just herself. She was helping build her family's legacy. How would she leave all that behind? She'd become a mom and then what? Scale back her work? Feel exhausted all the time? Not this pony.

"Something's off here. Doesn't this sort of thing usually happen with newborns?" Amber asked.

"I agree with the first part of what you said. But, no, this is a problem for the first year, to year and a half. Generally, kids older than that are safe from these kinds of people because couples want babies." Zach tucked his notebook inside his front shirt pocket and his eyes zeroed in on Amber. "If you insist on being here, I'll put extra security on the block just in case."

"Thank you, Zach." That should deter the jerk from making a return trip.

"Trust me when I say you don't want your brother finding out about this from someone other than the two of you," Zach said.

"Honestly, this situation might right itself by morning. We'll get Rylan's test results back and go from there." What were the chances he was the father anyway? They had to be slim, right? He couldn't remember being with anyone during the time in question.

And, besides, she'd make the call to Will.

Enough time had passed. Whatever had happened between her brother and Rylan would surely have blown over by now. How bad could it have been?

Chapter Seven

Zach was gone. The baby was fed, washed and asleep. Amber had washed her own face and borrowed a tooth-brush in order to brush her teeth. Thankfully, Rylan had an unopened spare. They'd dined on leftover pizza earlier, and the day's events had left her beyond tired, considering days on the ranch started at four o'clock in the morning.

"Got any clothes I can change into?" she asked Rylan, who stood at the bathroom door holding Brooklyn.

It was probably just the day Brooklyn had had, but trying to put her down to sleep on a makeshift bed on the floor was totally out of the question. That little girl's eyes had shot open the second there was no more human contact. At least she hadn't been so disturbed that she couldn't go back to sleep right away the minute she'd been picked up and cuddled.

Rylan had Brooklyn, and Amber was almost amused at how uncomfortable he looked. This was the first break from holding Brooklyn that Amber had had since meeting the little bean. Her arms burned and literally felt like they might fall off. Amber also tried to ignore how right it felt to spend the day with Brooklyn.

She was a good baby. That was the extent to which Amber would allow herself to examine her feelings. And it was most likely the marriage and family boom at the ranch that had her comfortable with a child in the first place. If this had been a few years ago... Amber stopped right there. *This* never would've been a thing.

The family cattle business had never been so successful, and her innovation with organics had heralded the ranch into the future and was a large part of the reason for the success.

Of course, she could admit to feeling like she was missing out on something lately. But that *something* couldn't possibly be a baby. Amber had spent a long time convincing herself of that. Even so, being with Brooklyn fulfilled a need Amber didn't realize she had. It was probably just the growing Kent brood that had her questioning her stance on no longer wanting children of her own. Besides, she'd never survive that heartache again if something went wrong.

"I can take her back once I'm settled," she said as he stood there looking at the two of them.

An emotion passed behind Rylan's dark eyes that under different circumstances she'd recognize as desire. But that was probably just her mind playing tricks on her, seeing what it wanted to see. Rylan had never seen her as more than a little pain in the rear who'd followed him and Will around like a lost puppy. Okay, the lost puppy bit was probably being dramatic.

"Follow me," he finally said. She did and tried not to notice how cute his backside was. It was, no doubt about it, but that wasn't what she liked about Rylan.

Her high school crush had that mysterious troubled

quality. He was a bad boy who was good deep down. Seriously hot. Wasn't that what every girl wanted? Finding a good bad boy was like owning a sweet horse that ran fast. Or meeting a unicorn.

Amber pushed those unproductive thoughts aside when she nearly bumped into said cute backside when Rylan abruptly stopped in front of her. It was probably her overwrought emotions that had her thinking about such silly things, like high school crushes.

First and foremost, she and Rylan had been friends. He'd been two years ahead of her in school.

And as long as she was admitting things to herself, she'd go ahead and say that he was a good guy. Sure, he'd started down a bad path but going into the military seemed to straighten him out.

A lesser man would've pushed this baby on the first person he could. He would've insisted Zach take her or allowed Child Protective Services to whisk the little girl away with a random family. No matter what Rylan said or thought of himself, he was a decent person.

"There are boxers in that drawer and T-shirts in the one below it." He motioned toward the dresser. She had to remind herself to breathe for seeing that baby sleeping so comfortably on his shoulder. A lightning bolt struck, like she needed to be more attracted to the man. What was it about a tough guy who could be so tender when handling something so vulnerable? A man like that was far more tempting than ice cream. And Amber liked ice cream.

Rylan walked to the door. He stopped at the threshold and hesitated for just a few seconds. Heat flushed through Amber, warming her in places she didn't want to think about with the baby in the room. With a sharp breath he left the room and closed the door behind him.

By the time Amber changed and walked into the living room, Rylan was studying his phone. He didn't look up, but he nodded toward the couch.

"You sure you don't want to sleep in the other room?" he asked.

"Definitely." She didn't want to sleep in sheets that had his masculine outdoorsy and campfire scent. She was no idiot. She wasn't doing that to herself on purpose. It was silly that she felt this strong of an attraction to Rylan after all these years. And embarrassing. Especially since he clearly still saw her as a friend. Even if he didn't, what would that mean? The two of them would never make it in the long run. They were about as opposite as two people could be. She loved the stability of the ranch and having family around, while staying in one place seemed to suffocate Rylan once he'd turned eighteen. As soon as he fixed up the Parker place, he'd get the itch to move on. Amber had no plans to get remarried. She'd shut that possibility off years ago when she'd married at eighteen, gotten pregnant almost immediately and lost both husband and child in less than six months. She'd begun her adult life as a divorcée, and that wasn't exactly a title she'd wanted to keep on her résumé.

She'd been young and infatuated. Amber had never been the type to sit around and dream about her wedding day. If she did get married again and, honestly, she couldn't see that as a possibility, then she'd go down to the courthouse and not make a big to-do over it.

Thinking back, her marriage had been the unhappiest time in her life. Before that, she'd felt free and full of possibilities. When she was little, her brothers used to tease her that she and Amy were like wild horses. Amber especially because she used to sneak into the barn and open the pens to let out the stock. Pop used to round them up and put them back in the stable. Amber would get in a whole mess of trouble, but she'd argue right back. When she was right, she was determined. When she thought she was right, she was unstoppable. She could hear her argument, her words to her father now. Wild horses had to be broken in order to be tamed. Not loved, broken. She couldn't think of a worse fate.

Being married had felt a lot like being shoved into a pen. Amber had accepted the proposal on impulse. The pregnancy came six weeks later, and she'd already realized being married wasn't for her. She'd kept quiet for the pregnancy's sake, figuring it was meant to be. That was the last time she second-guessed her instincts. They rarely failed her.

Amy and Isaac, from ranch security, had been on and off for the past couple of years. They were doing a terrible job of keeping their relationship a secret. Apparently, they were *on* again. What did it say about Amber that she was the Lone Ranger now?

There was a makeshift bed on the sofa. Rylan had pulled the back cushions off the couch and placed a rolled up blanket to soften the edge.

"You'll wear a hole in that carpet if you don't stop." Amber watched Rylan take another lap around the room.

"I was afraid if I stopped she'd wake up and cry

again. I didn't want you up all night because of my rookie mistake," Rylan said.

"You want me to take her now?" Amber held out her arms because one look in his desperate eyes gave her the answer. "Looks like you've finally met your match, Rylan Anderson."

He gave her a resigned look.

"What do you need?" Relief brightened his stressed-out features when he handed over the baby successfully.

"Nothing I can think of. We'll be good." She lowered her voice to church-quiet as she balanced the baby and positioned herself in a somewhat comfortable position on the sofa. "Other than maybe the lights."

Rylan shut off all lights but one, a side table lamp with a soft glow.

"You going to sleep?" Amber bit back a yawn.

"Doubt if I can." He settled into a side chair.

"Deputy Perry is parked out front. Zach will most likely patrol the area all night. It's probably never been safer to grab some sleep. But if it would make you feel better, we could go in shifts." Her cousin wouldn't risk anything happening to her. He'd always been protective just like her brothers. Things had gotten even more tense with the crimes that had seemed to follow the Jacobstown Hacker and that first heifer discovery weeks ago.

"I'll wake you if I get tired, but I'm used to going days at a stretch." Of course, he would be. He'd only just gotten out of the military. She was pretty sure a mission wouldn't have him sleeping every night at the Ritz.

Silence stretched between them. The only sound Amber could hear was the baby's breathing. So many thoughts raced in Amber's mind. Technically, she didn't know Rylan any longer. He had no idea about her life, what she'd been through since the last time she'd seen him. And she had no idea who he really was anymore.

"Why'd you call me?" she asked out of the blue.

"You want the honest answer?"

"If it's a good one," she teased.

"I have no idea. You were the last friend I had in Jacobstown and the first one who came to mind," he said. "You've changed—"

"Well, so have you," she quickly countered, hearing the defensiveness in her own voice.

"Hold on. I meant that in a good way. You're older—"

She issued a grunt, stopping him cold.

"You're not a little kid anymore. You're a grown woman. Beautiful."

"Well, now you're doing a little better." She figured he'd added that last part to keep her from giving him a hard time. She'd accept the compliment anyway. "You ever think about becoming a daddy, Rylan?"

"No. I'm not anywhere near where I want to be in life, and I don't want to do that to a kid. But if the test proves she's mine, it doesn't matter what I think, does it?" The question was rhetorical. His tone left no room for doubt that he'd do the right thing by Brooklyn.

There was another long pause where neither spoke. After all these years, it should be awkward to be in a dark room alone with someone she knew from her childhood. But this was Rylan. She couldn't feel anything but at home with him. An annoying little voice warned her that she was alone with a stranger, but it wasn't difficult to quash.

"What are we going to do if he comes back?" she asked.

"This time, we'll be ready." That statement had so much finality to it Amber had no doubt that Rylan meant every word. He had the skills to back it up, too.

Amber shut the thought down. Because Rylan's protectiveness over the baby lying across her chest stirred Amber's heart in ways she couldn't allow or afford.

Conversation trailed off when Amber could no longer hold her eyes open. When she opened them again, she heard Rylan's steady breathing. His shirt was off, and in the dim light she could see his muscled chest.

An ache welled up from deep within.

RYLAN BLINKED HIS EYES open the second Amber shifted her weight.

"You're awake," she said, sounding caught off guard.

"I was never asleep. My eyes were resting." He rubbed the scruff on his chin and then raked a hand through his dark, thick hair.

"Said every man I've ever met who was actually sleeping." She laughed. Her laugh, hell, her voice, had a musical quality to it. This wasn't the time to get inside his head about why it was her laugh he'd heard when an enemy gunman stood over him with an AR-15 pointed at the center of his forehead. He'd told himself it was natural for childhood memories to come back when a man faced death. And she did have a great laugh.

"I've been thinking about where I might've been about twelve months ago. I was stationed in San Antonio last year and had a few weekends off. Several of us guys used to drive over to Austin. They did some partying." The disappointment on her face struck like a physical blow. "I haven't had a drink in six years, three hundred and twenty-four days. Except possibly that weekend."

"Oh." The one word and the way it was spoken conveyed pity. He didn't want that from Amber. "I'm sorry. I didn't realize that about your drinking. I knew it had gotten a little out of control before you left but—"

"My low point was good for me because it made me realize that I had a problem. I saw the man in the mirror one sober morning and knew that wasn't who I wanted to be. Not on weekends, not on leave, not anymore," he said. "Before that I did a few stupid and reckless things. None of which involved not using protection no matter who I was with or how much I'd had to drink."

The women he'd spent time with knew the deal. He was upfront about his mind-set. He'd always shied away from any woman who was interested in anything more than one night of mutually consensual and amazing sex.

"I'm sorry you went through all that," she said, and the sincerity in her voice made him realize just how alone he'd been all these years.

It was fine. His choice. But this was the first time his life seemed lonely when he thought about it. The possibility of fatherhood was probably what had him going inside himself, searching for redeeming qualities that might make him worthy of bringing up that little girl on his own. He had no plans to let her down.

Amber tried to sit up and the baby stirred.

"I need to use the restroom. Think you can handle her for a few minutes?" she asked.

He nodded, deciding not to point out the fact that he might be doing that for a heck of a lot longer than a few minutes. The idea should stress him out, and it did, but not as much as he expected. He'd had a few hours to let the possibility sink in.

There was no going back now. If the call that came in said he was Brooklyn's father, so be it. He'd make sure that girl had a real childhood with dolls and dance classes even if he had to work two jobs to do it. Reality was a gut punch. Wasn't that what his mother had done? His father hadn't bothered to stick around long enough to get to know Rylan. That wasn't the life he wanted for Brooklyn. Staying in Jacobstown might not be an option. Work was sparse here. He'd have better luck and get more pay if he moved to Fort Worth or Dallas.

The thought of leaving Jacobstown hit harder than expected, but he could finish updating this house and then rent it out for income. He stopped himself right there. One step at a time. He didn't need to know how to finish the journey. He only needed to take the first steps. And that meant being okay with whatever news Dr. Logan delivered.

But first he needed to track down the baby's mother and find out what trouble she'd gotten herself into. Only a desperate mother would abandon her child.

Brooklyn squeezed her eyes shut before letting out a little cry. Panic set in. Was she hungry? Did she need a diaper change? Of course, she would need that. Didn't babies go to the bathroom almost constantly?

Thankfully, Amber returned before the baby could wind up a good cry. She brought a bottle back with her, and Brooklyn settled down almost immediately. She'd shown him how to feed the baby earlier, so he took her, figuring he needed the practice.

"You want me to burp her?" she asked him almost the second Brooklyn finished her bottle.

He nodded. There was an emotion behind Amber's eyes when she looked at the little girl that Rylan couldn't exactly pinpoint. Whatever it was ran deep.

"Will you teach me how to change her?" he asked as Amber passed the baby back to him. He did his level best not to sound as helpless as he felt when it came to taking care of the baby.

"It's easier than you think. Come on." The spark in Amber's eyes shouldn't stir his heart like it did. She could always make the most mundane thing seem like an adventure.

She dropped to the floor next to the diaper bag in the middle of the living room and waved him over. "Put her down on her back."

He was probably as awkward-looking as all hell, but he managed to set Brooklyn down gently without causing her to cry. The minute he withdrew his hands she kicked up a storm, and her sad face nearly broke him. "What did I do wrong?"

"Hold on there, little bean." Amber patted the little girl's tummy. Brooklyn wound up to cry, but Amber tickled her belly and Brooklyn laughed instead. The sound of her voice had a calming effect on the child, and he couldn't imagine doing any of this without Amber. He wasn't sure what he owed for the favor this had become. "Take a diaper from the bag next to me."

He did, ignoring the sizzle of attraction he felt when his arm brushed against her shoulder.

Amber unzipped the pink onesie pajamas and pulled each tiny foot out. Her motions were fluid, and she made it look so easy. She opened and closed the tabs on the diaper the baby already had on a couple of times as a demonstration.

"Open yours up. Figure it out. Pretend it's something mechanical and take it apart. There's not much to one of these." She leaned over and bumped his shoulder. The electricity pulsing between them from contact sent a jolt of heat rocketing through him. "My brothers' kids each seemed to have a different kind of diaper when they were this age. One needed a certain no-leak protection and another needed a specific night guard fabric."

"You mean there's more than one kind of these?" He couldn't imagine why.

"Afraid so," she said.

Rylan played around with the diaper, pretending he didn't just have the over-the-top chemistry reaction to Amber Kent. "This is pretty basic."

"Until you try to put it on a wiggly baby." Amber was making cooing sounds, and Brooklyn seemed enraptured.

He figured he could use the distraction to change a diaper.

Removing the other diaper was easy. The rest was a bit more complicated, but with Amber's help he managed his first successful diaper change.

"Does she have any other clothes in the bag?" Amber picked up Brooklyn while he checked.

"Nope. She has what she had on yesterday." There was nothing other than formula, diapers and wipes. But that was a lot, considering the way he'd received Brooklyn. "Someone cared about her, didn't they?"

"I hope so." Amber was busy putting the pj's back on her.

"Who takes the time to write a note, pack diapers and wipes but not extra clothing?" His mind churned. "For the most part it seems that someone wanted her taken care of. I mean, there are diapers at nearly every convenience store, but her mother wanted to make sure she had the ones Brooklyn uses."

"That's a good point. It makes me think she'd been considering her options for a few days at least," Amber said.

"Brooklyn might not be my daughter. Her mother could be someone I know. I still have no idea who she could be." Whoever the woman was must know that he wouldn't take a random person's word for it that he'd fathered a child.

"Maybe she figured it would take a couple of days for the paternity test to come back and by then she'd be out of trouble and able to take her daughter back," Amber agreed. "She could've picked you because you're loyal and might be the only one she knew who could handle himself in a dangerous situation."

Which made the odds Brooklyn wasn't his child drop pretty damn drastically if he was right. But then, he'd most likely spent one or two nights with the woman in question. Wasn't exactly a recipe for knowing him, and the idea that she'd been desperate didn't sit well.

A knock sounded at the front door.

Amber gasped.

Chapter Eight

Amber didn't mean to startle the baby. She reminded herself just how much little ones picked up on the emotions and energy of everyone around them.

"It's okay, sweet princess," she soothed.

"I'll take care of whoever it is." Rylan pulled a weapon from underneath the cushion of the chair he'd been resting in earlier. The sun was up but it was still early.

Several thoughts raced through Amber's mind. Was the baby's mother back? Amber should want that, but her heart squeezed thinking about Brooklyn leaving so soon. Had the guy from yesterday returned? That was all kinds of awful, too. It could mean that Deputy Perry had been jumped or worse. She didn't want to consider the possibility that he was outside somewhere hurt because of her.

It could be good news, like Zach had found the perp who'd tried to snatch Brooklyn from Amber's arms.

Rylan checked the peephole. "I'll be right there, Zach."

He returned his weapon to its hiding place before opening the door and ushering her cousin inside.

One look at the tension lines on Zach's face and she knew something was wrong.

"You need to come back to the ranch." His lips formed a grim line. "A body was found near Rushing Creek. Female. Early to midthirties. You can ride with me if you like."

"Oh, Zach. That's terrible." Every possible worst-case scenario fought for attention in Amber's mind. "Is everyone accounted for at home?"

"Yes. Your sisters-in-law and Amy have all checked in." Zach's brows furrowed. "You gave us a scare, though. I must've called your cell ten times trying to reach you."

"My battery must've died." She regretted her word choice under the circumstances and wished she could take that last one back. She couldn't, and it wouldn't change what had happened on the ranch. It was heart-breaking.

"Everyone would rest easier if they could put eyes on you. Plus, the family wants to meet and talk about what's happening," Zach said.

Amber picked up Brooklyn and held her to her chest to keep the little girl from crying, and to give herself something to do besides give into the mounting panic attack. A woman was dead. A family was about to receive the worst possible news and suffer an unimaginable loss. Her heart ached for the victim and her family.

"Everyone on staff has been accounted for," he added. She couldn't feel much relief considering some poor soul had been killed.

"He used the same MO as the Jacobstown Hacker," Zach continued.

Her gaze bounced from Zach to Rylan. His confusion was knitted across his forehead, and she realized he must not have kept up-to-date on Jacobstown. Of course, he hadn't. He'd cut himself off from the family and, as far as she knew, hadn't been in contact with anyone recently. "Over the past few weeks, someone has been killing animals. He's specific in the way he kills them by hacking off their left paw or hoof. Up to now, the jerk had focused on animals. Now everyone's fears that he would move onto people are being realized."

"I didn't know." There was so much compassion and reverence in his voice.

"Come with me, Rylan. *Please*." She added that last part as a plea because she didn't want to leave him or the baby. Whatever had happened between him and her brother needed to be set aside, and she'd remind him of that if push came to shove. She hoped it wouldn't come to that.

"I'll get your coat," he said. She expected an argument from Rylan and was pleased when she didn't get one. There was no time. Her heart hurt for the woman at the creek. Anger burst through her that someone could get away with that on her family's property.

Rylan located her coat, which he'd hung in the closet and helped her into it. Zach stood by the door, waiting for them to get themselves and the baby ready. Amber caught him watching her as she interacted with Brooklyn, and she knew exactly what was on his mind.

Amber stopped short of the door. "We don't have a car seat for her."

"I borrowed one from Deputy Perry. He's buckling it in my SUV now." Zach opened the door and the trio followed him, with Rylan closing in from behind. His home was a half hour from the main house at the ranch. This early in the morning Zach made good time cutting across town.

Isaac was working security at the front gate. He waved them by. Amber wasted no time exiting the SUV. She tried to help unbuckle Brooklyn, but her hands shook too hard. Rylan took them in his—a move that shouldn't calm her but felt like a lifeline to sanity—and caught her gaze. He didn't say anything and yet his presence comforted her.

Amber took in a calming breath and managed to usher in Rylan's masculine scent, all pine and outdoors.

"Go on in. I'll be right there," he said.

"Okay." She couldn't imagine that it was easy for Rylan to face her family home again, and it meant the world to her that he'd come along. Strange as it might seem to an outsider since she'd only been around him and the baby a short time, they felt like part of her family, too. She told herself it was because Rylan and Will had been attached at the hip for so many years up until the summer before senior year when Rylan's mother had passed away. Then, he'd stopped coming around and Will seemed a little lost without his best friend. Amber had confronted her brother about abandoning his friend when Rylan needed him most. That had gone over about as well as sriracha on a ghost pepper.

Mitch, the eldest brother, greeted Amber in the entrance to the main living room. She could hear low chatter coming from the kitchen area. The low hum buzzed toward her, and the tone made the air heavy, like dull gray rain clouds hovering in the sky before it opened up into a show of thunder and lightning.

"The kids are at my place with Joyce. Everyone else is here, including Will," Mitch said after a hug. Joyce had been their loyal caregiver since the day the twins were born. His twins had been the first babies in the Kent family. Being the eldest brother, he probably felt more responsibility for taking care of everyone in the family. Which was most likely the reason he'd taken Amber outside to tell her when his wife had become pregnant a couple of years ago. He'd chosen his words carefully. He'd been keenly aware of what she'd been through and even time didn't seem to heal the wound of losing her child. Amber appreciated Mitch for caring. But she really didn't expect the rest of the family to stop living their lives because of her loss. It was hers.

"Does he know where I've been and who I've been helping?" She wouldn't change a thing about the past twenty-four hours; she just needed to know what she was up against.

"Yes," Mitch admitted.

Amber took in a deep breath. "Let's go."

Four brothers and three sisters-in-law sat around the large hand-carved wooden table in the massive kitchen. Seven sets of eyes landed on Amber when she walked into the room. She picked Will first. Better stare him down straightaway so he knew better than to call her out. His wife, Kelly, sat to his right. The pair had been through hell and back when Kelly was almost forced to marry a Fort Worth millionaire who was out for revenge. Amber's brother Deacon and his wife, Leah, sat across the table from the others. Leah used to work for the city of Fort Worth as a detective. She'd been targeted by a murderer posing as a copycat. In the process of investigating her case, she'd met and fallen in love with Deacon. The other couple at the table was Nate and Chelsea. She'd moved to town after an inheritance from an aunt she never knew gave her a new lease on life. But trouble soon followed, and Nate stepped up to protect Chelsea and her daughter. In the process, she and Nate had fallen in love, married and the three, plus Linda, her mother, had settled into his house on the ranch. Which left Jordan and Amber, the single siblings in an increasingly small club.

Mitch and his wife, Andrea, sat side by side. He held on to her hands, and witnessing the comfort the pair—and all the couples—seemed to provide each other struck Amber. She'd never felt hollow inside. So, where was it coming from now?

Amber expected to find disapproval in Will's eyes, but he mostly seemed concerned. He acknowledged her with a grim smile. It was most likely the weight of the situation at Rushing Creek that had him casting his gaze down and not his disappointment in her.

Zach entered the room last, and all attention went to him as Amber took a seat at the granite island toward the back of the kitchen. She couldn't be in this room anytime around the holidays without thinking just how alive it had been in past years. Maybe it was time to change that, to bring some of that love and vibrancy back to the main house. It was a point worth considering because it was so easy in life to focus on what she didn't have instead of seeing and appreciating all that she did.

"Here's what we know so far." He looked up from his notes. "This information stays inside this room, by the way."

"Goes without saying," Mitch added.

"There hasn't been confirmation of the victim's identity." Zach paused. He took caring for the people of Jacobstown seriously, and a murder in his backyard was a big hit. Especially considering the murder had happened at the family ranch.

"She was found by Lone Star Lonnie on his morning rounds. He went farther north along the creek bed chasing wild boar." Lone Star Lonnie was the foreman of KR aka Kent Ranch. "Coroner says she'd been dead for less than twelve hours. I have deputies on the scene, and Lonnie refuses to leave."

Last night was Saturday. Amber's hands fisted in her lap. This shouldn't have happened. "I realize there hasn't been confirmation, but do we have any idea who the victim might've been?"

"Lonnie did the right thing by not contaminating the crime scene. He kept his distance. Mike will text me the minute he knows something." Zach referred to Mike Travis, the county coroner.

A thought struck that Amber couldn't ignore. Could the victim be Brooklyn's mother? The baby was outside with Rylan. Was that part of the reason he'd refused to come inside? Was he thinking the same thing? It was unbearable to know any life could be cut short. Amber's heart clenched thinking that Brooklyn's mother might be the one…

"Town will want answers today about the victim, her killer and how this happened," Mitch said. He was always thinking two steps ahead, and Amber appreciated that about her brother.

"Every woman will be looking over her shoulder from now until we catch the perp," Deacon chimed in.

"I'll help in any way I can," Leah offered.

Zach thanked her.

"My office won't release information until we have all the facts," he said. "But it never hurts to issue a statement about making sure folks lock doors and keep vehicle keys with them, like we've requested in the past."

Rylan walked into the adjacent room with Brooklyn in his arms. One look at his face, and Amber could tell she'd guessed right a few minutes ago. He wore a heavy expression like he carried the weight of the world.

"If y'all will excuse me." Will stood and then walked out the back door.

"Will," Amber started, but stopped when she saw the momentary hurt darken Rylan's features. For a split second, Amber considered going after her brother. Will needed air, and he needed to accept the fact that she and Rylan were friends. Granted, what was happening felt like more than friendship to her, and she thought Rylan experienced that same heat when the two of them were in the room together. But those were facts she didn't want to examine at the moment.

Amber refocused on Will. She knew her brother well enough to realize he needed space. Rushing out there now would only hurt her cause, and both of them could end up saying words they'd regret.

"Welcome back to town, Rylan." Mitch extended the first olive branch. "I'd offer a handshake, but I can see yours are full at the moment."

"Thank you," Rylan said, and she'd never heard two more sincere words from a single soul.

"Who is that sweet little girl in your arms?" Kelly, Will's wife, asked after introducing herself.

"That's a great question." Rylan gave a quick rundown of what happened yesterday. "All we know for certain is that her name is Brooklyn."

Leah seemed to catch onto the implication that Brooklyn's mother could possibly be the victim. She introduced herself to Rylan before saying, "If you need someone to go with you to the morgue, I was a detective in a past life."

"I appreciate the offer. I'm hoping it doesn't come to that," Rylan admitted after thanking her, as well. Seeing the family, save for Will, welcome Rylan so openly caused Amber's heart to squeeze.

Andrea introduced herself, followed by Chelsea.

While introductions were being made, Amber thought back to what Rylan had told her about his sobriety. The simple truth was that he may not be able to positively ID the victim if she was Brooklyn's mother. His mind was still fuzzy about what happened that weekend, and she took to heart the seriousness in his voice when he spoke about being sober. There was so much regret and self-reproach at the possibility he'd slipped up and had a weekend binge. The fact that he hadn't had a similar one since the very early days of his sobriety struck a chord.

Zach, who had been studying his phone, walked over to Rylan. "I put the description of the man who dropped Brooklyn off at your place in the database. I flagged the file as urgent. I also just heard back from the sketch artist. She can meet this afternoon if you're still game."

Rylan was already nodding. "Of course. I want to do whatever I can to help."

"I'm probably just being Pollyanna here, but maybe we'll get lucky and the baby's mother will show up to reclaim her," Chelsea offered.

"That would be a best-case scenario for the little girl. Of course, there are legal ramifications for dropping off a baby and disappearing," Zach pointed out.

"There are no easy answers on this one." Rylan held on to the little girl, who was starting to fuss. Her gaze was locked on to Amber. From the looks of it, she found a new friend.

Mitch issued a warning look. There would be concerns from her family. They loved her and were keenly aware of her loss. Deacon was discreet, but she caught him watching her a little too intently. For now, she wanted to keep the focus on the victim and not bring up what she was doing with Rylan—other than helping an old friend after the holidays who'd been put in an impossible situation.

"IT'S NOT SAFE back at my house." Rylan was finally alone with Amber in the kitchen after a round of everyone wanting to meet Brooklyn. He couldn't deny the kid was cuteness times ten. She'd reeled him in almost immediately. He appreciated the kindness the Kent family showed to the little girl.

Will walking out after Rylan had come inside was a blow. He couldn't say he didn't deserve it or have it coming. It just hurt.

"After what happened last night on the ranch, I don't think it's safe anywhere." Amber blew out a defeated breath. Then she looked up at him. "I'm going with you."

"I'd argue with you but I've seen that face before," Rylan said. His cell buzzed in his pocket. He fished it out and checked the screen. "It's the doctor."

He and Amber exchanged glances. This phone call had the ability to alter that little girl's future in a big way.

"I'll hold her." Amber took the little girl, who seemed more than happy to make the switch.

Rylan answered the call and walked over to the sink. He could see the sun bathing the yard in light. "Thanks for getting back to me so soon, Dr. Logan."

"I drew two samples, one for Zach to be locked up as evidence and the other to be sent to a lab for analysis. I had a friend open the lab and speed up the process as a favor. You deserve to know what you're dealing with, although this is unofficial word when it comes to the courts." Doc paused. "She's your daughter."

Those three words should be a gut punch. They weren't. He'd allowed that little bean to worm her way into his heart. Rylan had expected the news to hit hard. A piece of him was relieved. He tried to convince himself it was for Brooklyn's sake, that he would do a better job of protecting her than anyone else. That part was most likely true.

"Thank you, Doc," he said into the phone.

"I hope you got the news you were hoping for," Dr. Logan said.

"I appreciate the sentiment, Doc." Rylan stared out

the window for a long moment, absorbing the fact that he was someone's father. And then he turned to face Amber, who'd already moved beside him, and nodded. "She's mine."

"Are you okay with the news?" she asked.

"She's a great kid. She deserves to have someone looking out for her who cares. I'm ready to be that person." Rylan meant every word. "This might not be the way I'd envisioned becoming a father. Hell, I've never held the wife and kids fantasy. But here she is. I have every intention of doing right by her."

"Excuse me." Zach's voice came from behind them, interrupting their conversation. Based on his tone, he wasn't there for casual chatter.

Rylan turned around.

"My deputy just called. We got him. The man you described who dropped off the baby and ran yesterday morning is in custody." Zach put a hand up. "Now, I know what you're going to say and I'd probably want to do the same thing if I was in your shoes—"

"I doubt you do." Hearing the words inside his head that he was a father was about as foreign as it got. "I'm going down to your office with you."

"I wasn't about to say that you shouldn't come. I need you to identify him. All I wanted to be clear about is that you can't speak to him. You have to give me your word you'll stay on the other side of the mirror and not try to catch him in the hallway when he's being moved back and forth." Zach must've seen the tension building in Rylan's features because he kept talking. "Think of it this way. We make the right moves with this guy, and we find this girl's parents."

"Let me stop you right there, Zach. I just got a call from Dr. Logan. You'll get the official results soon enough, and they'll reveal that I'm Brooklyn's father."

Chapter Nine

After delivering the news that Rylan was Brooklyn's father, there wasn't much else that needed to be said. He had the rapt attention of everyone in the room. He turned to Amber. He'd tell her not to come with him, but he wasn't one for wasting time. She'd insist. "Are you ready?"

"Yes." The word was spoken in a firm and confident voice. No one could argue she knew what she wanted. "Can we borrow a few baby clothes before we head out?"

"We keep a few things here at the main house. I'll go grab some," Mitch said.

"While you guys wait for those, I'll get on the road. I need a five-minute head start." Zach left first.

Amber picked up the diaper bag and slid the strap over her shoulder. She looked at her family like she was daring one of them to speak. Will, the one person Rylan wanted to speak to the most, was outside somewhere, most likely in the barn. Work did a lot of good to clear the mind. It was also a great outlet for anger, an emotion Rylan understood all too well.

"Thank you for your hospitality." Rylan meant those words.

Mitch returned with a few items that he handed to Amber. He walked over and put his hand on Rylan's shoulder. "It took a lot to show up here, Rylan. You always were like family. If you need anything come back any—"

"Thank you, but I doubt everyone shares that sentiment." He motioned toward the barn.

"You know Will. He needs a minute. But he'll come around." Mitch set his jaw, looking confident in those words.

"Some people don't deserve forgiveness," Rylan said to Mitch.

"That's where you're wrong. Everyone does." Mitch squeezed Rylan's shoulder before leaning in close to his ear. "She'd kill me if she knew I said anything. But take it easy with her."

Rylan issued a grunt. "Amber can—"

"Hear me out," Mitch interrupted. "She probably didn't tell you but she was married before."

"Amber?" She never said anything about a husband. Why did it hit him so hard that she'd kept something so big a secret?

"It didn't go well for her. There was a child involved and—"

Those words hit like another rogue wave. It was starting to make sense why the family seemed so concerned when she'd taken Brooklyn in her arms. Anyone could see those two were natural together. Had she been married to a man who'd had a child in a previous relationship? It made sense as to why she'd been so cautious with him.

"Based on your expression I'm guessing you had no clue about either one of those things," Mitch said.

"Not a one." Rylan was still trying to absorb the first of the two revelations.

"I shouldn't have said anything. Those are not my secrets to share. I just don't want to see her heart ripped out—"

"You're trying to protect her."

Amber walked into the kitchen. She froze when she saw the two of them in intimate conversation. She balled a fist and planted it on her hip. "What's going on in here?"

"We were just talking," Rylan started, but she grunted.

"I figured that much out. You plan on telling me what you were talking about?" she asked.

"We can talk on the way over to Zach's office. Did you pick up your phone charger?" Rylan hoped the distraction would work.

It seemed to when she spun around and walked out of the room. She returned a few minutes later looking more than ready to go.

"Zach was our ride," Rylan pointed out. And he'd left minutes ago.

"I have more than one vehicle, Rylan. And I keep a car seat in the back of my small sport utility." Amber's gaze moved from Mitch to Rylan. "What were the two of you talking about?"

"I was just giving Rylan some kid advice," Mitch said, sidestepping the question.

"You sure that's all?" Amber asked her brother.

"I told him to be cautious with you and that if he hurt you I'd be on his doorstep." He walked over and put his hands on her shoulders.

"You know I'm a big girl, Mitch. I appreciate you having my back, but I'm capable of fighting my own battles," she said.

"Maybe I think you shouldn't have to fight anyone anymore." Mitch pulled her into a bear hug. "Love you, sis."

"I know you do." Amber returned the hug cautiously. "But we've gotta go."

Rylan took the lead, walking toward the door. Part of him needed to know what had happened to her. He wanted, no needed to know if what Mitch said had anything to do with the seriousness in her eyes. Years ago, she'd been all spunk and spark and fire. Her heart was bigger and more open than the Texas sky. And he could still see those qualities in her, but some of that spark had dimmed and he wondered how much it had to do with her ex, with having a child taken away from her.

Thinking about anyone hurting Amber caused a fire bolt to swirl through Rylan.

Leah stopped them at the front door. "Have you guys considered leaving the baby here until you figure out what's going on at Zach's office? We have plenty of qualified family members here to take care of her, and there are lots of kiddos on the ranch. I doubt anyone would notice one more."

Before Rylan could form an argument, Amber answered for him.

"She'll be safer with us, and Rylan wouldn't be able

to concentrate if she's away from him," she said. She was right, and he was surprised that she could read him so well. "But we're grateful for the offer."

"Let us know if that changes. Any one of us could come pick her up at Zach's office if the situation drags on or gets too tense." Deacon moved beside his wife, nodding his agreement with what she said. He put his arm around her, and Rylan was struck at how happy they seemed.

"Thank you," Rylan said, and he meant it for both of them.

Amber added an extra blanket over the baby. Rylan opened the door for Amber, who walked outside and into the brisk afternoon air. She shivered. "It's gotten even colder."

A blanket of gray clouds covered the sky, making it feel later in the day than it was.

Amber handed him the keys to her small sport utility after helping to buckle Brooklyn into her car seat. She stopped long enough to ask, "What did Mitch really say to you in the house?"

"Enough to make me curious about your past," he admitted before taking the proffered keys and moving to the driver's seat.

Amber put some muscle into closing her door after getting inside. "Did he tell you that I was married?"

"Yes. But that's all. He said it was a long time ago." Rylan turned the key in the ignition, and the engine hummed to life. He put the gearshift in Reverse.

"What else did he say?" she demanded, and her voice was a study in calm. He couldn't decide if that was good or bad.

There was no point beating around the bush, and he didn't like the idea of hiding information from her, so he came out with it. "Did your husband have a kid?"

"*I* had a child, Rylan. He was stillborn—"

"I'm so sorry, Amber. It's none of my business. You don't have to talk about it if you don't want to." His heart fisted in his chest thinking about the pain she must've endured as he pulled off the drive and put the transmission in Park.

He turned to her as she stared out the front windshield. "I was out of line bringing it up, Amber. And so was Mitch. He never should've stirred that pot."

"That's the thing, Rylan. I never talk about him. My family always tiptoes around the subject and I get it. They're afraid of dredging up the past, and I love the fact that they want to protect me. From what I can see that can be rare in families, and I wish more people had loved ones who would do just about anything for them." She paused and he let her catch her breath as a few tears rolled down her cheeks. "But I'm done talking about this for now. We have a little girl in the back seat who needs all of our attention."

"When you're ready to keep going, I'm here." A dozen questions fired off in his mind. This wasn't the time for any of them. He couldn't help but wonder if losing a baby was what caused the sadness in her eyes. It was a flash, and he'd almost missed it a few times already. There was another emotion present when she held Brooklyn that made sense to him now.

"That means a lot to me, Rylan."

She turned to face him, and he leaned over the armrest to brush his fingertips across her cheek. "I wish there was something I could say or do that could take that pain away from your eyes, Amber."

"No one can take that away, Rylan. But you can do something," she said.

"Name it. I'll do anything." He meant it, too.

"Kiss me."

"THAT'S NOT A GOOD IDEA," Rylan said, but there was no conviction in his tone.

She leaned toward him, and they were so close she could breathe the same air. His masculine scent filled her senses, destroying her ability to think clearly. "No. It's not. But it's too late for me."

With that, he dipped his head and claimed her mouth. She parted her lips for him and teased his tongue inside. For something that should be avoided at all cost, kissing Rylan sure felt right in the moment.

But then she'd thought about the one kiss they'd shared in high school more times than she cared to admit. She could be real about it. He'd most likely been drinking. In fact, back then she thought she tasted alcohol on his breath. When she'd accused him of kissing her because he was drunk, he'd laughed and told her he kissed her because he realized how beautiful she was. That night at the bunkhouse, where she'd often gone to clear her thoughts, he'd looked at her like it was the first time he'd really seen her. She'd changed over the summer and had grown two inches, to her current height.

And ever since he opened the door yesterday, she'd been wanting him to kiss her again to see if it would be as magical as it felt that night.

Rylan's hands came up to cup her face, and she brought hers up to get lost in his thick dark hair.

She'd never experienced so much passion in a kiss with any other man, not even the one she'd been married to.

The skill with which Rylan kissed Amber caused her mind to snap to other pleasures she figured he'd mastered, as well. She could only imagine the sparks that would fly in the bedroom based on the heat she was experiencing right then.

The baby cooed in the back seat, breaking into the moment.

Amber pulled back first, and he stopped her with his hands. He looked into her eyes, and it felt like he was looking right through her.

"Damn," he said under his breath. That one word was about the sexiest thing Amber had heard.

She laughed at herself and he cocked an eyebrow.

"That's not a response I'm used to in situations like this," he said, but then he smiled, too.

"I don't doubt you have a lot of experience in situations like this, Rylan Anderson," she quipped.

"That might be true. But none have ever felt like this."

Now it was her turn to say the word *damn*.

With that, he turned his attention back to the road ahead. He navigated back onto the driveway and onto the farm road.

Amber didn't ask how long Rylan planned to stick around. Staying in one place seemed to suffocate Rylan once he turned eighteen. He'd never been good at holding on to a possession for more than a few months. The pattern was always the same. He'd get a new motorcycle, and it would be all the rage for a few weeks. He'd tire of it and sell it only to buy a four-wheeler a few days later. The only certainty was that he'd get bored with his latest toy and move onto something *or someone* else. She figured some people didn't stick. They moved in and out of cities, jobs, lives. She would do well to remember that, because he'd moved out of hers once already. An annoying little voice reminded her that he'd come back to Jacobstown and that technically he didn't *leave* her.

Having a daughter would change him but nothing would tame him. He'd always walked the edge. He didn't grow up with money. He'd worked for every penny. But that didn't mean he spent it wisely. At least back then. She remembered the time he bought an old Jeep and then got bored with it before he was finished paying for it and lost money on the deal. It wasn't the money she worried about. Young people didn't have the same understanding of finances that someone with real responsibilities did. It was his attention span that bothered her.

Thick gray clouds rolled across the sky. Amber had a bad feeling in the pit of her stomach.

Luckily, Brooklyn had a full stomach. She was cooing happily by herself in the back seat. The two-lane farm road leading away from the ranch was empty at this hour on a Sunday. The temperature was dropping. The cold front was blowing through, and the temperature had dropped into the thirties. At least the temperature was above freezing and it was dry outside.

The conditions threatened to worsen, but the best

thing about Texas weather was that it changed on a dime. People always said if someone didn't like the weather, all they had to do was stick around for five minutes and it would change. And if not five minutes, then a couple of days before the sun would shine and the days would warm up again.

Rylan cursed as he checked the rearview mirror.

An all-black sporty sedan roared up behind them. There were no markings on the vehicle. Amber took note of the plate. "I think we should keep an eye on this guy."

"Maybe we should turn around and head back to the ranch where we have backup," Rylan said. They'd driven halfway to Zach's office.

Amber briefly thought about making a call for help. She'd charged her cell enough at the house to be able to make a call. This far away who would be able to get to them? Amber's heart galloped. Trees lined both sides of the road. Turning around was their safest, and only bet. She studied the car behind them. "It almost looks like an unmarked vehicle."

"Why would law enforcement be out here on this farm road?" Rylan made a good point.

"Wish I knew." She glanced back at the sedan. "This doesn't feel right to me, Rylan. We rarely ever have another agency here in town that Zach doesn't know about. Maybe we should give him a call just to check in with him."

"That's probably smart," Rylan said.

Amber called her cousin, who picked up on the first ring. "We have a suspicious vehicle on our tail and

Brooklyn is with us. Do you know anything about outside law enforcement being in the area?"

"I haven't heard a word. That doesn't mean another agency couldn't be involved, especially if Brooklyn was taken across state lines. We have no idea what we're truly dealing with, and I can't speak for another office," Zach stated. "What does the vehicle look like?"

She described it.

"What about the license plate? Maybe I can run it through the database and get a hit," he offered before seeming to think better of it and adding, "Although, any undercover operation would be blocked."

"It's worth a try." Amber chanced a glance behind.

Everything was quiet for a few seconds save for the sound of tires on the road and the unaware baby in the back.

"While I'm waiting to see if we get a hit, which vehicle is Rylan driving?"

"We're in my small SUV."

"Is that the one you take on cattle runs sometimes?" Most cattle ranchers used ATVs or pickup trucks and not horses like her family usually did. It was a tradition her father had started when they were young, and everyone kept it up most of the time.

"Yes."

"Have your weapon at the ready just in case there's trouble." She located her SIG Sauer in the glove compartment. Granted, it was normally her brothers going up against dangerous poachers, but she knew how to protect herself and she, like everyone else, carried anytime she went out on the property. A coyote could be lurking behind any tree or bush. Wild hogs were mean creatures, not to mention dangerous. And then there were poachers. She'd encountered the first two more times than she cared to count. She'd been spared the latter so far.

"I have DPS on the line. I need to put you on hold." Zach waited for acknowledgment, which she gave.

A grin lifted one side of Rylan's mouth. "I'd ask if you know what to do with that SIG, but I know better. Remember the time you shot a hole in my favorite ballcap?"

She couldn't help but laugh at the memory.

"You were just lucky it wasn't on your head at the time," she quipped, grateful for the momentary break in tension.

But then the sports sedan sped up toward the bumper.

"What do we do here, Rylan? What's our move?"

Chapter Ten

Lights swirled from the black sedan behind them. Amber wished Zach would come back on the line so he could tell them what to do.

"Anyone comes at us with a weapon we protect ourselves." Rylan pulled onto the shoulder of the two-lane road as he surveyed the landscape.

"This is bad," she said.

"If that little bean wasn't in the back seat and you weren't here, this would be right up my alley," he stated with one of those devastating smiles that was all Rylan. She tried to convince herself that it was the heat in the moment that sent a rocket of electricity shooting through her, and not the fact that she had a very real *and growing* attraction to the man in the driver's seat. "As it is, I have to consider both of you."

"Thanks for the confidence in my shot." Amber snorted.

"I just mean that if either of you got hurt because of me I'd never forgive myself. So, I can't be my usual self on a mission." His voice dipped when he spoke those words aloud. It always had a deep, musical quality that she could listen to all day. His voice poured over her like Amaretto over ice cream, melting her insides as it washed through her.

He covered her hand with his, and electricity pulsed through her. It was his masculine and all-male presence that did that to her, made her want things she knew better than to think about.

"I can take Brooklyn and run into the woods. No one would know this area better than me, and that would give you time to handle these guys on your own," she said.

The lights continued to swirl, but the driver didn't exit his vehicle. A pickup truck did come speeding up on the road in front of them, barreling toward them.

"Whatever happens next, I'm glad you came back, Rylan," she admitted. She wanted, no *needed* him to know that.

"Don't count me out yet, Kent," he countered with the sexy little smirk that dented the corner of his cheek. He was in his element.

A man in what looked like a state trooper uniform exited the vehicle. His tan uniform and hat seemed authentic.

"Something feels off, but I can't quite put my finger on it," Amber said.

The truck was getting closer as the officer walked toward them.

"Wouldn't he wait? I mean why get out of his vehicle on a two-lane road while a truck is steaming toward us?" Rylan had good questions.

"I'm concerned about this, Rylan." She scanned the officer and it struck her. "Zach never makes a traffic stop without his hand on the butt of his gun, in case of trouble. I've never seen any officer just walk up like this. Also, notice how much is missing from his belt?"

Rylan muttered the same curse she was thinking. Turning the steering wheel a hard left, he mashed the gas pedal. "Take the safety off and get ready to shoot if he so much as looks like he's about to pull his weapon and fire."

The tires peeled out as Rylan banked a U-turn and then navigated the small sport utility on the shoulder and past the black sedan.

"I sure hope you have a plan that doesn't involve getting rammed in the bumper by a pickup truck that weighs far more than my car." She braced for impact, and her thoughts immediately snapped to the little girl in the back seat. Even in a car seat she could be hurt by an impact.

The black sedan's engine revved, and then the vehicle spun around to follow them.

Rylan's reflexes were spot-on as he shifted to the right and swerved so that the pickup missed the bumper.

Zach returned to the line, and Amber gave her cousin the quick rundown and told him they were headed back toward the ranch with two vehicles on their tail. She ended the call. "He promised to send the closest deputy. He's also calling my brothers, so help should be here in a few minutes."

Rylan pushed the SUV as fast as it could go, outmaneuvering the other pursuing vehicles, and she could see why he was the best at what he did. His confidence was earned. She and the baby were handicaps that he wasn't used to accounting for.

Amber was ready with her SIG, but she really didn't

want to get a shooting match started. There was no telling where a stray bullet might end up, and she wouldn't risk Brooklyn's safety.

The road zigzagged ahead, and Rylan drove like an Indy driver on a hot track. He checked the rearview mirror a couple of times before she could visibly see tension leaving his shoulders as the other vehicles moved out of sight.

"They're gone. But I have bad news. You're stuck with me until this whole situation is settled."

"I get that we'll have to hide, but where can we go with an infant?" Traveling with a child wouldn't be easy. If Brooklyn cried at the wrong time, it could be game over. Even Amber realized that.

"Call Mitch. Let him know what just happened. Security needs to be made aware of another threat to the ranch. We can't take anyone's safety for granted." He was right.

The phone call home was short. She relayed the details. Everyone was already on high alert due to the murder that had happened last night. All Amber could think about was getting to her cousin's office and hearing what the mystery man who'd dropped off Brooklyn had to say. Certainly, he'd be able to describe the woman who handed over the baby, and that might jar Rylan's memory. Would she match the victim?

Right now, they had little to go on, and Rylan didn't seem able to remember being with Brooklyn's mother, or any other woman, during that time frame. He'd insisted that alcohol likely played a role in his memory loss, but after being around him she highly doubted that had happened. They would find another explanation if they looked hard enough. She believed that with her whole heart. "Do you think the guys who were following us will expect us to show up at the ranch? They could be circling back."

"I know a back way to Zach's office from here." Rylan made a couple of turns that would have them doubling back. His gaze was intense on the stretch of road in front of them. "I'm sorry I got you involved in this, Amber. I truly am."

"You didn't do anything on purpose." How could he have known how this would all shake out?

"I have no idea what Brooklyn's mother got herself into, but this isn't good and I'd bet anything now she got involved in something illegal." He gripped the steering wheel. That steel resolve was in his voice, but she didn't like the undercurrent of resignation that she picked up on, too.

"We'll find out soon enough. This guy at Zach's office will lead us to Brooklyn's mother—"

"Who might not still be alive," he stated.

"We can't think like that until we know for certain. I'm sure once you hear a description of her it'll all come back. We'll find her and figure out what made her leave this beautiful little girl and take off. I mean, she must've cared about her daughter because she did find a way to leave her with her father," Amber stated.

"What if—" He stopped himself. "No. Never mind."

"Go ahead. Say what you're thinking," she urged.

"I wasn't in a good place that weekend if I had a drink, Amber. There's a chance her description won't ring any bells. And then what? I've put you in danger for nothing." It wasn't exactly defeat in his voice that she heard, but she didn't like where this was going.

"If this guy gives us good information and if it clicks who he's talking about right away, then great. We still have to locate her, and from what I can gather so far, she seems to be in pretty big trouble. Look at that angel in the back seat. She's been well taken care of for three months. Her mother wouldn't do that if she didn't love her. And anyone who takes that good care of her baby can't be all bad. Maybe she got herself in a tough spot and went to the wrong people for help." Amber could only hope her words were sinking in. "It'll be okay. You'll see. This'll all be over soon, and you can start figuring out your next move. You can look forward to getting to know your daughter, Rylan. What could be better than that?"

Amber wiped away an unexpected tear as Rylan navigated into the parking lot of Zach's office, and then parked in a spot close to the front door.

THE SEDAN AND the pickup truck were gone for now. That most likely meant the drivers were on a scouting mission. Experience had taught Rylan that the men would return, ready to strike next time. They'd be better prepared. That was the only explanation for why they didn't shoot. Which led him to the conclusion that someone wanted Brooklyn.

They'd have to kill him to get to her. And based on the protective look on Amber's face as he walked beside her into her cousin's office, the same went for her.

Rylan had had bad days in his life. Hell, most of them could be considered bad once his mother passed away.

There was something about that little girl in Amber's arms that gave him a sense of hope. He chalked it up to the innocence children brought, the new perspective on life. Brooklyn was a good baby, which most likely meant she'd been well cared for up to this point. Her whole life was ahead of her.

A thought struck Rylan as he held the door open for Amber. What if her mother never turned up? Or, worse, what if she turned out to be the victim? What if the thing she'd gotten herself into caused her to lose her life? Other thoughts joined. What if she was sick? What if giving Brooklyn to him was a last-ditch effort to give the baby a chance at life?

All those thoughts amounted to a hill of beans when it came to thinking about anything happening to that little girl. Was there a court in the world that would take her away from him? He hoped the hell not. Because he was all-in when it came to Brooklyn from now on. It was a foreign feeling to him. He hadn't felt like he belonged to something bigger than himself in too long.

Shoving those thoughts aside, he entered Zach's office.

"We're going down the hall." Zach pushed off his desk, stood and focused on Amber. "There were no hits on the vehicles you described."

"They'll be back," Rylan stated.

"We'll be ready." Zach's resolve almost had Rylan believing the man could handle whatever entered his county. But Rylan didn't have time for false hope. This was bigger than Zach and his deputies. Besides, they had a murder to investigate. "But first, follow me."

Rylan put his hand on the small of Amber's back and

ignored the heat pulsing through his fingertips from the contact. This wasn't the time to notice the attraction sizzling between them or think about the kiss they'd shared. Or the fact that he'd never experienced a pull this strong to any other woman.

He forced the thoughts to the back of his mind and refocused on the man who started all this. The blond.

The small room down the hallway from Zach's office had low lighting, no doubt because of the one-way mirror. The room itself wasn't much bigger than a walk-in closet. The space on the other side of the mirror doubled in size. There was a table and two chairs placed opposite each other. The white tile seemed sterile and like what Rylan would find in a hospital hallway. The walls were barren and gray. The only wall decoration visible to Rylan was an analog wall clock. It was circular, about a foot in diameter with large black numbers. The timepiece hung above the only door in and out of the space.

Everything about the room was meant to make someone uncomfortable. It was damn smart because Rylan was uncomfortable looking inside.

The door opened and a deputy walked in with a man in cuffs shuffling behind him. Rylan recognized the man immediately as the one from yesterday, and he felt the tension stiffen his shoulders. He rolled them back to loosen the knots, but it didn't do any good.

"Is it him?" Amber was studying Rylan, and he figured she already knew the answer to that question.

"He's the one." Those three words confirmed what she clearly had already guessed.

The man wore a camouflage hunting jacket, blue

jeans and boots. He was much shorter than Rylan, not six feet tall if he had to venture a guess.

Deputy Perry instructed the suspect to sit. From opposite the table his shoulders were square with Rylan, which was good. The man was close enough for Rylan to see clearly. The interview room was small, and he figured it was designed that way on purpose.

He felt Amber move beside him with the baby in her arms.

The deputy's back was to them. "State your name."

"Chester Hunter III, but my friends call me Chess." Chess sat on the edge of the seat as he wiped his palms on his thighs. Rylan could only guess the man had sweaty palms. Chess displayed other signs of nervousness. Sweat beaded on his forehead, and he blinked at a rapid pace. He spoke a little too fast, and his voice was a higher pitch than Rylan remembered.

Zach opened the door and popped his head in the viewing room. He looked at Rylan. "Can I get a positive ID?"

"I'm certain it was him," Rylan responded.

"He's not denying his involvement. The deputy asked him to wait to give a statement until I could make it in." Zach put a hand on Rylan's shoulder. "Let's hope we get the answers we're looking for."

"Do you live in Jacobstown?" Deputy Perry continued.

"No, sir. I'm from Bremmer City." Bremmer City was to the south of Jacobstown. Rylan had done some partying there in his youth before signing up for the military and righting his life.

"Did you bring a child to a residence in Jacobstown

yesterday?" Deputy Perry jotted down a couple of notes. His posture was the opposite of Chess's. The deputy sat comfortably in the metal and plastic chair. His feet were apart, and he leaned forward on the table in between him and Chess.

"Yes, sir." Chess's right leg started shaking. The man looked to be in his late twenties.

"What's your occupation?" Perry asked.

"Mill worker," Chess replied. "I work for my father's construction company. He builds custom homes."

Perry asked a few follow-up questions.

"Can you describe the child in question?" Fact-checking was a routine part of any investigation.

"She was a little girl. Small enough to fit into one of those carriers you see people with all the time. Her hair was black, curly." He'd gone from a shaking leg to tapping the toe of his boot against the tile floor. "She was a cute kid."

"How old was she?" The deputy's voice was a study in calm. He was almost conspiratorial.

"I don't have enough experience with kids to tell. All I know is she was young enough and small enough to fit into the carrier." The words came out rushed.

"Did she have anything else with her?" Again, the deputy was confirming facts.

"Yeah. She had a diaper bag."

"Can you tell me how you came to be in possession of the child?" Rylan's ears perked up.

"Of course. I was pumping gas at the 401, the one by the Pig's Ear down on farm road 26. That's the one I always go to because gas is always cheaper than by the interstate." He blinked up at the deputy like competing gas prices were common knowledge.

The deputy nodded.

"So, I'm pumping gas when a woman holding a baby in a carrier comes up to me. She looked scared and her eyes were saucers, like a cornered animal's. She comes up to me and starts begging me to help her out. I'm looking all around expecting someone to charge up to us, or something—"

"Can you describe her?" Deputy Perry asked.

Rylan leaned toward the glass and listened.

"She was pretty. Her hair and eyes were brown, like coffee beans. She stood about yay high." He held his right hand up to his chin, which would make her about five feet five inches.

Rylan drew a blank.

The deputy scribbled more notes. "Can you describe what she was wearing?"

"Yeah. She had on some kind of shirt with jeans. The shirt was short-sleeved. Oh, and flip-flops. I noticed because I thought it was weird she wasn't wearing a coat or real shoes since it was so cold out." His gaze was fixed but there was nothing on the walls to stare at, and it was one of those blank stares like when someone recalled facts.

To Rylan's thinking, the guy seemed legitimate. He was definitely the man from the other day. There was no question. Rylan had wondered if Chess was involved. Based on his reactions and what he said so far, there was nothing to make Rylan believe that was true.

Deputy Perry glanced up. "Did you say flip-flops?"

"I thought that was weird, too," Chess stated. "The

kid was bundled up, though. She had a warm blanket over her and a hat on."

Flip-flops on a frigid day. No coat. The mystery woman was in a hurry, which supported the idea that she'd been in grave danger. Could she be from the area?

Chess's statement made Rylan think the mystery woman had found out at the last minute that someone was coming for her or the baby. The last thought struck a chord. Was the mystery woman in trouble herself and trying to off-load the baby, or was someone after Brooklyn instead?

The fact that someone was *still* after the little girl— his daughter—gave him the strong impression she was the target. Had they gotten to Brooklyn's mother? Had she disappeared in time, afraid to show up while the men chasing her were in town?

There were more questions than answers in this case.

Amber looked to Rylan expectantly.

He shook his head. "I don't know who she is."

"Did she have any distinguishing marks? Scars? Birthmarks? Tattoos?" Deputy Perry returned his focus to the notepad as he scribbled.

"Not that I can think of." Chess returned his focus to the spot it had been before. And then his face twisted. "You know, now that you mention it she did have a birthmark on her neck. It was low, close to her collarbone. On her left side because facing me it was on the right."

That struck a chord. A vague memory tried to take shape in Rylan's mind, but it was still a blur. He'd been running on no sleep for weeks during a mission in Kandahar. And then he'd gone to San Antonio for the last three months where he'd remained until getting his papers and moving to Jacobstown.

There was a time in his life when finding out he'd had a child after a weekend of partying wouldn't have surprised him. Granted, he wouldn't be proud of himself. But he wouldn't be shocked, either.

Looking back, shame for the way he'd handled his stress, his life, engulfed him like an out-of-control forest fire. Now that his head was clear, he could acknowledge that he'd used alcohol to deal with the stress of losing his mother before he was out of high school. He'd worked hard and partied even harder until that last time when he was so out of it he caught the Willows' crops on fire. He'd been so out of it that he'd almost died. It was a wake-up call. After that, he realized he needed to deal with his pent-up emotions in a healthier manner. Truth of the matter was that he'd wanted to be a better man. The desire had spread like a wildfire after Will had lied in order to protect Rylan.

Becoming sober hadn't been easy. He'd attacked it like everything in his life. He'd gone all-in. He'd realized that he needed to open up and talk, let people in rather than hold everything inside. He'd started talking after that instead of ignoring his pain and little by little was able to let the past go.

Admitting he'd needed help went against everything inside him as a soldier who'd been trained to rely on himself and take care of everyone else around him. Until he realized it made him far more of a man to own up to his mistakes, to his weaknesses. The hardest damn thing had been taking an honest look in the mirror.

Rylan would never be free of the shame, the guilt

until he made things right in Jacobstown. He had two apologies left to make. One to the Willow family and the other to Will Kent. He owed the Willows retribution. But how did he repay Will? How did he square with the man who'd stepped up and blamed his own negligence for the fire that devoured the Willows' crops and almost their livelihood?

Mr. and Mrs. Kent had stepped in to get the Willows back on their feet. He couldn't apologize to them or thank them for what they'd done. But he owed the Kent family. He sure as hell wasn't repaying them by getting Amber mixed up in his life. That made two Kents who should know better than to put their trust in Rylan.

Chapter Eleven

Amber stared at the one-way mirror. Hearing details about a woman Rylan had had a fling with shouldn't have this effect on her. So, why did it?

One kiss, no matter how electric it had been, did not a relationship make. Besides, getting involved with Rylan beyond friendship would be a mistake. He seemed to realize it as much as she did.

She bounced Brooklyn on her hip, reminding herself that she had no claim on Rylan. The two were friends and he'd come to her for help, not for a relationship. Was there chemistry between them? She'd be a fool to deny it. They'd always been able to laugh and joke around when they were younger. She'd always felt a little spark whenever Rylan was over. That spark had ignited into a full-blown attraction.

And how smart was that on her part?

Pretty damn stupid.

Rylan might have a child—and she had no doubt this little girl would be the one thing that Rylan would stick to—but that didn't change who he was. He would always move on. Those words, that honesty shouldn't feel like a knife wound to her chest.

Amber needed to create a little emotional distance. She took a step away from him as she examined the face of the man being questioned. Strange that he lived one town over but she had no idea who he was. It seemed like everyone knew each other in Jacobstown, but that wasn't exactly true. People moved in and out without being known.

Zach entered the viewing room. "How's it going in here?"

She knew what he was really asking. *Was any of this ringing a bell?*

"Not as well as I would like," Rylan responded.

"The coroner is sending over pictures of the victim in the hopes of a positive ID." Zach's voice held the respect of a deacon during Sunday morning church service.

Amber's heart went out to the little girl in her arms. It made sense that her mother would've given her to someone else if she suspected something was about to happen. Had her mother seen death coming? Was that why she'd made a bold move in making sure the child got to Rylan?

It was strange that Brooklyn's mother could be somehow tied to the Jacobstown Hacker. Or maybe she wasn't. Amber leaned toward Rylan and asked, "What do you think the odds of her mother being connected to the Jacobstown Hacker are?"

"I thought about that, too. Maybe she was an innocent victim of his, the perfect opportunity for him to finally strike." Rylan folded his arms across his broad chest.

Amber hugged Brooklyn a little closer to her. She couldn't imagine growing up without a mother. It was difficult enough to lose a mother as an adult. But as a child? Amber was even more grateful for the time she had with hers.

An argument could be made that Brooklyn's mother wasn't at the top of her game. She'd obviously gotten herself into some kind of trouble. She knew to stash her child away safely. Now that the paternity test had come back, it was certain that Rylan was the child's father.

What could Brooklyn's mother have possibly gotten herself into that could force her to hide her daughter? Coming to Jacobstown must've been a last-ditch effort. But showing up in flip-flops in late January, not wearing a coat?

Granted, it appeared as though she wasn't here on her own accord. She'd wrapped up the child in blankets and a hat before handing her off to a stranger and, what? Hoped for the best? That screamed of desperation. The woman didn't take time to put her own coat on.

The interview in the next room continued, and Amber realized she'd spaced out for a second.

"Did you ask the woman with the baby her name?" Deputy Perry continued.

"No. I didn't really think to at the time—"

"A woman thrusts her child at you and you weren't the least bit curious about her background?" Perry lifted a brow.

"It wasn't like that. She came up to me and begged me to take her baby. She said she needed help, but I told her to go inside the convenience store and tell the clerk. I told her to call the sheriff but—" His words came out faster this time. He'd already been rushing his speech, but he shifted in his seat and put his hands up to his face. "She said she couldn't involve the sheriff. Or something along those lines. I'd finished pumping my gas and was putting the nozzle back in the receptor by then. My first thought was that she was on something, but as she talked I realized she was scared."

"And what was your response?" There was no sound of judgment in the deputy's voice. Amber was too emotional to work in law enforcement. The thought of a man refusing to help someone in need riled her up too much. She'd never be so diplomatic. But then, that's probably one of many reasons she was a cattle rancher and didn't wear a badge.

"My mind immediately snapped to someone abusing her. That's when I looked for signs," he stated.

"And did you find any?" Deputy Perry spun the pen between his fingers as he waited for a response.

"That's when I saw the birthmark. No bruising, though. But that doesn't mean it wasn't somewhere on her body. She rattled off an address and said she needed to get the baby there ASAP." He paused for a beat. "She also said to make sure I wasn't followed."

"How did you respond to her?"

"I told her that I couldn't help her. She needed to go to the law." He flashed his eyes at the deputy. "I had a cousin who got shot for trying to help a friend of his who was in an argument with her boyfriend. I don't stick my nose where it doesn't belong."

Domestic violence was a serious issue. Amber had heard from Zach countless times those calls were the most dangerous. Domestic violence calls and traffic stops ranked up there as the most threatening to officers.

Still. Every one of Amber's brothers would stop to

help any person in need. There'd be no question. She could tell by the way Rylan tensed that he would've done the same. That was his personality. He might be the type to move around and never settle in one place for long but he wouldn't turn down anyone who asked him for a hand.

"What happened next?" Deputy Perry kept the interview on target.

"She got a panicked look. Started looking from side to side like someone might jump out from behind the gas pump. I'd finished my business so I told her that I had to go inside and pay. I told her to come with me and call someone. That's when she took off running." He paused another beat. "I figured that was the last I'd see of her or her baby. But when my back was turned she sneaked the baby in the driver's seat and took off."

"How'd you remember the address?" Perry made a good point.

"Easy. My mom moved out that way when she and my pops divorced. I'd been over there more than a few times to visit. Mom used to live next door to Mrs. Parker." Chess seemed satisfied with himself for the answer.

Amber turned to face Zach. "Any chance he could be *him*?"

"He would've been the last one to see her alive if the victim turns out to be Brooklyn's mother, which makes him our top suspect," Zach stated. "And he just admitted to being familiar with the area."

"I picked up on that, too." A shiver raced down Amber's back. She turned and studied the man sitting at the table. Would she even know if she was staring at a killer?

"Does your mother still live at the same address?" There was a slight difference to Perry's voice. She doubted Chess picked up on it.

"No, sir. She moved two years ago." If Chess was the Jacobstown Hacker, would he admit to knowing the area so freely? "My stepdad got work in Houston so they headed south."

"Do you come back to Jacobstown to visit friends?"

"Didn't have any. I'd stop by my mother's for lunch on Sunday a couple times a month. We didn't go out. I'd watch the game with Paul, her husband, and then head home," he admitted.

Zach's phone pinged. He checked the screen. "Coroner is sending over pictures of the victim."

Amber searched Rylan's face. He may not have had a relationship with the woman who could very well be the victim, but that didn't mean this would be easy. He'd spent time with her. They'd had a child. Granted, he didn't know about Brooklyn until two days ago, but a child connected people whether they wanted to be or not. She thought about the child she'd lost. About her ex, Red Coker. Losing their child had broken their relationship. Every time she thought about what happened to her baby, she ached. The pain hit her full force, like it had happened yesterday.

She shoved the thoughts down deep and refocused on Zach, who was pulling up an image on his phone.

He must've texted the deputy in the next room because he told Chess to sit tight and then left the room.

Chess fidgeted with his hands before leaning forward and resting his elbows on his knees. His right leg was going a mile a minute.

Zach stared at the image on his phone as he shared it with Rylan.

"There's no birthmark on her neck," Rylan pointed out. "It can't be her."

"Can I see? I might be able to help." She handed the baby to Rylan before walking over and standing next to her cousin. She wanted to protect the innocence of the child even though Brooklyn would have no idea what she was looking at. It didn't take but a second to recognize the victim. "I know who she is. That's Breanna Griswold."

Zach muttered a curse under his breath. "I remember that family."

"They moved away a few years ago saying they wanted a fresh start after Breanna got into trouble here. We were in the same grade in school, but we didn't hang out. She used to skip a lot. I think she got held back for nonattendance after freshman year of high school. I always felt so bad for her. She seemed sad all the time." Amber had invited her to sit together at lunch, but Breanna flat-out refused. "She kept to herself and never socialized. I saw her a few times hanging out with the McFarland boys, and we all know they turned out to be bad news."

Rylan suddenly got very still. She remembered overhearing a fight between him and Will about those brothers years ago. She figured this wasn't the time to reopen those old wounds. It was obvious by Will's actions earlier that he hadn't forgiven Rylan for whatever happened between them in the past.

She turned to Rylan. "Did you know her?"

He shook his head. "I have no idea why she would've been on the ranch."

Brooklyn tried to jam her entire fist inside her mouth. She started fidgeting in Rylan's arms.

"She's probably getting hungry," Amber stated, ignoring the look Zach issued. He could look all he wanted. It wouldn't stop her from getting to know Rylan's daughter. Besides, that man needed a hand if anyone did. He admittedly had no idea how to take care of a child. He didn't exactly have time to learn, either. She'd literally been thrust in his arms two days ago. "Can I help you get a bottle ready in the break room?"

Rylan glanced at Zach. "I don't want to get in the way of a family discussion."

He must've picked up on the feeling of being the monkey in the middle. She wasn't trying to put him in that position.

"Zach, you have anything else you want to say to me?" Amber's balled fist was on her hip now.

Her cousin shot a defeated look toward her. "I'm good."

"Then it's settled. I can take you to the break room. There's a microwave in there where we can heat up her bottle." Amber motioned for Rylan to follow. She thought about the offer to keep Brooklyn at the ranch and figured the idea deserved more consideration.

With a glance in Zach's direction, Rylan joined her in the hallway. He turned back to the sheriff. "Let me know if Chess says anything worth hearing."

"You bet."

"I can take her or the diaper bag. Which is a better help?" Rylan asked.

"You want to hold this muffin so I can figure out how to heat her bottle in that microwave? I never come here anymore," she admitted.

Brooklyn fussed the minute her daddy took her in his arms. "I don't think she likes me very much."

"You'll get the hang of it, Rylan. Give yourself a chance. The two of you just met." Amber looked at the baby, who was working up to belt out another cry. Her heart fisted while everything inside Amber rushed to comfort the baby. Yeah, she was in deep trouble. "I'll take her back and you can make the bottle."

"She met you *after* me." Rylan admitted defeat as he handed over the little girl. He followed Amber down the hallway and into the break room.

Amber rattled off instructions for heating the bottle as she rocked Brooklyn, offering what little comfort she could when all the baby really wanted to do was fill her belly.

Fifteen minutes and one crazy messed-up bib later, Brooklyn was sucking on a bottle of formula. It was dangerous to get too attached, Amber thought. And then she looked into those beautiful brown eyes that looked so much like the baby's daddy.

Thoughts of Breanna struck, of her family and how they would have to hear the worst news ever. Now Breanna's parents would suffer the heartbreak no parent should ever have to endure. Granted, Amber didn't wish that particular brand of pain on anyone. Having heard rumors about the family, she knew they wouldn't be described as close-knit. Did that really matter?

To her thinking, pain was pain. Loss was loss. And she wished she'd made even more of an effort to reach out to Breanna back in school. Would it have made a difference? Amber would like to think that everyone's actions could. Was she living in a fantasy world?

Maybe she didn't want to live in a world where they didn't.

Looking at Brooklyn, at her innocence, Amber had to believe that everyone could make a difference in someone else's life. She would already do anything for the little girl in her arms. The thought was dangerous.

Could she open up her heart again?

Chapter Twelve

Rylan studied Amber as Brooklyn slept against her chest. Ellen Haiden, Zach's secretary, had dimmed the lights in the break room, and Amber had moved to a leather club couch that was backed up against the east facing wall.

"I'm sorry about your friend," Rylan said.

"That's the thing—she wasn't."

He cocked an eyebrow.

"She had trouble at home. I heard rumors that she had it pretty rough. I invited her to sit at my lunch table, but she refused. I gave up even though I knew I shouldn't have." Her voice was laced with regret.

"How old were you?"

"I was in ninth grade. Old enough to know better," she said.

"Most kids that age can't be bothered to think about anyone but themselves. The fact that you noticed says how special you are." He took a seat on the arm of the couch and touched her cheek. Outside of the break room, activity was a blur. Here, with Amber, time seemed to slow and the setting felt intimate. It was just her. Being with her stirred places inside him. He still wasn't ready to figure out what that meant, but he was intrigued. No one had ever held his attention like she did. He'd never felt a draw this strong or wanted to reach out and touch a woman this badly.

And that's where he put on the brakes.

Amber was a friend, probably his only friend. He didn't need to go messing around with that. As long as he was in Jacobstown, and for the first time in his life he was thinking about sticking around somewhere more than a minute, he needed that friend.

Part of him wanted to say that he needed her, but he shut it down before it could gain any traction. Rylan didn't *need* anyone. He did, however, appreciate her help. So he wouldn't repay her kindness by taking her to bed, even though she gave him signs and his body tried to convince him it wouldn't end in disaster.

Besides, Will hated Rylan enough already. He didn't want to hurt his former best friend any further.

When Rylan had called Amber, he thought he was asking for a favor that might last a couple of hours. He never would've signed her up for what was going on. "You sure you want to keep doing this?"

"Doing what?" She bit back a yawn.

"Stick with me. I realize you're in danger, Amber. And you have a heart bigger than Texas, which is saying a lot. But there are places you could go to be safe," he said.

"Where? Like the ranch?" She twisted her mouth. "Look how well that worked out for Breanna."

She made a point. And he was still trying to figure out why she would've been on the family's ranch in the first place.

"Besides, Rylan, how do you know you didn't save my life?"

Now she was going overboard. "What does that mean exactly?"

"If I'd been on the ranch, that could've been me. This jerk was ready to strike. He's been ready. He's been biding his time, waiting for the right opportunity. What if that had been me out there instead of Breanna?" He couldn't argue the logic. And he appreciated her trying to take the burden off him.

"I hear what you're saying. We go back a long time," he started, "so don't take what I'm saying the wrong way. But I'd never forgive myself if anything happened to you because you were helping me."

She stared at him for a long moment. He expected her to put up a fight, but she seemed to be contemplating his words instead. She pursed full pink lips, and then she spoke. "I understand."

Silence sat between them, and he gave her a minute to rethink her position.

"I hear you, Rylan. I do. You've said it more than once. No matter how much this investigation heats up, I'm committed to helping you and this baby. You have a family, Rylan. How wonderful is that?" She put her hand up before he could comment. "Granted, I know the circumstances are not ideal. We'll find this baby's mother and figure out who she's running from. But at the end of the day you have a healthy and beautiful baby girl. That's a blessing some people never get."

Her words, her loss, was a gut punch. He must seem pretty damn selfish to her, considering she'd lost a child. He couldn't argue the point that Brooklyn was a beautiful kid. He had bigger fears about what the child's mother had gotten all of them into. From the sound of Chess's statement, Brooklyn's mother was scared half out of her mind. "We don't have any idea what's really going on. If I have a chance to protect you from it, I will."

"I know that, Rylan. I appreciate the fact that you care. Right now, you need me. You don't have the first idea how to take care of this little angel." Amber held that child tight against her chest. It was easy to see that someone would need pliers to pry Brooklyn from Amber's hands.

Rylan knew when he'd lost a battle. He wanted Amber's help, just not at the risk of losing her.

So, he conceded the argument for now and paced while he waited for word from Zach.

A half hour ticked by while they waited for Chess to work with a sketch artist.

The man was scared and, better yet, willing to cooperate. He was also the last known person to see Brooklyn's mother alive. Rylan could only hope she wasn't physically harmed. After hearing the story from Chess, it was clear that Brooklyn's mother was in serious danger.

About a year ago, Rylan remembered spending a lot of his leave time with a buddy. This was as good a time as any to make the phone call he'd been needing to make. Fishing out his cell, he told Amber about making the call and excused himself. It seemed wrong to talk about his time spent with another woman in front of her, like a betrayal.

Roger Hendricks answered on the first ring. "Rylan, man, are you in town?"

"Hey, Roger. Nah. I'm back in Jacobstown."

"Yeah? I heard you got out. Thought you might be up for a party," Roger said.

"Another time." Rylan had no plans to follow up on that. "I was hoping you could help me out, bro."

"Anything. You know I'd do anything for you, man," came Roger's response. The two had gone through basic training together before different deployments sent them to opposite ends of the world. They'd stayed in touch. Rylan had set his sight on elite forces, where Roger had served and then gotten the heck out, as he'd put it. His friend had said the only sand he wanted to see for the rest of his life was on a beach in the US. Rylan couldn't blame the man. Places like Kandahar weren't for everyone. "What's up?"

"I'm trying to locate a woman—"

"Who am I? Tinder?" Roger joked.

"Funny, bro. It's someone from last year. A friend of Sandy's." Sandy was Roger's girlfriend.

"Ah, yeah, Sandy. We had a good time together. But, man, we broke up months ago," he informed him.

"No worries, bro. What's Sandy's last name? Maybe I can find the person I'm looking for on her social media," Rylan explained. "It's important that I find her. I think she might be in some kind of trouble. I'd like to help her out."

"Good thinking. Bonds is her last name," Roger replied.

"Cool. Thanks, bro. I owe you one." Rylan didn't want to get into the whole baby business with his buddy.

Not yet anyway. He was still coming to terms with the fact that he was that little girl's father.

He ended the call and located Zach in his office. The sheriff had a serious expression as he studied his computer screen.

Rylan knocked on the doorjamb.

"Sorry, I didn't see you standing there." Zach seemed caught off guard. "I have the sketch."

He motioned toward his desk and studied Rylan as he walked over and picked it up.

"I don't know." Rylan racked his brain. She seemed kind of familiar but he wasn't certain. "It's not ringing any bells."

"Sorry," Zach said. His tone said he meant it.

"I have the name of my buddy's ex-girlfriend. I just got off the phone with him a few minutes ago. I might be able to use her social media page to locate our mystery woman. Do you have a tablet I can borrow? Amber and I can search social media sites and see what we can come up with," Rylan said.

"Great idea." Zach searched around on his desk, and had to move a couple of files before he uncovered a tablet. He held it up. "Here you go."

Rylan thanked him and returned to the break room with the tablet in hand. He sat next to Amber. "Let's see what we can find on this."

"Who are we looking for?" Amber's shoulder touched his, and he ignored the impact the contact had on him. When the time was right, he planned to address it. He also planned to see how far another kiss would take them even though he knew better than to go there in his mind.

"I have the name of one of Brooklyn's mother's friends. Sandy Bonds. I thought we could check social media now that we have a face to go on."

He set the sketch of the mystery woman on his leg while he pulled up a popular social media site on the tablet and performed a search for Sandy Bonds. Several faces popped up. He searched each one until he recognized her.

"There she is. There's Sandy Bonds." Amber studied the page.

"Who has seven hundred–plus friends?" Rylan asked under his breath. Close friends he could count on one hand. Okay, maybe his best friend was sitting next to him. And that was another reason why he shouldn't be thinking about the kiss they'd shared or wanting more than that from her.

"I never did get into social media other than for the ranch. I started our page and post every once in a while on it," Amber said. "It helped get word out when we were changing our practices in order to provide organic meats to our customers."

Rylan remembered that he'd read something about her being a pioneer in the beef industry. He admired her business savvy, but he also knew she respected her animals.

He scrolled through the faces, searching for a resemblance to the sketch. Zach strolled in and joined them, sitting on the opposite side of Amber.

And then it happened. The face he was searching for filled the screen.

"Alicia Ward." Zach said the name out loud most likely hoping to trigger a memory.

"We have a name." Rylan shrugged. "It doesn't ring any bells for me, but at least we have a face and a name to go with it. Let's figure out who she is. Click on her page."

"Mind if I?" Zach clicked on the tile with her face and a profile filled the screen. Rylan would call this progress, except there wasn't much on her page save for a few stock pictures of animals with cutesy quotes underneath.

"How much do people have to fill out in order to show up on one of these sites?" Rylan asked.

"Not much and any information can be faked," Amber said. "There aren't as many controls as you'd think there should be. Pretty much anyone can make a page as long as they don't put up strange or offensive material to get their page reported."

Zach scrolled through the animal pictures, no doubt looking for some kind of clue about the woman they searched for. "There's no information about who she is or where she's from. Do you know if she's even from Texas?"

"We met in Austin while I was stationed in San Antonio for a training exercise. I was in and out in a few weeks. Went to my friend's house a couple of times in Austin. Hit Sixth Street to listen to live music. I'd been through a stressful time overseas, and Roger thought I needed to get out more." Rylan tried to force the memory. He had a beautiful baby girl whose DNA matched his own. He ought to be able to remember the child's mother.

"Sandy should be easy enough to find. Her information is accessible." Some of Zach's confidence had returned. "You said Alicia is Sandy's friend."

"That's right." All Rylan could remember from those few times in Austin was hanging around with Roger. Most of the weekends were clear as a bell. There was one he couldn't make heads or tails out of, and that bugged him to no end. Guilt and a strong sense of shame slammed into him. Rylan had never considered himself weak, so a binge weekend seemed impossible. And yet the evidence sat in Amber's arms.

He fished out his cell and called Roger back. "Hey, sorry to bother you again. Do you mind if I ask a strange question?"

"Not at all, man. Go for it," Roger said.

"Was I sober when we hung out?" The question probably seemed out of the blue.

"You don't remember?" Based on the surprise in Roger's voice, Rylan had caught his friend off guard.

"I know I didn't choose to drink. But that's not the same thing as being sober—"

"Well, I didn't force anything down your throat," Roger joked.

Rylan let the conversation stay lighthearted. It was embarrassing to have to ask. He didn't remember falling off the wagon so why was that one weekend so fuzzy? Why didn't he remember the mother of his child or the making of his child? Hell, he should remember that, at least.

"Let me think back. Damn, it's been a while since we hung out, and you were definitely a saint. No drinking. But, yeah, there was that one time I wondered about you." His friend got quiet.

"What did I do?"

"Slurred your speech. You sounded… I don't know…*off*. Not like yourself. I even asked what you were drinking, but you denied having a beer." Roger paused. "Which was strange because I'm not the saint you think I am. I remember thinking there was no reason to lie to me."

"Was I with a woman that night? Do you remember me being with someone?" Rylan moved his lips away from the mouthpiece and focused on Zach. "Can you send that picture over to him?"

Zach nodded. He got Roger's number from Rylan and texted Alicia's photo.

A minute passed before Roger responded. "Wow, yeah, I remember this woman. What did you say her name was again?"

"Alicia Ward," Rylan said.

Roger drew in a breath. "Of course I remember her. A person remembers someone as good-looking as her. Especially when she comes on to his buddy. I was with Sandy then so it didn't bother me. But she was smokin' hot and seemed pretty locked on to you. You didn't stay in touch?"

"No. I don't remember much about her, and that's throwing me off because I quit drinking and got my act together when I signed up for the military." Rylan wasn't frustrated with his friend. He was frustrated with himself. "I don't remember drinking that night because I don't drink anymore."

"If a woman who looked like that came on to me, I'd remember." Roger's comment issued a strong response from Amber.

She grunted and Zach turned his head to face her. He seemed to know better than to say anything once he got a good look at her expression.

Hell, Rylan knew better than to poke the bear. Part of him—a part he shouldn't give much credence to—liked the fact that Amber seemed jealous. He knew better than to let the thought take seed. "I don't remember much about that weekend, to be honest. Do you remember if I did anything to embarrass myself in public?"

"I had my own thing going, and it's been a long time. Nothing that stands out," Roger said.

It was too soon to be relieved and Rylan wasn't any closer to answers, but if he'd slipped he was fairly certain Roger would've known it. Which didn't explain why he didn't remember Alicia. All he remembered drinking that night was soda.

"Thanks, bro. If you remember anything, will you give me a shout?" It was worth asking even though Rylan doubted anything would spark. A year was a long time to recall something that happened over a weekend. And to a buddy.

"Will do, man."

Rylan ended the call after saying goodbye.

"I'll be able to dig around now that we have a name. I'll get my secretary on a hunt for Brooklyn's birth certificate. That woman works miracles when it comes to research. Now that we know you're the father and we have a mother's name, there are two possibilities for last names, which will narrow the field." Zach's mind was clicking through his next steps. Those seemed like good places to start.

"I keep wondering why the unmarked car from earlier sat behind us for so long without making a move. When we bolted, he didn't try to shoot, either." That was just two of the puzzle pieces not clicking in Rylan's mind. "I keep coming back to the fact they were casing us." He turned to Zach. "There another reason you can think of?"

"I agree with you. They most likely wanted to see who is involved and monitor the threat level for when they come back," Zach stated.

"Why keep coming back at all?" Amber had been quiet for the past few minutes, and Rylan didn't necessarily see that as a positive sign.

"It's obvious that someone wants Brooklyn." Zach rubbed the scruff on his chin. "You want my honest opinion?"

Amber shot a look that dared him to go ahead.

"The mother got herself in some kind of trouble or decided to sell her baby to a ruthless baby ring. There's big money in black-market adoptions. A couple might have been promised this child and then the mother reneged. Maybe she didn't want to go along with this in the first place but felt she had no choice. So, she figures out another way, panics at the last minute and then backs out of the agreement. These guys aren't having any of that, so they come after the girl. Only these guys don't ask permission. They're used to taking what they want. They get things done. I'll send a deputy out to speak to Sandy Bonds and see if we can get any information about her friend. This could take a few days, so I want both of you to be prepared for that. I need a little time to investigate, and I need to know all three of you will be safe in the meantime. You're welcome to stay at my house."

Brooklyn woke up and started fussing, interrupting Zach. From what Rylan gathered so far about babies, she would need a bottle and a diaper change. "We appreciate the offer, Zach, but we'll figure out a good spot."

"How could anyone abandon a sweet little baby like this?" Amber's eyes sparked as she repositioned Brooklyn onto the couch beside her in order to change the little one's diaper. "Trouble or not, what kind of person could just drop her off with a stranger and run? She had no idea this man would come find you. He could've done anything he wanted to this little girl."

What did that say? Rylan let the thought sit for a few minutes. He liked to think of himself as a good judge of character. Going on a bender and having a baby with a near-stranger weren't shining examples of good behavior. Those weren't making the highlight reel of his life.

Again, he thought about the drinking and chided himself. How could he have allowed this to happen? He'd been to parties with beautiful women before and had never gotten out of control. The urge to drink never went away, but as the years went by sobriety got easier to maintain. He couldn't remember the last time he'd been tempted.

"If you two will excuse me, I have some work I need to get back to. I'll return as soon as I have something more to talk about." He extended his hand and Rylan shook it. "I said it before but welcome back to town."

Chapter Thirteen

"A sheriff's office is no place for a baby." Amber hugged the little girl tighter to her chest. She'd changed and helped feed Brooklyn, but the baby had a hard time settling back down. "She's probably just picking up on all this energy. We're too stressed, and she's reading us and there's too much activity for her to go to sleep."

"Can babies do that?" Rylan paced circles around the break room while gently bouncing Brooklyn. Seeing such a strong man being so gentle with a little one cracked a little more of the casing around Amber's meticulously guarded heart.

"Pick up on energy?" She looked at him. "I believe so. I've seen it with my nieces and nephews. If not that, she could have a fever."

Rylan stopped long enough for her to touch the baby's forehead.

"Is she hot?"

"No. Not that I want her to be sick, but that would explain why she's so fussy." Amber followed as Rylan made another lap.

"Everything she's known for the past three months

has changed. She might just be reacting to wanting her mother." He made a good point.

"I can't imagine what would have to happen for me to be willing to be away from my child." Amber's cheeks almost caught fire for how much she burned on the inside thinking about Brooklyn's circumstances.

"I don't remember her." Rylan stopped. "How much of a jerk does that make me?"

"It's weird. Don't you think? You don't remember drinking and, Rylan, I believe you. You vaguely remember spending time with someone, but it's all hazy. Have you thought about the fact that this woman might've slipped something in your—" she paused for a second "—Coke or tea or whatever you were drinking?"

"Coffee."

"At a party?" Amber wasn't a drinker but even she didn't drink coffee at night. And she loved her some coffee.

"It was winter. Cold outside and I'm not much on soda." His honesty shouldn't make her want to laugh. There was something pure in those words and she was more convinced than ever that he didn't drink, even though she couldn't prove it and all evidence pointed to him doing just that. "I'd just gotten back from a deployment and was undergoing some training in San Antonio. I had leave so I called Roger. I wanted to get the hell off base and away from anyone wearing combat boots."

Was he talking about something real with her? Not just cracking a joke when a subject got too intense like when they were kids? She liked the fact that he'd opened up to her. She could see the pain in his features when he talked about the possibility of him drinking.

"Did something happen overseas?" She wondered if that was part of the reason he'd doubted himself.

"A lot happened over there, most of which I can't talk about. But the worst of it, the worst of human kind came when a grandmother strapped an IUD to her grandson and sent him toward a bunch of us." He stopped like he needed a minute. Brooklyn fussed a little more, and he picked up where he left off pacing.

"That must've been horrific to watch." Again, she couldn't fathom a parent or grandparent who could do something so awful.

"The kid didn't make it near any of us. His life was sacrificed for nothing. Don't get me wrong, I didn't want any of my fellow SEALs to die—"

"I get it. You wanted his life to mean something. He was young, innocent. If he had to die, it should be for something," she said.

He stopped and locked eyes with her for a long moment. It was like time froze and the earth shifted. Sure, he was handsome and she'd been attracted to him from the time they were in high school. This grown-up crush just got real. And she couldn't allow the seed that had been planted to grow because her heart ached for Rylan.

So she cleared her throat and refocused on Brooklyn.

"She probably just needs to get out of here. Your arms must be breaking by now. Do you want me to take a turn with her?" She diverted her gaze because she didn't want to look him in the eyes when she felt so vulnerable.

"I got this. Looks like I'll have to get used to it just being me and her at some point. I appreciate all your help, but I have to learn how to care for my daughter."

"Rylan, do you want to hear a shock?"

He nodded.

"You're going to be an amazing dad."

"I doubt that. But I plan to give it my all. My failures won't be from lack of trying, that's for damn sure." He patted Brooklyn's back, but she only fussed more.

"Maybe try sitting down with her." She glanced at the wall clock. "It's time for another bottle."

It was getting late. They'd been at the sheriff's office for at least twelve hours. They both knew they needed to leave at some point. They couldn't stay there all night, not with a baby who needed some comforts.

Amber made a bottle. She needed something to do with her hands anyway.

Rylan settled onto the sofa with the little girl in his arms. He carefully positioned her so he could free his right hand in order to feed her the bottle. She settled down almost immediately as she latched on to the plastic nipple. He had that satisfied smile that dented his cheek. Her heart stirred even though she ordered it to behave.

That was the thing about being with Rylan. Her emotions were as out of control as he was. Amber wouldn't change a thing about him, either.

"It might be easier to transport her once she's sleeping. We'll have a few hours to make our move before she'll need tending to again," Rylan said, his voice a low rumble.

"Where should we go and how should we get there?" Amber asked as Zach walked into the room.

"I got a hit on the birth certificate. The baby's name is Brooklyn Ward, and she was born in a hospital in

San Marcos," Zach informed them. "Her mother listed her occupation as a homemaker. She didn't list a father's name."

"That's not surprising given the circumstances," Rylan said.

"The hospital where she gave birth has a reputation for covering up illegal adoptions," Zach warned. "It seems we were on track with the adoption ring."

"Can a baby be adopted without the father's consent?" Rylan made a good point. Amber didn't have a lot of knowledge of the adoption process, but the question was reasonable.

"In the state of Texas, when there's no father on record or at the birth, judges usually side with the mother," Zach informed him.

"How can we find out if paperwork was filed? Or if an adoption has been started?" Rylan started firing questions.

"She can't be taken away from you legally now that paternity is being established. Technically it already has been, but I'm talking about in the eyes of the law. My favorite lab should be able to confirm what we already know. Brooklyn is your daughter." Zach glanced from Rylan to Amber. "Why do I get the feeling the two of you were about to leave?"

"This place isn't good for a baby. She needs a bath and clean clothes," Amber stated.

"Were you thinking of taking her back to the ranch?" Zach asked.

"That's probably not a good idea. There will be a lot of attention as soon as news of Breanna's murder gets out," Amber replied. "This office will also be inundated. How will we be able to keep this little girl protected with people coming in and out? You know as well as I do the town has been uneasy. Everyone's been fearing what just happened on the ranch, and we have no idea how much pandemonium the news will stir up."

"You're right. We're already starting to get calls. Word will spread like wildfire from here," Zach admitted.

"Where is it safe for us to go?" Amber was thinking out loud.

"Maybe it's best if we don't say. I know a place we should be safe." Rylan sounded confident, and Amber wished she shared the feeling.

As it was, she felt like she was damned if she did and damned if she didn't. Tell Zach where they were planning to hide out and their location could end up compromised. Don't tell him and there'd be no extra patrol to count on.

Deputy Perry peeked his head into the break room. "Sir, there's a couple here that has requested to speak with you."

"Can it wait? I'm in the middle of something here," Zach said.

"This couple says they're Brooklyn Ward's parents."

"That's impossible," Amber said under her breath. She was on her feet in two seconds flat. "Zach—"

"I know," he reassured her. "Give me a minute to get them inside the interview room, and then I'll send for you. Wait here."

Willpower was in short supply when it came to waiting to see who claimed to be Brooklyn's parents. The expression on Rylan's face, the steel resolve in the face of the unknown made her wish for half his strength. This couldn't be easy on him.

Zach left the room, and she wheeled around to Rylan.

"Let's just hear them out. They can't be talking about her." She offered reassurance from a shaky voice.

"She's my daughter. They'll take her away over my dead body," was all he said, but those words were loaded with the kind of truth that took on a physical manifestation. There was no room for doubt.

Deputy Perry appeared in the doorway, signaling Amber and Rylan to follow him down the familiar hallway and into the room they'd been in not that long ago. The baby had fussed herself to sleep and was cuddled against her father's shoulder.

After depositing them inside the viewing room, Deputy Perry leaned into the interview room and gave a thumbs-up.

"Please state your name for the record." Zach's posture was relaxed as he leaned over a pad of paper that was sitting atop the table and looked at the male sitting across from him.

There were three people present. A couple who looked to be in their late forties or early fifties and a man wearing one of those crisp expensive buttoned-up collars tucked inside an even more expensive navy blue business suit. The man in the navy suit sat ramrod straight and had an intensity about him, like if he ordered a hamburger at a fast-food restaurant people would immediately get nervous about making it perfect.

The couple also wore suits, cut from material that would classify them as power suits. From what Amber could tell, there was a lot of money sitting across that table. She figured it was old money because everything the couple wore was understated, expensive and classic. There was nothing showy like people with new money gravitated toward.

Wealthy ranchers were a different breed. She noticed the differences all too well growing up. Her father would welcome anyone to the dinner table who was honest and worked hard. Ranch hands often got invited to her mother's legendary Sunday suppers, with food that Amber still could almost taste when she thought hard enough, and missed to this day.

Amber gravitated toward salt-of-the-earth types. If she and Rylan didn't have such a long history, he'd be the kind of man she'd want to date. But then, men she actually wanted to go out with had been in short supply in the past couple of years. Add to the fact that Amber worked fourteen-hour days and she had no time for socializing. It was fine with her except that she could admit to feeling like her life was missing something lately.

She chalked up her change of heart to all the happiness around her. Amy had found happiness with Isaac. Zach recently reconnected with the love of his life.

"My clients' names are Veronica and Cornell Robinson. They received information that their adopted daughter is here in your office." The Suit bent to his right and pulled a manila file folder out of his black briefcase. He set the file on the table between him and used two fingers from each hand to push the file toward Zach.

"What's the basis for Mr. and Mrs. Robinson's

claim?" Zach ignored the manila file, and that seemed to irk the Suit.

Amber had seen her cousin at work and in action many times before, and all she could say was the man had found his calling. He had a way of cutting through the layers and getting down to what was really important. He had a way with people and could get them to talk. Being sheriff suited him to perfection.

"Open the folder and you'll see for yourself." The Suit leaned back in his chair, folded his arms and crossed his legs.

"Whatever's in there won't hold up in court," Zach informed him, and Mrs. Robinson issued an over-the-top grunt. It was her turn to act indignant.

"We can do this the hard way, but I can see that you're a busy man and there's no reason to waste anyone's time." The Suit didn't realize he was already outplayed. At this point, this matchup was like watching a Little League team versus the Texas Rangers.

Amber could only see the back of Zach's head, and she wished for a better view of his face. It was his turn to lean back in his chair like he was in a hammock in the Caribbean. She could almost see his expression, having witnessed it so many times when he was on the verge of winning an argument. And growing up with five brothers and a male cousin who'd spent half his childhood at the ranch, she knew a thing or two about when someone was defeated.

"Do they look familiar to you?" Amber asked Rylan.

"I've never seen these people in my life." He seemed to be going to great lengths to keep a cool head, and she appreciated the fact that he'd taken her seriously about the baby picking up on emotions.

"Strange," she whispered. "The guys in the sedan and pickup from earlier might've been able to take her if they'd really wanted to, but they didn't. They let us go. Granted, you drove the heck out of my SUV in order to get around that sedan, but they let us go."

"I figured they were casing it and planning to come back in with muscle. I never saw this coming," Rylan admitted. "They didn't want to risk her being hurt because these guys want her in one piece is my best guess."

"My clients demand to take their daughter home, and if you would open that file, you'd see they're within their rights to do so and this mix-up can be resolved."

Mrs. Robinson wore her suit and pearls to perfection. Her hair was cut in a bob that flattered her oval-shaped face. She wore enough makeup to cover any blemishes on her face. It was almost too perfect. When Amber really looked at the woman, she noticed that she had on a considerable amount of foundation. What was she covering? Was she sick? Was Mr. Robinson physically abusive?

This couple looked like they could legitimately adopt a child. Based on appearances, money didn't seem to be a problem. So, if they'd used a sketchy adoption agency, there had to be something lurking in their background. Amber agreed with Rylan. Brooklyn would leave this office with them over her dead body, as well.

Zach extended his hand to the lawyer. "Forgive my manners. My name is Zach McWilliams."

The Suit obliged.

"What makes you so sure I have a baby here in my office?" Zach asked.

The attorney leveled his gaze. "Are you denying it?"

Amber rolled her eyes. It was just like a fancy over-dressed lawyer to dodge the question. "Zach has a good point. How do they know the baby they claim belongs to them is here?"

"Brooklyn Ward's birth mother, Alicia Ward, signed over parental rights to my clients," the Suit said.

"Sorry, I didn't catch your name." Zach picked up the pen in front of him and leaned forward again, ready to write.

"Teague Thompson." The man was playing it too cool. He was either as big of a deal as he would have Zach believe, or he was big-time bluffing.

Zach made a show of looking at his cell phone. Then came, "Will you folks excuse me?"

Teague Thompson pursed his lips and studied Zach before finally nodding.

Mrs. Robinson made a dramatic show of throwing her arms in the air.

"Do you see any real tears?" Rylan asked as he studied the woman's face through the mirror.

"Nope. Not one. I doubt she'd smudge her makeup with any," Amber said in a low voice.

Zach stopped in the hallway outside the opened door. The lights were dimmed inside the room, and it gave an almost intimate feeling.

Amber knew how this worked. As long as it was dark in the room, she was in the clear. The occupants of the adjacent room were none the wiser about who watched. By contrast, the interview room's lights were bright fluorescents.

Zach waved them into the hallway. Deputy Perry stood watch over the interview room door, arms folded against his chest and with his back to the door. He looked like a bull waiting to be baited, and it was obvious that wouldn't go well for the challenger. Amber knew from experience not to mess with a determined deputy. Her cousin hired only the best of the best, and the most loyal. He'd said that he could train someone how to do the job, but he couldn't train personality, work ethic or loyalty.

"This is an unexpected development." Zach raked his fingers through his hair.

"What's your take on the husband and wife?" Amber wondered if he picked up on the signs she saw.

"She's either sick or being abused." He didn't hesitate with his opinion, and it confirmed what she'd already been thinking.

"My thoughts exactly." Amber trusted her instincts but confirmation from Zach left no room for doubt. If Mr. Robinson had a history of abuse, no legitimate adoption agency in Texas would give the couple a baby.

"I can run a background check on him because they have a connection to Brooklyn's mother, who has gone missing. I can threaten to hold them both and interview them all I want. They've already lawyered up, and my experience tells me that they've been coached on how to answer any question I might bring up." Zach made good points. Even though she and Rylan were on the right side of the law, a good attorney knew how to manipulate the truth and find loopholes.

"Think we should stick around?" Rylan asked her.

Of course, in her mind the law always won out, but that was probably fairy-tale thinking mixed with good intentions.

"If you're not here, they can't accidentally see her. I can't lie to them, but I'm not obligated to volunteer information, either." Zach's face was a study in determination.

"I'd like to hear what they have to say. Why they think they have a claim to her," Amber interjected.

"Then stick around. Just know that they most likely will recognize the baby, and it could get messy," he informed her.

Brooklyn stirred and Amber's heart went into free fall. The last thing the little girl needed was to hear shouting or conflict. Zach was right. Even though she'd settled down for the moment, it was only a matter of time before she'd wake again and start fussing.

"What are the chances their claim is legitimate?" Rylan's jaw clenched, and she could see the question wasn't easy for him to ask.

Chapter Fourteen

"If all the players are on the court, I'd say we have the upper hand right now. I've learned not to take anything for granted when it comes to the law. I don't know who these folks might be connected to because I get the impression they're important. If they support someone in a higher office, I could get a phone call. My hands could be tied and that's not a feeling I like. A skilled lawyer could tie up the case for months, possibly years. And even if we get justice at some point, these two could relocate to Europe or Mexico and take Brooklyn with them." Zach spoke the truth and even though it wasn't what Rylan necessarily wanted to hear, he needed to consider every word carefully.

No one was prying Brooklyn out of his hands now that he knew she was his daughter.

"I wanted to give you a heads-up. I'm going back in that room, and at some point during the interview I'll be forced to open the file and see what evidence they think they've presented. If they know she's here, it'll make it more difficult for me to deny that I know her whereabouts. But something's brewing for them to come down here like this and demand custody. I took an oath to uphold the law. My instincts have to take second place."

Rylan figured as much. "What are you planning to tell them?"

"That this is my jurisdiction and every citizen, including the ones not old enough to defend themselves, deserve my protection. Here's the thing. I don't technically have proof that you're Brooklyn's father, and I might get caught in a legal loophole." He scratched his chin. "They might be bluffing, but I don't know what cards they have up their sleeves. Showing up here and boldly demanding custody of Brooklyn leads me to believe they haven't shown all of their hand yet."

Rylan nodded his understanding.

"I better get back inside. Think about what I said," Zach said.

Rylan thanked him and fisted his hands. The sedan and pickup could be outside waiting for them in case they made a run for it. He thought about their dwindling options. He and Amber couldn't take the baby back to his place. They couldn't take her to the ranch, either. There were too many witnesses, and Rylan would never ask another Kent to cover for him.

Amber urged him back into the small viewing room and closed the door.

"We have the right to demand to see our daughter." Mr. Robinson had the authoritative voice of someone used to being in charge at home and at the office. If Rylan had to guess, he'd figure the man for someone who ran his own business and not an abuse victim.

"How old is your daughter?" Zach asked.

"Three months and two days," Mrs. Robinson piped

up. Amber was right; there was something off about the woman that didn't sit right with him. The thought that the man seemed to be abusive with his wife sat like a nail in Rylan's stomach. Mrs. Robinson could best be described as…broken. She forced her shoulders straight, but Rylan could see that she wasn't used to being assertive. To make matters worse, Mr. Robinson's posture was tense, aggressive.

"When was the last time you saw the baby's mother?" Zach looked up from his notepad.

"No one said my clients have met the mother," the lawyer interjected.

Mrs. Robinson shot a nervous glance toward her husband, who held a solid glare aimed at Zach.

Mr. Thompson took Mrs. Robinson's hands in his. She bowed her head in dramatic fashion, and her shoulders rocked as though she was sobbing. She put on a good show.

"My clients were supposed to be given access to their daughter three days ago. The birth mother failed to show." It was the lawyer's turn to glare at Zach. "If you'd open the file, you could read all this in the report. As you can see, my client is distraught. We'd like to wrap this up and go home."

Wrap it up?

Rylan's daughter wasn't a present. He didn't like much about the adoptive parents and wondered if Alicia had gotten cold feet once she met them. It wouldn't do a lot of good to speculate, considering they were light on details. But his gut burned with fury.

"What kind of vehicle do you drive?" Zach asked.

"Excuse me?" The question seemed to catch Teague

off guard. "What myself or my clients drive is not relevant to this discussion."

"It is to me." Zach paused while Mrs. Robinson pulled out a packet of tissues from a designer-looking handbag. "What's the harm in telling me?"

"My clients don't have to explain what kind of car they drive or what they're doing in town. Their daughter is here—"

"How exactly do you know that?" Zach opened the file and looked at the first piece of paper. "It says here that you're from Fort Worth. Arlington Heights. How do you know what's going on here in my town if you live an hour and forty-five minutes away?"

Rylan knew enough about the city to realize that was an expensive neighborhood. That part didn't surprise him. He, like Zach, was curious how they'd tracked Brooklyn to Jacobstown if they weren't working with the drivers of the black sedan and pickup truck from earlier.

"Fine. We'd hoped that it wouldn't come to this, but we'd like to report a kidnapping." The lawyer had that card ready to play quickly. He'd anticipated some of Zach's moves. With an expensive suit like the one he was wearing, he looked prepared to earn his keep.

"I'm not admitting that the child is even in my county. However, if this alleged child is here in Jacobstown, you need to be very clear on one thing. She won't be leaving without a court order and/or DNA test—"

"My clients have rights, Sheriff. If you look at the second piece of paper in that folder, you'll see that a judge agrees." Teague looked a little too smug.

"And I have a right to investigate a missing person—"

"This is a kidnapping case—"

"I'm talking about Alicia Ward, the birth mother. My guess is that you already know she's disappeared. What I'm unclear on is why you believe her child is in my county." Zach slapped the folder closed and shoved it toward Teague.

Rylan turned to Amber. "Let's get her out of here."

"Okay. But where will we go?" she asked.

"Maybe it's best if we don't say. I know a place we should be safe." Rylan sounded confident and Amber wished she shared the feeling.

"THOSE PEOPLE COULD'VE ended up raising your daughter and you never would've known any different." Amber had been holding her thoughts in too long. She had no idea what kind of person Alicia Ward was, but the woman must've had some heart to back out of the deal at the last minute. "I have so many questions, Rylan."

"Like?" He got behind the wheel after she'd secured Brooklyn, and he'd made sure no one seemed too interested in what they were doing. It was past nine in the evening and they'd been at her cousin's office for thirteen hours. Her back was stiff and she was tired of sitting.

"If Alicia had known she was going to adopt out her baby, why wait three months? Why take care of her that long and then dump her on a family? Of course, the other question is why change her mind and have her brought to you? Was her pregnancy a scam? She gets herself pregnant and sells the baby but has been on the run for three months because she changes her mind and decides to keep the baby? And then she realizes that someone is after her or someone was getting close and so she tries to get the baby to you, who, by the way, has no idea she's coming or that he's even a father."

"All good points." He paused for a minute as he navigated out of the parking lot and onto the narrow street. "I still don't remember her or much about that weekend."

"And don't you think that's odd?"

"Look, I made a mistake. I must've fallen off the wagon—"

"What if you didn't, Rylan?"

"I'm not ready to let myself off the hook. It's happened before," he admitted.

"Years ago you slipped. But you said yourself that this time was different." Amber wasn't letting him hang guilt around his shoulders like that. Not if he was innocent.

"That doesn't mean anything—"

"You've been beating yourself up over this, Rylan. And if you did it, then that's fine. But—"

"No 'but.' I can't make excuses for myself, Amber. Don't you see that? It's too easy for a person like me to slip and fall down that slope again. I'd been under a lot of stress. I might've picked up a beer."

"You just don't remember it," she countered.

"That doesn't mean I didn't do it, dammit." Frustration poured off him in waves. Guilt and shame seemed to clock him.

"I believe in you," she said calmly.

"Well, don't."

She let that sit between them for a few minutes.

"Can you answer a question?" she asked.

"I can try."

"Those couple of other times that you said you fell off the wagon early on. Do you remember the first drink?" Amber gripped her cell.

"Yeah. I do. Clearly."

"But not *this* time," she continued.

"What, are you a prosecutor now? I already said that I don't remember any of it." His grip on the steering wheel tightened until his knuckles were white. "Are you satisfied?"

"Yes. I am." Amber gave it a moment to sink in.

"I hear what you're saying. It was different that time and that could've been because I didn't willingly take that first drink. It's a nice assumption, and one I want to be true with everything inside me. But I had a drinking problem at one time, and that means I can't make excuses. I have to take responsibility for my actions. Period. Until I know for certain that I didn't willingly take that first drink, I have no intention of cutting myself any slack."

The casual tone she was so used to in conversation with Rylan was gone. He usually covered what was going on inside with a wink and a smile. His charm was so good at seducing women, at making her fall a little bit harder for him. But this genuine side to him was an express train to hurt. Because she was falling for him hard. "I believe in you, Rylan. I believe that you've changed. And I believe that you're sober. I understand what you're saying, and I appreciate your perspective. I can only imagine how difficult it must be for you to think you might've jeopardized your sobriety. All I want you to do is open up to the possibility that it wasn't your fault. We have no idea what Alicia's intentions were. She might've signed up to get pregnant—"

"Why would anyone do that?" Rylan cut her off.

"We don't know her circumstances. Let Zach investigate. You know he's good at his job. He'll uncover the truth," she said, trying to soothe him. His commitment to his daughter only served to draw Amber toward him even more. When she'd given Red the unexpected pregnancy news, he'd come off as supportive in the early days. It didn't take long for his true feelings to surface. Red didn't want a child. Of course, she'd learned that after the wedding. At eighteen, she'd been young and naive. Had she been in love with Red? No. She cared about him, though. And she'd believed a relationship could grow from there. That they could grow to love each other after becoming a family. And then their child had been stillborn. Red had packed his bags and moved out before she made it home from the hospital. Looking back, he'd done them both a favor because being a Kent would've caused her to stick out their relationship. Kents didn't quit.

The divorce papers showed up a month later. Red had moved to California and moved on with his life. It should've hurt, but instead she felt relieved that he was gone. Ever since, she could admit that she never allowed herself to get close to anyone.

Speaking of family, there was something she needed to know before she made the argument that they might be safer at the ranch, just not at the main house. "Rylan, what happened between you and my brother?"

"It's between me and your brother." Rylan's tone had a definiteness to it that she ignored.

"I need to know."

"Why? What purpose could it possibly serve?" He white-knuckled the steering wheel.

"I changed my mind. I think we should go to the ranch for a few—"

"Forget it." Those two words had the sharpness of a blade and the finality of death.

"There's security at the main house. I know what happened to Breanna, and I reacted to that earlier but that was on the property, which we both know is vast," she argued.

"I still don't like the idea," he admitted.

"We can't just drive around all night. Being on the road isn't safe if those henchmen decide to come back and forcibly remove Brooklyn from our arms." Amber had no intentions of giving up easily.

"You said yourself there are flaws in ranch security." He could be a mule when he wanted to be.

Amber bit back a yawn. "There are baby supplies there. How are we supposed to take care of a three-month-old while being chased by these idiots?"

"We'll figure it out." Rylan checked the rearview mirror again, reminding her of just how much danger they were in.

"How?"

"You underestimate my abilities," he scoffed, and seemed genuinely put off by her lack of confidence in his skills as a soldier.

"I've seen how you handle yourself. Believe me when I say that if this was a one-on-one situation I'd have no doubts. But you have two handicaps, me and a baby who needs to eat every few hours and has to be handled with care. She could cry at the wrong moment, and you might not be able to cover in time. I'm not much use while I'm trying to hold her. You know that normally I know my way around a shotgun and I'm not afraid to use one. This is different, Rylan. Even a tough guy like you can see that we'll hold you back and quite possibly cost us everything. I know you're strong physically and mentally."

He grunted at that last word.

"You are, Rylan."

"We need to find Alicia Ward, and we can't do that from the ranch," he argued.

"That's a good point. We can't find her and offer the best protection for Brooklyn. If the Robinsons or their henchmen catch up to us, we might be forced to hand over your daughter and let the courts decide. You heard Zach. That could take months or years. Our family attorney would tell you the same thing if we called him." She gave him a few minutes to let those words sink in.

He concentrated harder on the stretch of road in front of them. She was getting through, making progress.

"The ranch is the safest option for Brooklyn," she added.

"That's playing dirty," he finally said.

"Maybe, but I'll do anything to keep that little angel safe and so will you. The Robinsons are going to leave Zach's office without their baby. They believe, right or wrong, that they have rights to her. Until your official DNA test comes back and proves to the courts that you're the father, we don't have any aces in our hands.

Can you live with yourself if someone takes her? We only assume the vehicles were linked to the Robinsons. What if they weren't? Brooklyn could be sold off into some baby ring and literally disappear from our lives forever before we have a chance to find her." Amber risked a glance at Rylan, and she could see that her filibuster was working.

So, she stopped in order to let her argument sink in.

After circling a block three times, Rylan turned east, the direction of the ranch.

"I don't like the idea of putting your family in harm's way," he said.

"Breanna Griswold might argue that you can't protect everyone." Amber's heart fisted thinking about Breanna, about her family, about her lost life even before her death. "We need to get some rest and give Brooklyn a break. I can get enough supplies from the main house to get us through the night without alerting anyone to our presence."

"Where do you expect us to sleep without someone realizing we're there?" he asked.

"The bunkhouse." She could've sworn she saw him tense at the idea of going to the last place they'd been alone together before he left eight years ago.

Chapter Fifteen

The rest of the ride to the ranch was silent. All the noise was going off inside Rylan's head. Thoughts battled for attention. Frustration nailed his gut. And he'd be damned if he wasn't thinking about the kiss he'd shared with Amber that had been so much better than the one in the bunkhouse. There'd been so much promise and intensity and chemistry in that kiss. Rylan could honestly say there'd never been a kiss like it. He wondered if that was what it was like to have something more than a physical attraction to someone. Although he had that, too. In spades.

He had to remind himself that he was falling down another slippery slope and as silly as it sounded, even to him considering he was a grown man, the promise he'd made to Will at eighteen still mattered. The fight the two had had and the position Rylan had put Will in still mattered. Even more so now that Rylan was a man.

But this wasn't the time to dwell on an inappropriate attraction to his former best friend's baby sister. He almost laughed out loud at the *baby* part. Amber Kent was all woman. She helped expand the successful family cattle ranch into the powerhouse it was today and had yet to hit thirty years old. She was a force to be reckoned with. She had a sharp wit, an easy laugh and a heart that knew no bounds. And even though she'd closed off parts of herself, which he assumed had to do with the baby she'd lost, she was still the most open woman he'd ever met. One look into those eyes and he could see right through her.

Rylan refocused his attention. Dwelling on Amber's good points wasn't doing anything to quell his attraction to her—an attraction he needed to keep in check.

His thoughts were weighted with other issues. He wondered if there was a court in Texas that would take his daughter away from him. He didn't remember the girl's mother. How would that make him sound? His playboy ways might catch up to him, and Brooklyn could pay the price.

But then, if the adoption wasn't on the up-and-up, would the Robinsons want to bring this to court? Was that why they'd brought the big guns now? They'd walked into that interview room like they owned the place. When he really thought about it, Teague Thompson had played the confidence card. Mr. Robinson had seemed angry and put out. Those were understandable emotions given the fact that they'd been promised a baby who'd then disappeared. Mrs. Robinson seemed troubled. Rylan got a bad feeling every time he thought about her. And Zach had made a good point about the family's possible political connections.

"I know a private investigator who might be able to help us dig into the Robinsons' background," Amber said as they approached the gate to the ranch. "That way we won't feel like we're wasting time resting."

"That's a good idea." Rylan stopped at the guard shack.

Isaac Vanguard stood six feet one inch. He worked security at the ranch. With short, light brown hair and powder blue eyes, he would likely be considered attractive by most women.

Isaac stepped out of the building. He bent down as Rylan opened the window.

"Amy's worried about you," he said to Amber. "Said you two were supposed to be planning a lunch to benefit a women's shelter, but she hasn't been able to reach you."

Amber leaned toward the driver's side and filled Rylan's senses with her flowery and clean scent. Had she always smelled this good? "I'm sorry. I totally forgot. My cell battery died, and I keep forgetting to charge it. If you see her before I get a good charge, would you mind telling her I'll be in touch as soon as I can?"

Isaac glanced in the back seat. "Will do, ma'am."

He moved back inside the shack and pressed the button to open the gate. There was another security guard in the background, a man Rylan recognized from the other day. It seemed the Kent family was serious about adding extra security, and he saw that as a good sign they could handle almost anything that came their way. "Who was the other guy?"

"That's Blaise Dillinger." Amber rubbed her temples.

"You okay?" Rylan picked up on the tension. Granted, what they'd been through would have anyone stressed. Adrenaline had long faded from their encounter with the pickup truck and sedan, and the surprise of the Robinsons showing up at Zach's office.

"I was just turning over ideas in my head, spinning

out. What if my cousin has to follow through with an investigation? The Robinsons could get a search warrant and surprise us. My family would never give us up, but they'd also be put in a bad position if they knew we were here. They'll protect us no matter the cost. They won't hesitate to stand up for us, and that could cost them if they're found in contempt of court."

"We're here. What now?" Rylan figured they were already well in over their heads.

"Would you mind doubling back to Isaac for a second?"

Rylan put the gearshift in reverse and navigated backward toward the iron gate.

Isaac must've realized something was up because he hopped out of the guard shack and jogged toward them.

"Need something?" he asked.

"If anyone asks who's at the ranch, you don't have to answer—"

"Yes, ma'am. I know." He nodded.

"I would never put you in a position to lie, Isaac—"

"I took an oath to protect this family. I've been advised of my legal rights and am aware my actions could be contested in court." Isaac's dedication was noble. "I don't have to answer any questions I don't want to. Ever. Unless I'm in a court of law being asked by a judge. It's my decision whether or not I want to put myself in jeopardy with the system. And in case you're wondering what that means, my loyalty lies with this family."

"I'm not asking whether or not you're loyal, Isaac. I already know the answer to that question. I wouldn't want you to put yourself in a bad position over me," Amber said, clarifying.

"With all due respect, I can decide the risks I'm willing to take." The man's loyalty would never be in question, and Rylan couldn't help thinking that Isaac would've made a good soldier. He had all the right qualities: honesty, loyalty and bravery. Everything else could be taught.

Amber pursed her lips, no doubt wanting Isaac to think of himself first but obviously realizing he wouldn't. When she finally spoke, she said, "Thank you, Isaac. You're a good man, and you can't know how much I appreciate everything you do for my family."

Isaac allowed himself a small smile before nodding.

Rylan pulled away and navigated around the house toward the barn. Between family members and ranch hands, there were enough vehicles at the Kent main house parking lot to slip into a spot and have a reasonable expectation no one would be the wiser.

"There are sleeping quarters in the barn if you'd rather go with the men—"

"I know." He'd worked three summers in that barn alongside his best friend, Will. Damn. Everything good about Rylan's childhood always came back to the Kent family—a family that had always made him feel like one of their own despite him being from the wrong side of the tracks, coming from a no-good father and having a decent hardworking mother who had no gas left in the tank to spend time with him on the rare occasions she wasn't at work. "I don't want to be separated from you, Amber. Not right now."

Amber gave a small smile before fishing out her key ring and fanning out the keys. After sliding a couple around the ring, she selected one. "I'll grab a few things from the main house and meet you in the bunkhouse."

The thought of being alone with Brooklyn set his stress levels on high alert. This was his daughter, and he had to learn how to be alone with her. Rylan had been to a hostile country. He'd encountered enemies with every kind of face-to-face weaponry. He'd endured hostile, unforgiving terrain.

But he'd never imagined something that weighed next to nothing would be the thing to take him down.

Rylan brought the whole car seat inside with him. The bunkhouse was actually an apartment over the Kent Ranch offices.

In a few hours, Lonnie would be awake and ready to start the day. It wasn't uncommon for one of the Kents to sleep over in the second-story apartment, so Lonnie most likely wouldn't be the wiser as to who was actually there. He wouldn't bother the occupants.

It didn't seem right to sneak around the same ranch he could practically call home. Being here brought back so many memories, most of them were good. His last year in Jacobstown had been hell after his mother had passed away.

The offices smelled the same, hay and horses. With a diaper bag over his shoulder and a baby carrier in his left hand, he would be a sight. No one from his past would believe this to be possible. Hell, he was still trying to digest this one.

He shuffled up the wooden stairs, looking over the offices where he'd spent so much of his childhood.

The apartment was small but cozy. The furniture was arranged just like he remembered. There was an open-concept living room with a kitchenette. A flat screen was mounted on one wall, with the most comfortable couch Rylan had ever slept on across from it.

The kitchenette was in the corner. This close to the offices and barn it only had a sink, a fridge and a microwave, but that was good enough to get by in a pinch. The apartment was never meant to be a permanent residence. The rectangular dining table had one of its long sides pushed up against the wall. Two chairs were at opposite ends, and two were tucked into the same side. It was comfortable for two, maybe three people to eat there. Four was a stretch even though there were four place settings.

And Rylan had crammed at the table with Will and a couple of ranch hands more than once. Being here reminded him of everything he'd lost, his mother and then his friends, and anger welled up inside him at his past weakness.

He couldn't help but glance down at his daughter and feel nothing but pain at the fact she would never meet her grandmother. Had his mother been around for him? No. But she'd worked hard to keep food on the table and never asked for anything in return. As far as Rylan was concerned, the woman was a saint. It mattered little that he didn't really know her. He loved her the same. Losing her had sent him into a downward spiral that had cost him everything he cared about, and most of his self-confidence.

The door opened and Amber slipped inside carrying a full armload of baby items.

"That was quick," he said, ignoring the way his heart

fisted when he saw her again, and how much he didn't want to think about her but did while she was gone.

The kiss they'd shared on that couch had been out of nowhere and one he'd never forget as long as he lived. She'd turned to him, locked gazes and then pressed her lips to his. He should've stopped her and eventually he did. But not before a bone-searing kiss that left him wanting more than he could allow.

"I knew where everything was." Before she could finish her sentence, he was by her side, helping her unload the supplies. She had a smaller and softer version of the baby carrier. She set it up next to the couch. "When she wakes and has a feeding, which should be any minute now, we'll change her and move her to where she'll be more comfortable."

Rylan stood by helpless as she unfolded the cloth seat and opened the straps, so it would be ready for Brooklyn.

"Dinner's in that bag," she continued. "I grabbed a pan of Joyce's lasagna from the fridge."

"I miss her cooking," he said.

"Heat it up and I'll get everything ready over here." This wasn't the time for old memories. Rylan knew better than to allow Amber's voice to roll over him like it was. He knew better than to think about the kiss they'd shared. And he especially knew better than to compare it to all the others since, because they came nowhere close to matching until she'd kissed him again the other day.

Amber Kent proved to be trouble he didn't need in his already overcomplicated life. Damn that life could change with the snap of a finger. It had been like that when he'd lost his mother and had caught him completely off guard.

Being here on the Kent property, Rylan couldn't help but remember the past—a part of his past that he wasn't exactly proud of. He wouldn't go back and change it if he could, mistakes and all. It had made him a better person. It had made him the man he was today. The kind of man who would step up and take care of his responsibilities no matter what else it cost him. A man who wouldn't think twice about offering a helping hand to anyone in need.

Amber's words from earlier started to take root. Maybe he hadn't taken that first drink. Rylan hoped like hell that was true because if he had, that said there'd been no change in him, no growth, and after everything he'd been through to earn his sobriety, he didn't want that to be true.

Brooklyn started to cry, and Amber went right to her while he fixed a bottle. They were getting pretty damn good at parenting together, and he couldn't imagine doing any of this without her. Reality was a gut punch. Because once this ordeal was over, she'd go back to her life here on the ranch and he'd go back to his. For the first time, he felt unsettled about his decision to come back to Jacobstown. But where else would he go?

He chalked his feelings up to not facing the Willow family yet. It was part of his commitment to his sobriety to apologize to those he'd hurt in the past. He'd saved the Willows for last along with Will. Facing those two was going to be the most difficult, and he'd wanted to be strong.

Amber fed his daughter while he set the table.

Rylan's cell buzzed, and he stopped long enough to answer. "What's going on, Zach?"

"I did some digging around into Mr. Robinson's business—"

"Hold on a sec while I put you on speaker," Rylan interrupted. He moved to the couch and sat on the arm while holding out the cell between him and Amber while she burped the baby. "Amber's here. You were saying that you poked around in Mr. Robinson's business?"

"That's right. It turns out that Alicia Ward was one of his employees. She left almost a year ago," Zach informed them.

"That would be around the time Alicia got pregnant." Amber looked up at Rylan, and his fingers flexed and released from wanting to touch her.

"There've been domestic violence and assault claims against Mr. Robinson by his wife and a woman by the name of Charlotte Pemberton. I traced her to an escort service out of Dallas. Most of the claims came from his wife, but she dropped each one. It's the same story for Ms. Pemberton," Zach said.

A picture emerged that made Rylan's gut twist into a knot.

"Would those cases be enough to stop the Robinsons from being able to adopt a child since they didn't stick?" Amber asked.

"A legitimate adoption agency would have a difficult time getting over physical violence charges. A good interviewer would be able to see right through the Robinsons." Zach paused a beat. "Mr. Robinson also chairs a reelection campaign for the judge who resides over his county. George is influential in Texas."

Several thoughts raced through Rylan's mind. Had Robinson paid Alicia to get pregnant when he and his wife couldn't have a child? And then had Alicia decided not to go through with it? That she couldn't do that to a child? To the man she'd targeted to be the child's father?

"I also found out that Alicia has a sister who lives in Austin. Her name is Adeline. The two were reportedly close until last year. Adeline claims not to have seen or heard from her sister in the past six months," Zach stated.

"We know she's alive," Rylan stated. "Or she was. Otherwise, Brooklyn wouldn't be in the world. We know Alicia was alive a few days ago because she fits the description given by Chess."

"That's what I've found out for now. Technically, I can hold Mr. Robinson for seventy-two hours, but that's a risky move. For now, the Robinsons are in my office. I'm treating them like victims rather than suspects. I thought you should know where we stood," Zach said.

"I appreciate it," Rylan offered.

"Zach, before you go. Can I ask a question on a different subject?" Amber asked.

"Go ahead."

"It's about Breanna. With everything that's going on, have you been able to locate her parents?" Amber's voice was low and reverent. Rylan could see the sadness in her eyes when she spoke about the victim.

"No, I haven't. I have a deputy dedicated to searching for them, though," he said.

"Word was that they moved to San Antonio a few

years ago." Amber paused a beat. "I'd heard Breanna was back and that she was still using. I know that won't affect how vigorously you work to bring justice to her killer, Zach. I'm just saying we might want to look into that community to see where she's been and who she's been hanging around with lately."

"I'll make a list and start there, Amber. Thanks for the information." Zach's voice was somber.

"You're welcome, Zach. Are we back to the same suspects?"

"Reggie Barstock still tops the list. I'll look for any connection between him and Breanna. There were no signs of a struggle, which leads me to believe she was familiar with her killer." Amber visibly shivered, and Rylan figured it was the thought someone she knew could do something so unimaginable.

"There's one more thing," Zach said. "I had Deputy Perry poke around in Teague Thompson's practice, and he's been associated with illegal adoption rings in the past. The guy is dirty but he's also connected. His uncle is a senator, and their connections in Texas run deep."

"Sounds like one hell of a web," Rylan stated.

"It is, which means we have to build a solid case for you and Brooklyn in order to keep the two of you together. Perry is on his way over to Alicia's sister's house in Austin. Turns out Alicia's laptop is at her sister's place." Zach was a miracle worker and a damn fine investigator once he had a trail to follow. "Hang in there a little longer. I'm tying up the Robinsons here, but I don't have enough evidence to hold them if they decide to walk out the door. If I can support the emerging picture, I'll have enough evidence to make an arrest."

"Any sign of Alicia?" Rylan asked. The unspoken possibility was that Mr. Robinson had already gotten to her and she was already dead.

"Nothing yet but her laptop might give us a few leads," Zach said.

Rylan ended the call after thanking the sheriff for the update.

"I vaguely remember Reggie Barstock growing up. What's the deal with him?" he asked Amber.

"He was Maddie's boy," Amber told him.

"I remember her. Sweet lady." Rylan didn't know the family very well, and he had no memories of Reggie. "She had that business downtown for the longest time."

"That's right," Amber agreed. "All I remember about Reggie is that he stuck to himself in school. He didn't play any sports, and I don't remember him being much of a student. I think Deacon was a little surprised he graduated from high school. My brother said there'd been some talk of Reggie being held back for grades or absences. Maddie Barstock was a saint. No one could figure out how Reggie had turned out so opposite except that he'd had a no-good father. You know how the town can be once they lock on to something. Anyway, his mom's reputation was golden, and she'd been a kind employer to everyone who'd worked for her. She passed away last year and left Reggie out of the will. Ms. Barstock left everything to her grandniece, Chelsea."

Rylan perked up at hearing the name. "The same one I met at your home the other day?" he asked.

"That's her. She's an amazing person, and she owns the craft pizza restaurant on the town square." Amber practically beamed with pride. She'd always been all about family. But then the Kents were a tight-knit bunch. Rylan had seen it firsthand even though he'd learned to appreciate so much more now that he was a grown man.

"I'm sure Reggie didn't take too kindly to what he would view as his inheritance going to someone he didn't know," Rylan concluded.

"It was strange knowing he'd been slipping in and out of town without anyone seeing him. Zach found out last year and since Reggie has a limp on his left side—"

"Those are easy dots to connect, considering you said it was always the left paw or hoof. And now Breanna's left foot was—"

She flashed her eyes at him like she could hear the details even though they both knew what had happened because of the crime scene photos.

"So, yeah, the guy disappeared after high school and most had believed him to be gone for good. He resurfaced last year full of bitterness, and not the least bit sad about his mother's passing. All he seemed to care about was his inheritance. He tried to scare Chelsea into leaving town, which was awful. Apparently, he's been living in Louisiana all this time getting in and out of trouble," she said.

"What kind of crimes was he committing?" Rylan asked.

"Zach said it was small-time stuff. But everyone agrees that he needs to be watched. I mean, he knows Jacobstown, having grown up here. And, sure, a picture has been emerging that he's the one, but Zach isn't convinced yet. No one can reconcile the fact that he didn't come across as the smartest guy, and the profile of the

Jacobstown Hacker indicates someone with a higher IQ." She blew out a breath in frustration, and he realized how taxing it was for her to talk about this.

Brooklyn started fussing, and before he could react Amber was at the little girl's side. It was a good time for him to think about getting a meal into Amber and making sure she got rest. He could see that she took care of everyone around her. But who took care of her?

"The baby's settled," Amber announced with pride that stirred places in his heart he thought long since dead. He'd been dead inside far too long.

"Come eat." He'd set the table, and the lasagna smelled damn near out of this world.

Amber joined him and took her seat. Tired and frazzled, she was still beautiful. She must've been starved because she didn't say a word until she'd cleared half her plate. Rylan liked watching her enjoy a good meal. There were other things he liked about her that he didn't want to focus on.

"I know Joyce is an amazing cook but this food is beyond good," Amber said. The sound of appreciation in her voice stirred his heart.

Rylan glanced down at his empty plate with a forced smile. "Like I said, I haven't had this good of a meal in longer than I can remember."

"I'm going to finish eating, take a shower and then I want to talk about why that is, Rylan."

Chapter Sixteen

Rylan made a pot of coffee. He'd been successfully avoiding the topic of his and Will's blowout up until now, but he figured he owed Amber an explanation. She deserved to know the reason because he could see an emotion stir behind her eyes that he hadn't been able to pinpoint until now. It finally dawned on him that she blamed herself, that kiss, for him running off to join the military. So, she most likely blamed herself for the fight between him and Will.

He'd showered in the spare bathroom downstairs while Amber used the one in the apartment. He knew his way around the Kent Ranch, so it was easy to navigate even with little lighting. He also knew where all the supplies were stocked. He'd found an extra set of clothes that roughly fit, brushed his teeth and had settled at the table with his first cup when Amber emerged from the bathroom.

Her hair was down. It fell well past her shoulders. She had on a Grateful Dead T-shirt and shorts that were almost hidden by the oversize tee. Her long legs looked silky and smooth. He clenched and released his hands. Then, he picked up his coffee mug and forced his gaze away from her attributes. After taking a sip, he stood up. "You want a cup?"

"Stay right where you are, Rylan. I'll get it." She shot a smile that was a dagger to his heart. It was difficult to maintain objectivity when she was in the room and everything about her was temptation.

After pouring her cup and doctoring it up, she joined him at the table.

"You should probably get some rest," he said to her.

"I highly doubt if I could. I keep thinking about Breanna and what happened. And then this situation, the uncertainty... Besides, if I'm really that tired, I could drink a cup of coffee on my way to bed and still sleep," she said with a half smile. It didn't reach her eyes and he knew why.

"You want to talk about it?" He liked talking to Amber even though he was normally the silent type.

"I know you and my brother got into a fight but you left and never looked back. I didn't think I'd see you again." Her voice hitched and her cheeks flushed as though the admission, the sadness, embarrassed her.

When she looked up at him with a mix of hurt and defeat in her eyes, his heart fisted in his chest.

"I'm sorry I disappeared on you," he admitted. "My life had spiraled down a bad path and..."

"Was it because you kissed me? Because I've been thinking about that night here in the apartment a lot lately and it was my fault, Rylan. You didn't kiss me. I distinctly remember that I kissed you." Suddenly, the rim of her coffee mug became very interesting to her. Her cheeks flushed with what looked like embarrassment, and he'd be damned if it didn't make her look even more beautiful.

"There was so much more to it than that," he said, hating that she'd carried a sense of shame with her all these years. "My life became a mess. That's why I kissed you back and—"

"Oh. You don't have to explain—"

"Hang on. I didn't mean it to come out like that," he said, backpedaling. "What I'm trying to say is that there are lines that shouldn't be crossed. Kissing your best friend's little sister behind his back is not exactly a stand-up thing to do. Mine and your brother's relationship was already strained. I had no right to do that."

Amber stood, picked up her dish and silverware from earlier, and said, "You don't need to defend yourself."

"Is that what you think I'm doing?" He stood and followed her into the kitchenette where there was barely room for one.

She turned on the faucet and rinsed her plate, keeping her back to him. The only time she ever did something like that was when she was too angry or too embarrassed to talk, and his heart took a hit thinking he'd caused her reaction.

He'd gone and made a mess of the situation.

"Amber—"

"Don't, Rylan. I'm not in the mood to be insulted by the person I'm in the middle of helping. A person who won't tell me why he won't sleep inside the main house. A person who disappeared into the military after a blowout with my brother and never looked back and won't tell me what happened in the first place." She kept her back to him as she stood in front of the sink.

"You think I walked away and never looked back?" He was so close behind her that her flowery scent filled his senses. He could reach out and touch her, so he did. He put his hands on her shoulders and felt her skin heat a little under his touch. Her body's reaction to him stirred an already awake part of his anatomy that was difficult to hide underneath jogging shorts.

"Isn't that what you did, Rylan? Isn't that what you're going to do as soon as the dust settles again and you get bored or whatever it was that caused you to go to Collinsville in the first place? Isn't that exactly how you got into trouble before?" Her words rushed out like they did when she was stressed.

He took a step closer and was almost body to body. It was taking all his self-control not to reach out and touch her. It would be so easy to move her hair away from her neck and start kissing her there.

Before he could drum up the willpower to turn away, she took a step back and leaned against him.

Rylan had to admit his feelings for Amber were always brimming underneath the surface. Seeing her with his child did things to his heart that he knew better than to allow. He had no business falling for a Kent.

Honestly, she was too good for him but she'd never see it that way.

"Are you going to answer me?" Her pulse drummed underneath his fingertips.

"What can I tell you, Amber? Do you want to hear that I think you're beautiful? That you make me want things that I don't deserve? That I will never deserve and, by the way, your brother agreed with me? Because I'll say it. And then what? You'll feel sorry for me—"

Amber spun around with all that ire in her eyes that was so damn sexy. "I couldn't possibly feel sorry for you, Rylan. As far as my brother goes, he has no idea what's best for me."

This close, her body was flush with his, and he could feel her breasts rising and falling when she spoke. He dropped his hands, looping his arms around her waist. All he could feel right then was the desire sweeping through him, consuming him with need.

"All I can feel is the same thing you do." Looking into her glittery eyes wasn't helping his situation any.

"This is a bad idea," he said.

AMBER BROUGHT HER hands up to Rylan's chest and smoothed her fingers over the ridges beneath his T-shirt. She blinked up at him. "Is this a bad idea, Rylan? Because I can't think of one good reason why this shouldn't happen. We're adults now. Adults who are capable of making the decision to have one night of amazing sex together."

She pushed up on her tiptoes and kissed him. His body went rigid at first, but then he pulled her tighter against him.

"I won't deny that you've grown up, Amber. You're incredible. You're smart. Beautiful," he said.

Pulling back, she looked directly into his eyes and realized just how much trouble she was in. The more time she spent with Rylan, Amber could sense herself falling further down that slippery slope of feelings. The heat that had been burning between them was like nothing she'd ever felt in her past relationships. Their chemistry sizzled, and she assumed the sex would be beyond anything she'd ever experienced.

It would be so easy to get lost with this man in this moment and forget about the past, about their history.

And that's exactly what she planned to do for at least one night.

She dropped her hands to the hem of Rylan's T-shirt while locking gazes with him. His hands joined hers, and a few seconds later his shirt was on the floor.

His hands went to the hem of hers, and her fingers trembled with anticipation as she fumbled with the fabric, trying to help. He captured one of her hands in his and brought it up to his lips. He pressed a kiss on the tip of her fingers and then on her palm. He peppered kisses on her exposed wrist. Sensual shivers skittered across her skin and her stomach went into free fall.

"I said it before and I'll say it again—you're beautiful, Amber Kent." His voice was low, raspy and sexy as hell. "You're even more beautiful than I remembered, and that's saying a hell of a lot."

He pulled her T-shirt up and over her head, and it joined his shirt on the floor. He palmed her breasts and she released a moan as she unhooked her lacy bra. His hands were rough from working on his house. She liked the feel of them against her skin as they roamed.

He toed off his boots and she followed suit.

"Why did you disappear after you kissed me?" She couldn't help but ask the question that had been on her mind far too long.

"You really want to talk about this now?" He ran his finger along the waistband of her shorts. "Because I have something else entirely on my mind, and it's a hell of a lot better than dredging up the past. It's the here and now, you and me. And I've been waiting a long time for the chance to do this."

He sure knew the right things to say as he dipped his head and ran his lips across her collarbone and then along the base of her neck. Warmth coiled low in her belly.

"It can wait." She wanted this to happen, this thing that was happening between them. She wanted it more than she wanted air.

Maybe she was caught up in the moment, but she didn't care. She'd denied herself too long. She moved her hands to the waistband of his shorts, and a few seconds later those were on the floor in a pile with their clothes. Her shorts joined his.

He hooked his thumbs on either side of her panties, and those went on top of the pile along with his boxers.

Rylan Anderson stood there, naked, and in front of her. His glorious body glistening in the moonlight streaming in from the top of the window. Shadows highlighted a strong male body. His erection pressed against the soft skin of her belly when he pulled her close to him. Again, their bodies were flush and she could feel every time he took a breath.

How many times had she wished for this when she was still naive enough to believe in wishes? One of the biggest problems with her relationship with Red was that he wasn't Rylan, would never be Rylan. She'd told herself to get over her crush and move on. And she believed she had until now. Now she realized she'd just stuffed her feelings down so deep that she'd become numb.

She brought her hands up and dug her fingers into his thick hair and breathed. Her breasts pressed against him as his hands roamed around her back and then cradled her bottom. A thunderclap of need exploded inside her and all she could think about was this man, his weight on top of her, pressing her deeper into the mattress.

Amber had no idea the air could heat up so quickly or the chemistry between two people could be so explosive until Rylan. She'd call it attraction or chemistry, but there was so much more to it than physical. Although, he was one damn hot man. With Rylan, there was a deeper connection.

He lifted her up and she wrapped her legs around his toned midsection. She could feel his erection pulsing against her heat. With her arms around him and his hands cupping her bottom, he walked her into the bedroom and set her down on top of the covers.

It took less than a minute to retrieve a condom and sheath his stiff length before Amber wrapped her arms around his neck and kissed him. His response? He kissed her so thoroughly that if she wasn't already on the bed, her legs might have given out from underneath her. He cupped her breasts with his right palm as he balanced most of his weight on his left hand. Her nipple beaded as he rolled it between this thumb and finger, teasing her. Her back arched and she let out a mewl.

He captured it with his mouth.

"I want to feel you moving inside me, Rylan," Amber coaxed.

It didn't take much encouragement.

He pinned her to the mattress with his heft, careful not to overwhelm her with his weight. She wrapped her legs around his midsection and he drove his tip inside her heat. For the first few seconds he just teased her, driving her to the brink of craziness.

Amber bucked her hips as she dug her fingers into Rylan's shoulders. He drove himself deeper inside her as he lowered his head and captured her mouth. He tasted like a mix of coffee and peppermint toothpaste.

Bare skin to bare skin, he groaned as he thrust harder and faster. She matched his pitch as they practically gasped for air.

His stiff erection drove to her core, and she rode the feeling to the brink. Faster. Harder. More.

"Rylan," she rasped.

He pulled his head back far enough to really look at her. "You're incredible, Amber."

She loved the sound of her name as it rolled off his tongue. She heard something else that sounded a lot like, "I love you." But she was probably just hearing what she wanted as he pushed her over the edge and rocketed her toward climax.

It was then he drove himself faster and harder until his entire body tensed...and then sweet release seemed to wash over him as he let out a guttural groan.

Rylan collapsed alongside her. She rolled onto her side to face him, and he pulled her into the crook of his arm. He kissed her again and she memorized the look on his face. It was the first time she could remember seeing him with a smile that lit his eyes. It was addicting and dangerous, making the pull to him even stronger.

"Amber Kent, I hope you're not tired because one time is not nearly enough with you."

Chapter Seventeen

Making love with Amber changed things for Rylan. Now that he'd cracked the lid on that pot, he could only hope she felt the same. Lying there, skin to skin with her, he knew he was only beginning to scratch the surface of his feelings for her.

Amber's steady, even breathing said she was asleep, and he didn't want to disturb her. Brooklyn would be awake soon, needing another bottle. He peeled himself away from Amber and out from under the covers, moving slowly and quietly so as not to disturb her. She needed rest. If she heard the baby, she'd hop up before he could throw his shorts on.

Rylan walked into the kitchenette area and put on a pot of coffee. There was no way he could sleep thinking that Brooklyn's mother might already be dead. His mother had passed away while he was in high school, but looking back as a man he was nothing but grateful for the time he got with her.

It was taking all of Rylan's self-control to stop himself from going down to Zach's office and forcing the smug Mr. Robinson to talk. The sheriff had laws to follow whereas Rylan had better ways to make the man talk. And if the Robinsons weren't still there, he'd hunt them down. But then, he hadn't let his temper rule him since those bad decisions he'd made in high school. He'd finally realized letting his temper control his actions hurt him and the people he cared most about in the long run. But times like these tried his patience, and a woman's life could hang in the balance.

Patience had never been his strong suit.

He was deep into his second cup of coffee when Brooklyn stirred. Staring down a baby alone was enough to make this strong man crumble.

But he was nothing but proud when he made her bottle, fed her and burped her, before changing her diaper. Since he'd acted fast the little girl had never properly woken up and that made changing her diaper a hell of a lot easier. He had Amber to thank for helping him get the hang of things.

Pride filled his chest when he placed her back inside her infant bouncer and successfully strapped her in. For the first time since having her handed to him out of the blue, he was starting to think he might not be awful at caring for her.

It was even better that Amber was still sleeping. The thought of being her shelter and taking care of her stirred his heart. Not that Amber Kent couldn't take care of herself. It was sexy as hell when a strong woman could open herself up and allow herself to be vulnerable. And he liked the feeling of taking care of someone who did so much for others.

Rylan thought about Mr. Robinson. A picture emerged that made him sick to his stomach. Had Alicia been forced—or pressured might be a better word—into having a child for her boss? A man with his temperament and dominant tendencies would see no problem in forcing one of his employees to do something she didn't want to. If the man didn't treat the woman he was supposed to love above all else with respect, how was he supposed to treat people he would see as pawns?

There were other thoughts that popped into Rylan's mind. Why did Alicia have a change of heart? Although, looking at the way Amber had almost instantly bonded with Brooklyn, he figured there was a built-in protection hormone for mothers. Had Alicia bonded with the baby during the pregnancy? He'd heard about rogue hormones in pregnant women. They served a purpose, and he figured most of them were to ensure survival of the child.

Thinking about Zach's phone call earlier got Rylan's mind spinning. He wasn't quite ready to let himself off the hook about the slip last year in his sobriety. Evidence was mounting that Alicia might've been desperate to get pregnant. She could've locked on to him after seeing him at the party. And she could've slipped something into his coffee.

Until he had proof, Rylan couldn't afford to let himself off.

He grabbed a small notebook and pen from the junk drawer in the kitchenette, and then started jotting down notes.

By the time he looked up fifteen minutes later, Amber stood in the doorway to the bedroom staring at him.

"Hello, beautiful," he said, and she broke into a smile.

"Rylan." Her voice had a tentative quality to it, and he figured he knew why.

"You're important to me, Amber. Last night changed things for me. I just don't know what that means yet," he offered, and thought he saw a flicker of disappointment behind her eyes as she approached.

He grabbed her hand and tugged her down onto his lap. He kissed her, wishing he could say what was really on his mind, that he'd had a hell of a time going all-in with anyone. But the thought of losing Amber was a knife stab to the center of his chest.

The sound of boots shuffling up wooden stairs had Rylan reaching for his weapon. Amber immediately went toward the baby.

"Will you take her into the bedroom?" She had her SIG and could protect them both given the time.

"Be careful, Rylan."

"Close the door but wait to see who opens it before you shoot." He fired a wink and it was meant to break the tension.

She frowned.

"Don't count me out yet, Kent. I'm actually damn good in these situations."

Amber smiled but it didn't reach her eyes. Worry lines creased her forehead as she picked up the baby in her bouncer and glanced back one more time before closing the door. He could've sworn she whispered that she loved him, but it could've been his imagination.

A knock sounded.

"It's Will. Open up."

The bedroom door cracked open. "I'll let the two of you talk while I hang out with this sweet girl."

Amber stood there holding Brooklyn in her arms. The baby smiled up at Amber. And a fire bolt struck Rylan square in the chest.

He walked to the door and answered. "How'd you know I was here?"

"Where's my sister? Is she safe?" Will's concern touched Rylan. Although, he shouldn't be surprised a Kent would look out for another Kent.

"She's here." Rylan opened the door all the way. "You want to come inside?"

Will glanced at him before nodding.

"A lot has happened since we last spoke." Rylan motioned toward the table. "You want a cup of coffee?"

The sun wasn't up yet, but days started on the ranch at 4:00 a.m. Rylan should've known they couldn't fool her family, thinking they could go unnoticed on the property.

"I'll take a cup if you've got it. Black." Will took a seat.

Rylan poured two and joined Will. He set down one of the mugs in front of his former best friend.

"Before you say anything, I'd like to apologize to you," Rylan began.

"There's no reason to rehash the—"

"I believe there is. And it's an important step in my sobriety."

Will's eyes widened in surprise.

"That's right. I've been sober for many years now, but facing you has been the most difficult part of the journey," Rylan admitted.

"Why is that?" Will took a sip and studied Rylan's face.

"I needed to be ready to forgive myself if you accepted my apology. And I'm not there yet but—"

"Losing a friendship, hell, a brotherhood has been punishment enough. Don't you think?" The sincerity in Will's words struck like a physical blow.

Had he missed the friendship as much as Rylan?

"You covered for me that night. What I did was wrong, and you stuck up for me even though I didn't deserve it. I was a stupid kid—"

"You lost your mother, and I couldn't seem to help pick you back up or get you on the right path again," Will said.

"I let you down, not the other way around. And I let the Willow family down by catching their crops on fire." Saying those words still hurt. "I had no business—"

"Hold on a second. You think it was *you* who lit that fire?" Will's voice was steady.

"I was the one there. You said it yourself. That's where you found me. You took the blame so I wouldn't end up in juvenile detention." That's how Rylan remembered it.

"The McFarland boys set that fire, and they did it on purpose. I just couldn't prove it. They were drunk and seemed to think it would be real funny to destroy the field. You were passed out. I found you before the flames got to you, or they would've let you die. I was angry with you at the time for choosing those jerks over our friendship. You never had anything to do with the fire. My parents helped the Willows get back on their feet. But you almost lost your life." Will smacked his palm on the table. "I was almost too late that night, but it never should've gone that far. I should've been a better friend."

Rylan let those words sink in. All the guilt he'd been feeling these years for the fire had been wasted? Damn, those were a lot of years to be carrying around shame for something he didn't do. Looking back, they'd been for nothing.

He didn't regret his time in the military. He'd gotten his act together there. His service had been good for him. "Thank you for telling me, Will."

"I tried to talk to you before you left, but you said you didn't want to look back."

If only he'd known. "Being stubborn isn't my best trait."

Will chuckled and it broke the tension. "You think?"

"I'm sorry for the pain I caused, man. I missed our friendship. It's one of the main reasons I decided to straighten up my act."

"That means a lot to hear." Will offered a handshake. "How about we pick up where we left off, but from the good times?"

"Now that's a deal." Rylan took the hand being offered. "For the record, I had no idea I was getting your sister into a mess when I called her the other day for help." Those words couldn't be truer.

Will didn't respond right away. He seemed to take a minute to think. "I realize you would never put my sister in harm's way."

"She means a lot to me, Will."

"I saw that the other day. That's why I walked outside to clear my head. I'd imagined a different scenario happening if you and me were ever in the same room again." Will's face brightened. "It involved fists."

"Yeah, I deserve it after the way I messed things up in our friendship," Rylan said.

"Well, I thought you'd be throwing the first punch," Will admitted.

"I guess I had a lot of pent-up aggression in high school." Rylan took a sip of coffee. "The only punch I want to throw now is at the person who's trying to take my daughter away."

He updated Will on the situation with Alicia and the Robinsons.

"Zach promised to call when he got further into the investigation." Rylan set his mug down. He looked up at Will. "Your sister's in the other room if you want to talk to her."

"I don't have anything to say, except take it easy on her. She went through a lot and, strong as she is, none of us want to see her hurting like that again. It nearly cracked us in half when we saw her after she lost the baby. Her son-of-a-bitch ex took off, not that she ever cared about him the way she does about you." Will lasered a look at Rylan. "You do realize my sister has feelings for you, right?"

"I hope so." Rylan sure as hell had feelings for her. What that meant in the long run, he had no idea. Right now, all he could think about was putting Mr. Robinson behind bars and making sure that both Amber and Brooklyn were safe. For his daughter's sake, he needed to find her mother.

"Good. Because even when she was married I never

saw her look at him like she does you." Those words broke through the walls he'd carefully constructed.

"The truth is, Will, I'm not nearly good enough for your sister." He kept his tone church-quiet because he knew she'd argue if she heard.

"You know what, buddy? There was a time when I would've blindly agreed with that statement. Not anymore. For what it's worth, I think you're exactly who she needs." Will set his mug down and stood up. He turned toward the cracked bedroom door. "Did you hear that, Amber?"

"I sure did," she said with all that stubbornness and ire he loved about her.

Will left and Amber walked into the room.

"We need to talk," she said. "Later."

Rylan wasn't sure he liked the uncertainty in her tone. Was she shutting down on him? Was this—whatever *this* meant—moving too fast? He felt caught up in a rogue wave. For now, he was riding on top but how long before it sucked him under and tossed him out to sea?

AMBER HELD BROOKLYN to her chest. She couldn't allow this angel to cloud her judgment and yet how could she not? Holding this baby felt so right. Being with Rylan felt so right. But what didn't feel so right was the fact that Amber wasn't Brooklyn's mother.

Boots shuffled up the stairs and Amber's gaze went to the table, searching for whatever it was that Will forgot. She made a move toward the door, but it swung open and Mr. Robinson stood at the entrance.

Amber stared at the barrel of a gun.

"Hold on there, buddy," Rylan said. His cell buzzed on the table.

"Come over here," Mr. Robinson ordered. His eyes wild and angry, he looked like a hungry predator closing in on prey.

Amber was paralyzed with fear. All she could do was hold the baby tighter to her chest. If danger involved only her, she wouldn't hesitate to fight back or try to duck for cover. But holding the baby ensured Amber would move slower. A half-second hesitation could give Mr. Robinson the upper hand. Damned if he didn't already have it, and that just burned Amber up inside. She'd never played the victim role and had no plans to start now. She would, however, do whatever was necessary in order to ensure Brooklyn's safety.

Rylan was near the table on the opposite side of the sofa. His cell was buzzing madly on the table. Even a skilled soldier like him couldn't make that leap before Mr. Robinson got off a shot.

"You don't want her," Rylan interrupted. "I'm the one you want."

Mr. Robinson's hand trembled, and she could almost visibly see his blood pressure rise. "I'll decide who's going with me."

"Where's the baby's mother?" Rylan asked.

"She's not coming back." Robinson's face twisted when he said the words. "I killed her with my own hands. Stupid bitch couldn't follow simple directions. All she had to do was have the baby and hand her over. I would've preferred a son. Women are so weak. But my wife wanted her anyway."

Amber glanced at Rylan, half expecting him to make

a move but knowing he couldn't. Her heart ached for how calloused this man sounded about taking Brooklyn's mother's life. No matter how bad of a mother Alicia might've been or undeserving of this angel, the woman didn't deserve to have her life cut short.

Amber was close to the door. The gun was pointed at *her*.

There was no way she'd allow this man to shoot the baby. Amber turned to block Brooklyn and give Mr. Robinson a clear shot at her instead.

"It's okay, Rylan," Amber said in as calm a voice as she could muster. If anyone made a wrong move, Mr. Robinson could get spooked and pull the trigger.

"No one told you to speak," Mr. Robinson seethed.

Didn't those words grate on Amber. This man needed to wake up. It wasn't 1950 anymore. Women could vote. They could run ranches and have a variety of careers. And, at least in her case, could shoot a gun. So, he'd better watch his mouth.

"If anything happens to me, you won't get what you came for." Amber motioned toward the baby. "I go down and I take her with me. You lose. You'll be arrested. My cousin, Zach McWilliams, won't sleep or stop until he hunts you down. So, it seems we're in a bit of a stalemate."

"Her cousin might go after you legally, but I'll go after your family. Your wife. Your mother. Any living relative you hold dear. And then I'll come after you. You'll know it's coming. It's going to happen but you won't know when and you sure as hell won't be able to stop me." Rylan's voice was a study in calm composure.

"You'll come with me and bring the baby with you."

Mr. Robinson practically spat the words. His voice was filled with the tension of a man on the edge.

And then he shifted the barrel of the gun toward Rylan and fired.

Chapter Eighteen

Rylan was hit. He made a show of flying backward and landing hard against the back wall. He dropped onto the dining table and then rolled off of it. The bastard had to pay. No matter what Alicia had done, she didn't deserve to lose her life. He, of all people, knew what it was like to make mistakes. There should be second chances and not the finality of death.

Amber gasped. The horrific look on her face slammed guilt into him. Yes, he'd taken a bullet, but he'd been in worse tactical situations. A good soldier could detach emotionally and stay logical. So, he'd gone back to his training the minute he realized Robinson was going to walk out the door with Amber and Brooklyn.

Playing up his injury gave him an advantage when there weren't many to be had.

Robinson pushed Amber out the door, and the look of horror on her face would keep Rylan awake at night if his plan failed. It would be the last time he saw her if he didn't play his cards right.

The minute Robinson got Amber into the stairwell, Rylan jumped into action. He moved stealth-like toward the window behind the kitchen sink. He opened it, climbed on top of the counter and slipped out.

Hanging on to the outside of the window, he was able to cut some of the distance to the ground. He'd landed behind the offices. Damn, the sun was coming up, and that meant Lonnie and the ranch hands would be out on the property.

Where was Will?

Fire shot through him at the possibility that anything had happened to his friend. No, that wasn't possible. Rylan and Amber would've heard something. Robinson must've hid in the shadows and waited.

Blood dripped from his left wrist where the bullet had grazed him. Even one-handed he could take down Robinson.

Rylan moved along the shrubbery line at a healthy clip until he saw movement. Robinson had Amber's elbow in his grip. Seeing that shot more fire through Rylan.

He dropped and crouched low so he'd stay below Robinson's line of sight through the brush. He caught his first break when he saw that Robinson was walking Amber toward Rylan's position. The man was a hothead and not a career criminal. All Rylan had to do was exercise patience and wait for the man to slip up.

With a useless left hand, Rylan would have to rely on his right. It wasn't his dominant hand anyway, but one hand down wasn't ideal in any fight. He didn't doubt his skills. Emotions had gotten the best of him in the apartment. How could they not? It was Amber and his child, a child he didn't know about last week and now couldn't imagine living without. The little bean had wiggled her way into his heart.

Steady, Rylan controlled his burst of adrenaline. Part of it came from the pain in his left wrist and the other part was due to the circumstance unfolding. He couldn't allow himself to consider any other outcome than a successful mission. And yet his heart was engaged. It was too late for going all-logic and no-emotion. Which was funny because Rylan had never been one to get caught up in emotion.

Guess he was a changed man now that he could see a future. And his future involved Amber and the baby in her arms, if Amber would have him.

He'd work double time to make up for the loss of Alicia in Brooklyn's life.

Robinson drew near and Rylan caught his second break. The man's nerves were getting to him. It was possible he'd never shot anyone before. Although, he'd admitted to killing Alicia. Was that big talk for a small man?

Rylan had no doubt that Alicia was gone, but one of Robinson's henchmen might've done it. Most people who'd actually taken another life found no need to brag about it.

As the increasingly nervous man looked from side to side, he let the gun barrel point away from Amber.

In a split second, Rylan leaped out of the brush and tackled Robinson before the man's brain could send a message to his finger to pull the trigger.

Rylan disarmed Robinson with ease, knocking the gun loose and causing it to tumble a few feet away onto the grass. It fired and he heard Amber scream.

"Take Brooklyn away from here," Rylan said to Amber. He wanted both of them as far away as possible.

Engaging in death rolls to disorient Robinson, Rylan stopped when he was on top of the older man and squeezed his arms to his sides with the force of his thighs. He might've been one wrist down, but his legs were far more powerful.

Robinson tried to buck, but Rylan just smiled down at the man.

Amber was already shouting for help.

"You're going to spend the rest of your pitiful life behind bars. You're going to make new friends with that winning personality of yours. And if one of your henchmen so much as drives through this county, he won't drive back out alive. Are we clear?" Rylan reared a fist back and punched the jerk who'd killed the mother of Rylan's child and had almost killed the love of his life.

When he looked up at Amber, he saw her handing over the baby to her cousin Amy. And then he saw a red dot flowering on Amber's shirt. What? When?

The next few moments moved as though in slow motion. A security team descended on the scene in less than a minute. Isaac pressed his knee into Robinson's back as he zip-cuffed him.

Rylan flew to Amber the second Robinson had been secured.

Nothing in Rylan's life made sense without Amber. He dropped to her side on the green turf.

"Don't you leave me," he said to her. "I love you, Amber. I *need* you." Rogue tears broke free and fell from his eyes. "Please, stay with me."

Her eyes fluttered and a ghost of a smile crossed her

purple lips. She was losing a lot of blood. He pulled up her T-shirt and saw a bullet wound the size of his fist where the bullet exited. Rylan wasn't a religious man, but he cupped her face in his hands and said a protection prayer that he'd learned as a kid.

He vaguely heard crying in the background along with shouting.

"Come on, Amber."

When she didn't respond, he took off his own shirt, balled it up using his good hand and gently pressed it into her wound to try to stem the bleeding.

"I need an ambulance," he shouted as the shirt was almost immediately soaked.

Rylan couldn't be sure how long it took for the EMTs to arrive on the scene. Time slowed to a standstill as Amber lay on the grass. She had a pulse, but her breathing was shallow.

And his heart nearly stopped beating in his chest.

The EMTs went to work immediately, giving Amber oxygen. They put pressure on the wound and stabilized her enough for her to be transported to County General, which was a twenty-minute drive.

On the way, Will instructed Rylan to pull a shirt out of the gym bag in the back seat. Rylan did as instructed. Pulling it over his head with one hand was tricky, but he managed.

The ambulance driver made it in half that time as Rylan followed. Will had practically dragged him to his vehicle. And then he'd chased that ambulance all the way to the hospital.

Will offered reassurances along the way, but the words were as hollow as the space in Rylan's chest. He pulled into the ambulance bay at the ER. "Go. I'll park and be right up."

"Thank you." Rylan tore out of the passenger seat and was next to the EMT as he brought Amber's gurney out the back of the ambulance.

Lights blared, twisting together as Rylan followed Amber inside. A team waited for her, and he figured that wasn't a good sign under the circumstances.

"Sir, are you hurt?" The intake nurse seemed to notice the blood all over his arm and wrist. Some belonged to Amber and some was his own. The nurse's gaze landed on his wrist as he favored it. No amount of pain could distract him from why he was really there.

"I'm fine. This isn't my blood."

The nurse cocked a concerned eyebrow.

"I'm Ophelia and I'd like to take a look at that wrist if you'll allow it," the nurse said.

"The only person who needs treatment is behind those doors. When can I get an update about her condition?" he asked. He was locked on to a target and nothing else mattered.

Will burst through the ER doors. "I'm with him."

"Any chance you can convince him to accept treatment on his wrist?" Ophelia asked.

"Not until he hears a positive report on my sister, Amber Kent," Will told her.

The last name seemed to register because Ophelia's eyes lit up. "Your family has been so generous to this hospital. Please, follow me."

For once in Rylan's life, he was grateful the Kents had money. He'd sign over his own life savings if it meant getting information about Amber's condition.

"She's brave, Rylan," Will said as Ophelia led them into a private lounge. There were leather chairs instead of hard wooden ones. There was a nice coffee bar off to one side and a fridge with a glass door next to it. Every popular soda was in there along with all the sparkling waters a person could drink.

"Help yourself to a drink or a snack," Ophelia said. "I'll check with the nurse on duty and see if I can get an update for you gentlemen."

Every half hour from that point on, a nurse showed up in the waiting room to talk to Will and Rylan. After two visits, the room was filled with Kents and their spouses. Rylan learned that Brooklyn was safe on the ranch with Joyce, who couldn't stop doting on the little girl. Brooklyn seemed happy as a lark in Joyce's care. She'd been there from day one for Mitch's twins and the other babies as the Kent brood grew.

Zach was the only family member missing, and he was busy arresting Mrs. Robinson for being an accomplice in Alicia's death, a death Zach had confirmed by the coroner's office. He phoned with an update that Alicia's laptop browser had searches for date-rape-type drugs like ketamine. She'd also done research on fentanyl.

Knowing that Rylan had maintained his sobriety felt hollow without Amber to talk to. He missed the sound of her voice, the feel of her skin. He missed her quick wit and even faster smile.

The light that had always been Amber might've dimmed, but in the past twenty-four hours he'd seen it return full force.

After Amber's loved ones waited an agonizing

twenty-four hours and she had had three blood transfusions, a nurse walked into the waiting room. Chatter stopped and the room fell silent.

"She's in recovery and she's asking for Rylan Anderson and her brother Will," the nurse announced.

The pair had been hovering over the coffee machine, waiting for news. Rylan had allowed his wrist to be tended to an hour ago once he'd learned that Amber was out of surgery to remove bullet fragments from her hip.

Rylan took the lead and Will followed the nurse down the hall.

"The doctor will be in to speak to the family soon, but he was pleased with how the surgery went," the nurse stated. "She'll be moved into a room soon. He wants to keep her here for a few days to make sure her recovery is smooth."

The middle-aged, short redhead stopped in front of a door. "She's right in here."

Rylan wasted no time walking in, and Will was on his heels.

Amber's eyes were closed. Seeing her in that room with all the machines beeping and tubes hanging out of her gutted him.

He and Will flanked the bed, and Rylan took her hand in his.

She blinked her eyes open, locked on to Rylan and smiled.

It took another fifteen minutes for her to open her eyes again. This time, she kept them open a little longer.

"Did you mean what you said, Rylan Anderson?" she finally said. She coughed. "My throat is dry as a cactus."

Rylan couldn't help but crack a smile. He picked up a water container and helped her get the straw to her lips.

"Thank you. That's better," she said after taking a drink. "Where's the baby?"

"You gave us a scare," Will said.

"Believe me, I wasn't trying to." The smile faded too soon. "Is everyone else okay? Brooklyn is good, right?"

"Yes. The Robinsons are going to separate prisons where at least Mr. Robinson will spend the rest of his life. Brooklyn is with Joyce, waiting for you to get better so you can hold her again," Rylan said. "And I meant what I said. I love you, Amber. I can't imagine my life without you."

Amber's eyes lit up.

"You heard that, right, Will?" she asked.

Will couldn't help but laugh. "I did."

"Then you can go," she teased.

"I'd like him to stick around if you don't mind," Rylan said, and the room fell quiet from the seriousness of his tone. "Your father was a good man. He was kind to me. I wish he was here all the time, especially now because I'd like to ask him for your hand in marriage. But if Will can step into his father's shoes for a minute, I'll ask him instead."

Will practically beamed as he looked at his sister. Her smile displayed a row of perfectly straight, perfectly white teeth. Not everything was so perfect about Amber, except that she was perfect for Rylan. "Permission granted."

Rylan bent down on one knee. He was still holding on to Amber's hand when he said, "You're my best friend and the first person I want to speak to no matter what kind of day I've had. My heart is yours, Amber. I can't imagine loving anyone more or finding a better partner to spend my life with. So, if you'll do me the honor, I'm asking you to marry me."

"It's ALWAYS BEEN YOU, Rylan. Ever since that first kiss at sixteen years old I knew there was something special, something that I'd never find with another man." Tears streamed down her cheeks. "So, yes, I'll be your partner, your wife. And I promise to love you with every breath until my last."

Rylan stood up and leaned over the bed to kiss the woman he loved. He finally found where he belonged.

"What do you think about a Valentine's wedding?" Amber asked.

"That's not far off. You sure you don't want time to plan a wedding?"

"I don't want a big wedding. I want a marriage. And I can't think of a better Valentine's present than to make our family official," she said.

Those were all the words he needed to hear. "Valentine's it is."

Will moved around the side of the bed and gripped Rylan in a man hug. "You've always felt like a brother to me. Welcome to the family."

Rylan couldn't think of a better way to spend the rest of his life than with a real family, his daughter and the woman he loved.

* * * * *

BACKCOUNTRY ESCAPE

NICOLE HELM

For the helpers.

Chapter One

Felicity Harrison had learned two things since coming to live with Duke and Eva Knight when she'd been just four years old, with a broken arm and black eye courtesy of her father.

First, she loved the outdoors. She could hike for days and sleep under the stars every night given the chance. Didn't matter the season or the weather. In her mind the winds of the South Dakota Badlands had made her, and she was part of that stark, awe-inspiring landscape.

The second thing had taken her a little longer to figure out, but once she'd hit puberty she'd been sure.

She was desperately, irrevocably in love with Brady Wyatt.

Despite the fact she was nearing thirty and he'd never shown any interest in her that he didn't show all of her foster sisters, Felicity hadn't fully given up on the prospect that Brady might notice her at some point.

It was possible. She had made changes in her life the past few years. Between her epic shyness and intermittent stutter, high school and college had been a bit of a disaster but she'd found her passion in parks and recreation—as much as people would laugh at her zeal for nature.

In finding her passion at an early age, and making it her career, parks and rec had ended up being the thing that gave her some confidence. The drive to succeed had helped—or maybe forced—her to overcome some of her issues and bumps in the road.

After years of seasonal work in the national park system, she'd finally landed her dream job as a park ranger at Badlands National Park, her home. The job had been hard and challenging, and it had *changed her*.

She wasn't the same Felicity she'd been.

Brady hadn't noticed yet because he was so busy. Being a police officer and EMT in Valiant County took up a lot of his time. Plus, he lived a good hour away and spent free time at his grandmother's ranch even farther out.

She just needed the opportunity to show him who she'd become, and *surely* he'd fall for her the way she'd fallen for him all those years ago.

She daydreamed about that opportunity while she took her normal morning hike. Summer was inching its way into the mornings so she didn't need her park jacket over her sweatshirt. It was her favorite time of year, and that put a smile on her face and pep in her step.

The sky was a moody gray. Likely they'd have storms by afternoon, but she imagined the sky was a bright summer blue and Brady was hiking with her. He'd hold her hand and they'd talk about what birds they were hearing.

Her fantasies about Brady were always just like that. Soft, sweet, relaxing. Brady was steady. Calm. His five brothers were wilder or edgier, even Jamison. As the oldest, Jamison was serious, and seriously noble, but there was a sharpness to him that had taken Felicity time to grow accustomed to.

But Brady? He was even-keeled. He didn't shout or swear. He believed in right and wrong, and he appreciated the importance of his duties as an EMT. He took care of people. *Healed* people.

Calm and good and healing were definitely things she wanted in her life.

She was so caught up in her fantasy she almost tripped over the boot in the middle of the path.

She regained her footing and looked down at the brown boot. It was unlaced, and the soles were caked with dirt.

Felicity stared at it as the slow roll of cold shock spread out through her body. For a second her vision blurred and sound disappeared. She couldn't suck in a breath. She could only stand and look at the boot.

She'd seen this before, done this before. It was happening again.

No.

Her mind rejected the possibility and she managed to breathe in, let it slowly out. It was just a boot. People lost weird things on the trail all the time. Maybe it had gotten too heavy. Maybe it was broken.

There were a million reasons. A million. Besides, it wasn't even the same kind of boot as…the last time. This one was clearly a woman's, if the bright pink laces were anything to go by. It was an accident. A coincidence.

You have to check.

She nodded to herself as if that would make her move. Make this okay. As if she could will away all the similarities to last year.

There wouldn't be a body this time. Couldn't be.

Just keep walking.

You can't just keep walking!

Her mind turned over and over, reminding herself of a Felicity she didn't like very much. She stepped purposefully away from the boot. It wouldn't be like last year.

She would turn to the right and look off the path. She would see nothing but rocks and the stray scrubby flora.

First she looked left. Because…because she had to work up to it. There was nothing but mixed grass prairie that existed on that side of the trail. It was fine.

The right side was where the last body had been. There wouldn't be one. There *couldn't* be one. She forced herself to turn, to take the few steps to the very edge of the trail.

This side was rock, geological deposits that brought people to the Badlands in droves every summer. There wouldn't be a body. Couldn't be.

But there was.

She stared at the mess of limbs all at wrong angles. She stared, frozen, willing the image to disappear. The canyon to the side of the trail was narrow and deep, but you'd have to be sincerely not paying attention to fall down it, or…

Or.

She finally managed to squeeze her eyes shut, last year's memories rushing back like a movie in her head. Unseeing eyes and a black beard then. Now, a woman facedown in the rock, hair moving in the wind.

Nausea rolled through her, but she swallowed it down and tried to think. Tried to remember where and what she was.

Don't touch anything. Don't touch. Don't touch.

She took a few stumbling steps back on the trail.

Last time, she'd checked the body with a thought to help. Last time, she'd compromised the crime scene trying to identify the person while waiting for the cops. Last time, she'd made so many mistakes.

Not this time.

She nodded to herself again. This time she'd do it right. Not mess with anything. Not ruin anything.

How could it be *happening again*?

"One step at a time, Felicity. One step at a time."

She was calmed by the sound of her own voice, even if there was no one around she was talking to. She pulled out her phone, called the local police department and radioed her boss so he could get someone out to seal off the area.

Then she called Brady. She couldn't help it. When she was in trouble—when she or any of her foster sisters were in trouble—they always turned to the Wyatt boys.

They always came, and they always helped. Because they were good men, and Brady was the best of them, in her estimation.

When he answered, she managed to tell him what had happened, though she felt detached and as if she was speaking through dense fog. He promised she wouldn't have to be alone.

She tried to allow that reassurance to soothe her, but mostly she settled in to wait, hoping she wouldn't throw up.

"SHE CALLED *YOU*," Gage Wyatt grumbled at his brother through the phone receiver tucked between his ear and shoulder as he navigated the highway in front of him.

Summer had turned the hills green, and the tall grass waved in the wind. Gage had always gotten a kick out of the fact that's exactly what his ancestors would have seen when they'd arrived here by cart and horse.

He couldn't find amusement today as his twin brother tasked him with something he most especially did not want to do.

"I can't make it," Brady lectured. "I called Tuck, but he didn't answer. He's likely on a case. You're closer than Jamison, Cody and Dev—not that I'd send Dev. She needs someone there ASAP, Gage."

Gage swore inwardly, not sure how out of the six Wyatt brothers he was the *only* one available. He kept his voice light and offhanded, the Gage Wyatt special. "She's moon-eyed over you. That's why she called *you*."

There was only the briefest of pauses in return. "She found a body." Brady's tone was flat, the kind of flat his voice got when no amount of coaxing, arguing or nonchalance was going to irritate him into caving. "Another body."

"All right, all right," Gage muttered. "I'm not too far off." At least in the grand scheme of things in South Dakota. An hour, tops. "Same place?"

"No." Brady related where exactly in the park Felicity had stumbled across a body. Not too far from her park ranger cabin.

She'd found *another* body. The same thing had happened to Felicity last year, and it was horrible, to say the least, that she was dealing with that again. Gage listened as Brady explained where he'd need to go to get to Felicity. He turned his truck around and started heading for the park while Brady spoke.

"Be gentle with her," Brady said. "You know Felicity."

"Yeah." He did, he thought grimly as he hung up and tossed his cell phone onto the passenger seat. He knew her better than his brother did apparently.

Felicity wasn't the same shy wallflower she'd been growing up. Ever since she'd gotten that job at Badlands and moved home—well, closer to home—she'd been more sure of herself, more…something. He didn't like to dwell on that considering she was so hung up on Brady.

Who apparently didn't even notice she'd grown up, no matter how long it had taken her.

She'd held up really well last year when she'd found the body. It had seemed like a freak accident, and she had seemed able to handle it, especially admirable since she wasn't used to dealing with dead bodies. As a police officer, he had dealt with quite a few, not always violent or tragic. Sometimes as simple as someone going to sleep and not waking up.

It was part of the job, and even if it wasn't, he'd grown up in a biker gang until his oldest brother had gotten him and Brady out when they'd been eleven. He'd seen worse there living among the Sons of the Badlands those eleven years, especially considering his father ran the group. Ace Wyatt didn't deal in mercy—he dealt in his own warped version of justice.

Thanks to his oldest brother, Jamison, Gage had never believed in his father's justice. But he'd had to survive it, and the body count, before he'd had the maturity or the badge to cope with it.

Now he had both, but no matter how much Felicity had come into her own lately, she wasn't supposed to have to deal with dead bodies.

Plural. The pattern here made him uneasy. It was rare park rangers found bodies when not part of a search for missing people. Rarer still to have it happen to the same ranger twice.

She did need someone, but Gage didn't know why Brady hadn't called one of her foster sisters. Most of them would do better with the whole soothing and reassuring task ahead of him.

Likely Brady had called him because he knew some of the police officers with Pennington County, and none of the Knight fosters would. They might soothe, but Gage would be able to get some answers.

Gage would get those answers for Felicity. It was the

soothing and reassuring part he wasn't so keen on. He tended to keep a hands-off policy as much as possible when it came to her.

"Grown woman," Gage muttered to himself, tapping his agitated fingers against the wheel as he drove. "Did this before. She'll do it again."

He pressed the gas pedal a little hard.

"Didn't she just help save Cody and Nina's butts?" he demanded in an imaginary argument with Brady. "She's capable. More than." Wasn't that half the reason he kept his distance? Capable Felicity in love with his twin brother was dangerous to his well-being.

He muttered to himself on the long, empty drive to the Badlands. Usually he'd marvel at the scenery. Even living here his whole life, he didn't take for granted the rolling grassland that turned into buttes and the grand rock formations that made up the park and its surrounding areas. But he was working up a good irritated steam—mostly as a defense mechanism against Felicity in particular.

She *was* moon-eyed over Brady. So it made sense that since she'd grown a spine and begun showing it off, Gage had started having a little more than friendly thoughts about her. What didn't make sense was harboring those more-than-friendly feelings knowing full well she worshipped the ground Brady walked on.

Who could blame her? His brothers were saints as far as he was concerned. Oh, Cody and Dev had a bit of an edge to them, but at the heart of it they were all good men.

Then there was Brady, something better than a good man. Smartest of all of them, honorable without being hard about it. By the book and serious, yet affable enough that everyone *loved* Brady. He never said the wrong thing, never offered an inappropriate joke to ease the tension. If all his brothers were saints, Brady was the king saint.

On the other hand Gage was the one who said the wrong thing for a laugh. Who didn't take anything as earnestly as his brothers took their breakfast choices.

Of *course* Felicity had a thing for Brady, and it seemed inevitable that Gage had the bad luck to be hung up on someone in love with his perfect twin.

He rolled his shoulders as he pulled into the parking lot for the trail Felicity had been hiking. This wasn't about him, his issues or even his stupid feelings.

This was about Felicity. Helping her with a sad co-incidence. Coming across her second dead body in as many years.

He ignored a tingly *this is all wrong* feeling between his shoulder blades and flashed a broad grin to the cop stationed at the blocked-off trailhead.

He pulled out his badge, did some sweet-talking and was heading toward Felicity in a few minutes.

Once he reached the area where the cops and park rangers were huddled, he stopped short and took a minute to observe Felicity. She sat on a rock away from the circle of people. She was deathly pale, her fingers twisted together, and she stared hard at them.

His heart ached, very much against his will. As a sheriff's deputy for Valiant County, he'd dealt with his share of victims and innocent bystanders of awful things. He knew how to deal with the walking wounded.

But he actually *knew* Felicity, and had since he'd escaped to Grandma's ranch. He'd been eleven to her nine. He'd witnessed her nearly mute elementary years, an awkward-at-best adolescence and then eventually this change in her. Now, in front of him sat a woman who was not falling apart though she had every right to.

That twisting feeling dug deeper so he pushed himself forward. "Hey."

She looked up slowly, her eyebrows drawing together in dawning confusion. "I called Brady."

The twist grew teeth, and he might have grinned negligently in a different situation. But she'd just found a body, so Gage shrugged instead and didn't let the burn of her disappointment settle inside of him. "He sent me. I was closest."

She stared at him for a few seconds before she finally jerked her chin in some approximation of a nod. "They already—" she swallowed, a slight tremor going through her body "—moved the body out."

"Any ID?"

Felicity shook her head. "Nothing on her."

"Her. So, this is different than…" He winced at how insensitive he sounded. Sure, it worked when you were a cop. Not so much when you were here as a friend.

She paused. "Yes," she said finally, in a way that was not convincing at all. "Different."

"Let's get you back to your place, huh?"

She gestured helplessly at the team of cops and park officials. "I have to…"

"They know where to find you if they need more information. Come on. You probably haven't eaten since breakfast." He pulled her to her feet and easily slid his arm around her shoulders since he knew she'd balk at moving if he didn't give her a physical push.

She smelled like flowers and summer. Quite the opposite of the situation they were dealing with.

She pressed a hand to her stomach, her heels all but digging in where she stood. "I couldn't eat. I can't."

"We'll see. You want to walk back?"

She looked around, dismay clear as day on her face. "No, but I need to."

He understood that. If she didn't walk back the way

she'd come, she'd be afraid of returning this way even when her job necessitated it.

Still, he had to give her a push, and he tried not to feel a bit sick over the fact he was forcing her to do something she didn't want to do. Even if she needed to. He followed the trail back toward her cabin, keeping a tight grip on her shoulders as they walked.

A cold drizzle began to fall, but neither of them commented on it or hurried their pace. It felt like a slow trudge through chilled molasses, and Gage didn't have the heart to speed her up even as she began to shiver.

When they got to the authorized-user-only trail, Gage took it without qualm. It would lead to her park housing, and he'd get some food in her. Encourage her to rest.

Then, when she wasn't so pale, he'd head back to the ranch. Felicity wouldn't want him to stay anyway. She'd either handle it on her own, or he'd call one of her sisters for her.

Her little cabin was situated in a small grove of trees. It was old, but she'd infused it with a kind of hominess, though he couldn't identify how. Just that it looked like a nice place.

He reached the door and waited for her to pull out her keys. She unlocked the door and stepped inside.

He'd hoped the walk would have helped put some color back in her cheeks, but she still looked pale as death and like a stray wind might knock her over. Her red hair was damp, and the tendrils that had escaped her braid stuck to her ashen skin.

"Go change into something dry."

She looked up at him, her green eyes lost and sad. She didn't say anything, just stood there looking at him.

"Go on. I'll fix you something to eat while you change."

She shook her head. "I'll just throw it up."

"We'll see. Go on now." He shooed her toward where he figured her bedroom was, down a short, narrow hallway.

He went to the cramped kitchen and poked around for something to make that would go down easy. He found an unreasonable amount of tea and picked one that looked particularly soothing. He followed the instructions, trying not to feel claustrophobic in her closet of a kitchen.

When she returned she didn't look any less lost, but she was in dry sweatpants and a long-sleeved T-shirt for Mammoth Cave National Park. She stood at the entrance to the kitchen taking in her surroundings like it was somewhere she'd never been before.

"Sit," he ordered, uncomfortable with how fragile she seemed.

She nodded after a time and then took a seat at her tiny table. He set the mug of tea in front of her. "You'll drink all of that," he said, trying to sound as commanding as his grandmother did when she was forcing food on someone.

She didn't drink, just stared at the mug. "They think I have something to do with it," she said, her voice so quiet he almost couldn't make out the words. "I can tell."

"No. You've been through this before. You know how it goes." He found a loaf of bread and dropped a slice in the toaster. "They have questions they have to ask just to make sure, but—"

"It's the second time." She lifted her gaze to meet his, and there was nothing timid or uncertain about her, as there had been in the past. No, she was in complete control, even lost and scared. "The questions were different. And they're right. It does. It has something to do with me. I know it does."

Chapter Two

Something about Gage's large form taking up almost the entire space in her tiny kitchen made Felicity want to blurt out everything that was going on in her brain.

He was making her tea and toast. She wanted to lay down her head and cry. She expected her sisters to take care of her. She even expected Duke to take care of her—he'd had to step in as mother along with father when Eva had died. He'd done his best.

Her foster family had always done their best, just like their friends the Wyatts.

But this was Gage. Gage always made her feel edgy. Like she was on uneven ground. You never knew what Gage was going to do or say, and she preferred knowing exactly what was going to happen.

Sometimes she blamed his size for the discomfort she felt. He was so tall and broad and, Lord, he packed on the muscle. But Brady was the exact same size, just as strong and broad, and Brady only ever made her feel safe. Comfortable.

Gage set down a plate with a piece of buttered toast in front of her. Her cheap, cute floral dishes looked all wrong in his hands.

Today was all, *all* wrong.

"Why do you think it has something to do with you?" he asked as he took a seat across from her.

"You made me tea and toast." She could only stare at the wisps of steam drifting up from the mug. Gage Wyatt…had made her tea and toast?

"You're lucky. If Grandma Pauline was here, she would have made a five-course meal and insisted you eat every bite."

It was true. His grandmother soothed with food—whether you wanted food as soothing or not. Tea and toast was a lighter option, and her stomach might actually be able to handle it. So she sipped the tea, took a bite of toast and avoided the topic of conversation at hand.

"Felicity."

She winced at the gentleness in his tone. "Why did Brady send you?" She squeezed her eyes shut. "I'm sorry. That sounds ungrateful."

He shrugged again, just as he had outside when she'd made a point of telling him he wasn't who she'd been expecting. There was something in his gaze when he gave those careless shrugs that made her heart feel weighted. Like she'd said something all wrong and hurt his feelings.

Which was ludicrous. Gage did not get hurt feelings, especially at her hands.

"Like I said outside, I was closest." He tapped his fingers on the table, the only sign of agitation.

"You've been very…nice," she said, not even sure why she wanted to try to make him feel better when any hurt or agitation had to be her imagination.

"I'm always nice."

"No. That is not true. Not that you're mean, but I'm not sure anyone would describe you as nice." Gage was challenging. He was irreverent. He made her jumpy. Even when he was doing something nice.

"Felicity. Why do you think this crime connects to you?"

The toast turned to lead in her throat and she had to work to swallow it down. She didn't want to talk about it, but she needed to. She needed help. From someone in law enforcement who would listen to her. "It was the same."

"A woman this time," he noted. "So, not exactly the same."

"Maybe not the *who*, but it was my morning hike. My routine. I've changed it a little since last year, but I always have a routine." Routine steadied her. Made her feel strong and in control, and now she wasn't sure she'd be able to have one or feel that ever again. "The last time, it was my routine hike. My personal routine hike—not work related. Just like this time."

He nodded and waited patiently for her to work up to say the rest of it.

"The boot in the trail. Unlaced. That happened last time, too. I stumbled over the boot last time. This time I saw it in the nick of time—probably the pink laces." Those laces would haunt her forever.

"Okay. So you saw the boot, and then what?"

She'd already told the Pennington County deputies and her boss the answer to that question. Over and over in a circle. But she hadn't explained to them what she was about to explain to Gage. "I told them I looked on the sides of the trail to see if anyone had had an accident."

"You told them…"

"I knew where the body would be. I looked on the left side first because that wasn't where the body was last time. I looked to the left and there was no one there, but

I had to check. It would be on the right side of the trail. I didn't want there to be, but I just… I just knew the body would be where it had been last time. Only a few feet off the trail." She shoved away the tea and the toast and got to her feet. "I can't…"

There was nowhere to go in her tiny cabin. Stomp off to her room like a child? Tempting.

But Gage walked right over to her, putting his big hands on her shoulders and squeezing them enough to center her in the moment.

He was so dang tall, and it was unreasonable how broad-shouldered he was. When he was clean-shaven, he looked so much like Brady it got hard to tell them apart. But their eyes were different. Brady's hazel edged toward brown, and Gage's green. Gage's nose was crooked, and he had a scar through his eyebrow.

Brady's face was perfect. Gage's was…

"You know, Brady told me I needed to be gentle with you."

Those words felt like cold water being splashed in her face. "I'm not a shy little girl anymore," she snapped, trying to shrug off his hands. When would they all see that? It wasn't enough she'd helped save Cody and Nina from one of the Sons last month? Honestly.

"That's what I told him," Gage said, which had her looking up in confusion.

"You…"

"Anyone who's paying attention can see you've changed, Felicity. You're an adult. You've found yourself or whatever you want to call it."

Did that mean *Gage* was paying attention? Impossible.

"Now. You've done this before. So, don't say you can't when we both know you can and you will."

She sucked in a breath. He was right. It didn't quite

steady her, though. Why was Gage of all people right? And why were his big hands on her narrow shoulders?

As if he'd read her thoughts, his hands slid away and he stepped back, shoving his hands into his pockets.

"Why couldn't it be random? I mean, it looks like the killings connect. It's not accidental and it's not suicide. It's murder—even I could see that no matter how much they tried to BS me. But just because it's murder, doesn't mean you're the key. Maybe Badlands is the common denominator. Maybe you're just…"

"Unlucky?"

"Sure. Why not? The bodies aren't showing up on your doorstep."

"Just on trails I walk as a matter of course," she returned, wishing she could believe his coincidence theory. "That boot wasn't an accident, and it wasn't placed there yesterday when anyone could have come across it. It was put there so *I* would come across it."

"Okay." He nodded, taking a few more steps away from her.

It seemed odd, the forced distance, but she could hardly think about anything going on with Gage when she had a dead body to worry about.

"If you're being targeted…why?"

"I don't know." She didn't have a clue. Maybe she'd believe it was her connection to the Wyatts. She'd shot one of the Sons of the Badlands men to help Nina and Cody escape Ace Wyatt's machinations. Except she'd never had a personal interaction with Ace Wyatt, the president of the gang and Gage's father, who was now in jail.

But jail hadn't stopped Ace from making things happen on the outside last month. Why would she think he couldn't reach her now?

The problem was that last month was the first time

she'd ever interfered with Sons business, which didn't explain the first body from a year ago.

Unless that *had* been an accident and this was a copy-cat?

"You think it's Ace."

Felicity looked up at Gage because his voice was so flat. Even when Gage got angry he usually hid it under that natural irreverence. It was why she preferred Brady. Brady was rather stoic, but when he showed an emotion you knew what emotion you were getting. Gage was unpredictable.

Even now. She didn't know what that cold, flat voice meant. She only knew it was possible this connected to his crime boss of a father, even if Ace was in jail and the Sons of the Badlands seemed to be getting weaker.

"I don't know. I don't know, but I interfered last month."

"It wouldn't connect all the way back to last year." He kept talking before she could offer her theory. "But it wouldn't have to—it would just have to look like it. Sounds like Ace."

She nodded. "I need you to help me figure out if it is, Gage. I can't trust the local police to do it. I'm sure they're fine at their jobs, but they don't know Ace, and they're afraid of the Sons. You aren't."

"Everyone is afraid of the Sons, Felicity. It's stupid not to be." He sighed, presumably at the horrified look on her face. "We'll figure it out. Okay?"

SHE WAS STANDING still as a statue, looking at him like he'd slapped her across the face when he'd simply told her the truth.

Even if the Sons were weaker than they'd been, they

were still dangerous. Too dangerous, and anyone with a connection to Ace Wyatt was definitely in the most danger.

They were working on getting more charges leveled against Ace, thanks to three of the men who had been arrested after trying to hurt Cody and Nina and their daughter last month. But it still wouldn't add up to a life sentence, even if he was found guilty at his upcoming trial for the first round of charges.

Unfortunately, no matter how sure Jamison and Cody were that the law would keep Ace powerless—when Ace had already proved jail couldn't—Gage had doubts.

Major doubts.

Felicity *had* been integral in the arrest of one of those men who was potentially going to take the stand against Ace. It made sense she'd be targeted.

Gage's phone chimed and he looked down at the text from Brady.

I can relieve you if you want.

Felicity would want Brady. She deserved the Wyatt brother she preferred even if her crush was hopeless. Brady didn't have a clue who Felicity really was. Gage wasn't convinced his twin could ever look at the Knight fosters and not see a *sister*. Or at the least think, *Hands off.*

Brady would always toe the unofficial line. Gage never did.

No worries, he typed and hit Send before he could talk himself into doing the right thing.

Maybe Felicity wanted Brady, but Gage would be the better helper in this situation. He was willing to bend a few more rules than Brady. Besides, she'd said she needed *his* help. Maybe it was only because he was here, but hell, he was here.

"Once they ID her, we'll want to see how she connects to the first victim."

Felicity shook her head and took a seat. "I don't think the victims matter. I mean, they matter. To their families. To me. But they're not the point to whoever is doing this."

"Maybe not, but we'll research it all the same. We'll go over things. Maybe you should stay at the ranch until this blows over."

She was shaking her head. "I have a job to do. If I run away from that—"

"They're going to put you on leave. They did last time, didn't they?"

"They can't. It's summer this time. It's busy season. I'm scheduled for programs and…" She trailed off as her phone buzzed. She swallowed and looked at the screen. "It's my boss."

Gage didn't say *I told you so*. He didn't need to. Didn't want to after having to stand and listen to her desperate attempts to change her boss's mind.

When she finally hung up, she stared at her phone. "I can't work for at least a week."

"That's not such a bad thing."

Her head whipped up, fury in her green eyes. "It's a terrible thing. On every level. I can't *be* here. It will haunt me—her body. Every night. You can't get rid of something you never face. It puts my job, my *dream* job, in jeopardy. Do you have any idea how hard I've worked to get this position?"

The color had come back to her face, the faintest blush rising in her cheeks. She was breathing a little heavier after that tirade, and she had her fingers curled into fists.

She was possibly the most beautiful woman he'd ever

seen, and he knew that made him a jerk. "Yeah," he finally managed. "You worked your butt off."

His simple affirmative had her slumping in her seat. "I don't want to go to the ranch. Duke will worry. Sarah and Rachel will worry and fuss. Your grandmother will make a feast for seventy and expect a handful of us to eat it all. Worst of all, you Wyatt boys will push me out of this when it is my fight."

"It's our fight."

"And yet I'm the one with blood on my hands." She held them up as if she'd been the one to do any kind of killing.

He knelt in front of her and, though he knew it would be a mistake, took both her raised hands in his. "There's no blood here."

"There might as well be," she returned, her voice breaking on the last word. She blinked back tears. "I can't sit idly by. If you take me back there, you'll push me out. All of you."

Brady would lead that charge, but Gage didn't tell her that. He held her hands in his, irritated that both were so cold. She should have drunk the tea. He should have made her.

"No, you can't sit idly by," he agreed, if irritably. "But that doesn't mean we can't go to the ranches and work through it. Let the police do their jobs here. Let your boss do his job for the park. Back home, we'll work together to figure out what this really is. Together. I promise. No one will push you out."

She stared at him, eyebrows drawn together, frown digging lines around her mouth. Her eyes were suspicious, but she sat there and let him hold her hands. She sat there and stared at him. Thinking.

While she was *thinking*, he was *feeling* quite a bit too much.

She tugged her hands out of his grasp and stood abruptly. She stalked away from him, though it ended up being only a few steps because the cabin was so small. She whirled and pointed at him. "You promise?"

"I promise," he replied solemnly.

Because Gage Wyatt would break rules and didn't mind lying when it suited, but he wouldn't break a promise to Felicity. Not even if it killed him.

Chapter Three

Felicity sat in the passenger seat of Gage's truck, brooding over the lack of her own vehicle. The lack of her job for at least a week. The lack of her little cabin that wasn't her home exactly. It wasn't *hers* to own—it was the park's.

But neither were the ranches hers, though they made up the tapestry of her childhood and adolescence. The Wyatt boys and the foster girls of Duke and Eva Knight had run wild over both ranches. They were a piece of her, yes, but she didn't own them.

She'd gotten into the wrong business if she was worried about owning things, though. Apparently, the wrong business if she didn't want to find dead bodies.

She closed her eyes, but that only made said bodies pop up in her head, so she opened them and leaned her forehead against the window. She watched the scenery pass, from the stark browns, tans and whites of the Badlands to the verdant green and rolling hills with only the occasional ridge of rock formations that would lead them to the ranches they'd grown up on.

"Brady said for us to meet at my grandma's."

Felicity sighed. "I don't want a fuss." She didn't want all the attention or the attempts at soothing. Right now she wanted to be alone.

Except then her company would be the images of the dead bodies she'd found, and that didn't exactly appeal, either.

"Maybe it'd be a good time to tell them about our Ace connection theory," Gage offered as if he was trying to make her feel better. Which was odd coming from Gage, who was known more for making a joke out of serious things. Still, if she really thought about it, he often did that in a way that made people feel better, even if only momentarily.

"So it's *our* theory now?"

Gage lifted a negligent shoulder. "We can call it yours, but I agree with it."

"Will they?"

"Not sure. Don't see why they wouldn't. It makes sense. We'll look into it one way or another."

"*We* or you guys?"

He spared her a look as he pulled through the gate to the Reaves Ranch. Pauline Reaves had run this ranch since she'd been younger than Felicity, and though she'd married, she'd kept the ranch in her name and never let anyone believe her husband ran things.

As the story went, her late husband had been in love with her enough not to care. Felicity had never met the Wyatt boys' grandfather, who had died before Felicity had come to live with the Knights.

Felicity loved Grandma Pauline like her own. Not such a strange thing for a girl who'd grown up with the care and love of foster parents to love nonfamily like family. Pauline had always represented a strong, independent feminine ideal to Felicity. One she'd thought she'd never live up to.

But the older she got, the more Felicity felt that if she worked hard enough at it, she could be as strong and determined as Grandma Pauline. She could forge her own path.

Thoughts of Pauline's strength disappeared as the line of cars in front of Pauline's old ranch house came into view. Despite its sprawling size, piecemeal additions and modernizations over the years, and the fact only two people lived full-time in it, the house was well cared for. The boys always made sure repairs were done quickly, and Grandma kept it spick-and-span.

Still, it showed its age and wear. There was something comforting in that—or there would be if there wasn't this line of cars in front of it.

"Everyone's here."

"I mean, not…everyone," Gage said, trying for what she assumed was a cheerful tone.

He'd failed. Miserably. Everyone or almost everyone's vehicle being here meant something…something big at that. It was more than her stumbling across a dead body.

Felicity frowned as Gage parked in line. Based on the vehicles she recognized, Tucker and Brady were here, as was Duke and potentially Rachel and Sarah if they'd driven over with him. Dev and Grandma Pauline lived on the property, but it was Cody's truck that really bothered her. Why would he come all the way out from Bonesteel? The only vehicle missing was one belonging to Jamison and Liza. Hopefully they were at home in Bonesteel, safe and sound, taking care of Gigi, Liza's young half sister. "What is all this? Why is everyone here?"

"I don't know," he replied, sounding confused enough that she believed him. He got out of the truck and she followed. Dev's ranch dogs pranced at their feet, whimpering excitedly as they'd been trained not to bark at Wyatts or Knights.

Felicity wanted to dawdle or trudge, spend some time

playing with the dogs, or maybe make a run for it to the Knight Ranch, where she knew she still had a bed waiting for her.

But that was cowardly, and it wouldn't change whatever this was. It would only avoid it for a while.

She followed Gage's brisk pace to the back door, which led to a mudroom. The dogs wouldn't follow inside at this entrance since you had to go through the kitchen to get to the rest of the house—and Grandma Pauline did *not* allow dogs in her kitchen.

Felicity stepped into the kitchen behind Gage. A very full room.

Duke and Rachel were there, sitting at the table. When Felicity had been younger, she'd been jealous of Rachel. She was Duke and Eva's only biological child, and she looked like she belonged in the Knight family. Even though with the fosters they'd been a conglomeration of black, Lakota and white—no one looking too much like anyone else—Felicity had always felt the odd man out with her particularly pale skin and bright red hair.

But she was older now, and today she was glad to see the people who were her family.

It was a little harder to be grateful for the presence of the Wyatt brothers. All of them being here in this moment only meant trouble. They brought it with them, and though they fought it as much as they could, it was always there.

Tucker stood next to Cody *and* Jamison—so they must have driven together from Bonesteel. Dev and Brady sat at the table while Grandma Pauline bustled around the kitchen.

They all looked at Felicity with smiles that were in turn sad, sympathetic or pitying. Felicity's chest got tight and panic beat through her, its own insistent drum of a heartbeat. "What's going on?"

Grandma Pauline all but pushed her into a chair and set a plate with a brownie on it in front of her. Duke took her hand and patted it.

All the eyes in the room except Gage's turned to Tucker.

His smile was the most pitying and apologetic of all. "When Brady told me what happened I asked a buddy over in Pennington County to let me know if they found anything out."

Felicity had to pause before she spoke. Getting upset often made her stutter return, but if she kept herself from rushing, she could handle it. "And they did?"

"The victim's name is Melody Harrison."

Everyone was quiet. So quiet and this was usually a noisy group.

"It's a common enough last name," Felicity forced herself to say slowly and calmly. "It might be a coincidence." She didn't know anyone named Melody, even if they shared a last name. Of course she'd been taken away from her abusive father at four. She hardly knew her biological family.

"It is common. Unfortunately, the next of kin who identified her..." If it was possible, the pitying expression grew worse. "He was her father. Michael Harrison."

"M-my father. B-but that's common, too, and—"

Tucker nodded grimly. "I confirmed it, Felicity. Your father. Melody was twenty-two, so she was born after you were placed with the Knights."

"Y-you're s-saying that..." She winced at how badly the stutter sounded in the quiet room. She made sure to take breaths between each word as she spoke. "The dead body I found is my sister."

"At least by half. Which means…" Tucker scraped a hand over his jaw.

She didn't let him say it. She might have before last year. Let him say it. Let the Wyatt boys take care of it. But no one could really take care of what was going on in her head. Even when she was weary enough to wish someone else could.

"The cops will try to connect me to it even more now."

GAGE SWORE AND felt a stab of guilt when Felicity flinched as if she'd received some kind of blow.

This was ludicrous. "How? When she didn't even know the sister existed?" Gage demanded.

His brothers gave him *that* look. The *you should know better, Gage* look. Because he was a cop. He knew how to investigate a suspicious death, and Felicity tripping over her alleged half sister was certainly suspicious.

He looked at Felicity. She'd made him promise that she wouldn't get elbowed out of dealing with this herself, so he waited for her to bring it up.

Though mostly he wanted Grandma Pauline to shove her full of brownies while he took care of everything.

However, he had enough women in his life to know they didn't particularly appreciate that method. Besides, he'd promised. So… He all but bit his tongue.

He gave Felicity a go-ahead nod, and then gestured when she simply stared at him. She blew out a slow breath.

"It could be Ace," Felicity finally said. She looked down at the plate and the brownie on it, but her voice was clear and steady no matter how little eye contact she made.

"How?" Jamison returned.

She looked up and met Jamison's gaze. "I interfered.

I helped Nina and Cody. I don't know *how* it's Ace, but I know why it could be. It makes sense." Her gaze shifted to Gage, looking for some kind of support or backup.

Me not Brady. Which was very much not the point. "Obviously, the timing of the first one doesn't work, but it could be a copycat type thing. It could be a way to make it look like she's involved—and I think the family connection only makes that more plausible."

His brothers mulled that over.

"Possibly a setup. To get Felicity in trouble. A punishment for interfering," Jamison said, clearly trying to work out the logistics. "I buy that. It's Ace's MO. But how would he have orchestrated it? Since the attempt on Nina's life, we've been keeping tabs on everyone Ace talks to."

Gage had thought about that on the long, silent drive over to Grandma Pauline's. "We keep tabs on everyone who visits him in jail. Not who he talks to inside. He could be paying off a guard or threatening another inmate. Problem is, until Ace is sentenced and sent to a more secure facility, he has ample ways to outwit the system *and* us."

"His lawyer keeps getting the trial pushed back," Tucker said, disgust lacing his tone. "They're going to drag it out as long as they can."

"Don't you have any informants on the inside, Detective?" Gage asked, infusing the word *detective* with only a little sarcasm.

Tucker rolled his eyes. "Not anyone I'd trust enough to tangle with Ace."

"What do we do?" Duke asked. Demanded.

"The park forced me to take a week's leave of absence, and then they'll *reevaluate*," Felicity said miserably.

"So, you'll be home." Duke didn't have to say *where you belong* for it to be heard echoing in the silence.

Felicity smiled at Duke, but surely everyone saw how sad that smile was.

"There's not much we can do right now," Jamison said, always the de facto leader, no matter the situation. "Tucker will keep his ear to the ground when it comes to the investigation. Cody and I can look into getting some more information about who Ace talks to in the jail."

"What about…" Gage hesitated at the word *father*, considering he barely liked to call his own one. "Michael Harrison. Where did this guy come from?"

"He was the victim's father."

Gage shook his head. "That's an awful big coincidence. There was a reason Felicity was removed from his care. Was this girl?"

"Okay, point taken. We'll look into both of them."

"And what will I do?" Felicity asked, and though Gage thought she tried to turn it into a demand like Duke had done, it didn't quite hit the mark.

"Come home and rest, girl," Duke instructed.

Gage opened his mouth to come to her defense because he'd *promised*, but she shook her head.

She smiled at her foster father. "That's a good idea, Duke."

They both stood up from the table, and since she hadn't taken even a single bite of the brownie Grandma had put in front of her, Grandma immediately shoved a plastic container full of brownies into her hands.

Felicity smiled and gave Grandma a one-armed hug. "Thank you, Grandma Pauline."

"You eat, you hear me?"

"Yes, ma'am." Felicity glanced back at Gage. "Keep me up-to-date?"

He ignored the fact he got a little something out of her asking *him* and not Brady. He was very good at ignoring things he didn't particularly care for.

He gave her a nod, and Duke, Rachel and Felicity left Grandma's kitchen. Leaving Gage with his brothers and Grandma.

Dev stood first. "I've got work."

"I'll help," Gage offered. "I was supposed to anyway." He paused and looked at Jamison, Cody and Tucker. They had the best ways to get information. Gage had a few buddies over at Pennington, but Tucker knew the detectives. Jamison and Cody had been integral in getting Ace arrested in the first place, so they had a lot of ways to find information on the Ace side of things.

Gage rode the road. He had a bit too much of a mouth on him to receive the promotions Tucker and Brady seemed to rack up without even trying.

It didn't bother him. He preferred the in-the-trenches view from the bottom, but right now the lack of resources to get information made him superfluous.

So why not sweat away some frustration on ranch work? He'd spend the night, check in on Felicity tomorrow morning, then head back to his apartment to pick up his take-home car for his evening shift.

If that itch between his shoulder blades stayed there all through the afternoon and night, well, he'd deal.

WHEN HE WOKE up the next morning and trudged down to breakfast, Brady was waiting at the breakfast table. Gage rubbed bleary eyes and knew the news was bad without even a word passing between them.

"They searched Felicity's cabin," Brady said without preamble.

"And?"

"They found evidence of clothing being burned in the fire grate outside the cabin. They've collected some hair they found—clearly not Felicity's."

"Doesn't mean it's that woman's hair. That doesn't mean anything. Good Lord, she's not a suspect."

"They've sent the hair and what was left of the burnt clothes in for DNA testing," Brady said, his calm poking at Gage's agitation.

Brady sighed and shook his head, showing his first sign of emotion. "I've got a bad feeling about this."

"So do I." It smelled of a setup. But not enough of one to tip off cops who didn't know Felicity. Or Ace, for that matter.

"We've got to get her a lawyer," Brady said. With a straight face and everything.

"A lawyer? Are you insane? We have to get her out of here."

Brady's expression went carefully blank. "You can't run from the police, Gage. You *are* the police."

"Yeah, and I know this is garbage. *You* know it. Felicity wouldn't hurt a fly, and I'm not going to let her be arrested and God knows what else. Can you imagine her stuck in a cell somewhere? It's not happening."

Brady didn't move even as Gage paced the room. Cody often called them two sides of the same coin. The way they reacted, or acted in general, was often in big sweeping opposites, but when it came to it—twin junk or just the way life worked—they were the same deep down.

They might not *react* the same, but they understood.

"Where would you go?" Brady asked, without Gage even having to say he'd be the one to hide her.

"I don't know yet, but I'll figure it out."

He had to.

Chapter Four

Felicity woke up in her childhood bed. There was a deep, soothing relief in that familiarity, that cocoon of safety…for about five seconds before the anxiety started to creep in.

Luckily, there was plenty to do to keep a mind occupied when you woke up on a ranch. Though Duke and Sarah ran the cattle operation with their seasonal workers, Felicity knew a chore or two could always be picked up.

It wouldn't keep her mind from running in circles, but it might help exhaust her enough she could manage a decent night's sleep tonight instead of tossing and turning as she'd done last night.

She rolled out of bed and looked around the empty room. She'd once shared it with Sarah, but when Liza, Nina and Cecilia had all moved out, each of the remaining girls had gotten their own room instead of sharing with one other sister.

Felicity had learned how to be alone, but she did it best and most comfortably when she could be outdoors. When she could listen to birdsong and watch the stars move across the sky. When the fresh air and unique landscape made her feel *awe* at her place in the world.

Indoors, alone was just alone. Too quiet and too claustrophobic.

The thought had her walking into the hallway, determined to find someone to eat breakfast with and then find chores.

She ran into Rachel in the hallway and raised an eyebrow at her notoriously bad-at-mornings sister. "Aren't you up early."

"That class I'm teaching at the rez this summer started last week." Rachel yawned. "It might kill me."

"I thought you were going to stay with Cecilia while you did that." As a tribal police officer, Cecilia lived on the rez. Though she wasn't Duke's biological daughter, she was Eva's niece. Neither Cecilia nor Rachel would have ever said it aloud, but they had more of a connection with each other than with her, Sarah, Liza and Nina. Blood mattered, even in a foster family.

"I've been spending weeknights with Cee, and weekends here. But Daddy was grumbling last night so I stayed an extra night. I'm staying there the rest of the week after class today." Rachel yawned again, then her eyes brightened. "Hey, drive me over instead of Sarah? You can spend a few nights with us at Cecilia's, take your mind off everything. We'll have a sleepover. Sarah won't stay because of the ranch, and Liza and Nina have their girls to worry about, but the three of us could have fun."

"I don't—"

"I won't take no for an answer."

Felicity smiled. It wasn't such a bad idea. She could clear her head, enjoy her sisters. Maybe Rachel and Cecilia had a deeper connection, but Felicity only seemed to feel that when she was alone and overthinking things. When they were all together, they were sisters.

Maybe all those thoughts about deeper connections were more her own issues than the truth.

"Well, then I guess… Damn, I don't have a car."

"We'll take Duke's. He can use Sarah's truck for the

weekend. You drop me off at the school, then you can do whatever. I'm sure the park will let you go back to work next week once the police have figured this out."

Felicity smiled, though she was not at all sure. Nothing about what was going on felt like last time. Last time had been a shock. It had been scary and a little traumatic, but she'd been able to convince herself it was a one-time thing. She'd just had the bad luck to be the one to find him. Bad luck was life.

Twice in two years felt a lot less like random bad luck.

"Come on," Rachel said, slipping her arm around Felicity's taller shoulders. "I'll make you breakfast. Pancakes."

"You don't have to go to all that trouble."

Rachel shrugged. "Daddy and Sarah will sing my praises. Neither of them are very good at taking care of themselves."

"What do they do when you're not here?"

"I'm hoping one of them learns through sheer necessity. I guess we'll see."

They headed downstairs together. Though Rachel was legally blind, she knew the house so well she didn't need her support cane when walking around inside and most of the grounds outside, as well.

Duke and Sarah were likely already out doing chores, but they'd be back in a half hour or so to eat and get more coffee. Felicity set out to help Rachel make pancakes and they chatted about Rachel's art class.

It felt good and normal, and Felicity almost forgot all her worries. Everything would be fine. She had a great family. Maybe the real issue wasn't so much what had happened, but how she'd allowed herself to feel solitary and singular when she had so many people who cared about her.

Since she hadn't done anything wrong, she just had to wait out the investigation. Maybe the time off would even be good for her. She'd been so focused on having her dream job that she'd neglected her family.

She'd spend time with her sisters, with Duke, do some work around the ranch, and when she was cleared to go back to work, she'd focus more on balance.

As she turned to put the bowl of strawberries she'd just cut up on the table, she saw a truck cresting the hill to the Knight house. Not one of Duke's trucks.

"Who is it?" Rachel asked.

"Gage." Why he was suddenly the one in charge of this whole thing, she didn't know. She'd called Brady originally because she'd wanted someone to take care of it, but Brady wouldn't have just taken care of it—he would have taken over.

She'd thought she'd wanted that in the moment, but she realized as Gage's truck pulled to a stop in front of the house, she was glad Gage had included her. He'd encouraged her to speak. He believed her theories. It felt more like she was on even ground with him.

"It's early," Rachel commented. "But that doesn't mean—"

"It means he has bad news. If it's bad news, it's about the dead woman." *My sister.* Felicity really couldn't wrap her head around that part yet, so she kept pushing it away. Kept pushing the involvement of her father out of her mind. Over and over again.

Despite knowing it was coming, the knock on the door made Felicity jump.

"We could pretend we're not here," Rachel offered.

"It would only delay the inevitable. Besides, he knows we're here." Felicity steadied herself on a deep breath before opening the door.

Gage looked disheveled, which wasn't that out of character for him, but considering the circumstances it felt foreboding. His grave expression didn't help. Gage was almost never grave. He was the one who cracked a joke to break the tension or told a bizarre story to take everyone's mind off things.

Brady was the grave twin, the one who took everything seriously and was weighed down by it. She'd always admired Brady's willingness to accept responsibility.

But wasn't trying to lift the weight of a room its own kind of responsibility?

"Pack a bag," Gage said, his voice rough. "You've got five minutes before we need to be on the road."

Those harsh words, with no preamble, had Felicity frowning at him. "What are you even talking about?"

"We have to go. Now. Unless you want to spend the night, or a few nights, in jail."

GAGE SHOULDN'T HAVE put it so bluntly, but time was of the essence. He hadn't even had his coffee, which might have accounted for some of the bluntness.

"Go pack your things, Felicity," Rachel said when Felicity stood motionless.

Felicity left the kitchen at Rachel's words, and Rachel turned back to whatever she'd been doing. It looked like making pancakes.

Gage didn't know what to say in the face of a nice domestic morning Felicity should have been able to share and enjoy with her sister. This was really more of a *do* situation, and the fewer people who knew what they were doing, the better.

When Rachel turned back around, she held two travel mugs he was pretty sure were filled with coffee. *Thank God.*

She held out both to him. He stepped toward her

and took them. She angled her head up, looking at him thoughtfully even though he knew she couldn't see him clearly.

The scars that had caused her loss of sight were such a part of the face he knew so well, he only noticed them now because things were bad. It made him think about all those years ago when a freak mountain lion attack had taken Rachel's sight.

Grandma had started teaching them all to shoot the next day—Wyatt brothers and Knight girls side by side, armed with various guns and starting at ten paces away from a row of tin cans balanced on a fence.

When bad things happened, you did what you could to learn how to protect yourself from the next one. That was the lesson of his life. That was why he'd become a police officer. He knew what awful, horrible things could happen—from animal attacks to cold-blooded murder—and he'd wanted to be one of the ones who set things to right.

Sometimes he had. Sometimes he hadn't. Life wasn't perfect, and being a cop didn't mean he could fix everything, even if he wanted to.

But he could fix this for Felicity. First, he had to get her out of harm's way. Then the Wyatts would work to make sure this got cleared up. But he simply couldn't stand the thought of her in a holding cell. Not Felicity.

"You'll take good care of her," Rachel finally said.

It wasn't a question, so he didn't answer it.

Felicity returned with a backpack. She'd changed into jeans and a T-shirt and was wearing her hiking boots, which was a good thing. They'd be doing some considerable hiking. "You'll need a coat. Light one, but a coat nonetheless."

"Where are we going?"

"We'll talk about it in the truck."

She blew out an irritated breath as she walked away and then returned with a windbreaker. "Good?"

He nodded.

Felicity turned to Rachel. "Duke is going to—"

"I'll handle Daddy. You be safe."

They hugged briefly, then Felicity turned to him, grasping the straps of her backpack, a grim determination on her face. "All right. Let's go."

He led her out to his truck. He'd fixed Dev's camper shell onto his truck bed and stuffed it full of a variety of things. Hunting gear, fishing gear, ranch supplies. Hidden under all of that were two backpacks set up for backcountry camping. Brady was under strict orders to pick up the truck at the drop-off point and park it at the local airport. Make it look like he was really taking the vacation he'd lied to the sheriff about.

They reached the truck and got in. Felicity hadn't asked any questions—not that he would have answered them until they were in the truck and on their way.

She hefted her backpack into the back and folded her hands on her lap. She looked straight ahead as he started the engine.

Gage began to drive, knowing he should explain things. Instead, he took a few sips of coffee to clear his morning-fogged brain and waited for Felicity to demand answers.

"Where are you taking me?" she finally asked, which wasn't the question he thought she'd lead with.

"I figure you know some pretty isolated areas in the park we could hike to and camp without anyone finding us."

"If you backcountry camp you have to get a permit," she said primly.

He wished he could be more amused by it, but in the

moment he could only be a little harsh. "Felicity. You don't honestly think I'm going to waste my time with a permit."

"It's about safety and the park's environmental integrity. We have to know how many people—"

"Well, safety and the damn environment are going to have to take a back seat." He spared her a look, hoping it got across how dire this situation was.

"I'm a suspect," she said flatly. "We already knew that was a possibility."

God, he wished that was all it was. He rubbed a hand over the scruff on his jaw. He hadn't had a chance to shave this morning, and it didn't look like he'd be shaving any time soon.

"It's worse than that."

She swallowed. Her words were careful as she spoke, and he knew she was trying to keep her stutter under control. "How so?"

"The investigators searched your cabin."

"I d-don't have anything to hide. What does that matter?"

"They found some things anyway."

"What? How?" Felicity demanded, outrage making her cheeks turn pink. He liked it much better than the stutter, which sounded more like fear than fight.

"Someone is setting you up as a murderer." He shifted his gaze to the road. "Still want to get that permit?"

Chapter Five

Felicity didn't speak for a while after that. She let Gage drive her back to the Badlands, just as he'd driven her home from them yesterday.

Today he took the long, winding backroad to the southern portion of the park. It was far less trafficked and technically on reservation land. There would be no actual way to get into the park the way Gage was driving without doing some serious off-roading.

She looked at the grim line of his mouth and knew that was exactly his plan.

Because someone had planted evidence that she was a murderer.

A *murderer*.

The more that word spun around in her head, the more she didn't understand it. "There has to be some kind of mistake."

"What those cops found? It was no mistake. It had to have been planted, Felicity. And if it was planted, someone is purposefully trying to frame you for murder."

"It also means that poor woman was murdered."

"Felicity."

She hated the pity in his tone. *Poor, silly Felicity.* "It is still possible she just fell. It is still possible…" Yes, she was silly, because there was a part of her hoping for tragic accident over premeditated evil.

"You're the one who told me the boot in the trail was the same as the last time. Surely you knew it wasn't an accident."

"Don't you ever entertain a hope no matter how unreasonable it might be? Don't you ever think, well, *maybe* it's not as awful and dire as it looks?"

"No," he said flatly.

She didn't have to ask him why. In the silence she could hear Ace's name as if Gage had uttered it himself.

Gage had spent his formative years in the Sons of the Badlands against his will. He'd been eleven when Jamison had saved him and Brady from the gang, gotten them to Grandma Pauline. So by the time he had a real home, with an adult who truly loved him and would care for him, Gage had likely already seen too much to believe in hope.

She'd been young enough that memories of her father's beatings were vague. Sometimes she wasn't sure if they were actual memories or nightmares she'd had.

But she'd definitely been in a cast when she'd come to live with the Knights at the age of four. So, it was all true enough.

No matter her past, she could always hope for the best outcome. That's what the Knights and their love and security had given her.

"If it's Ace setting me up, I don't understand why. I don't understand."

"You said it yourself. You interfered. You helped Nina and Cody outwit his plans. That puts a big red *X* on your back, and there was already one there for being a Knight."

"But I'm not a Knight, by name or blood."

"By love you are. Which makes you a friend to the

Wyatts. One who fought for us. That's all it takes to make you Ace's target."

She knew all that rationally. Though she'd assumed Ace had targeted Liza and Nina because they'd had relationships with his sons, Liza and Nina had also defied Ace's plans.

And now she'd joined their ranks.

"As for the how... I don't know how Ace does anything, let alone get hundreds of men to follow his particular brand of narcissism and contradictory insanity for years and years on end. But here we are, and you're unlucky enough to have connections to us. Maybe Ace never paid much mind to the Knights before this, but he's certainly making a case for it now."

Gage brought his truck to a stop in the middle of nowhere. Actual nowhere.

"Why are you stopping?"

"We're going to hike the rest of the way."

"And just leave your car here?"

"It'll be taken care of."

"But what if we need to get out? What if there's bad weather? Did you even pack a weather radio? Enough water? Floods, tornadoes, lightning. Rattlesnakes. You know bison are dangerous, right? And prairie dogs carry the plague."

He gave her a sardonic look and slid out of the truck without responding.

She scurried after him. There were two parts of her brain fighting it out. The one that understood he was doing what he could to keep her out of harm's way, and the part that had taken an oath to treat the park and its denizens with respect and integrity.

"Backcountry camping is serious business," she said

to him in her firmest park ranger voice as he opened the camper shell on the back of the truck.

"I've been camping before," Gage replied, moving things around and barely paying any attention to her.

"Backcountry camping?"

"Yes."

"In the Badlands?"

He hefted out a sigh, stopped what he was doing and turned to her. He folded his arms over his chest, which was a distraction for a moment or two. The cuff of his T-shirt ended right at a bulge of muscle, made more impressive by the crossed-arm pose. Something wild and alarming fluttered low in her stomach.

Which wasn't important when he was talking about hiking without a permit and without taking the appropriate safety precautions.

"Sweetheart, my father left me in the Badlands for seven nights when I was seven years old. I can handle this. So can you." Then he went back to his rummaging, pulling out one backpack and then another. They were bigger backpacks than the one she'd brought—these were clearly designed for backcountry camping.

"Put anything you brought that you'll need in the green one," he said, as if he hadn't just confided something truly awful about his childhood.

Since Felicity didn't know what to say, she did as she was told. She pulled out the things she'd need: a dry set of clothes and a sweatshirt, her knife, hat, water bottle and water treatment supplies.

They were silent as she added her things to the backpack Gage had given her. He shouldered his pack, then helped her with hers, working with her to adjust the straps so it hit her where it should.

"You ready?"

She nodded, though it was a lie. She didn't think she'd ever be ready for being framed for murder. For hiking, illegally and ill prepared, through the Badlands with Gage Wyatt.

But here she was, and she'd have to face up to it. Ready or not.

GAGE THOUGHT HE'D managed to escape the uncomfortable piece of his childhood he hadn't meant to share with her. He didn't talk to anyone about his father's rituals. The initiations, the tests. Not even Brady, because though they'd had to go through them at the same times, what with being born on the same day and all, Ace had always kept them separate.

None of his brothers had ever truly discussed it. They mentioned it and laid out the bare facts when need be. But there was no looking into what it had felt like to jump through Ace's hoops.

Gage had no interest in ever going *there*.

"Why did he do it?" Felicity asked, as though she could read his thoughts.

Gage shrugged. If he never discussed it with people who'd understand, he sure wasn't going to discuss it with Felicity. But as they hiked, using a topography map and GPS tracker and his own internal sense of the land, silence ate away at his resolve to forget he'd ever brought it up.

"He called it our initiation," Gage grumbled, stopping their progress to determine if they should head east or go ahead and climb the column of rock in front of them.

"Initiation to what?"

"To the Sons." *To the Wyatt dynasty.* Gage pointed at the map, his father's voice echoing in his ears. He had to point at the map so he didn't give in to the urge to cover his ears with his hands and block out Ace's insidious voice. "What do you think? Around or over?"

Felicity peered over his shoulder. She'd fixed a baseball hat on her head and pulled her hair through the hole in the back. She'd tied her windbreaker around her waist. Underneath she wore a dark red T-shirt. She'd always been a shade too skinny, but working at the park had packed some muscle on her.

She looked more capable park ranger than inconsequential waif. It was a good look for her, one he had no business noticing at all, let alone here and now.

"Looks like around will be better," she said, reaching over his shoulder and tapping her finger on the paper. "Best place to camp is going to be over in this quadrant."

He took her advice, ignoring the flowery scent of her shampoo or deodorant or something that shouldn't be distracting but was.

They started around the column of rock. The sun was high in the sky, beating down on them. It would have been a good time to stop for water, but it seemed like a better idea to find a good spot to camp.

As far away from this conversation as possible.

"Did you want to be in the Sons?"

"Of course not," Gage snapped at the unexpected question that felt more like a dagger than a curiosity.

"I mean, when you were little. When you didn't know any better."

"I always knew better." You didn't spend most of your childhood watching your father threaten your mother's life—knowing she got pregnant over and over to keep him from going through with it—then watch her lose everything when her body simply couldn't carry another child into this world.

And you couldn't believe it was the right way of the

world when you had an older brother like Jamison, who had spent his first five years with Grandma Pauline, telling you the world could be good and right.

"I'm sorry," Felicity said after a while, her voice almost swallowed by the wind. Unfortunately, not enough for him to miss it. He didn't want her apologies, or this black feeling inside of him that threatened to take his focus off where it needed to be.

He ignored her sorry and these old memories, and focused on one step in front of the other. It wasn't the first time in his life he'd counted his steps, watched his feet slap down on scrub brush. He'd thought those days were over.

But was anything ever really over? Ace could die and there would still be the mark he'd left on hundreds—if not thousands—of people.

And first on that list were six boys with the Wyatt name who had to live with what they'd come from.

"Do you know anything more about… It's just I never knew my mother. When they placed me with the Knights they said she was dead. I don't know how. I thought I didn't want to know. No. I *don't* want to know what happened to her or why. But this connects to my father. This half sister I didn't know I had and who's now dead. Who was her mother? Did my father beat her like he beat me?"

"Jamison's working on it," Gage said, trying to infuse his words with gentleness. What terrible questions to have to ask yourself.

"It should be me. I should go up to my father and ask him those things."

"Well, maybe you can at some point."

"Some point when I'm not going to get arrested, you mean?" she demanded irritably.

"Yeah, that's what I mean."

She sighed heavily next to him. "I don't ever want to talk to him."

Gage gave her a sideways glance. She wasn't just certain, she was *vehement*. Her jaw was set, her gaze was flat and those words were final.

"Then let Jamison do the research on the woman and your father."

She wrinkled her nose, looking at her feet as they walked. "Isn't that cowardly?"

"There's nothing cowardly about your family helping you out, Felicity. Where would Jamison or Cody be if they hadn't let each other help? Where would Cody and Nina be if you hadn't helped them?"

Felicity frowned, but she nodded. "Water," she said, stopping their hike and shrugging off her pack. Gage did the same. They took a few sips from their water bottles and passed a bag of beef jerky back and forth. When they were done, Felicity dutifully sealed the empty bag in a plastic zipper bag and stored it in her pack. Ever the park ranger.

"Ready?"

She nodded, and they started hiking again, in silence for a very long time. When Felicity spoke again, he could tell it was a question she'd been turning over in her mind.

"How do we prove I didn't do it if we're all the way out here?"

Gage didn't know exactly how to respond. He'd promised Felicity the Wyatts wouldn't take over and leave her in the dark, but the nice thing about leaving people in the dark was they couldn't take actions that might undermine what you were doing until it was too late.

Still, a promise was a promise.

"This is just step one."

"Step one?"

"When they come to arrest you, the story will be you went backcountry camping to get your head on straight. By the time they send a team out to find you—if they even do, they might wait—you'll be gone."

"Gone where?"

"That's step two. Let's focus on getting through step one."

"Gone *where*, Gage?"

He sighed. There was no way getting around it. "Back to the scene of the crime."

It was a very strange thing to set up camp with Gage. As a ranger Felicity had done this with all sorts of people—friends, coworkers, strangers.

But never a Wyatt.

Which shouldn't be different or feel weird. The Wyatt brothers were her friends. She'd shared meals and *life* with them.

Trying to convince herself this was all normal came to a screeching halt when they had everything unpacked. "Wait. There's only one tent."

She looked at Gage, a vague panic beginning to beat in the center of her chest. He merely raised an eyebrow, the sunset haloing him in a fiery red that made the panic drum harder.

"Safest if we're in the same tent," he said after a while.

She wasn't sure how to describe the sound that escaped her—something strangled and squeaky all at the same time.

"Problem?"

"No. No. *No.* Of course there's no *problem.*" There was a catastrophic, cataclysmic event happening inside of her, but no *problem.*

"Afraid I'm going to try something?"

She tried a laugh, which came out more like a bird

screech. "I like Brady," she blurted, as if that had anything to do with *anything*.

"I'm very well aware."

"And you like..." She thought of the women she'd seen Gage with. Rare. He never brought girlfriends home.

Still, every once in a while for a birthday or something, the Wyatt boys and Knight girls would get together in town. Go to a bar or something. Gage's dates were always... "You like breasts."

He choked out a laugh. "Yeah. Crazy that way. Hate to break it to you, you have those."

She looked down, even though of course she *knew* she had breasts. Not ever on full display or anything, but yes, she had them. They were there. And why was *she* looking at them while her face turned what had to be as red as the sunset?

Had Gage noticed her breasts? Why did that make her feel anything other than horrified?

"If it bothers you, I can sleep outside."

"It doesn't *bother* me." She was pretty sure she'd have the same ridiculous reaction to sharing a tent with Brady. Sharing a tent was *intimate* and she didn't have an intimate relationship with...

Anyone.

But there was one tent up, and perfectly rational reasons for them both sleeping in it. It would be fine, regardless of the jangling nerves bouncing around inside of her. She'd survived those for almost her whole life, even learned to overcome them for the most part.

She was struggling today because people thought she was a murderer. Someone was trying to make it look like she was a murderer. It was messing with her brain in many different ways, not just one.

"Hungry? I can cook up some dinner," Gage said,

acting as though this was normal and fine and not at all scary and weird.

"I hope you know you can't have a campfire. Backpacking stove only. We can't go breaking every park rule just because we're in trouble."

Gage didn't respond. His mouth quirked, his eyebrow raised, and he pulled a backpacking stove out of his pack.

Brady never did that arched eyebrow thing. Brady's lip never quirked in that sardonic way at her. And his eyes never went quite that shade of brown, as if there was a hidden intensity under all that...

What on earth was *wrong* with her?

She was camping with Gage to avoid being arrested for a murder she darn well didn't commit.

"Park rules are important," she insisted, though he hadn't argued. "People try to get away with all sorts of things that hurt the cultural and ecological integrity of the land and threaten the safety of the park."

"Believe it or not, I'm well versed in what people will try to get away with."

"I suppose you think your laws are more important than mine?"

He cocked his head as he set up the stove and measured out water into a pot. "Why do you assume that?"

"Because..." She trailed off because she didn't have a good answer. Gage had never given any indication he thought his job was more important than hers. Nor had any of the other significant people in her life. Certainly she'd had a few park visitors who liked to sneer at how not important she was to them, but—

"Sit. Eat. Stop...that."

She blinked at him, startled by him interrupting her thoughts. "Stop what?"

"Whatever it is you're doing standing there with your mind whirling so hard I can *hear* it."

"You cannot hear my brain."

"Near enough. If you're going to occupy yourself, might as well focus on the problem at hand, not how much more you'd rather spend a night in a tent with Brady than me."

"That isn't what…" But she couldn't explain in a way that made any sense.

She acquiesced and sat, then took the tin bowl he offered her. She *was* hungry. Tired, too. And though she knew he couldn't *hear* her brain moving, it felt like it was galloping around at rapid pace, and she wasn't sure why.

She'd sleep under the same canvas roof as Gage Wyatt. So what?

So someone wanted to frame her for murder—she had a big group of people willing to help her prove she hadn't actually done it. She had Gage to make sure she didn't spend a night in jail.

They ate in silence, watching the sun go down. It might have been peaceful, but she didn't feel any kind of peace. Just anxiety and something else. Something edgier and sharper than the sheer manic ping-ponging of anxiety.

"He doesn't get you, Felicity," Gage said quietly, staring intently at the bowl in his lap as the last whispers of light faded away. "I'm not saying that to be cruel. I just think you could find a lot better focus for your… It's not going anywhere."

It took her a minute to realize he was talking about Brady, and then another minute before full realization hit.

She couldn't find the words to argue.

"He can't ever…" Gage swore under his breath. "Brady

is too noble to ever see you as anything other than Duke's foster daughter."

It should hurt. She should be outraged and embarrassed and feel horrible. Intellectually, she told herself that. But there was no crushing pain of a heart breaking. No heated moral outrage that he didn't know what he was talking about.

She was under no illusion Brady looked at her and saw the real *her*. She'd never asked herself why she liked him anyway, why she convinced herself he might someday.

It wasn't comfortable that Gage had been the one to point out having a crush on Brady didn't make much sense. Her face was on fire, and she couldn't find a way to defuse her embarrassment.

She didn't think Gage's words were cruel. In fact, she knew he was trying to be kind. Trying to show her it was never happening.

She was in the middle of the stark Badlands with his twin brother of all people telling her things she already knew.

Because she did know. She told herself she didn't. She told herself she was holding out hope for Brady to come around, but she was aware of the truth.

Brady was safe. In more ways than one. Safe because he wasn't edgy or volatile. Because he was exactly what Gage said. Too noble to ever consider one of Duke Knight's daughters in a romantic way.

She didn't want Brady in reality. She liked the idea of him. Liked pining after him. She could tell herself she had normal feelings for a guy and never actually have to deal with it. *Know* she'd never ever have to deal with him reciprocating.

The truth was Brady was never going to break his code of honor and see her as different—and she'd known that.

She'd liked him *because* she'd known that.

"Maybe I don't need him to get me," she managed to say, when what she really meant was, *Maybe I don't want anyone to know me*.

Gage shrugged. "None of my business," he muttered.

Which was more than true. Totally and utterly true.

She couldn't for the life of her understand why he'd brought it up.

GAGE DID NOT sleep well. The tent was small, and it smelled like a woman. He'd never camped with a woman before.

Never will again.

Maybe if you were all wrapped up in the woman it would be nice enough, but with a platonic friend you had some more than *companionable* feelings for it was too crowded, too all-encompassing. Who'd want to be right on top of anyone like this?

He looked at Felicity, who was fast asleep only a few feet away from him.

She was too pale—he could tell that even in the odd cast the faint light made against the blue nylon of the tent. Her freckles were more pronounced than usual, and though she slept deeply and quietly there were shadows under her eyes.

He felt a stab of guilt, a twist of worry that he'd done something rash without fully considering the consequences. He'd put her through too much just so she didn't have to spend a few nights in jail.

Jail. Whether it was a holding cell or the facility Ace was at, she'd look worse in there. She was an outdoorsy person. Better to be hiking through the rigorous Badlands backcountry than locked in a cell, that he knew for sure.

Thunder rolled in the distance, making the tent seem all that more intimate.

Felicity's eyes blinked open, and he knew he should probably look away. Try to pretend he wasn't a creeper staring at her while she slept.

But he didn't.

Worse, she stared right back. For ticking seconds that had his breath backing up in his lungs. Her green eyes were dark and reminded him of Christmas trees, of all damn things.

"It's raining," she said quietly, still holding his gaze.

"So it is."

She pushed herself up into a sitting position. Her red hair tumbled behind her, the rubber band she'd had it fastened back with yesterday falling onto the floor between them. She didn't seem to notice.

Gage couldn't help it. He reached out, picked up the band and held it out to her. She took it with one hand, patting the unruly state of her tangles with the other.

He watched a little too closely as she bundled it back behind her, fastening the band around it again. Then way too closely at the way her shirt pulled over her breasts.

He looked up at the top of the tent and blew out a breath. Rain pattered there and he focused on counting the drops, on considering how heavy the rain was and if they should hike today or stay put. Anything that wasn't this totally pointless, impossible attraction to the woman head over heels in love with his twin brother.

Yeah, it figured he was *that* messed up.

"If we go out today, we'll have to be very careful," Felicity said primly.

He didn't dare look at her, because something about that park-ranger-lecturing voice really did something to him.

He was *seriously* messed up in the head.

"You know, the Badlands are made up of bentonite clay and volcanic ash. Which means, when it rains the rocks become very slip—" She stopped herself, frowning at him. "What are you grinning at?"

He shook his head, trying to wipe the smile off his face. "Nothing."

"You're grinning about *something*."

"You don't want to hear it from me."

"What does *that* mean?" she demanded, hands fisted on her hips, though she was kneeling.

He should keep his mouth shut. Go outside into the storm if he had to, but that would be stupid. Almost as stupid as the words that tumbled out of his mouth. "I just remember when you couldn't string two sentences together—especially around a Wyatt—without turning bright red and running to hide in your room. It's nice you found your passion. Even if it's bentite clay."

"Bentonite."

"Right. Sure." He couldn't help laughing. "You're doing all right, Felicity. That's all I'm saying."

"Why wouldn't I want to hear that from you?"

"Anyone else notice?"

She squared her shoulders as if gearing up for a fight. "I don't need anyone to notice."

"But I did notice, is all I'm saying. And I like it." Which was better than everything he wanted to say, like *and I'd like my hands all over you.*

Their gazes met and held. She opened her mouth as if she was going to say something to that, but no sound emerged.

He should say something. A joke. God, he should tell a joke, but it was as if every coping mechanism he'd built to defuse a tense situation had evaporated simply because he'd spent the night under the same fabric roof as her.

She cleared her throat and looked away. "What's the plan? It isn't safe to stay here with a storm. You do have a weather radio, don't you?"

"I wouldn't think it'd be safe to go hiking through a storm, either," he said, opening his pack and rummaging around until he found the radio. He tossed it to her.

She fiddled with it and he unzipped the door. They had a rain flap, and he could feel the wind blowing in the opposite direction. He could use some fresh air and a glimpse at how heavy the storm was looking.

He heard the static of the weather radio, then the low, monotonous tones of someone going on about warnings and watches.

"Gage."

"What?" He reached for his gun, sure that the gravity and fear in her voice meant there was someone coming, a physical, human threat. But as he turned to her, she was pointing at the sky.

And a very distinct funnel cloud.

Chapter Seven

For precious seconds, every training Felicity had ever received on the subject of what to do in case of bad weather simply fell out of her head. Her mind was blank as she watched the distinct form of a funnel cloud whirl on the horizon.

It was far away now, but it wouldn't stay that way.

Fear and dread skittered up her spine. She knew fear and dread—had been born into it. It was acknowledging the feelings when reality sank in—whether it was the violent look in her father's eye or a funnel cloud, first was fear.

Then, she'd learned to act.

"We need to break down the tent and get to lower ground, but not too low. More rain could come in right after it and we don't want to be caught in any flash flooding," she shouted above the sound of the wind and rain.

"You load up both packs and I'll take care of the tent," Gage said. It felt less like an order and more like two people working together to survive.

Lightning flashed, something sizzled far too close, and thunder boomed immediately after—the hard crack echoing in her ears.

Her hands shook as she shoved the weather radio back into Gage's pack and hurried to roll the sleeping bags into their sacks. He had the tent down in record time, which left her open to the elements. She pulled up the hood of her windbreaker.

Fat drops fell from the sky on their packs and their bodies. Felicity looked at the funnel cloud. It was still there. Closer.

"Rain is a good sign," she said, knowing it was more hope than reality. "It means the funnel itself is still a long way off."

"Is it?" Gage returned, shoving the packed tent into his pack. "None of this feels like too good a sign." He settled a cowboy hat on his head and looked around. "Where to, Ranger?"

She'd looked at the topographic map when they'd camped last night and oriented herself to the area. She'd listened to the weather radio and tried to get an idea of the trajectory of the storm. "Follow me."

Though they hiked in silence, the storm raged around them. Thunder booming, lightning cracking and sizzling too close. She let out a screech against her will when she *saw* lightning strike in front of her.

"Steady," Gage said, his voice low and close to her ear. "All that slippery benzonite."

"Bentonite," she ground out as her heart beat so hard against her chest it felt like a hammer trying to break through her rib cage.

The rain slowed, the noise quieted. The air got still and the sky was tinged an unearthly green. Felicity walked, forcing herself to breathe slowly in and out as she began to shake with fear.

"Don't look back," Gage ordered.

She listened, because she knew what was coming. Especially when the still silence suddenly turned into a slow-building roar.

"We should take cover," Felicity shouted over the thundering wind. Dust swirled around them and she had to close her eyes against the debris flying into her face. "We can't keep walking."

"There isn't any cover."

"Kneel. Put your pack over your head—just like tornado drills in school."

"I—"

There was the sickening sound of a blow and a grunt. Felicity whirled around and out of the corner of her eye saw Gage go down. He stumbled, rolled and hit the ground too hard.

He was swearing when she skidded down next to him, which she'd take as a good sign. Swearing meant breathing and consciousness.

"Don't move," she ordered, still having to yell over the sound of wind and rock.

He swore some more, most of it lost to the roaring tornado around them, while he followed her instructions and didn't move.

He was bleeding from a nasty cut on his temple, but it didn't look deep enough to worry over a severe head injury.

"Can you roll onto your stomach?"

He didn't respond, but he rolled over.

"Loosen your straps," she instructed, already scooting up so she could reach his pack. "I'm going to pull your pack up to cover the back of your head."

Small rocks and dust pelted her, seemingly from all sides, though nothing like what had taken Gage down. He grunted as he got the straps off his arm, and she tugged the pack up to cover the most vulnerable part of his head.

Then she lay down next to him and situated her own

pack over the back of her head and neck. She closed her eyes and focused on her breathing.

It reminded her too much of a time she'd tried to forget. The first four years of her life. They were a blur and she had always been happy to leave them that way. Eyes closed, careful breathing, and terror ripping through her while noise raged around her…

She could remember, clearly, hiding in the back of a utility closet. It had smelled like bleach, and she'd scrambled behind mops and brooms. He'd found her. The creak of the door, the spill of light that didn't quite make it to her.

And still unerringly he'd stepped forward and grabbed her by her shirt and dragged her out of the closet. For a few seconds, she was back there, struggling against her father, against the inevitable.

Then a hand closed over hers. In the here and now and roaring winds. She opened her eyes to look at Gage. Blood was trickling down his face since he was lying on the uninjured side. And he was trying to give her some comfort.

"I've survived worse," he rasped over the sound of the tornado.

"Have you?"

"Human nature is worse than Mother Nature."

Felicity shook her head as much as she could in her prone position. "You don't know enough about Mother Nature then, Gage."

She had no idea if he'd heard her, but she didn't let go of his hand, and he didn't let go of hers. As the world heaved around them, they held on to each other.

She wasn't sure how long they lay there or how much longer after that the roar faded into a light wind and pattering rain. The rumble of thunder was distant.

Eventually she felt the groundwater begin to seep into her pants and knew they had to get up. She gave Gage's hand a squeeze before letting it go, then got to her knees. She looked around.

The Badlands stretched out before them looking no different than it had before the tornado had blown through. In the distance, the sun peeked out from the clouds, its rays shining down in clear lines.

Felicity let out a long breath. They'd survived.

"Hopefully, it stayed out here," she murmured to herself. Out here in the Badlands, nature took its course and few things were irrevocably harmed. Tornadoes and extreme thunderstorms were *part* of the shape and heart of the landscape.

But Pennington County and the reservation were in the path of the tornado. People and things could be irrevocably damaged. People and things she loved, even.

But before she could worry about that, she had to worry about Gage.

She tugged the pack off him. "Can you sit up?"

He didn't answer in words. He rolled to his side and leveraged himself up, wincing and swearing. Then swearing some more when she moved to help him.

"Don't stand yet," she said, pushing him against the rock behind him. "Sit right here so I can clean you up."

"You're beautiful. Both of you."

She startled for a second, then shook her head, realizing he was attempting a joke despite the fact blood still oozed from the cut on his temple. "That's some head injury."

"I see double. But at least I'm not blind, right?"

"Not exactly the joke I'd make right now, Gage."

"That's my job. Make the joke no one else would make. Get a little laugh to diffuse the terror."

She felt both relief he was trying to make light of the situation and a bone-deep worry at how much blood was on his face, how deep the cut was under further inspection, and the fact he hadn't even tried to get to his feet.

She rummaged in her pack and retrieved the first-aid kit. She couldn't waste potable water on washing blood off his face, so she had to hope the antibacterial wipes would be enough. She crouched in front of him with some regret.

"Not to sound like a cliché, but this is going to hurt."

IT DAMN WELL DID. He hissed out a breath as she pressed the antibacterial wipe to the nasty wound on his head.

He didn't know what had hit him, a rock probably. It had been sharp and hard and taken him down in the same way. His neck and back hurt, probably from the fall.

And the fact you aren't getting any younger.

"I'm sorry," she murmured, wiping the blood off his face. The wound throbbed and stung in turns, but Felicity's fingers were on his face and that wasn't so bad.

"A pretty woman is patching me up. I'll survive."

Her worried expression transformed into a frown. "Stop saying that."

"What?"

"Beautiful and pretty. You don't need to suck up to me. I'm going to tend your wound either way."

"Don't you think you're beautiful and pretty?"

She stared at him for a good minute, her mouth hanging slightly open. "I… Oh, just shut up and let me do this."

He smiled, couldn't help it. Irritated Felicity made him feel better.

No matter her annoyance, her hands were gentle as she wiped up as much blood as she could and then applied the bandage. She touched his forehead and his cheekbones as if checking for more damage.

He watched her, woozy enough that he didn't even try to hide that his attention was on her face. On her, fully and wholly.

She finally looked him in the eye, opening her mouth to say something. But it evaporated before any sound came out. For seconds they simply stared at each other, silent and still, stuck in the moment.

He couldn't remember the last time he'd felt this. Middle school maybe. The desperate need to *do* something. Make a move, because it felt almost as if he'd cease to exist if he didn't. A profound fear of coming up short left him frozen in place.

Because he wasn't Brady, and Brady was always the better option. Gage was more of a backup.

Felicity deserved first prize, even if that particular prize didn't have a clue of the woman she'd become.

Felicity straightened, stepped back and wiped her hands on her pants. She looked around. The rain had tapered off, and though clouds mostly covered the sun, it occasionally broke out in soft rays as the clouds moved with the furious wind.

"We need help. We need cell service." She nodded with each sentence as if making her own mental list.

"Good luck on that front."

"We should consolidate to one pack. Your vision is messed up so your balance will be off. I'll carry one pack—water is most important. We're going to be slow moving, but I know where to go. We can hopefully get to cell range before nightfall."

"I can carry my own pack. My vision is fine." He blinked a few times. The doubling came and went, but he could walk just fine.

"No. It isn't smart. We have to be smart."

Gage struggled to his feet, ignoring the wave of dizziness and making sure not to reach out for balance. She was watching him too closely and he needed to prove to her he was fine so she didn't worry. So she didn't try to help.

"One pack," she muttered, crouching in front of the two packs, and pulling things out and shoving other things back into hers. "We'll mark this place on the map and come back for what we leave."

He watched her move—each gesture jerky. Each sentence sounded a little more... *Tight* was the only word he could think of. Like there was some invisible string pulling her in tighter and tighter.

Until she broke. Except Felicity wasn't going to break. He could see that as she babbled on and on about what they had to do. She would keep that rein on control through this whole thing, then be left with a hell of a breaking point when all was said and done.

He knew her well enough to realize she'd see that as a failure, especially if she broke in front of their family or whoever finally picked them up.

He wanted her to break now. She'd still be embarrassed that it was in front of him, but it wouldn't be as bad as Duke or her sisters or the whole Wyatt clan.

"Felicity. Take a breath."

"I'm breathing," she retorted, as he'd predicted. She made a move to sling the newly rearranged pack onto her shoulders, but he grabbed it and pulled it off her.

"Hey, I said I was going to—"

He dropped it on the ground to the side of them and stepped toward her. She scrabbled back, almost tripping in the process.

"What are you doing?" she screeched.

He didn't answer, because the more she worked herself up the better chance she had of actually letting it go.

Gently he folded her into his arms. "We're okay," he murmured. He rubbed a hand up and down her back, cupped the back of her head and held her there against him as she struggled a bit. He understood the manic look in her eyes, understood what she needed to do before they moved on. "We're okay."

"I know it," she squeaked, wriggling against his hold. But her breathing was ragged and it only took a few more seconds of holding her there for her to break. A sob, the slow surrendering of her forehead to his chest.

"That's it," he murmured, resting his cheek against her hair. "Let it out."

She did. As he held her there, hand in her hair, cheek on her hair. Soft and curling against his own skin. He wanted with an ache he didn't fully understand because it was so deep, so wide, so *nonsensical*.

Still, he held her while she cried, and though time wasn't in their favor he didn't rush her. He let her have her moment.

Finally, she pulled away with a sniffle, wiping at her cheeks with her palms. "I'm stronger than that," she muttered.

"Nothing weak about crying. I mean, I know that goes against Grandma Pauline's code of badass conduct, but I've helped too many people in too many dire situations to not know crying is essential sometimes."

"Eva always said so. More to Sarah than the rest of us."

"Sarah tries too hard to be tough," Gage returned, speaking of the youngest Knight foster.

"She comes by it honestly, between being Duke's second hand on the ranch and helping Dev when he needs it."

"Maybe we should lock her and Dev in a room and

tell them we won't let them out till one of them shows an emotion that isn't categorized as pissed-off grumpy."

Felicity chuckled, which had been his hope. She sucked in a breath and let it out loudly. "All right. We've got a long way to hike."

"You're in charge."

She gave him a suspicious look. "Really?"

"You know where you're going and, frankly, you're better with that kind of map than I am. So, lead the way, Ranger. You'll get us where we need to be."

She blew out a breath and nodded. "All right. Follow me and be careful. One injury is enough."

She was right about that.

Chapter Eight

The hike was brutal. The rocks were slippery, and they couldn't find much grass to walk on instead. Added to that, no matter what Gage said, he was clearly not at 100 percent. He was slow and he'd stopped arguing about her being the only one carrying a backpack.

Felicity hated to admit it, but crying it out had certainly calmed her. She felt exhausted but determined. Worried but not panicked. They would get where they needed to go, even if Gage wasn't 100 percent.

Because she was.

She eyed the sun, and how quickly it was heading for the horizon. Maybe they'd have to hike at dark for a bit. Dangerous, but so was surviving a tornado blasting through the Badlands. Which they'd done with only minor injuries.

"How you holding up?" she asked. Though she wanted to look back and get an idea for herself, they were in a particular slippery canyon area. One wrong step would mean a nasty fall. So, she listened carefully to his response and any pain that might be threading through his voice.

"Fine and dandy, gorgeous," he said breezily.

She gripped the straps of her pack, trying to tamp down her irritation. "Stop that."

"But see, now that I know it irritates you I *can't* stop."

She kept her gaze on the landscape in front of her. If he was joking around he couldn't be that bad off. "This isn't a joking situation, Gage."

"Well, it's not a joke. It's me saying something true that irritates you for some reason," he returned so *reasonably*, as if it was reasonable when it wasn't at all. "Anything can be a joking situation if you're funny enough."

She knew there had to be a good response for that, but she couldn't find it. Not even a lecture about jokes.

Both their phones began to chirp, and they stopped in their tracks.

"We should probably keep hiking and get to the ranger station before dark," Felicity said. No matter how badly she wanted to check their phones, they were running out of good hiking time.

"People are worried about us, Felicity," Gage returned.

When she turned around to lecture him, he already had his phone to his ear. She eyed the sun again, then took out her own phone.

She had fifty text messages, ten missed calls and five voice mails. She winced, then began to type out a text to everyone at the ranch that she was okay. Something quick, then they could be on their way again.

But Gage swore, so vehemently that Felicity stopped midtap.

"What is it?"

He shook his head, held up a finger and returned the phone to his ear. "Jamison. You've got to be kidding me with that message," he said viciously into the receiver. He paused, his expression fury personified as he listened to whatever Jamison was saying in return. "Yes, we're fine. What's being *done*?"

He was silent for so long Felicity had to bite her tongue

to keep from demanding answers immediately. He was getting them. She had to be patient.

"Stay put. Take care of your own. We'll handle us." He ended the conversation and shoved his phone into his pocket.

When he didn't immediately speak, she stopped holding back. "Gage. Tell me what is going on."

He shook his head, his jaw working for a few seconds before he finally spoke. "The tornado hit the jail."

Felicity felt as if the ground fell out from underneath her and she was descending through an endless canyon. Though she was standing on her own two feet, the sound of the long-gone tornado roared in her ears. "What?"

"It hit the jail in Pennington. Ace is unaccounted for."

"As in dead or as in…"

"Escaped. He's not the only one." Gage shoved a hand through his unruly dust-covered hair. "But he's the one we have to worry about."

"All right. We have to get back," Felicity said, doing her best to sound calm and sure. "Back to the ranches, work out a game plan with everyone."

"If our theory about Ace being involved in framing you for murder is correct, he's coming for *you*, Felicity."

That revelation hit hard, but she wouldn't let it show. She straightened her shoulders and firmed her mouth. "If he's behind this trumped-up murder charge, hasn't he already hurt me enough? He won't be after me—he already got me. He'll be after one of you."

Gage stared at her for a long time before finally inclining his head. "Fair point."

It felt like a victory when none of this was a victory. It was only problem after increasingly threatening problem.

"Okay, we head back to the ranch," Felicity said. "Someone can pick us up at the ranger station. It's better if we're all there, working together to keep everyone safe from Ace. Especially Brianna and Gigi." Cody and Nina's daughter and Liza's half sister had already been through enough.

"If you show up at either ranch, you'll be arrested."

Felicity tried to play off the wince inside of her. "I... I can handle that. You should be with your family." She tried to smile, though she knew it faltered.

She could handle jail. She could handle it because she knew she was innocent. It was fine. Okay, *fine* was an overstatement. But it would be bearable. She could bear it. She could. Because eventually the truth would come out.

Eventually.

"I'm not letting you go to jail, Felicity. Not ever."

She blinked at his sheer vehemence. Her entire stomach seemed to flip over at the look in his eyes.

She didn't know what that was. Didn't want to know because it scared her. It...vibrated through her. Too big and too much.

"It wouldn't be so bad," she choked out.

"If they convicted you, do you understand how many years you could be stuck in there? Do you have any idea how long it would be before you could come out here?" He pointed to the land around them. "Think about it— you'll come to the same conclusion I did."

She looked around at the Badlands, at the vast gray, moody sky. At her heart, laid out in the world around them, even when it did things like throw a tornado at her. "I wouldn't survive," she murmured.

She didn't need anyone to understand her, to see her as the woman she'd become because *she* knew who and what she'd built herself into. Being a somewhat solitary person meant she didn't need people to constantly validate her choices or tell her she was doing great.

But she hadn't realized how nice it would be to have one person actually…get her. Not in some demanding way, not showing off how much. Just a simple, true understanding.

She didn't know how to fully accept that it was *Gage*, who was nothing like her. He was all confidence, with a certain brashness that *was* charming but certainly nothing she understood.

How could he look at her and see…it all?

She didn't want to know. She didn't want to think about it, but all she could seem to do was stand here and stare at him, something big and bright and terrifying shifting in her chest.

Ace was free, and she was wanted for murder. That was her focus right now.

Or so she told herself.

Felicity looked at him like his understanding was some kind of gift when it couldn't be. When his father was on the loose, with everyone he loved a target.

Including her.

Not that Gage was *in love* with her. Liking and appreciating someone and being attracted to someone did not add up to *love*.

Besides, loving anyone while Ace existed was a pain and fear he didn't intend to take on. He'd watched Jamison and Cody survive, barely, and maybe they were happier on this side of things, but how could that fear of Ace really ever go away?

It couldn't. It didn't. Not until the man was dead. Gage was half convinced he'd never die.

"All right," Felicity said at length. She sounded shaky

at first, then her voice strengthened as she spoke. "Still, you're hurt. You need to go back and have that looked at."

"Hey, I can still see. I can still walk. Cody did a lot more with a lot worse."

"Because he had to," Felicity said with a gentleness that made his skin tight and prickly.

"Are you suggesting I leave you out here on your own?" he asked, trying to keep the sheer volume of rage out of his voice. All that rage wasn't directed at her—it was at Ace, and himself—but he was in danger of losing it anyway.

"It wouldn't be the first time I've hiked, camped and survived the Badlands on my own, Gage."

"It won't be *this* time, either," he returned. "Listen to me. There's no splitting up here. No leaving anyone on their own. That isn't how you beat Ace. Haven't Jamison and Cody proven that? We have to work together best we can. And whether you like it or not, you and me are together for this one."

She didn't respond as she chewed on her lip and mulled it over. He couldn't stand the quiet, so he kept on her.

"Jamison and Cody are going to protect Liza, Gigi, Nina and Brianna in Bonesteel. The rest of my brothers will be at the ranches with Grandma Pauline and your family. It makes sense for us to keep to our plan. We have to prove you didn't murder this woman."

He took a step toward her, told himself at the last minute not to grab her hands like he wanted to. "Just think. If we prove this—we can go home to the ranches. Ace being on the loose makes things nerve-racking. But it doesn't change our objective. It doesn't change what *we* have to do."

"I don't want to be the reason you're not working with your brothers on this."

He didn't understand the things she did to him. He'd avoided personal vulnerability all his life because, good Lord, life was too tough to be worried about weakness. She was tough, but she was also…this: the broken little kid underneath all that tough exterior.

He understood it too well.

"We're in this together, Felicity. Now, how long will it take us to hike to your cabin?"

"Days."

He knew it was long, but he'd been hoping doable. They couldn't hike days. Especially after leaving one pack behind.

"Another park ranger would give us a ride if we get to the visitor center," she said, though she sounded uncertain.

"Are there any park rangers you trust? That you're willing to put in the path of both the police *and* Ace?"

She wilted. "No."

He didn't want one of his brothers making the trek, which had been the original plan. With Ace on the loose, they needed to stick together, protect Grandma and the Knights. Having one or even two come pick them up was risking too much.

"What about Cody's group?" Felicity asked. "Nina said there was some woman who helped them, and Brady mentioned a doctor who video chatted him through patching Cody up. Call Cody and see if they can help. Even if they can just offer a ride if we can meet them a little south of the visitor center."

"If they can't, he'll come himself."

"Not if you remind him his job is to protect Nina and Brianna."

It wasn't the worst idea. Besides, what would it hurt to ask?

"We have to keep hiking, though," Felicity insisted. "The minute we lose daylight, we're in for trouble. I had to prioritize water over sleeping bags and dry clothes in the pack. We can eat and we can drink, but we won't have any way to protect ourselves if another storm comes through."

He studied the sky. Another storm seemed more likely than not. Hopefully, they'd survived their one and only tornado, but rain and lightning could be just as dangerous in the wrong circumstances.

"All right," he finally acquiesced. Her plan was sound, and it was a compromise between what they both wanted to do. "I'll text Cody, then we'll get moving."

"You text him. I'm going to change your bandage." She dropped her pack and rummaged around in it while he texted Cody to ask for backup south of the visitor center.

She pulled off the bandage slowly, clearly trying to keep the adhesive from hurting his skin.

It was hard to focus on the throbbing pain when her chest was in his face and he had much more entertaining things to distract himself with.

"I'm worried about infection more than the cut itself," she said conversationally as she used another stinging wipe around the wound.

He bit his tongue to keep from hissing or groaning in pain, then let out a slow, steady breath as she smoothed a new bandage over the cut.

"There." She cupped his chin and tilted his head up as she examined the bandage. She gave a little nod, clearly satisfied with her work. She brushed at his scruffy jaw, presumably trying to get dirt and debris out of his whiskers, but her other hand gently traced the bandage.

He was sure she was making sure no dirt had gotten into the bandage, but it felt like a caress. Like she cared.

And his libido certainly didn't seem to know the difference between *trying to stave off infection* and *trying to get in his pants.*

Irritated, he squirmed. "If you expect me to be able to walk straight, you're going to have to stop touching me like that."

She pulled her hand away so fast her whole body jerked and she stepped back, landing awkwardly on a rock. She started to fall backward, arms windmilling, so he grabbed her and yanked her toward him.

Which sent her bumping into him, sending *him* falling backward. Luckily, he knew how to land after a blow well enough. Unluckily, she was now sprawled on top of him.

She was on top of him, breathing a little heavily, her eyes wide and her cheeks pink. He thought not kissing her might kill him.

But she wants Brady.

"I'm going to get you out of this mess." He didn't know why he had to promise her that, to vow it here and out loud. He just had to get it out. Better than kissing her, he had to believe.

She stared at him, green eyes dark and steady, still lying on top of him, soft and warm and wonderful. "I believe you," she said quietly.

And he was doomed. So he went ahead and pressed his lips to hers anyway.

Chapter Nine

Felicity had never walked through fire before, but she was pretty sure it would feel like this. Completely enveloped by sensation.

In this case not burning to a crisp, painful and fatal, but melting into someone else entirely. Maybe it *was* fatal—she wasn't sure—but she couldn't help following it. The wild sensation of freedom like standing in the middle of grass and rock with no one else around. Just her and the wind and sky and utter glory.

Except it was Gage. *Gage.* Gage Wyatt. Kissing her. Kissing *her.*

She blinked her eyes open, trying to push herself off him. He stopped kissing her, but his hand curled around her arm, keeping her in place.

"We have to… Getting dark," she croaked.

He did his raised-eyebrow thing, and all she wanted to do was run away from him, but his big hand was still curled around her upper arm, keeping her all sprawled out against him. He was very…hard and warm and… She had to get up.

"Hike. Before dark. We need to get moving."

"You kissed me back."

"I…" She didn't know what to say to that. How to process *any* part of today. "L-let me go."

He did. Immediately. She scrabbled off him and onto her feet. She was shaky and shaken, and God knew she didn't have a clue what to say.

Gage had kissed her. Voluntarily. And…seriously. Devastatingly. Like he'd been waiting half a lifetime to do it.

Oh, boy. Oh, no.

If she went home she would be arrested for a murder she didn't commit, and Gage Wyatt had kissed her.

She *knew* she hadn't killed anyone, and as much as the world wasn't always right and good, she simply had to believe someone could prove that.

What she didn't know was how to deal with this…kiss.

She'd let Asher Kinfield kiss her when she'd worked at Mammoth Cave for a summer. It had been nothing like this. It had been kind of stiff and fumbling. Off-putting.

Not like fireworks. No, bigger than fireworks. A volcanic eruption. Destructive and totally altering.

All because of Gage Wyatt.

She looked back at him as he got to his feet. She'd jerked away not so much because of his words. More because she'd lost herself in touching him and had forgotten she was supposed to be bandaging him up, not caressing his wounds. She *had* been touching him like a lover, and she didn't know what on earth had possessed her.

Gage stared at her, his face hard and unreadable. "I'm not Brady," he said sharply.

That snapped through some of her panic. She scowled at him, insulted and maybe even hurt. She couldn't name half the feelings pulsing inside of her. "I was under no illusion you were, *Gage*."

"You sure about that?"

"Yes." She grabbed the pack and fastened it onto her back with jerky movements. She was not going to argue with him about Brady. She hadn't even *thought* of Brady until Gage had brought him up. "W-we have to m-move."

She didn't wait to see if he followed, and she refused to acknowledge her stutter. She started marching along, carefully avoiding slick spots. She was entering more familiar territory as they neared the ranger station.

She kept them away from the main road even as they approached the station. She was tired, parched and starving, but she didn't want to stop. Darkness was approaching and there was no time to stop.

So she told herself. Better than thinking about what she might have to face if they stopped.

Felicity came up short as she saw a figure in the distance. At first she thought it might be another ranger doing rounds, but the figure was wearing a baseball cap, not a park uniform.

"Just keep hiking. Act casual. Normal," Gage instructed. "It might be our ride. It might not be. If she approaches us, just act like you would with any other hiker."

Felicity swallowed at the nerves fluttering in her throat, but she nodded and kept hiking again. No matter where Felicity and Gage walked, the figure moved so their paths would cross.

When Felicity saw that she was a woman dressed all in black, with no signs of backpacking gear, she prayed to God it was someone from the secret group Cody had worked for last year.

Because if not, it was bad news indeed.

"Howdy," the woman greeted as they finally met on solid ground covered in grass. "Nice evening for a hike, isn't it?"

"Getting a little late," Felicity offered, working hard to keep her voice steady and without stutter.

"It is." The woman tipped her unnecessary sunglasses

down. "You guys need a ride?" She jerked her chin in the direction of the road. "You're looking a little worse for wear, and I've got a truck not far off."

Felicity exchanged a glance with Gage.

"Sure, Shay," Gage said.

The woman smiled and winked. "Follow me, Wyatt."

Felicity blew out a breath. It was their ride, thank God. They still had a good mile walk, and exhaustion pounded at her temples. She had no idea what Gage had in mind once they got to her cabin. They'd been through a tornado, and miles and miles of hiking. All she wanted to do was sleep.

Shay led them to a big black truck with tinted windows Felicity doubted were legal. She climbed into the back of the truck anyway, Gage getting into the front seat. Gage and Shay spoke in low tones and Felicity tried to pay attention, but she couldn't stop herself from dozing as the truck began to drive.

She awoke with a start when she realized the vehicle had stopped. Shay and Gage were outside, heads together as they spoke. Felicity looked around. They were in the grove of trees not far from her cabin.

When she pushed the door open and stepped out, Gage and Shay immediately stopped talking.

Felicity frowned at them.

Gage leaned close to Shay and whispered something.

Shay nodded. "Thanks. Good luck." She smiled at Felicity as she walked back to the truck. "Especially for you."

Felicity didn't know what to say to that, but Shay was gone in a flash anyway. "What was that?" she demanded of Gage.

He shrugged, studying the trees. "Don't worry about it."

"Don't worry about... Are you... You can't..."

"Calm it down, Red."

"I'd like to punch you."

"I'd like to see you try," he returned mildly.

She was tempted. She'd convinced Tucker to teach her how to land a decent blow before she'd gone off on her first seasonal park ranger job in Kentucky. But something told her even if she threw a decent jab-cross combo, Gage would never let them land.

"Come on. Let's get to the cabin."

It was dark now, the air cool. Everything felt wrong and eerie, and she had a flash of the woman's body at the bottom of the canyon.

The woman who was apparently her sister.

She shuddered as they walked as silently as possible. The tornado clearly hadn't been through this way, though a few downed branches suggested some heavy storms. She hoped her cabin hadn't sustained any damage.

When they reached the edge of the trees and she could detect the outline of her cabin in the moonlight, she felt her stomach sink in despair. Not because of damage, though. "There's police tape," she whispered.

"Lucky for you, I'm the police."

"Gage."

He was already striding forward. He went to the back door and began untying one side of the Do Not Cross tape. Felicity stood in the clearing of her cabin and stared, openmouthed. "You can't—"

He cut off her directive. "Come on now. We've left following the rules behind. Keep up, Felicity." He motioned her forward.

SHE STOOD AS if she wasn't going to listen to him. But Gage knew there was no other way right now. Maybe they wouldn't find any leads in her cabin, but it would give them a place to sleep for the night—a place no one would dream of looking for them.

Finally Felicity moved forward.

"Got your keys?"

She didn't answer, just frowned deeper and pulled keys out of her pocket. She unlocked the door and gingerly stepped inside. Gage tied the police tape back to the banister and walked in behind her.

She stood, miserably surveying her tiny kitchen. "They moved things," she said. "Went through my home and…" She shook her head.

He gave her shoulder a squeeze, though it made her jump. Still, he couldn't stand to see that look of utter defeat on her face. She'd gotten through the past forty-eight hours on grit and determination and strength. He knew how hard it was to hold on to that when things seemed bleak.

But she needed to.

"Don't get sad. Get mad, Felicity. Someone came through here and planted evidence against you. The cops are doing their job, and it sucks that's their job, but let's focus on who's trying to make you into a murderer."

She didn't say anything for the longest time. When she finally did, she did it moving toward the fridge. "I'm hungry." She opened it, studied the contents and shook her head. She slammed the door, wrenched open the freezer, then brought out a tub of ice cream.

She grabbed a spoon, settled herself down at the tiny table in the corner and went to work.

"We might want something a little bit more nourishing."

The look she gave him could have melted that ice cream in front of her.

"I do, anyway."

"Help yourself," she said through a mouthful of ice cream, gesturing at the small refrigerator and pantry.

Gage poked around, found some mixed nuts and a beer, and helped himself. Not exactly nourishing, but maybe she was right that comfort food was the way to go tonight. He settled into the chair across from her, wondered if she ever had any cabin guests that necessitated another chair and kept his opinions on that to himself.

He lifted the beer. "You sit around drinking a lot of beer by yourself?"

"Slugs," she replied. "Kills 'em."

He chuckled. He had no earthly understanding of why he found that endearing or why he could so easily picture her putting out little trays of beer for slugs just as Grandma Pauline always had.

"I'm giving myself five minutes to wallow," she said, scooping up another large glob of ice cream. "I survived a tornado. I'm wanted for murder. A murder I didn't commit. You…" She trailed off before she finished that sentence. "I get five minutes to wallow." She shoved the entire bite of ice cream in her mouth.

"Then what?"

She swallowed and looked down at the container. "I don't know."

"I tell you what. Let's extend the wallow. Ten minutes with the ice cream, then about—" he checked the clock on his phone "—five hours of sleep in a bed."

"Then what?" she asked, echoing his own question back to him.

"In the morning, we check in with my brothers and see if they've made any progress or have any idea where Ace is. We'll go through your cabin and see if we can find anything off or missing. Then… I want to go look at where you found the body."

She shoved away from the table, abruptly sticking the lid on the ice cream and putting it back in the freezer.

"Felici—"

She whirled to face him. "Tell me one of your stories."

"Huh?"

"Those crazy stories you pull out whenever everyone's down and you want to get a laugh." She pointed to herself. "I'm depressed." Then to him. "Now, cheer me up. Make me laugh."

"I can't do it on command."

"Why not?"

"Well, for starters, it's not what you need right now."

"Oh, really. What do I need?"

He stood. He could do without the beer and they'd have a chance to eat in the morning, so he left both on the table. He walked over to her and, as gratifying as it was that her eyes got wide and dropped to his mouth, he didn't do what she was clearly expecting him to.

He simply wrapped his arms around her and gave her a squeeze. "We need sleep," he said. Much as he wanted to hold her a little closer, stroke a lot more than her hair, it wasn't the time.

He pulled back from the friendly hug and she blinked up at him. "I guess you're right," she said at length. "I have extra sheets for the couch."

He snorted out a laugh, which he tried to bite back when she glared at him. "Bad news. We've still got to be careful. We'll want to be out of here before sunrise, and we need to be close. No separate rooms, Felicity."

"Just what are you suggesting?"

"I'm not *suggesting* anything. We're going to have to sleep in the same place. Whether it's your couch or your bed, you've got a sleeping buddy tonight. So, pick your poison. My guess is your bed has more room."

"You're not going to sleep in *my* bed. With *me*," she returned, all shrieking outrage.

Gage didn't figure arguing with her was going to get him anywhere, so he shrugged and headed for the door he was pretty sure led to her bedroom. She scurried after him, blustering without forming any actual words.

He opened the door, walked over to the bed, toed off his boots, gave her a look that said *try and stop me* and settled himself onto one side.

She stood there and stared at him, mouth open, little sounds of outrage escaping.

God, he was too tired for her outrage. "You can tie me up if it'd make you more comfortable. Might give me some ideas, but if it'd make you feel better, be my guest."

She scowled at him. "I'm not *afraid* of you."

She certainly seemed it. Well, maybe *afraid* was harsh. She was nervous. Jumpy and high-strung—keeping as much space between her and him sprawled out on the bed as possible.

"Want to talk about earlier first?" He couldn't say he particularly *wanted* to talk about that kiss, but it was muddling his mind when he needed to be lucid and think about how on earth they were going to clear her.

"No!" she squeaked.

The squeak amused him even if it shouldn't. "Suit yourself."

"Fine. *I'll* sleep on the couch."

"No, you won't, Felicity. You're in here with me, if I have to tie *you* up." He might have ended it on a joke, but he was deadly serious and she seemed to understand that.

After huffing and crossing her arms over her chest, then throwing them up in the air a second later, she finally stalked to the bed. She wrenched off her boots, muttering the whole time, then lowered herself onto the bed.

In Gage's estimation, the full-size mattress was hardly adequate for one person let alone two.

No matter, she was putting as much space between them as if they were on a king-size.

It was dark in here, but it smelled like her. And if she thought *she* was ticked off about the sleeping arrangements, she had *no* idea what was going through his head.

He was almost asleep when she finally spoke.

"You kissed me," she said, as if it was some grave accusation.

"That I did." And he didn't regret it in the slightest, even if she hated him for it. She'd kissed him back.

Him. Not Brady. There might be a little sibling jealousy there, but when he'd said he wasn't Brady earlier she'd looked so shocked he had to believe she hadn't been thinking about Brady when she'd kissed him back.

"Why did you do it?" she asked, her voice soft, and he would have said *timid* if he didn't know how damn strong she was.

"Because I wanted to."

"That's hardly an answer."

"Why?"

"Because you don't just suddenly want to kiss someone after never wanting to kiss them."

"Who said I never wanted to?"

She was quiet at that, so he rolled onto his side with an exaggerated yawn. "Night, Felicity."

She didn't respond, and he fell off into a deep sleep.

HE AWOKE TO something vibrating against him and realized it was his phone.

He swore internally when he saw it was four in the morning, but it was a text from Jamison: Call ASAP.

He slid out of the bed, tempted to spend a little too

much time staring at Felicity in the glow from his phone. She was still dead asleep, face relaxed, hair a mess around her head.

Prettiest damn thing he'd ever seen, and he did not have time to dwell on this too-soft feeling going on inside of him.

He moved into the living room and called Jamison. "What do you have?"

Jamison didn't waste time or words. "Prints came back last night—one of Tuck's friends sent him an email. Tuck just got off another case and called me." Jamison was in full cop mode, and Gage didn't interrupt. "They found Felicity's biological father's prints on the evidence they sent for DNA testing. They'd also found his prints in her cabin. Tucker's going to go talk to the detectives this morning, explain that Felicity hasn't had a thing to do with her father so this is unusual. With the tornado damage, Felicity isn't high on their list of priorities—which is good and bad. Good, you guys should be able to remain undetected. Bad, they're not going to worry about dropping the warrant yet."

"Her father had something to do with it?"

"It's looking that way to me. Added to that? He's disappeared since the tornado, and I doubt he's a casualty."

"Why do you doubt that?"

"We've done some digging. The real reason I called you. There's something bigger at play."

"Something bigger than someone framing Felicity for murder?"

"Bigger or more connected anyway. Gage, Michael Harrison visited Ace in jail. Before the murder."

"How? We've been tracking that."

"He signed in to speak to another prisoner, but after

looking deeper into it, there was a switch and he managed to talk to Ace thanks to a paid-off guard."

Gage let that sink in. Felicity's biological father had
visited Ace in jail. His father and hers were connected.
And he had no doubt his father was behind it all.

Chapter Ten

Felicity had never been a particularly good sleeper. Night terrors had plagued her as a kid, and while she'd grown out of those for the most part, vivid dreams still afflicted her often. Not always bad ones, just clear and real-feeling.

She opened her eyes, her body hot and heart racing, more than a little embarrassed at just *what* her vivid imagination had been up to. Steeling herself, she turned her head, but Gage wasn't there.

She told herself she was relieved, even blew out a breath as if to convince herself she was. But some echo of the dream was still thrumming inside of her and at the center of that thrumming she was most definitely not relieved.

Then from somewhere outside the room she heard Gage swear, quietly but in an uncharacteristically serious tone she knew meant bad news.

There was no rest from the true, important, pressing issues in their lives. But the words that rattled around in her head as she slid out of bed weren't anything to do with being accused of murder or Ace being on the loose.

It was Gage's voice, grave and completely unflinching, saying *because I wanted to* over and over again.

She didn't have to work to silence that voice when she stepped out to the living room, though. Gage turned to face her. The pure gentleness in his look might have totally undone her if it didn't scare her to the bone.

"What is it?"

"Why don't you have a seat?"

"What is it?" she returned, trying to do his one-eyebrow quirk.

He didn't say anything. She wasn't sure he even breathed, which made it very hard for her to.

"Jamison and Tucker have been busy," he said, with a hesitance in his voice that felt very un-Gage-like and even more disconcerting. "Looking into things and… there are things."

"Be specific, Gage."

"They found your father's prints in the cabin and on the evidence."

Felicity wished she'd taken that seat he'd wanted her to. "I don't understand."

"No one does, just yet. But I assume you haven't been entertaining your father here?"

"Here? Entertaining? I haven't had any contact with my father since Child Protection Services took me away." She crossed her arms over herself, trying to keep all the awful parts of that sentence tightly under her control instead of at the will of her emotion.

"That's what I thought. Well, he was here. Your father was *in* your cabin at some point."

"That's… If he was here, he planted the evidence." Which meant he could be the killer. Why would he kill his own child? He'd beaten Felicity herself when she'd been helpless and small, and still she had a hard time wrapping her mind around the possibility he'd gone so far as to end his own child's life. "He planted the evidence?"

"That's the angle Tucker is going to press upon the detectives, and at least that there's no good reason his prints should be here. But with the tornado, everyone's busy. This case has fallen in priority."

"My father was here?" Why would he... After all this time, why would he be causing her trouble now? And such awful, horrible trouble. She wrapped her arms around herself, trying to find some center of fight or determination when all she felt was unaccountably sad.

That's when she realized Gage remained very still, watching her with a dark hazel gaze that looked pained. "There's more." She didn't even have to put it as a question. She knew. There was more.

Exhaustion threatened despite the sleep. This was life exhaustion. This was how many blows could one person take and keep going.

The answer was always *as many as life hands you*, but that answer sincerely sucked right now.

"Jamison found out..." He cleared his throat. "Michael Harrison went to visit Ace before you found the body."

Felicity had never fainted in her life, but the room spun and faded to black and her knees went to jelly. Before she could collapse, Gage was at her side, his strong arm around her waist leading her to the couch.

Her father and Ace? It made a horrible, terrifying kind of sense. This wasn't isolated. It wasn't just her father or just Ace. It was them together. Why were Ace and her father acting together?

Gage crouched in front of her, but she didn't know what to say to him. All she really wanted to do was press her forehead into her knees and cry.

She'd cried enough. She'd wallowed enough.

But how did she keep going forward knowing that it wasn't just Ace against her, it was her own father. That the life of a woman—a sister she'd never known—was over because of her in some warped, weird way.

"You can't start blaming yourself," Gage said sharply, as if he could read her thoughts.

"You don't know what it's like to have a father who…" She trailed off and mentally kicked herself.

"Don't know what it's like to have an evil murderer for a father?" He made a considering noise. "It just so happens I know a thing or two about that."

"I don't. I never thought my father was *that* bad." There'd only been four years. Years she didn't fully remember.

"He beat you," Gage said flatly.

"I know, but…" She didn't know how the next words came out, when this was Gage, not her therapist and not her sister. But Gage. And still, the words tumbled into the silence. "Sometimes you have to… I had to tell myself it was just a bad temper. I had to tell myself it was just bad luck, extraordinary circumstances that made him snap. I couldn't make him the bad guy because what did that make me?" She realized, again, that was the worst thing to say when she looked up at him and there was a kind of desolation on his face.

Because he knew. He understood. All those feelings she'd never been able to fully articulate in the therapy Eva had made her go to when she'd first been with the Knights, when she'd talked with Nina or Liza about their less-than-stellar childhoods. She didn't even have to articulate it for it to make sense to Gage.

Suddenly she had to know, to fully understand, the breadth and width of Ace Wyatt. "Did Ace hit all of you?"

"Yeah."

"And worse?"

"I don't know how to quantify worse, Felicity." He raked a hand through his hair, a rare sign of discomfort and frustration. "It was only eleven years."

"He abandoned you in the elements when you were seven as some kind of initiation."

"Yeah. But see, I only had five years of that. Jamison? He did thirteen. Each year it went up one."

"Went up one?" She could tell he didn't want to say more, that he'd already said more than he wanted to, but she needed understanding. For both of them. "Please, Gage."

"You stayed on your own one night for every year of life. It wasn't so bad. It was a week plus without Ace. Without those people. Maybe it was hard to find food and water. Maybe..." He shook his head, as if to shake it all away. "It was awful. But it was all awful. Beatings, whippings, initiations. Trying to pit us against each other. He's a terrifying man. A sociopath with a deep understanding of people—how to manipulate them, inspire them, twist them."

She didn't know how she understood him. What he spoke of was longer, truly more awful than her four sketchy years under her father's care. But she understood that he worried what all that twisting had done to him, no matter how hard he'd tried to fight it. She reached out and touched his cheek on the side of his face that wasn't bandaged. "He didn't twist his sons."

The look of anguish on his face, as if he wasn't so sure, just about broke her heart. "You're good men," she insisted. "Regardless of what our fathers are—evil sociopaths and murderers or what all—it doesn't matter. We're good." She took his large, rough hands and squeezed as hard as she could. "I know we are."

He looked at their joined hands, then up at her. He had a heartbreaking look in his eyes, as if he was the personal cause for everything bad that had ever happened.

"I hate that you're on his radar, because this will hurt. Even when we win, this will hurt."

She couldn't help feeling some bubble of hope, the curve of a smile. "*When* we win?"

"We're not going to lose, Felicity. I won't let it happen. Whatever it takes."

She had no cause to doubt him, because they'd gotten through this far. But she understood in that vehement promise, that Gage cared. Not just about himself. Not just about winning against Ace. But about her. Period.

She leaned forward and pressed her mouth to his. It was nothing like the kiss in the Badlands. She was too shy for that. Didn't know how to lead and run with all that wild heat. But she kissed him anyway, with what little skill she had. And he let her—he didn't lead her anywhere else, just kissed her back as gently and carefully as she'd kissed him.

When she pulled back, he didn't say anything. He stared, and nerves crept in to dismantle all that surety about him caring, about him wanting to kiss her for a lot longer than she'd ever thought of kissing him. "You said you wanted to kiss me."

"Yeah." He reached out, rubbed a strand of her hair between his thumb and forefinger. His mouth was curved, not in a full-blown smile, because even here there wasn't anything to smile about. But it was softer than *whatever it takes*. He looked from her hair to her eyes. "I like kissing you," he said so seriously, so simply, she couldn't do anything other than believe it was the truth.

"I think I like it, too." More than anything as simple as *like*. And it centered her, reminded her that outside all of this terrifying situation, she had a real life. Was a woman. Maybe even a woman who ended up kissing

Gage Wyatt as much as she pleased. But she had to fight for that possibility first.

She was ready. She had to find a way to be ready. "All right. What's the plan now?"

GAGE SUPPOSED STAYING here and taking her to bed wasn't much of a plan when their murderous fathers were on the loose, Felicity their target.

But it was tempting.

Sadly, time wasn't on their side.

"First things first. It's nearing dawn and we've got to clear out in case any detectives stop by. I want to take a look at where the woman's body was. See if we can find any clues of our own."

Felicity winced, but she nodded.

"You don't have to—"

"I'll go with. Two people searching for clues is better than one. I guess it's just that she was my sister. I can't fully grasp it. When I try to think about it, when I try not to think about it. I don't know how to feel."

"You didn't know she existed, Felicity. I'd give yourself a break on that, and if you don't want to relive it, you don't have to."

She shook her head, her hands still in his. It was a nice weight, a sign of partnership, of some level of caring about each other.

It wasn't the time or place to delve into how much, but there was a nice certainty to being in this together.

"We shouldn't be apart. Not with Ace on the loose. Don't you think it's dangerous with him out there?"

He hated that she was right. "He wouldn't necessarily know we're here—I don't know how he could—but you're right. We should stick together. Keep an eye on each other until we know more." Letting her out of his sight wasn't an option.

"So, it's a promise. We stick together, no matter what?"

He nodded. "It's a promise."

She squeezed his hands and then released them. Her face was all determination now—the sadness and fear buried. She stood and slapped her palms on her thighs as if to say *let's go.* "I'll grab my own pack from here. You can carry the one I had. We really should arrange for someone to pick up what we left behind after the tornado."

He didn't know why her stubborn insistence on park protocol warmed his heart like it was damn Christmas or something, but it did.

"Is there an anonymous way to let a ranger know? Hey, maybe it'd even get Ace thinking we're dead. We could have been blown away in the tornado, shattered who knows where, and all that's left is the backpack we dropped."

"What an awful thought." She shuddered. "I guess it'll be okay another few days. Go get the other pack. Grab what might work in my pantry. Load up on water. Water is most important. I'll pack mine with camping gear and bandages and disinfectant so we can keep your wound clean. That should see us through another few days if we have to."

"You didn't ask me what's next after we check out the murder site," he said, slowly standing.

She looked up at him, eyes so green and serious. "We'll go to Sons territory, of course. Ace likely went there. If my father is working for him, or they're working together—they're probably there right now. Maybe not. I don't know them, don't understand them, but we go where their power is. Regardless of whether they're with the Sons or not, someone in the Sons knows something. That's where we have to go."

"That doesn't scare you?"

"It terrifies me. But so does prison. I want to act. I don't want my fight left up to someone else. What other options are there?"

The only one he could think of involved locking her up far away, and he knew she'd never go for that. "We could just hide until Jamison and Cody figure it out."

She actually rolled her eyes as if this wasn't life and death they were talking about. "As if you could stay sane waiting for your brothers to handle everything for you. For *me*, actually. This is my mess. I'm glad you're here with me. I couldn't do it on my own, but it is my mess."

"A mess you're in because Cody called you for help."

"My father—"

"Are we really going to stand here and argue who's more to blame for a mess created by our fathers?"

"Fair point. All right. Pack up."

They went in opposite directions—her to her room, him to the kitchen. He focused on the practicalities, food and water, and trusted her to take care of shelter.

If he entertained himself by thinking of sharing a tent again, well, a man deserved some distraction from all the garbage heaped on him.

She returned to the kitchen, a pack already strapped to her body. She was wearing new khaki pants and a tan sweatshirt that would often blend right in with the landscape they'd be hiking.

She held out a similarly colored lump of clothing. "It won't help with your jeans, but it's an extra large. You don't have to wear it just yet, but it's a good idea to have. Tie it around your waist."

"Men do not *tie* sweatshirts around their waists."

She raised an eyebrow at him. He was not amused at her mimicking him. When he didn't take the sweatshirt at first, she shoved it at him.

"Take a hit on your manliness, Gage. For the sake of—oh, I don't know—surviving, maybe."

He scowled as he took the sweatshirt and tied it around his waist. "Happy?"

"Downright celebratory. Woo-hoo, time to inspect a murder scene!"

Her sarcasm cheered him even if it was at his expense. "Ready to head out?"

She nodded, and though he could see the nerves in her eyes, her hands were steady. Her expression was determined in spite of the fear.

"Oh, one thing first," she said, her expression grave as she walked toward him. She stopped in front of him, looking up at him as if he was supposed to have an idea what that one thing was.

Then she put her hands on his shoulders, rose to her toes and pressed a kiss to his mouth. It was soft, a little timid like the one in the living room, but sweet. And sweet was just as potent as anything else when it came to her.

She lowered back to flat-footed. Her cheeks were edging toward red, but her smile was satisfied even if she was embarrassed, too.

If he didn't die from Ace, he might from this.

He wanted to tell her…everything. How watching her change and find her strength had shifted something inside of him. Had set a spark to this feeling he didn't quite understand. Something bigger than himself and the fear of being Ace Wyatt's son.

He didn't have the words for any of that. So, he grinned at her and then made a move for the back door.

He stepped out, his mind still fuzzy with *feelings* he didn't know how to verbalize.

He heard a shuffle, but before he could react, the cold press of steel was at his temple and his father's amused voice in his ear.

"Well, hello, son. Funny running into you here."

Chapter Eleven

Felicity tried to scramble back and run in the opposite direction, but Ace was too quick. His arm snaked in and grabbed her by the shirtfront.

"Not so fast." Ace laughed and the sound made her stomach turn in utter terror.

She wanted to fight him, but the gun pressed to Gage's temple kept her frozen in fear. Even if he didn't want to kill his own son, any struggling from her could have him pulling the trigger—purposefully or accidentally.

Then there was her own father standing in the yard, a much larger gun than Ace's slung over his arm. She hadn't seen him in years, didn't recognize him on a visual level, but she knew it was him.

Ace gave her shirt a jerk, sending her pitching forward. The weight of the backpack added to her inelegant loss of balance, and she landed hard on the ground. She struggled to get up. Maybe she could run for help? But that would leave Gage here. Alone with them.

Her father moved close and stood over her. He didn't press the gun to her temple like Ace had his to Gage, but he pointed it at her all the same.

"Can you believe it, son?" Ace was saying to Gage, grinning from ear to ear even with a gun pressed to his own son's temple. "A tornado busted me out of jail. A *tornado.* Can you understand the absolute significance of that divine intervention?"

"I'm sure you'll enlighten me whether I want you to or not."

"When my parents left me to die, it was the land that protected me, built me. Now it's the land, the fearsome power of this land, that's given me my freedom back after my sons were too weak, too soft to do what they were meant to do."

Felicity shuddered at the words, at how reasonable they sounded to her. She understood what it felt like to be made new by the awe-inspiring landscape around them. The preacher-like way he spoke those words had her listening, rapt. Understanding.

She had something in common with Ace Wyatt. What a horrible, horrible thought.

"You think it's a weakness not to be you, Ace. But you're outnumbered, because the sane ones among us consider it a strength to be able to battle back our worst impulses. To not believe ourselves the ultimate judge, jury and executioner."

Ace cocked his head as he studied Gage. "A nice story you six have told yourselves. But there are six of you. One of you will have to face the music. Or the end will come."

"Endings always come. And the most poetic ending for you will be rotting in a cell for the rest of your insane life."

"The land provides. It provides the willing and the worthy, and it has provided me my freedom, again."

He sounded so rational, so utterly sure, Felicity had to remind herself he *was* insane. Evil, surely, if he'd killed people and done some of the things the Wyatts said he did.

"Then, after the land anoints me yet again, frees and

provides and gives to me, *yet again*, I'm lucky enough to stumble upon exactly who I was figuring out how to find."

"I thought you didn't believe in luck," Gage said, his voice cool and detached as if a deadly weapon wasn't pressed to his head.

Ace chuckled. "Oh, I believe in it. I also believe it favors the prepared and anointed. I am both. What are you?"

Gage muttered disparagingly under his breath. He was staring straight ahead so he couldn't see the way Ace's eyes gleamed.

Crazy. Evil. Felicity didn't know what it was, but that sheen made everything inside of her ice, made the hair on her arms and back of her neck stand up on end. All that reason she'd almost thought he'd been speaking evaporated when she looked at him.

She focused on breathing evenly in an effort to keep panic at bay. She had to find a way to survive this. A way for both of them to survive their fathers.

There wasn't much that could be done with Ace holding a gun to Gage's head and her father pointing a gun at her.

Don't panic. Don't panic. Think.

The Wyatt brothers had always said their father didn't want them dead, or they'd be dead. There were multiple theories, though most centered on the idea Ace Wyatt wanted slow, painful revenge on his sons, not just a violent death.

The likelihood of Ace actually pulling the trigger was low. And since neither had shot her, maybe they didn't want her dead, either.

Still, she could visualize Ace shooting Gage—see it

happening before her, and that kept her from moving. From hoping.

Two against two might have been a fair fight if she had a weapon of her own, but all she had was a back-packing knife stuffed deep within the pack on her back. Was there any way to get it without drawing attention to herself? And even if there was, what was the point of bringing a knife to a gunfight?

"I don't know what brand-new break you've had with reality," Gage drawled, "but—"

Ace's free hand jabbed out so fast Felicity barely saw it. She wasn't even sure where the punch landed, only that it had Gage gasping for air and falling to his knees.

"You weren't next on my list, Gage. But you mixed yourself up with this one and messed up my plan. You know how I feel when people mess up my plan."

The only thing that came from Gage was horrible gasping noises as if he was struggling to breathe.

Without fully realizing she was doing it, she moved toward him. Until an excruciating pain in her hand stopped her. She looked at the source of the crushing, terrifying pain and found her father's boot pressing harder and harder against her hand.

"You stay put," he said.

She tried not to sob, not to react, but he ground the boot harder against her hand. He was going to break her fingers with much more pressure. The only thing currently saving her was the give of the soil after the rain.

"Got it?" he demanded, jabbing her side with his gun.

She nodded, tears streaming down her cheeks. But she didn't make a noise.

The pressure eased off her hand, and she wanted to sob with as much relief as throbbing pain, but she breathed through it.

"Felicity, I need you to break your promise to me," Gage said, his voice clear and calm, which earned him another punch from Ace, right against the throat.

Her promise? Her promise. To stay together no matter what. No. No, she couldn't break it. She couldn't leave him here.

But as he gasped for air against his father's horrifying blows, she realized that in this case, splitting up was the only chance they had. Ace would have somewhere to take them, somewhere to torture them.

If she could get away, she could get all the Wyatts here. She could save Gage. She didn't want to leave him with Ace, even for a second. But when they'd promised each other to stick together that had been when Ace was out there. When the threat was from the outside, not the inside.

She couldn't save Gage with brute strength, but if she could get away she might be able to save him some other way.

She met his gaze. And nodded.

GAGE DIDN'T LET the nerves show, didn't let on how afraid he was because God knew this was going to hurt.

But she'd be safe—or safer. It was the only chance he had to survive. Maybe he wouldn't, but if she was safe that would be okay.

So, he had to make sure he did enough damage to Ace that Michael came over to save him. He had to give Felicity enough time to really run.

The two men holding guns on them would kill her, no doubt. They'd kill him, too, but Ace would want to make it hurt first. Maybe he'd want it to hurt for Felicity, too, since she'd gotten in Ace's way with Nina and Cody, but that only made her being here, in their grasp, that much more dangerous.

"Have you had your dramatic mom—"

Gage interrupted his father's comment by throwing his head backward, and straight into his father's.

It rang his bell—stars dancing and pain radiating down to his toes, but the gun dropped from his temple. Gage took the opportunity to pitch his body forward hoping his legs would hold him.

He still had the damn pack on his back and wished he'd had the foresight to drop it, but when Michael came charging at him, Gage managed to get an arm out of the strap and use it as enough of a force to knock the gun pointed at him from Michael's hands.

Gage didn't stop to look and see if Felicity ran. There wasn't time for him to look, so he just had to trust that she'd understood him and that she'd nodded because she knew she was going to run.

Michael swore at him and charged.

Felicity's father did not appear to be the smartest man, but he had fists like mallets, and was all bulk and muscle. Though he'd lost his gun, he used his body as a weapon against Gage, landing two punches to the gut before Gage could block them.

Gage was not a small man, but he felt like one for a second. Michael making him feel small only reminded him that Felicity had been small. A tiny girl and this man had used his fists on her—enough that protective services had intervened—which was a bit of a feat in isolated rural areas with low government funds.

Gage used that rage, that utter disgust to propel him forward with a blow that knocked Michael back two steps.

A gunshot rang out too close, but no blast of pain

followed the noise. Still, Gage knew well enough Ace wouldn't miss twice. Even to forward his precious plans.

So Gage grappled with Michael, finally landing a knee to the most vulnerable part of his attacker. He managed to flip him off and then got to his feet, only to come face-to-face with Ace's gun barrel.

"Well, shoot me then," Gage snarled. His mouth was bleeding, and God knew what other parts of him were bleeding and broken. Every cell of his body hurt, and this was all so pointless.

Not pointless. Felicity is gone. He didn't dare look around and verify. He just *willed* it.

Ace's own face was bleeding, and Gage got morbid satisfaction from knowing his head had caused that gash on Ace's brow.

Ace's gaze whipped behind Michael, from the gun that had fallen to the ground, to the pack that had been ripped from Gage's back.

"You let her *go*?" Ace growled.

Michael was struggling to get to his feet. "He practically knocked you out. I had to—"

"You worthless moron! Go after her! Go!"

Gage couldn't help smiling even as blood dripped down his face. He wasn't sure he'd ever heard Ace sound so furiously disgusted. Usually his anger was deadly, eerie calm, but Gage had clearly put quite the crimp in Ace's plans.

Who wouldn't grin at that? Especially as Michael scrambled to retrieve the gun and then ran off more in panic than with any thought as to which way Felicity had gone.

She'd be faster and far more knowledgeable of the terrain. She was gone and on her way to find help. Gage had to believe it.

"What are you smiling ab…" Ace trailed off, rage and disgust sinking into the lines on his face.

"Jail didn't agree with you, Daddy," Gage offered, hoping to throw Ace off.

"You care about her." Ace sneered. "What is it about you boys? Where did I go so wrong? Weak. Stupid. Undone by any woman who opens her legs."

Gage couldn't keep the easy grin on his face, and it morphed into a sneer. But he bit his tongue to keep from saying anything that might give Ace more ammunition to rail against and agitate Gage into making a deadly misstep.

"What a mistake you've made," Ace whispered, a vicious fury dancing in his eyes, that Gage only remembered seeing once before—when Ace had realized Cody had escaped.

Jamison had worked hard to get Cody, the youngest of the six boys, out from the Sons before he had to go through the ritual they'd all had to survive on their seventh birthdays. Jamison had managed, managed so well Ace had assumed Grandma Pauline had paid one of his men to betray him. He'd never suspected Jamison.

At first.

That moment Ace had learned Cody was safe and out of his grip, Gage had seen this exact look. And known he'd be lucky to survive it.

But he had then, why couldn't he now?

Which was the last thought he had before pain exploded at the side of his head, and the world went dark.

Chapter Twelve

Felicity tried to keep her mind off the lack of water. Once she found cell service, she'd have help and water.

Her head pounded along with her thundering heart. She knew she could outrun her father, but he had a gun, which meant she had to do a lot more than just outrun him. She had to get away completely.

Now, Ace, he could probably catch her if he was the one chasing her. Her father was a big man, and though she remembered a certain agile precision in landing a blow, she doubted it extended to endurance running.

But Ace was tall and lean and crazy. That was the worst part, really. He seemed almost normal sometimes. She'd found herself listening too intently to what he had to say.

Charismatic wasn't the right word because that had too positive of a connotation. Compelling maybe. Even knowing everything she did about Ace—which was probably only the half of what Ace was and had done—she'd been *compelled* to listen to what he had to say.

It made her feel sick. Or maybe that was the dehydration.

She allowed her pace to slow, then stop, turning in a careful circle to study her surroundings.

She'd gone straight for the canyon land, which may

not have been her smartest choice what with the lack of water, but it was better than the wide-open grassy plains. There were a million places to find cover in the rocks, crevices and caves.

And that was only if her father found her.

She was currently in a long, deep crevice. Some of the wet from yesterday's storm had dried, but there were still damp places where the sun hadn't touched. Not safe drinking water, but she considered it for a minute.

Maybe she should go back. Knife in hand. They weren't supposed to split up. This was all wrong.

She climbed up a portion of the rock wall that would allow her to see out over the horizon while still keeping her mostly out of sight. She scanned the area, the tall spires and rocky hills. The sky was a brilliant blue, as if a tornado hadn't blown through less than twenty-four hours ago.

The air was hot, but it was *Badlands* air. Home. Heart. She'd be okay.

The land provides.

The thought comforted her for a second or two before she realized it was Ace's voice. Ace's words.

She pushed out a breath, nausea stealing over her. How could a madman's words be comforting? Had she gone crazy? Was she that weak?

She shook her head. Maybe she was, but she could choose not to be. She could fight it. It was like being shy, and her stutter. Those things still existed within her, but she fought them away.

So she would fight the terrifying idea she had something in common with Ace Wyatt. Just as for years she'd fought the terrifying idea a man who'd beat his young daughter was her own flesh and blood.

And that flesh and blood had come after her, no doubt.

She looked around again, a double check to make sure her eyes weren't deceiving her.

She caught the hint of movement to the east and squinted at it. Then, since she had time, she dug through her pack and pulled out her binoculars. She focused on the area where she'd sensed movement.

In between two spindly spires of red rock, a figure was moving. He was still far enough away the binoculars didn't magnify features enough for identification, but based on the size and location, she had to believe it was her father.

He didn't look like an adept hiker. He stumbled and picked his way over rock. She could continue to outrun or out-hike him if she chose.

But she would no doubt become too dehydrated to function after a while.

What were her options? He had a gun and he was clearly stronger than her. She couldn't fight him. She had no gun to ward him off. Just that knife in her pack.

She considered waiting till he got close enough and then throwing it, but she'd never thrown a knife in her life and it seemed too big a risk to just start throwing her one and only weapon.

Rocks might work. She was strong and had good aim, but he'd have to be really close for them to do any damage.

She kept watching him through the binoculars. Maybe she wouldn't have to do anything at all. One good fall and he'd be out of luck.

One good fall. What if she *created* the fall? She could take him out. Even with him having a gun, all she'd need to do was give him a little push. Well, more than a little, but a push. Or trip him somehow. She could incapacitate him or trap him in a deep crevice.

It would be tricky and dangerous, but it would be a better option than trying to find cell service without any water to drink. If she took out her father here, she could get back to the cabin. Close enough to it and she could access her Wi-Fi and send a text.

If she was careful and quiet, she could do it without Ace even knowing she was back. Surely he wouldn't take Gage anywhere until her father returned with her in tow.

She'd hope, anyway.

In the meantime, she'd take her father out.

THE PAIN EBBED and flowed, excruciating waves of it, dulling into something almost bearable. Almost reasonable enough he could fight through, open his eyes and figure everything out.

Then another wave would take him under. Black, black, vicious black.

But then something happened, a familiar sound, a familiar panic. He found consciousness gasping for air and eyes flying open. His vision swam for a good few seconds before it cleared.

And there was Ace.

With the whip.

Gage tried to remember he wasn't seven years old any longer. He was an adult. Whatever his father could dish out, he could take.

But that whip was the nightmare he thought he'd escaped. He wouldn't let those old memories rush into his brain. There was enough pain there. He had to focus on the present. Where he was and if Michael was here—because if he wasn't, he was still somewhere after Felicity.

Felicity. He'd focus on her and not the echoing crack of that whip.

"Good morning, son. Or should I say, good afternoon?"

Gage didn't say anything, though he wanted to demand to know how long he'd been out. He wanted to demand a whole myriad of things, but he didn't trust his voice with that whip in his father's hands.

Ace shifted it from one hand to another. "Did you think I'd forgotten? You never forget your son's weaknesses." Ace smiled, a grin that was all sharp edges and sure as hell crazy.

Except Ace always knew what he was doing. So maybe he was just evil. Maybe all his talk about being anointed and chosen and born from the dust were the things he used to justify all that potential for horror he had inside him.

Gage had never really cared to find out. Especially when that whip was involved.

He wasn't a child anymore. He was *not* a child anymore. The whip would hurt, but it couldn't break him. He couldn't let it. That was what his father wanted, so he wouldn't give it to him.

But his body wasn't getting the message. There was the nausea, which he could blame on the concussion he had to have been given. The heart-pounding, sweaty-palmed terror making his limbs weak—that was all whip.

It's just a weapon like any other.

But it wasn't. Not for him.

"Why do you get the whip, Gage?"

Gage wouldn't respond. He wouldn't. He didn't have to give in. Not anymore. This wasn't the same game it had been when he'd been a defenseless boy.

Maybe he was tied up in what appeared to be some kind of cave...always a cave. But he was thirty-one years old. A grown man who'd fought drug addicts and arrested child molesters and done what he could, *everything* he could, to right the wrongs he came across.

He had to survive this wrong. He'd done it once, much younger but with his brothers' help.

Now he was an adult, and if Felicity had gotten away, it could be with his brothers' help again.

If Felicity and his brothers could find him.

Big, *big* if.

Ace stepped forward, still moving the whip handle from hand to hand.

"The rules are the same, boy."

Gage shuddered as if he was still that little boy. As if the years meant nothing. His size meant nothing. There was Ace and that whip, and Gage was nothing in its wake.

No.

"I ask a question, you answer it. Why do you get the whip?"

"Because my father's a psychopath?"

The crack slammed through the air the same time the stinging, breath-stealing pain lashed over his leg. He couldn't hold back the hiss of pain, despite knowing it was exactly what his father wanted.

It would be worse—get worse. His father's whip was weighted and could break bones with the right slap.

Gage could survive it. Better to survive it than give in like he'd had to as a kid.

"Why do you get the whip, Gage? You and no one else?" Ace cracked the whip between them, and though Gage cringed at the sound, no blast of pain followed it.

Psychological warfare. It wasn't enough to just hurt his sons—he wanted to break them. The problem was, if you were broken, the pain would stop.

For a time, but the war never stopped. There would always be this war between Ace and his sons, because they'd dared to be good instead of capitulate to his evil.

He'd promised himself never to be weak in the face

of his father again. But giving Ace what he wanted without truly believing it wasn't weakness. It was survival.

What wouldn't Gage do to survive? To make sure Felicity had survived?

"I get the whip because I'm the smartest," Gage said, his voice already battle weary.

"Good," Ace replied in the same tone a teacher might use when a student finally succeeded with a difficult concept.

It made Gage feel slimy, slick with self-disgust and the ever-present heart-pounding fear. But if he threw up, he knew exactly what Ace would have to do.

He had to be tough. Tough enough to survive. Tough enough so that Ace would leave him alone and torture someone else. Anyone else.

It was his own fault. If he could make more mistakes, be more of a disappointment, Ace wouldn't try to mold him, make him. If he could be less, this wouldn't happen.

Sometimes he even believed that, no matter that it was a sad, self-serving lie.

You are not a child.

But he felt it. Felt those old feelings and thoughts taking over as if they were a spirit set on possessing him. He couldn't get the words out of his head, the pleas he'd offered as a child desperate for the pain to stop.

"So much potential in you, Gage. And you failed all of it. What you could have been. What you could have done. You've failed. Just like Jamison and Cody. Did you know they could have killed me? Both of them. It'd all be over. Instead, here I am."

"Do you want to see if I'll kill you?" Gage asked, giving the bonds that held him a little jerk. "I'd be happy to oblige that little experiment."

Ace laughed. "We'll get to it. We will. I'll give you

all a chance to end me, because only the one who ends me could ever take my spot."

"We don't want your spot."

"One of you will. I was chosen for a reason, Gage, and one of you will be, too. Perhaps you six are my great challenge. My cross to bear. Every leader faces them."

"I can't decide if you're crazy or just evil, but *you* barely run your own gang anymore. You're hardly a leader. Seems to me, the Sons don't need you, Ace. Hasn't jail taught you that?"

The next hit was so quick and vicious Gage howled in pain and shock. Ace's grin widened.

"The pain can end. You know how it can end."

"I'm not worried about your pa—" Another crack and painful slap, though this one wasn't as hard or unexpected. Gage breathed through it, even as he felt blood begin to trickle down his thigh inside his pants.

Based on his father's reaction, Gage knew one thing. The Sons *were* struggling without Ace at the helm. Ever since Jamison and Cody had managed to get Ace behind bars, the Sons had been sloppy.

Or maybe…

Could it be that the *Sons* weren't struggling at all. It was Ace, losing power over the group that had followed him blindly. Wouldn't that be worse to Ace—continuing on just fine without him and so many of his top men dead after a planned explosion by Cody's former North Star Group?

The thought—the utter possibility—almost made Gage laugh. It reminded him that *everything* had an end. And maybe he wouldn't live out his father's end, but his brothers would.

Felicity would.

She wasn't here, and neither was Michael. There were

too many scenarios, too many possibilities of where Felicity could be and what she could be facing.

He had to survive this next little while just to make sure she survived. To make sure.

Then he did the thing he'd sworn to never do again.

Because sometimes you had to break a promise to yourself to keep a more important one to someone else.

"I get the whip because I'm the biggest. The smartest. The one best suited to take over, but the weakness of my mother needs to be beaten out of me."

Another blow, but he'd been expecting that, too. Giving in to what Ace wanted never truly offered relief. If it were that easy, life would be a heck of a lot different. For all of them.

"Isn't that how it goes?" Gage asked, failing to make his voice sound properly deferential.

"Try again. Try to mean it this time. Feel the truth. The weakness will be whipped out of you, Gage. Here. Or you'll die. Jamison won't save you this time. Brady won't save you. Even that little redheaded dimwit can't save you. It's you and me."

"And one of us will end up dead."

"Oh, son, now you're speaking my language."

Chapter Thirteen

Felicity may have lived with her father only until she was four years old, but as she waited to take him out, she realized she'd learned quite a few things from him.

Silence was the first thing. Stillness the second. If you were silent and still, it was hard to become a target. And in a house with her father, she was always a target.

He had to find her first, though.

She'd learned to fold in on herself, to meld into her surroundings with everything she had. She'd learned and honed those skills before she'd learned how to speak or walk—or so she thought. So she *felt*.

Life with the Knights, and the slow—very slow—bloom of maturity and adulthood had helped her unlearn those impulses. She'd figured out how to speak and move and dream and believe without folding in on herself. Without hiding.

But a person never unlearned their early impulses completely. As her father huffed and puffed toward her, she struggled to stay in the present. Hard when she was hiding just as if she'd been that toddler struggling to hide from another one of her father's rages.

But she had a plan this time. She had fight this time. Her father didn't get to terrorize her anymore.

She moved with his movements, keeping her body

shielded by the large rock she was hiding behind. She was careful of where and how she stepped—even a pebble tumbling down the side of the crevasse she was tiptoeing around might bring his attention to her.

Though, based on all his heavy breathing, maybe not.

She kept her breathing even, that old hiding trick in full force as he passed the rock she was behind—as she moved around it so she could surprise him from the back.

She didn't even need to push him. As she jumped out, guttural scream piercing the quiet air, he jerked, tripped and tumbled down the steep cliff.

He landed with a thud, and then moans of pain that echoed and grew louder and louder. He writhed on the hard ground below and Felicity looked down at him. She felt inexplicably *furious*.

She'd won, for the moment. Done exactly what she planned to do, and still the fury swept through her like a tidal wave.

"Do you feel big and powerful now?" she called as she considering kicking some rock down on top of him. Or maybe throwing the heaviest rocks she could lift. She wanted to torture him. She wanted to cause him all the pain he'd caused her. She wanted to...

She stopped herself, and the fury. She wasn't like him—didn't want to be. She didn't need to terrorize him just because he'd terrorized her. It wouldn't solve anything or erase anything.

Still, it surprised her how badly she wanted to.

"Felicity." He said it in the same tone of voice she remembered. Pleading. Apologetic. Therapy had taught her that an abuser's strongest weapon was his ability to make himself seem truly sorry, truly sympathetic.

"Maybe you should answer the question. Do you feel big and powerful now?"

"I was only following orders, Liss. That's all. Ace is a powerful man. I had to do what he said. Please. Don't… I'm sorry. I had to."

He was a big lump on the ground, holding on to his leg. She stood quite a few feet above him. He was begging and pleading, and it was only the therapy she'd had that kept her from falling for it.

"You didn't *have* to do anything. Ace doesn't own you. You weren't…" Then it dawned on her, what she'd never fully considered. "You're *in* the Sons?" He had been. All this time. Somehow? Or was it new?

Did it matter?

No. What mattered was he'd killed his daughter—a sister she'd never known—and then tried to frame Felicity for murder. Regardless of Ace's influence, he had done those things. She was sure of it.

"You *killed* her," Felicity said, her voice vibrating with an emotion she wished she could bury for right now.

"Killed who?" His eyes bulged in horror down there in the canyon. "I ain't killed *no one*."

She believed him, for a split, stupid second when she felt a moment of relief and hope. She desperately wanted to believe her father wasn't capable of murdering his own daughter, despite all the evidence to the contrary.

But that was so utterly ignorant she hated herself for even thinking it, no matter how briefly.

"Is Ace telling people I killed somebody?" He scrambled to stand and howled in pain. Presumably he'd seriously injured his leg. "I didn't kill nobody!" he shouted, panic and desperation tinging his words.

"And yet your fingerprints were all over my cabin. *And* the evidence. You're the one who identified her body."

"I didn't! I didn't! Whose body? What are you talking about?"

Felicity faltered. Michael seemed utterly confused and lost, and it wasn't beyond Ace, even in prison, to be able to make things happen. But how could someone have impersonated her father to identify a body? How could prints be dropped without her father being culpable?

"What about your daughter?"

"You're my daughter, Felicity." He managed to get to his feet, leaning on one leg over the other. He put his hands together as if praying. To her. "Please. You gotta help me. Ace made me do all this, but I didn't kill anyone. Please."

"You beat me. I was three years old, probably younger when it started. You beat me. A little, defenseless girl."

He had the decency to drop his arms to his sides. He made a helpless gesture. "I… Yes, I did that. I know it makes me a monster. I was messed up. I still am. I get it." He didn't make the pleading motion again, but he did look up imploringly, shading his eyes against the sun with his hand. "But I didn't commit *murder.*"

Maybe he hadn't. Maybe he had. She didn't know.

She wasn't sure she cared.

"You deserve what you get," she said, but it was a whisper and she knew he didn't hear her down there. "You deserve what you get," she repeated, still whispering, feeling tears sting her eyes.

But it seemed more than possible that her father was just a pawn in Ace's scheme. Not an innocent one. He was in the Sons, had to be, whether he'd always been or had joined up recently. He deserved anything he got—and more than that, he didn't deserve even a second of her concern or help.

"I didn't kill anyone," he said, his voice wavering as if he was about to cry.

"Maybe," she agreed, feeling detached. As though

she was floating above herself or as if there was cotton shoved into her chest instead of a heart and lungs. "It doesn't matter."

She could hear the way she sounded. Flat. Emotionless. There were emotions—she could feel them swimming under all that cotton—but she was afraid of what would happen, what she would allow herself to do if she accessed them.

She stepped back from the ledge.

"Felicity. Where are you going? You can't leave me down here!"

She took another step.

"Please! Please. I'm hurt. Don't... I'll die down here. I'm *hurt*. Please. Please!"

"I remember begging," she said. The sun was beating down on her, but all she felt was ice. Brittle, stinging ice. She had to get away from it.

Away from him.

"You'll probably die down there."

"Then it'll be you committing murder, Felicity," he yelled from his spot down in the canyon as she walked away.

"So be it," she whispered to herself.

GAGE WEAVED IN and out of the pain, out of consciousness. The blows kept coming, and would, until his father was ready to fight.

Usually at the point Gage was his weakest. But when a boy was at his weakest, that's when he fought the hardest. Or should.

According to Ace.

He'd be brought to his weakest point, then be given a weapon. A smaller, less useful weapon than his father's, but a weapon nonetheless.

Gage had survived this a few too many times to count. His own personal hell. His punishment for having a quick mind. For being born big and strong.

Gage was under no illusion he was special. Ace had picked on them all for separate reasons. Doled out punishments specific to each of his sons.

Gage had never told his brothers the whys of his personal hell. Instead, he'd worked to make himself the opposite of everything Ace said he was.

Once he'd finally got into school, he'd failed. Over and over again. He'd skimmed through graduation from high school to the police academy. He never let himself excel, and since Brady did, and so well, no one ever thought twice of the underperforming twin.

Thank God. A saving grace.

Now he was back here, in the exact position he'd escaped, the exact position he'd proved to everyone he didn't belong to be.

He couldn't think about being back in this same place he'd escaped. Couldn't think about how unfair it was.

Maybe Ace was right all along. He was anointed somehow. Chosen. Because somehow Ace always·got what he wanted, even if it took years to get there.

No. No, it wasn't true. Jamison was alive and well, getting ready to marry Liza and make a family with Liza's half sister. Cody was back with Nina and their daughter Brianna, building a life in Bonesteel.

Ace didn't get everything he wanted.

Gage fought off the nausea, reminded himself not to float away from the pain because that would only prolong the inevitable.

This standoff was inevitable.

Always had been. Always would be.

And if he ended it, maybe he'd be like Ace, but maybe

he'd end this for his brothers. Would that be so bad? So wrong? Couldn't he live with anything if it meant saving his brothers?

"I think you're ready, Gage."

Gage laughed. It was all so ridiculous. He'd been whipped and beaten bloody—he could feel the blood covering him. Like a film.

This was Ace's language, Ace's currency. Blood and pain.

It could be Gage's, too. If he killed Ace, by some grace of God, it would be his language, too.

He didn't want it. He'd rather die. If he just knew Felicity was safe, he'd rather die. But he wasn't sure. He had to fight to be sure.

He was tired of fighting the insanity of his own father. Tired of fighting, period. He just wanted…life. He'd taken for granted the years since his escape when Ace had left him alone thinking they'd just keep lasting.

Gage looked at the man who'd fathered him, tortured him then and now, and had no doubt murdered Gage's mother. Gage didn't understand any of it. Top to bottom. "Why didn't you just kill us, Ace? You had the chance. Over and over and over. You've always had the chance."

Ace stepped closer, looking at Gage as if he'd missed some important life lesson along the way. "What's life without the chance? You've made me into a monster in your own head, Gage. You all did. None of you ever tried to understand. I don't want you dead. I want you reborn as only mine."

Reborn. It was such insanity. As if his own mother could be erased from him even if he wanted her to be. After all, she'd been weak enough to love a monster, to keep giving birth to son after son this monster would torture. Just to stay alive. And for what? To die anyway.

In the moment, he had no warm feelings for the mother who'd allowed this, but she hadn't been a monster. She hadn't been *this*. "She was better than you, you know," Gage said, expecting the blow to follow.

It didn't. Not yet. Ace got very still. "She was weak. And so are you."

"It isn't weak to survive you, Ace."

"She didn't, did she?"

"She did. She knew who and what you were. She couldn't break free of the spell of that, but she knew. She used to tell all of us that when she died, that when *you* killed her, you would try to make us into you. She said we never had to turn into that, if we didn't want to. She was stronger than you where it counted. We didn't escape until she was gone. Why not, Ace?"

"You really want to play the why-not game?" Ace smiled, the chaotic, gleaming smile that made Gage's stomach roil completely separately from the concussion symptoms.

If Ace was talking, though, he wasn't whipping or beating, so Gage nodded. "Yeah, let's play."

"Why didn't your mother escape? Why didn't she run you all to your precious grandma? She could have."

"Of course. She wasn't a prisoner to you *at all*," Gage said, letting the words drip with sarcasm.

"You six escaped. Why couldn't she?"

Gage opened his mouth to rage about how Ace had warped his mother, twisted her until she didn't know *how* to escape. Maybe that made her weak, but she'd given Gage himself the belief that something better existed out there. He just had to get there.

Maybe it was Jamison who had proved it, over and over again, but it was his mother's seed of truth that he'd first believed.

But he was tired. God, he was tired. And his mother was dead. What did this matter? What did any of it matter? Why couldn't he give up?

He, of course, knew the answer. Felicity was out there, and as much as his brothers would survive and thrive without him, they would blame themselves. They would want to avenge him.

"Maybe she didn't want to bring your insanity to her own mother's household."

Ace snorted. "Your mother thought as little of Pauline as I do."

"And yet Pauline lives. Thrives. She raised us. And you let her. Why is that?"

Ace's face went dark, the terrifying fury Gage had once known better than to poke at. But he couldn't hold himself back, not when his own fury was beginning to bubble under all the pain and exhaustion.

He smiled at Ace in that same way Ace was always smiling at him. "You're afraid she really did curse you." Gage laughed. "That's just sad."

A blade flicked out—Gage didn't know from where—but it was at his throat, sharp and deadly.

"I was wrong, Gage. Rare, but we all make mistakes. Even me. I thought you were the smartest. But you're the weakest, and now you'll die. Say your last words, son. Because I'm done trying to make you into something."

Chapter Fourteen

Felicity licked her lips even knowing it wouldn't help the dry, cracked texture. It wouldn't magically make water appear or make everything swirling around in her mind make sense.

She was close to her cabin. Close to water. That was all that mattered as the sun beat down on her from above.

She squinted against the sun and stopped in her tracks when she saw what sat outside her cabin in the distance.

A police cruiser.

For a moment she felt relief so potent tears stung her eyes. She started forward, then remembered she was still wanted for murder.

Even if the police had saved Gage, that didn't mean things had been cleared up.

But they could be. Wasn't water more important than getting arrested? Gage would clear it up and everything would be fine.

Eventually.

Maybe.

I didn't kill anyone.

Her father had seemed so desperate. So surprised. So confused by what little she'd said about the murder. Was it her own bias doubting he'd killed, or was it just reason? *I didn't kill anyone. I didn't kill anyone.*

Ace had to have framed him, but how could she prove Ace was behind anything when he'd been in jail? And why would she want to? Her father deserved whatever he got.

Dying of exposure?

She pushed that thought out of her head, but the roiling nausea that accompanied it stuck around.

She slowed her pace as she moved toward her cabin. There was no sign of Ace or Gage. She used as much cover as she could to creep closer and closer to the small grove of trees that had been planted on the east side to give the cabin some shade back in the days before air-conditioning.

She hid among the trees, straining to hear something that might give her an idea of why the police were here. Had they found Gage? Ace? Was everyone okay?

Or was it all much worse than that?

The vehicle was a Pennington County cruiser, so there was no chance it was one of the Wyatt brothers, who all worked for Valiant County.

She didn't realize two men were in the cruiser until the driver's side door opened, and the passenger side next.

Two men got out. They clearly weren't in any hurry. Had they just driven up before she'd crested the rise for the cabin to come into view? That would mean Ace had taken Gage somewhere before the police had shown up.

She closed her eyes against the pounding panic. She had to figure out what was going on.

"Doesn't look like the tornado disturbed much here," the taller officer said to the other as they moved slowly toward the cabin. Not out of fear, but as if they weren't in any hurry to get to work.

"Lucky for us."

"Going over the house again seems overkill, doesn't it?"

The shorter one scratched his head. "That detective from Valiant County was adamant. Hard to blame him. Seems off if it's true the suspect didn't have any contact with her father."

"Seems *convenient* more than *off*, given he's friends with the suspect." The officer stopped short and swore. "Someone's been here. The tape's off."

"Could have been the wind," the other one said, but he was already pulling on rubber gloves and reaching for the caution tape fluttering in the slight breeze.

Tucker was the detective from Valiant County they were referring to. It seemed they were here only to search her cabin again. Look for more clues.

What might they find?

Didn't matter. She had to find Gage. There was no indication they had any idea he'd been here, or that Ace had.

Before she went in search of Gage, she needed backup. She had to forget about the desperate need for water and connect to the Wi-Fi.

But she'd need to be closer than the trees. Somehow, without getting caught. She could wait them out, but how long would that be? How long could Gage survive whatever and wherever Ace had presumably taken him?

Maybe he'd fought Ace off. Maybe...

Well, she couldn't entertain maybes until she knew for sure. She had to get a message to the Wyatts, then figure out what happened.

Without getting caught.

She closed her eyes for a second, letting herself pray to anything and everything she believed in, then she grabbed her phone. She pulled up the Wi-Fi and watched the screen as she crept closer and closer.

"Come on," she muttered, waiting for her Wi-Fi name

to come up. She was easing out of the trees, her gaze moving from the cabin to the phone, back and forth, back and forth.

"Someone was definitely in there."

Felicity jumped back, pressing herself behind a tree. She squeezed her eyes shut and held her breath. She couldn't hear over the pounding of her own heart in her ears. She was light-headed and afraid for a moment she might faint.

Then the engine started.

She dared peek from behind the tree and watched as the police cruiser drove away.

She nearly wept in relief. Still, she waited, making sure they were gone for good before she ran forward. She had to stop, drop her pack and dig for her keys. With trembling hands, she found them and ducked under the caution tape.

It took a while for her hands to stop shaking enough to insert the key into the lock. She pushed it open and went straight for the faucet. She flipped on the water, ducked her head under the stream and drank with messy, greedy gulps.

Once she cooled off a little bit she remembered herself and her priorities.

She pulled up the text messages on her phone and sent a group text to everyone—Wyatts, Knights.

Ace was at my cabin. Took Gage. Don't know where. Going to track. Need help.

She paused, stupidly, then took the time to explain where she'd left her father and that he'd need help and medical attention.

She couldn't be that cold to let revenge take over her.

He beat you. Gage's words, flat as they'd been when he'd first delivered them, echoed in her head.

She shook her head. What was done was done. She'd sent the text and now she had to find Gage.

She grabbed the few water bottles she had left and went back outside, locking the door behind her. She ducked back under the tape, pushed the water into her pack and studied her surroundings.

She could see a myriad of footprints. Had the cops even looked at them? She focused on them now, remembering this morning.

Ace had tossed her down, and there was the indentation in the grass where she'd slid. There was a boot print—presumably one of the cop's—in the middle of it.

She moved there, then turned to look at the house. Ace had held Gage, that horrible gun pressed to his temple, right there and—

Gun.

She bolted back into the house, knowing it would take too long and knowing she had to do it. She got her gun and holster, then returned to where Ace had held Gage.

She tried to determine whose footprints were whose, followed the two sets that veered off behind the house. One had to be Gage's, didn't it? If her father had followed her, his prints wouldn't be aligned with Ace's *or* Gage's.

There was mud here, not sloppy mud, but slowly drying mud. Still wet enough to make deep marks, but more of a clay texture. A flurry of footprints, a few indentations she couldn't figure out, but it all ended in a set of footprints and two long trenches.

Like heels being dragged. Fear snaked through her, but she couldn't give in to it.

She followed them.

They went for a way, into the patch of grass behind

her cabin. Still, the ground was soft enough she could follow it.

Until the grass gave way to rock. The millennia of wind and rain, soil and rock. Erosion and deposition in its grand, epic scale.

Her heart, stretching out before her, and the absolute worst landscape she could encounter when trying to find someone. Rock was vast, virtually trackless. Too much wind to follow any kind of idea of which way they'd gone.

Then she saw it. A little bit of fabric under a rock. Black, like the T-shirt Gage had been wearing. Just a bit of it, clearly ripped off.

You're being unreasonable. If he was being dragged away, how could he rip his shirt *and* stick it under a rock?

Unless he was doing the dragging, but wouldn't he have gotten help? Not dragged Ace off alone?

It was probably just something blown by the wind—a hiker tearing his clothes on a rock, or the remnants of a ceremonial object. Granted, those occurred more often in the southern portion of the park. Still, with the winds in the Dakotas it was hardly impossible.

But this fabric was under a rock. Specifically. Purposefully.

If she went in the direction of the piece of fabric, she'd be heading back out into the canyons and rock formations.

That didn't scare her. She was a park ranger. She was equipped, now, with water. She knew how to navigate. She knew how to get back if she went in the wrong direction.

She glanced warily at the sky. She was prepared to camp. No food, but she had water. She had a weapon now. Everything would be fine.

Because she wouldn't stop until she found Gage.

She followed the bits of fabric, almost sobbed with relief as she found a car insurance card with Gage's name on it. He had really been Hansel and Greteling it through the Badlands while Ace dragged him along.

How hurt was he, though, that he didn't fight off Ace?

She kept going, ignoring that thought as she followed the bits of Gage's things. She had to double back a few times when she couldn't find anything for a while. It was exhausting, and she should stop for water, but every time she found the next hint she pushed forward, desperate to find the next one.

She didn't touch them, hoping the Wyatt boys would be able to find them and him. If *she* could, *they* could, she was sure of it.

When she reached a clearing of sorts along a long wall of rock, she almost doubled back, but in the distance she saw something black and out of place against the tan, reddish and brown landscape.

She moved toward it, then stopped a few feet away.

It was a wallet. It sat in the open, which she thought was strange. It wasn't hiding. It wasn't under a rock—so technically the wind could have blown it.

Right above the wallet was the entrance to a cave.

Slowly Felicity lowered her pack to the ground, taking care to move quietly. She pulled the gun from the holster and crept toward the cave, her heart in her throat.

GAGE KEPT HIS gaze on his father as he waited for the pain. Would Ace slit his throat like he had the knife poised to do? Or would it be slower, meaner?

It could go either way, but for right now Ace simply held the knife there, waiting for Gage's last words.

He didn't have any. Not for his father anyway.

"Cat got your tongue? Maybe that's where I'll start."

Gage shrugged, even as he felt the blade of the knife scrape against the tender skin of his neck.

Ace paused, frowning. There was a noise, some kind of skittering like pebbles falling, toward the mouth of the cave. Likely some kind of animal, but Ace tilted his ear toward the sound.

Gage was weak, beaten, bloody, and still he knew a moment when he saw one. With enough of a push, he couldn't escape, but he could get that damn knife off his throat.

He used the bonds that held his hands tied behind his back and to whatever was behind him to hold his weight as he managed to slowly and quietly rear his leg back.

He made noise as he kicked, which was inevitable. Ace tried to sidestep the blow. Gage planned on that and managed to pivot with enough time for his kick to land, knocking Ace over, with some help from a rock formation behind him.

Ace snarled up at him. "You think you can win with your hands tied behind your back?" Ace demanded, a vicious, piping fury that overrode his usual distressing calm. *"You."* He got to his feet, searching the cave floor around them for his knife.

When he didn't see it, he began to reach for the gun at his side.

"He might not be able to. But I can."

Gage was sure he was hallucinating. The sun shone behind her like she was some kind of red-haired guardian angel, complete with firearm.

It wasn't possibly happening, but there Felicity was, stepping away from the streaming sunlight and into the dim light of the cave. She held her gun pointed at Ace.

She didn't shake. She didn't waver. She didn't look

over at Gage himself. She just kept that gun pointed at Ace, her gaze cool and calm and locked on him.

Ace's sneer deepened. "You won't shoot me."

"I shot your man last month. Isn't that why you're after me now? Trying to pin a murder I didn't commit on me."

Ace laughed mirthlessly, and the sneer stayed put on his face. "Don't flatter yourself. You're a bug."

"A bug you can't squish." Her voice was so cool, so controlled, it very nearly sent a shudder through Gage. He wasn't sure he *knew* this Felicity. She was like a different person.

"Felicity—"

She shook her head, still not looking over at him. "I want you to loosen the holster, let it fall. Then you'll walk out of this cave, Ace. Hands up, walk slow. I'll follow. Then we'll all wait."

"You must have mistaken me for one of my sons. I'm not going to simper and follow along. You think that sad excuse for a gun scares me? *Me?* Do you know what I've survived? Do you know what I am?"

"I don't really care, Ace, because my finger is on the trigger and if you don't move in five seconds, you'll have a bullet to the gut."

"Let's see what you got, sweetie." He began to move for his gun—not to drop it, Gage was sure. "I'll be the nightmare you—"

The shot rang out and Ace's body jerked, stumbled, then fell.

Gage made some kind of noise—horror, shock, relief and a million other things wrapped up into whatever expulsion of sound escaped his mouth.

"Felicity."

She took a step back. She didn't seem so cool and calm now as Ace writhed on the floor. He held on to his stomach, blood trickling over his hands. She still had the gun pointed at him.

"Felicity," he repeated, trying to keep his voice calm. "Get the gun."

Ace was reaching for it, but every time his arm moved, he groaned or grunted in pain. Color and blood drained from him with equal speed.

Felicity moved forward and slid his gun out of his holster without much of a fight from Ace.

She stared down at him, both guns in her hands now. "Felicity. Come untie me."

She didn't move. She stared down at Ace's body as if she was in a trance. Ace writhed, made awful noises, but he didn't attempt to fight Felicity. Her finger was still on the trigger, the gun still pointed at Ace.

Gage didn't know whether she planned to shoot him again, and he certainly didn't know whether he wanted her to or not, but the pale, lifeless look on her face was killing him.

"Felicity. Look at me."

Finally, she turned. A breath escaped her, shaky and pained. Then she sucked it in. She was pale, the color of death. Her eyes were glassy and her breath was coming in shallow puffs now.

He couldn't make his way to her and it cut him in two.

"I had to." She flicked a glance at Ace again.

"You did the right thing," Gage said, trying to draw her attention back to him. "Grab his knife. Then come untie me, okay? We'll figure it out. One step at a time."

She nodded too emphatically for him to feel any better about her mental state.

"Right over there. By that big rock."

"It's a sediment pile."

"Sure, sure." Hearing her using the technical term was some kind of relief. "Bring the knife here, okay?"

She nodded again, and this time actually moved for the knife. Gage glanced at Ace. He was still moving, writhing and groaning.

She'd shot him in the gut, just like she'd warned.

Felicity slid her gun into her holster, still holding Ace's in her hand. She picked up the knife, both her arms shaking now.

"Felicity. Untie me. Come on. Felicity?"

"Right." She approached him, all shaking limbs and too pale complexion. When she finally reached him, still holding the knife and gun in either hand, she met his gaze.

"God...you're... Gage." She inhaled shakily, tears filling her eyes.

"I'm okay. Kind of. I mean, I'll be okay. Look at me. I'm doing better than you, at the moment."

"You're covered in blood."

"It's okay. Don't cry, sweetheart. God, it's killing me. Just untie me. Okay. Untie me. I need you to untie me."

"I'm sorry. I'm sorry." She scrambled forward and began to work on the ropes with the knife. "My brain's in a fog. I can't seem to think."

"You're fine. You saved me. You're all right."

"Saved... I... Did I kill him?"

They looked over at Ace. He'd stopped writhing, but his eyes were open and full of hate. Directed at them.

"Get me untied, Felicity," Gage said flatly.

"I'm trying. I'm trying." She was practically chanting it, but he could *feel* her shaking behind him as she worked.

Gage kept his eyes on Ace. Ace didn't move. When

he opened his mouth as if he was trying to speak, little more than a groan escaped.

All this time, Gage had dreamed of Ace's end, and he didn't know what to feel in the face of it actually happening.

When Felicity finally managed to cut and untie the bonds, Gage at least felt relief instead of uncertainty. He stumbled a little forward, shook the rope off, then turned to Felicity.

She was staring at Ace, anguish written all over her. She kept looking at Ace as she spoke. "I texted your brothers. I followed your trail, surely they'll be able to. But we should head back if we can. I don't know what to do about..." She trailed off, swallowed and then looked up at him. "You're so hurt."

He held her face in his hands and studied her eyes. Too unfocused. She was in shock and they had to get out of here. She shook underneath his palms as if she was falling apart.

He wouldn't let that happen. He pressed a kiss to her forehead. "Felicity. Hey, I'm here."

She inhaled sharply and let it out on something like a sob even though no tears fell onto her cheeks. "I left my father to die. I shot Ace. You're so hurt." She looked up at him imploringly. "I don't know what to do."

He wanted to scoop her up and carry her away, but he'd be lucky to walk out of this cave on his own. "We just gotta get out of here. You got a message to my brothers. They'll be here. Let's get out of this cave. You just need some fresh air. Come on." He let go of her face and winced at the blood he'd accidentally left there.

His body screamed in pain, but he couldn't let her see it. He took a step and tried to breathe through the shooting pain, but with the next step his leg buckled. He cursed and glared over at Ace, who'd made some gurgle of a sound. Almost a laugh.

He was smiling, but he wasn't moving. The color was draining out of his face and he just lay there, clutching the bleeding wound.

"You're going to die. A slow, painful death," Gage offered.

Ace's smile didn't die. It widened. "And won't that be funny?" Ace said, his voice a rasp. "This little girl with more strength of spirit than you worthless weaklings did what you couldn't."

Gage struggled to his feet with Felicity's help. She didn't speak as she helped him limp toward the cave opening. Gage refused to engage with his father.

Gage made it without falling again, though the opening of the cave required some climbing that had him trying to bite back groans. He wasn't successful, and by the time they were a few feet away from the cave, where he'd left his wallet, Felicity was crying, silently, the tears streaming down her face.

He couldn't stand any more, and he lowered himself to the ground in something more like a crash. She stumbled over to him, presumably to help him, but he just folded her into him.

She let out a sob, and then another, and Gage held her while she cried—while he kept an eye on the mouth of the cave.

He was pretty sure Ace was completely incapacitated, but he wouldn't put it past the man to magically heal himself and come out of that cave whole and ready to fight.

"We should head back," Felicity said, her voice a squeak.

"Not sure I can do that. Let's just wait."

"It's getting dark. They might not see the trail."

Gage held her close despite the pain ricocheting in his body. "They will. They will. Let's just rest up a bit." He felt like he was fading, but he held on to Felicity and she snuggled into him as they waited.

It didn't take too terribly long. The sun was beginning to set when he saw someone in the distance.

"There shouldn't be just one person," Felicity said, fear and concern lacing her tone. She got to her feet. "I only see one figure."

"They might have split up to track."

"I left my father, Gage. He was hurt. But it could be him. He said he didn't kill anyone. Didn't even seem to know about someone being dead."

"But Tuck said he ID'd the body."

"I know. I know. I don't understand any of this, and if Ace dies, we may never know."

"If Ace is dead, Felicity, everything will be okay. That I can promise you."

Chapter Fifteen

Brady reached them first, then was able to radio emergency services with directions. Though she protested, Felicity was whisked away to the hospital just like Ace and Gage.

She was discharged a lot quicker than they were, and then bustled away to the Knight Ranch, where Duke and Rachel and Sarah fluttered all over her before forcing her to go to bed.

Felicity hadn't slept. She tried. She closed her eyes, lay completely still and emptied her mind of *everything*. But in that numbness she couldn't find the release of sleep.

Still, she stayed in bed for a full eight hours. Awake. After that exercise in futility she was up and ready to just…do anything else.

Sarah was at her door before Felicity had even made it across the floor.

"You shouldn't be up."

"I stayed put eight hours," Felicity said, wincing at how much she sounded like a whining child.

Sarah's expression was disapproval, but she didn't push Felicity back to bed, so that was something.

"Is Gage home?"

Sarah nodded. "I just talked to Dev. They released him this morning. Brady took him home and Grandma

Pauline's ordered him to bed. Tuck is staying at the hospital to make sure police are guarding Ace at all times."

"So…" Felicity had to say it, had to accept the strange dichotomy of feelings swirling inside of her. "Ace is alive."

Sarah nodded, a scowl on her face. "He went through surgery. The prognosis isn't great, but the longer he survives, the higher his chance of survival goes. Or so says Brady."

"I want to see Gage."

"Duke—"

"I'm going over there," Felicity said. She didn't know what it would do. She'd be fussed over there just as much as here, but…

She only knew what she had to do.

Sarah convinced her to take a shower first, and Felicity knew that while she was showering, Sarah was likely telling Duke what Felicity planned.

He'd want her to stay put, but she just couldn't.

When Felicity was out of the shower, dressed and ready to go, Sarah was waiting for her in the kitchen.

"I hope you're not missing chores for this."

"Chores can be made up. Besides, I'm just going to drive you over. Then I'll come back and do my work. Duke or I will pick you up later."

"You both know the doctor said I was fine."

Sarah pursed her lips as if considering what to say in response, an odd thing for outspoken Sarah. Eventually she just shook her head. "Come on."

They drove to the Reaves Ranch. Felicity insisted Sarah not walk her to the door. If it had been Rachel or Duke, insisting wouldn't matter, but Sarah understood something about a woman needing to do things on her own two feet. "Felicity?"

Felicity paused before she slipped out of the car. She looked at Sarah, who kept her head straight ahead and her shoulders hunched practically up to her shoulders. Which Felicity knew meant she was going to say something genuine and meaningful.

"I hope you know you don't have to go through this alone."

Since it made her want to cry, especially coming from Sarah, Felicity shook her head. "What I was going through is over," Felicity replied, and got out of the car.

It might have been the biggest lie she'd ever told, but it felt right to say it. She walked across the yard and stepped into Pauline's kitchen without knocking—Pauline considered knocking a grave offense among her friends.

"There's a girl," Pauline greeted, standing in her normal spot by the stove. "You're looking peaked yet."

Felicity forced a smile. "I'm all right. Where's Gage?"

"Upstairs," Brady answered from his seat at the table, a mug of coffee next to his elbow and his phone out in front of him. "Still asleep or should be."

"Can I go see him?"

"Let's give him some time yet," Grandma Pauline said, nudging Felicity into a chair. A plate loaded with a country breakfast appeared in front of her.

Felicity could hear the sounds of little girls playing in the living room, so Gigi and Brianna were here, which meant Liza and Nina were, too.

She stared at the plate, knowing she should eat it for Grandma Pauline's sake. But despite her internal coaxing, she couldn't seem to force herself into actually doing it.

The back door opened and Dev stepped in, stomping his boots on the mat. "Any news?" he asked.

Brady shook his head. "Not since the last."

"Why are they trying to save the SOB?" Dev groused. "Worthless waste of resources."

"Doctors take a vow to heal anybody," Brady lectured.

Felicity felt numb. She didn't know why. Everything she'd done was what she'd had to do. Leave her father to die. Shoot Ace. She'd had to do all those things, and if two monsters ended up dead, didn't that make her a hero?

But she didn't feel good. She didn't even feel terrible. She felt empty, and being here didn't help.

She just wanted to see Gage. Make sure he was all right. If she did that, maybe everything would click back into place somehow. Maybe she wouldn't feel as though she were walking through a cloud.

Dev sat down and ate his breakfast, and Brady poked around on his phone and drank his coffee.

No one tried to fill the silence with conversation. The only sounds were the girls in the other room and Grandma Pauline cleaning up after breakfast.

After typing furiously on his phone, Brady set it down and cleared his throat. "Jamison and Cody are on their way back to rest up for a bit before heading out again."

"Did they find my father?" Felicity asked, even though she knew the answer. Why would they head back out if he'd been found?

"No. Not yet. A few agencies are still looking, though. And they'll keep at it."

"He should be where I left him." They'd told her they hadn't found him when she'd been at the hospital last night, but she'd hoped by morning things would change. Daylight would make finding him so much easier.

Maybe the numbness would go away once she knew

what had happened to him. "I don't understand why he wouldn't be."

"It could be he tried to find a way out, a way to safety. There are a lot of possibilities, Felicity. You said your father didn't kill that woman."

"That's what he said." She had no reason to believe it, no reason not to. What did it matter? Obviously, Ace had set him up one way or another.

"We'll keep looking for him."

Felicity nodded, the knot in her stomach becoming tighter and heavier.

"If you're worried or don't feel safe, you can stay here. We can—"

"I'm not worried. There's no reason to worry." She stood and pushed away from the table with too much force—everyone in the kitchen looked at her and it made her skin crawl with the feel of their stares and assessment. "I need to talk to Gage. That's okay, right?"

Brady's brow furrowed, but he nodded. "I'm sure it'll be fine."

Felicity didn't even wait for instructions. She didn't know which room Gage would be in, but she'd figure it out. Of course, as she stepped into the living room heading for the stairs, Liza and Nina stopped her.

Liza enveloped her in a hug almost immediately. "We're so glad you're okay." She pulled back and studied Felicity's face. "You need to sleep."

Felicity tried to muster a smile. She didn't bother to lie to Liza, who'd always seen through them all with a mother's knowledge. "I tried."

It had been hard to lose Liza when she'd gone back to the Sons to save her half sister. Hard to have her back, too. Felicity hadn't fully accepted Liza's return at first—

she'd still felt a little hurt and betrayed. In the moment, she couldn't access any of that bitterness.

She was just glad someone could see through her. If someone could, maybe she'd make sense of herself, eventually.

"What's wrong with Aunt Felicity?" Brianna asked, forgetting her dolls with Gigi and coming to stand next to her mother. "Did Grandma Pauline make you some magic cocoa?"

Felicity managed a smile and slid a palm over the girl's flyaway blond hair. It was amazing how quickly and easily Brianna had slid into the family. Despite spending her first almost seven years away from Cody and the Wyatts, she'd had no problem accepting he was her father, accepting the crowd of aunts and uncles she now had.

It warmed Felicity some to remember what family and love could do. "No magic cocoa yet. I'm going to go check on Gage first."

"His head got smashed," Gigi said seriously.

"Not exactly," Liza replied on the long-suffering sigh of a frustrated parent. "The Wyatt boys need to learn to choose their words a little bit more wisely around small ears."

"Can we go up and see Uncle Gage?" Brianna asked. "I can give him my magic necklace."

"Uncle Gage has his own magic for now," Nina said. "We call them high-voltage painkillers that make him sleepy. You go on up, Felicity. I'm sure he'll be glad to see you."

Liza linked her arm with Felicity's. "I'll show you which room."

That tone, which meant *I'll drag all of your secrets out of you* had Felicity hesitating. "I can find the room. I—"

"Come on now," Liza said cheerfully, pulling Felicity toward the stairs.

Felicity had no choice. Liza pushed her in front to take the narrow staircase first, and she followed right behind.

"You know, Brady had to sedate him to keep him from charging over to the Knight Ranch and seeing you this morning."

For the first time in something like twelve hours, Felicity felt *something* pierce the numbness. Not much, but a little spread of warmth. "Oh."

"Oh."

"That's what I said. Oh."

"Felicity." Liza stopped her at the top of the stairs. "As someone who's been on the receiving end of a Wyatt man's concern, that was *not* friendly concern."

"What was it then?"

Liza narrowed her eyes and folded her arms across her chest. A very formidable *mom* look. "Care. Serious, love-type care."

"Love." Felicity's face got hot and the word came out like a croak. She didn't particularly want to feel embarrassment, but she supposed it was nice to feel anything. "You're being ridiculous."

"Am I?"

"Yes. He just kissed me is all."

"Is all." Liza took Felicity by the shoulders before she could continue down the hall. "But you've always liked Brady."

"I..." Felicity looked imploringly down the hallway. "I didn't even really *know* Brady, you know? It was just a safe crush."

"There is nothing safe about a Wyatt."

Liza laughed at the horrified look that must have

crossed Felicity's face. Then she pulled Felicity into a hug.

"Babe, you *shot* Ace. There isn't anything safe about you, either. Revel in that a bit." She pulled her back. "You saved Gage's life. But this one? It's still yours. Don't—"

"It isn't like that." Felicity didn't have the words, but she knew what she felt, what Liza was worried about. "It isn't like that. You know... How it feels like no one understands you? Deep down, I think all us foster sisters *could* have understood each other, but we were too self-absorbed to realize that. We weren't mature enough or something to access understanding, even when we had love."

Liza nodded sadly. "It's hard to see past your nose when you're that young, and that wounded."

Felicity nodded. It hurt she hadn't realized it before, but at least she understood it now. "He's the only person to make me recognize other people understand what I was feeling. To suck me out of feeling like I'm the only one who knows what certain things are like. To actually look and see all of me, not some half version. It's not transferring feelings or anything. It's... He just got me. And that matters. Does that make sense?"

Liza nodded, her eyes suspiciously shiny. "All the sense in the world."

GAGE STRUGGLED TO wake up. Something had changed. In the air. Inside of him. Something had changed, and he had to wake up to figure it out.

When he finally managed to blink his eyes open, the room swam. Back at the ranch. Last night at the hospital was a vague blur, but Brady had driven him home this morning, with strict orders to rest and heal.

It didn't sound so bad in the moment, his temples

pounding and his mouth dry as dust. His body ached everywhere. He was pretty sure his hair hurt.

Then a cool hand brushed his forehead, featherlight and soothing. He sighed into it a moment, half convinced it was some guardian angel.

But God knew he didn't have one of those.

He managed to move his head, and there was Felicity, sitting on the floor next to his bed. All he could see of her was her red hair, and the arm she'd put up on his bed to stroke his forehead.

"Am I about to have an illicit dream?"

She tilted her head up, giving him a skeptical if amused look. "I don't think so."

"Darn." He tried to move, but it all hurt too much. "What are you doing sitting on the floor? I can't see you down there."

She got to her feet, moving a few steps down the length of the bed so he could look up at her without having to crane his neck.

It hit him now, safe at home in his childhood bed, in a way it hadn't back in that cave. "You saved my life." He'd been prepared to die, if she was okay, but instead she'd stepped in and saved him.

It awed him straight through. Even if she didn't seem all that pleased.

She looked down at her hands. "People keep saying that. I don't remember much of it, to be honest. It just kind of happened." She shrugged helplessly.

She was too pale. She looked frail, like she had in that cave. Shaken and in shock, though she had a better grip on it now. She still wasn't... Felicity.

"Why don't you come sit down?"

She didn't. She just stood there, staring at him as if

figuring out some great mystery. "Liza said you wanted to come see me. She said you had to be sedated."

He tried to shift in the bed, but just ended up wincing in pain. "Liza exaggerates. God, you smell good. Come here." He patted the bed next to him.

She studied the small spot, lips pursed, then carefully eased a hip next to him on the bed.

"If you wanted to, you know, caress my forehead again, weep a little over my wounds, I wouldn't be opposed."

He managed to get a snort out of her. Not quite a laugh, but an improvement to the seriousness. And even better, she drifted her fingers across his forehead.

They stayed like that for a few minutes, her moving her fingers back and forth on his forehead, a kind of balm even painkillers didn't offer.

And since it was making him relax, and he was too tired, too hurt to fight it, he reached up for a handful of her T-shirt and pulled her down until they were nose to nose. Then he kissed her, with all that softness.

She kissed him back, and something in her shifted or relaxed. Lightened, like a weight lifted. At least it seemed to him.

She pulled back a fraction, green eyes studying him with a kind of meaningfulness that might have sent him running far away if he could. But he couldn't. He was pretty much stuck here, and she made him feel...

She made him feel. Which meant it was time for a joke. "Still like it without all the mortal danger clouding your judgment?"

Her mouth curved, and she didn't back away. "Yeah, it's okay."

"What's wrong, Red?"

She exhaled shakily. "I don't know. They can't find my father."

"If Ace put him up to everything, that's not so bad, is it?"

"I guess." She swallowed, searching his face as if the answers she needed were somewhere in him. "He could be dead out there. Because of me."

"You could have been dead a long time ago because of him. No matter what he did or didn't do in *this* moment. What happened to him, he brought upon himself."

She sat so still, didn't suck in a breath or let one out. It was as if she froze completely. But after a moment or so of that incomprehensible reaction, she gave a small nod. "You should rest," she said, easing away.

"You're looking a bit like you could use some yourself."

"I tried." She lifted her shoulders, then dropped them. "I can't."

He pulled her close and tugged the covers up around them both. "Give it a shot."

And they both slept.

Chapter Sixteen

As the next few days passed, everything was a bustle of activity.

Ace was going back to jail, more charges heaped on him. It would be harder and harder for him to hurt people on the outside. Though she knew no one fully believed he was powerless in jail, it was still safer having him there than in the hospital. And she knew the Wyatts were hoping the attempted murder charges would get him transferred to a federal prison.

She hoped so, too, but while they waited for the bureaucratic tape to be cleared up, Gage was healing. All the Wyatts were still insisting he stay out at the ranch instead of his apartment in town, but everyone knew he wouldn't acquiesce that much longer, nor would he need to.

The police had canceled the warrant for Felicity's arrest, which had been a relief on every level. And, best of all, she'd been cleared to go back to work starting Monday.

Added to that back-to-normal, she seemed to have come out on the other side of this whole ordeal with something almost like a boyfriend, though she hesitated to say that word aloud, especially since they hadn't exactly told anyone about them.

Still, while she stayed at the Knight Ranch and Gage healed at the Reaves Ranch and everything cleared up, they took walks, exchanged kisses and had gone for a picnic lunch yesterday.

The Wyatts treated her like some kind of conquering hero, and somehow shooting Ace, even if she hadn't killed him, seemed to get it through everyone's head that she was not still the shy, stuttering Felicity.

Everything was fine and good. Better than it had been before this whole nightmare started.

Except that her father was missing. And while there was an APB out for him, and he was considered a missing person *and* a person of interest in a murder investigation, there was no trace of Michael Harrison. Even with Jamison and Cody and even Brady spending time searching for him.

It was like being stuck in limbo. Had she killed her father, no matter how inadvertently? Or was he still out there? And would that make him dangerous?

Felicity had no answers, and no one else seemed too concerned about it, so Felicity could only pretend that life was good.

She seemed to be fooling everyone—even Liza—that she was happy as a clam. With Ace out of the hospital and back in jail as of this morning, the Wyatts were darn near jovial. So much so that they were having a big family dinner, complete with the Knights.

It was raucous and good. Felicity had hoped the large group of people in Grandma Pauline's kitchen would make her feel better. Instead, the noise and cheer was just making her feel more like she'd lost her mind somewhere in that cave.

She forced herself to smile, even forced herself to eat, though her stomach roiled and cramped at the idea.

She didn't know why she couldn't let it go. Why she couldn't have some well-deserved celebration like everyone else in the room.

Except, their father was in jail. Hers was mysteriously missing.

He had to be alive or they would have found him. Why would he be alive and hiding? Was it because he thought he'd be blamed for the murder? Was it because he'd lied to her and he *had* murdered someone—his own daughter at that?

Felicity's head pounded with all the what-ifs and emotions they stirred up. When Grandma Pauline brought out dessert, Felicity excused herself, pretending she needed to use the bathroom.

She headed away from the dining room, bypassed the bathroom, and went toward the rarely used front door, instead. There was a rickety old porch swing out there. It didn't get much use, but sometimes Grandma Pauline did her mending there when she didn't have enough people to cook for.

Felicity lowered herself onto it. She needed to get it together, but she didn't know how.

She should be happy. She should be ecstatic. Maybe concern was normal, but…

It was just that she knew the Badlands. She knew what it would have taken to survive, if hurt. He hadn't even been able to stand when she'd left him there.

Left him to die.

Somehow Ace was alive and her father, who probably hadn't killed that woman—her sister—was dead because of her.

Maybe the woman wasn't even her sister. Her father had said he hadn't identified any body. Tucker had looked into that, interviewing the morgue employees. None had been able to confirm or deny that Michael had been the one to identify the body. Might have been, or it might have been someone pretending to be him.

Felicity closed her eyes and let herself rock on the swing. She heard the dogs clatter up onto the porch and she leaned forward to pet them, trying to find some comfort there.

Something had to change. She couldn't go on pretending. Eventually she'd just explode.

But her feelings didn't seem to want to listen to her rational thoughts, and she simply felt stuck in this awful place of...

Guilt.

She turned her head toward the door when she heard it creep open, forced all her heavy thoughts away as Gage stepped out onto the porch.

He didn't seem surprised to see her there, or even confused. "Got room on that swing?"

Felicity managed her fake smile. "Of course."

Gage slid into the seat next to her, draped his arm around her shoulders and gave her a little squeeze. He petted one of the dogs that put its head on Gage's thigh. "That smile's getting a little rough around the edges, Red. You might want to just let it go."

Somehow he made it easy to do. The smile died and she let herself lean into him. She didn't know how to explain what was going on inside of her, but he didn't seem to need her to.

"I know you're worried your father's still out there."

She wrinkled her nose. Okay, he didn't need to see through her *that* easily. "It's fine."

"If it was fine you'd be inside or enjoying even half of this shindig. Do you think he's going to come after you or something?"

Wouldn't that make things easy? Well, maybe not easy, but different. It made more sense than guilt. "Maybe."

"Ah."

She tilted her head up to look at him. "Ah what?"

"It isn't that they haven't found him, and that he may be alive. It's that he might be dead. And you'd have to blame yourself."

She blinked at him, then looked out at the late summer sunset. "Neither are particularly positive potential outcomes, Gage."

"No," he agreed. "But I'm having trouble wrapping my brain around how you're feeling guilty for doing what you had to do to someone who made your childhood a living hell. Who could have made it a lot worse if the state hadn't stepped in."

She was supposed to blame him for that. And maybe he would have been bad enough to kill her back then. She only had hazy memories of living with him. She'd done her best to push them away when she'd been younger, and now they were hard to access.

She could remember pain. Hiding. Fear and confusion, but it was hard to attribute it to a specific face. All those reactions and impulses had come back easily enough when he'd been after her, but it still hadn't been the same.

The monster from her childhood was a faceless one. The man she'd left to die had been flesh and blood. She knew that didn't make sense, that it wasn't *right*, but it was all inside of her anyway.

She inhaled and let the breath out just like her therapist had taught her. "I—I don't like the i-idea I used the Badlands against him." The deep breathing didn't take away the stutter in the moment, but she'd gotten her feelings off her chest.

"Oh, Felicity," he said on a chuckle as he leaned his temple on the top of her head. "Leave it to you."

She slumped in the seat, but his arms stayed tight around her. "It sounds stupid," she muttered.

"No, it sounds like you. And I get it. It isn't like I don't understand. I can stand over here and think you shouldn't feel guilty that you might have left your father to the fate of the Badlands, since I know what he did to you. But I didn't experience what he did to you. Hell, everything we had with Ace is fifty kinds of warped. I wanted him to die, but I'm not sure it would have been any kind of relief if he did."

It was strange to have someone give words to feelings she didn't know how to articulate, but that's just what Gage did. When he did, it helped her find her own words. "I hate feeling this way, but I don't know how to make it stop. Not until I know for sure. Everyone expects me to be happy, and I just—"

"Sweetheart, you don't have to pretend to be happy just because everyone expects you to be. And let's be clear, Dev never expects anyone to be happy."

She managed a true smile at that. "I should be happy."

"If you're not, you should take your time to get right inside." He squeezed her shoulders again. "Give yourself a few breaks. We clawed our way through a rough few days there—it's okay if you're not ready to jump right back into normal life."

"You are *not* my normal life." This, him… She liked it, more than liked. But it didn't feel like her life to have a hot guy want to spend time with her, to slip his arm around her, to kiss her brainless.

"I am now," he said firmly.

It didn't *fix* her problems, but that determined sincerity eased some of the tightness. She'd still have to deal with whatever had happened with her father once they found him, but she'd have someone who understood the complexity of emotions over it...right next to her.

She tilted her head up. "You sound pretty sure about that."

He tapped her chin. "I am."

It was nice. Something and someone to be sure about, so she pressed her lips to his. He kissed her back, but he let her lead. He seemed to know the difference—when she wanted to be swept away, when she needed to be in control of something.

More than that, she understood the same about him. When he was content to sit back, and when he needed to push forward on something.

She sank into that kiss. Pushing forward. She'd been sitting around sulking, basically, but that was over. She had to act. She had to grab her life—*her life*. Why did bad men get to rule her life?

Not anymore.

She pulled away a fraction. "Are you going back to your apartment tonight?"

"Um." He cleared his throat. "I wasn't planning on it."

"Maybe we should." She didn't give him a chance to answer. Instead, she pressed her mouth to his again. When he deepened the kiss, pulled her so close she could scarcely catch a breath, she figured that was a *yes*.

The door creaked open, and though Felicity jumped back, Gage kept his arms around her and gave a withering look to Brady, who was staring at them with bugged-out eyes and a wide-open mouth.

"Help you?" Gage prompted.

"Grandma Pauline told me to—um." Brady cleared his throat. "Well." He rocked back on his heels and shoved his hands in his pockets. He looked embarrassed, which was kind of funny.

Felicity couldn't remember Brady ever looking embarrassed or uncomfortable. She couldn't remember ever seeing him with *any* elevated emotion, and it solidified what she'd been finding with Gage.

Brady was, on the surface, easy and nice. But Gage was... Real. To her. Likely Brady would find someone to be real for, but it wasn't her.

"Grandma Pauline wants to shove us full of dessert," she supplied for him.

Brady did not look directly at them, still sitting on the swing with their arms around each other. "Yeah."

"Ready, Red?" Gage asked, giving her hair a little tug.

She was ready. Ready to stop wallowing and wondering and actually do something. A few somethings, in fact. She got to her feet. "You bet."

GAGE MOVED TO follow Felicity, but Brady stepped in between them, allowing Felicity to move forward and stopping Gage from following.

Gage couldn't say he expected the censure on his brother's face, but seeing it now wasn't such a grand surprise. Brady had a lot of internal rules—not just for himself, but for everyone.

"Looks like I'm staying outside to talk to my twin brother, darlin'. You go on inside."

Felicity gave him a disapproving look. "Don't do that. You don't have to do that." She turned to Brady. "And you don't have to do whatever it is you have it in your head to do."

Brady's expression remained carefully blank. "If you'll excuse us, Felicity."

She rolled her eyes, muttered something about Wyatt men and headed inside.

Gage matched Brady's pose—stuffing his hands in his pockets, rocking back on his heels. He gave a cursory glance at the dogs sitting between them, tails wagging. "Nice night," he offered blandly.

"What exactly are you doing here?"

"Well, Brady, as I've known you to do the same with a handful of pretty women, I'm going to let you spell that one out yourself."

"You shouldn't—"

Gage might have had patience for Brady's lectures if he wasn't grappling with something bigger, broader than he was particularly ready for. "She's not your responsibility. And she certainly doesn't need your protection. Not from me."

"No. She isn't and doesn't. She isn't your responsibility, either."

"And that means what exactly?"

"What *is* this?" Brady gestured helplessly. "Felicity?"

"Yes, Felicity." He didn't have doubts there. Maybe he had some doubts about himself, about how right or ready he was for what he felt, but his feelings were there. And Felicity was too important to allow himself or Brady or anyone to convince him he should run away from them.

"You can't *fool around* with one of the Knight girls. I never thought I'd have to tell you that. Duke only tolerates Cody at this point because he's Brianna's father, not because Duke *approves* of Nina and Cody. I don't think he has any reason to tolerate you fooling around with Felicity."

Gage was about to make a joke, even opened his mouth to do it. But Felicity had told him he didn't have to do *that*, and he'd known what she meant. Not to make a joke to diffuse tension. Not to be *Gage* about it, all things considered.

So, maybe instead of a joke he could just settle in with the truth, no matter how uncomfortable. This was his twin brother after all. They had survived the same things. Side by side. Two sides of the same coin. Sometimes it felt like they spoke a language no one else understood. He loved all his brothers with all that he was, but what he shared with Brady was something unique.

Surely, Brady's censure was concern. Just veiled in that very Brady disapproval. "Well, I guess it's a good thing I'm hardly *fooling around*," Gage ground out.

"What? You're in love with her or something?" Brady snorted, but it died halfway through as his jaw went slack. "Gage…"

"Look—"

"Felicity, of all damn people."

"What's it matter if it's Felicity?"

"You can be impulsive, and this is not the time to be impulsive." Brady jerked a thumb toward the door where Felicity had disappeared. "She's not the girl to be impulsive with."

Gage shook his head. He'd never felt sorry for Brady. Brady was the smartest, the most even-keeled of all six of them. Everyone liked Brady everywhere he went. He was the best of them.

If Brady didn't understand that love was impulsive and just plain inconvenient, but *there* and necessary and impossible to ignore, well, he did feel sorry for Brady and hoped his twin would learn someday what love—inconvenient, out-of-the-blue love—could do.

"She's not a girl, Brady."

"I know that."

"I don't think you get it. Even with everything she

did—including save my life—I don't think you get it. That's okay. You don't need to. This is not a situation where we require your input."

Brady opened his mouth, but Gage shook his head.

"Input. Not. Required."

"Fine," Brady replied tightly. "Then I guess we should get back to dessert." He turned for the door. "And Duke kicking your butt," he muttered under his breath.

Maybe. But it was a risk Gage would take—couldn't help taking. Still, with honesty came the need for more of it.

"Did he have a weapon—just for you?" Gage asked before Brady could go back inside.

Brady paused at the door. When he turned around it was slow and careful, his expression carefully blank. He didn't meet Gage's gaze when he spoke. "He threw knives. To teach me to expect the unexpected."

There was more to that, and Gage wanted to know it all, but they didn't have time to get that deep into it. "Did he tell you *you* were special, so he had to be harder on you?"

Brady let out a long breath, but when he spoke it was detached and rote. "He said I was stupid and worthless, so he'd do what he could to make a man out of me."

Gage could only stare at his brother at first. He'd never imagined. Brady. By far the smartest of them, at least the one who tried the hardest. He could have gone to medical school and become a doctor if Grandma had had access to the money or the understanding of how college worked.

But it made a sick twisted sense, in that Ace way things clicked together. They were twins and Ace had somehow used that against them. Make Brady work harder. Make Gage shrink away from what he was.

Brady shrugged, an out-of-character, impatient gesture for him. "We don't talk about this. What's the point?"

"I would have said there wasn't one just last week, but now I think we should. All of us. It would make us stronger against him. When you can... When you can let it go and someone understands, it changes something, Brady. And we all understand."

Brady met his gaze then, something wry in his expression. "Yeah, maybe, but good luck getting through to Dev on that score."

"We'll work on it." Gage was certain they needed to. "And there's something else we need to work on. I want you to help me find Felicity's father. She can't rest until he's found one way or another."

"We're looking."

"I don't mean casually or leaving it up to Pennington County. I mean you and me. Really looking."

"You aren't up for it yet." Brady tapped his temple. "That concussion was serious, Gage. The rest will heal no problem, but you don't want to take chances with your brain."

"Okay, so I'll take a few days. But..."

Brady sighed heavily. "She needs closure. And you're going to make sure she gets it."

"Damn straight." She'd saved his life. He loved her, as uncomfortable as he was with *that*. He owed her something. He'd give her this. Whatever it took.

Chapter Seventeen

By the time they managed to convince everyone that Gage was well enough to spend the night on his own, and that she would be fine going back to her cabin in the park alone—though neither precisely planned on being alone—Felicity was wound tighter than a drum.

But it was good to feel something—even anxiety and a weird giddiness. She walked outside with Gage, Grandma Pauline and Brady still in the kitchen grumbling about that fool boy and his hard head.

Most of her family had already headed back to the ranch, and she'd need to have Gage drop her off so she could get her car. She couldn't very well tell anyone Gage drove her back to her cabin. It wouldn't make sense.

"You're going to have to drive me over to my car. Otherwise, everyone is going to figure out where I went."

"I don't think we were fooling Brady any. He very clearly knows."

"So does Liza," Felicity murmured, tilting her head up and staring at the giant spread of stars above. Liza, Jamison, Gigi, Cody, Nina and Brianna had all headed back to Bonesteel earlier, but Felicity had to wonder how long Liza would keep what Felicity had told her a few days ago to herself.

"So…" Gage took her hand in his as they walked to his truck.

She looked down at their joined hands, marveled at how quickly that just felt right. But with rightness meant she owed him the truth. "I'm not ready for Duke to know."

"Ah."

"It's just… All those years ago? Everything with Nina disappearing on the heels of losing Eva *and* Liza really messed him up, and we both know no matter how much he loves Brianna, he hasn't quite forgiven Cody for being part of the reason Nina stayed away with her so long. I don't want to hurt him." She owed Duke so much more than she'd ever be able to repay, and that seemed reinforced by seeing her biological father again.

"I don't think you being happy would hurt him, Felicity. Even if he shot daggers in my direction for a while."

"Maybe." Maybe Gage was right, but… "I need to do a few things on my own, *really* on my own, right now."

"You do understand that what you're suggesting by coming home with me is not something you do on your own?"

She swatted his arm, unable to contain the laugh. "Yes, I'm aware."

He took her by the shoulders, and rubbed his hands up and down her arms. "Are you sure you want to do this? Now."

She didn't hesitate, because Gage was the only thing that made sense right now. If she went after what made sense, then she'd find herself on even ground again. "Yes. I'm sure."

"Brady seems to think I'm being impulsive, and that I shouldn't be…with you."

"Well, it's a good thing Brady doesn't get a say." She

saw some hesitation in him, and she knew it wasn't his own. It had been put there—that he should be careful, that she couldn't handle it.

She wouldn't let anyone push her back to that place where people thought she needed to be protected or handled with kid gloves just because she was shy or stuttered or had been abused as a child. No. "I know what I feel when you kiss me, Gage. And I know how much it means that you understand me. And I understand you. I think we both know how special that is."

He stared at her for a long time, then he nodded. "Yeah. Listen, I've got an idea. Trust me?"

She nodded.

"Get in the truck."

They both climbed into Gage's truck, and Felicity decided to relax, enjoy the nighttime drive over the short, rolling hills of the Reaves Ranch. She had a spiritual connection to the Badlands that existed for some unknown reason deep inside, but she'd been raised and loved on these rolling grasslands of the two ranches that had been her childhood. If the Badlands were her soul, the ranch lands southeast of there were her heart.

He drove out, deep into the heart of the ranch. All the way through the pasture, to the tree line that ran along what had once been a creek but rarely got a trickle these days. The Knight land was on the other side of the creek bed.

It was so distant people rarely came out here unless a cow was missing. He stopped between the old creek and the pasture fence. He turned off the ignition and made a broad gesture.

Felicity's eyes widened. "Outside?" She couldn't school the squeak out of her voice.

"Seems...right."

It did. She'd rather be out here than anywhere else, and it was coming to be that she wanted to be with him more than anyone else—even herself, a rare thought for an introvert like her.

He slid out of the truck and grabbed a blanket from the back seat, and she followed. The night was warm, though the breeze was cool. The world smelled like summer— grass and wild. And though it was very much night, sunshine lingered in the air.

He spread out the blanket, looking something like a ghost in the silvery moonlight. But he was no ghost. No apparition. He wasn't even a dream. Gage Wyatt was very real, and all hers.

Not what she'd planned, certainly. Not at all what she'd expected. And yet perfectly right, down to this. Understanding her enough to give her this.

The fog she'd been muddling through these past few days was gone, and while she still had fears and concerns and complex emotions over what had transpired, this was simple. And true.

She rose to her toes and kissed him. The stars and moon shone, the breeze slid over them, and Gage kissed her until there was only him—her own universe for the having.

He laid her out on the blanket, covered her. There was no room for nerves—why would there be? Unlike everything else in her life, she was sure of this, sure of him.

Because he undressed her with reverence, whispered all sorts of wonderful things against her skin. He made her feel beautiful and whole and strong.

She'd always wanted to feel strong, and it wasn't that he was *giving* her strength—it was that he was showing her all the ways it already existed. And now that she saw, now that she knew, what couldn't she do?

She kissed him, touched him—tracing his bandages and the wounds Ace had marked on him with her fingers, with her mouth. She tried to imbue some sort of healing property to the touches, but when she opened herself to him, she knew what true healing was.

Acceptance. Understanding. Finding where you belonged. Building hope together.

She let herself surrender completely to pleasure and that hope, gave herself over to the wave of it. The immensity of it.

She'd been through too much for that to scare her—how much she felt, how much she wanted. There was no room for fear when he moved inside her, with her, together until a sparkling, all-encompassing pleasure pulsed through her.

He gathered her up close, wrapping them in the blanket, the stars vibrant and all but vibrating in their velvet South Dakota sky.

She snuggled into Gage, breathed the mix of him and outside. This had been the first step toward her future.

She knew what the next was, though she didn't want to think about it in the happy, sated afterglow.

Unfortunately, Gage wasn't going to like that one.

She'd ignore it for now, and she wouldn't tell him yet.

There were some things you had to do alone, no matter how nice it felt to be together.

GAGE HAD DRIVEN her back to her car so she could follow him to his apartment if only because she'd been fretful over his head wound.

He wasn't sure what sleeping out under the stars would do to make it worse, but he hated to see all that worry on her shoulders because of him. Even if he didn't mind a little fretting on her part, like she might feel some fraction of the care blooming inside of him.

Hell, it wasn't care, it was love. He kept wanting to deny it, but how could he when her red hair was spread out over his pillowcase? Her face was slack in sleep, one arm tucked under her pillow and one pressed up against his.

Felicity had spent the night in his bed, snuggled up to him like she belonged there. It felt like she did. It felt like *she* thought it did.

Still there was a sheen of anxiety to it. Whether it was her missing father, the ever-present threat of Ace— no matter how many high-security prisons they put him into—or Gage's own nerves at the idea of loving someone so...

Perfect wasn't the right word. He'd be afraid to touch perfect, but she was perfect for him somehow. Matched.

He'd never thought he'd be in love—especially not with someone who'd been hung up on his brother not all that long ago. He'd never thought he'd find himself dreaming of a particular kind of future that wasn't: be a cop, have fun, protect his family from Ace.

He touched the bandage on his head. He was still achy and knew he wouldn't be cleared to work for a while yet. Maybe he could be doing desk hours by the end of the week, but Gage hardly looked forward to that.

So, he wouldn't look forward. He'd enjoy his present.

Felicity moved, yawning and stretching as she rolled into him. Her eyes blinked open, that dark, intoxicating green. Her mouth curved. "Morning," she murmured sleepily.

"Morning," he replied, his voice rusty—and not from sleep.

She pressed a kiss to one of the scratches on his arm.

She didn't fuss over the marks Ace had put on him. Instead, she treated them with a kind of reverence that made him feel vulnerable, but not in that fearful way he had as a child. This was something else. Not weakness, not fear, but hope and love, he supposed.

"I need to get up and get going," she said, yawning again as her eyes seemed to focus and engage.

He had no doubt Felicity Harrison was a morning person.

"What's the rush?"

"I want to give my cabin a good clean, and I need to get my uniforms ready for tomorrow." She gave him a quick peck and slid out of bed. She grabbed her T-shirt from the floor and slid it over her head.

A pity.

She shook out her sleep-and-sex-rumpled hair and then began to separate it into sections. It was mesmerizing, but his brain kicked into gear over what she'd just said.

"Are you sure you should be out there all alone?"

She pushed out a breath and began to braid her hair. "No. But I think I have to. I can't live scared Ace might get through again and…" She paused twisting the band around the end of her braid and looked at him, a heartbreaking desolation in her gaze. "I haven't said this to anyone, but I don't think my father could have survived, Gage. I really think he has to be dead. Which means they might never find him. Not if animals got to him. It's so big, so vast, and I just have to live with the uncertainty I guess, but I'm mostly certain."

It killed him that she blamed herself, but he knew how sneaky and hard to shake blame could be. He got out of bed, didn't bother with his shirt and just pulled his boxers on. "Okay, but I want you to take one of those button things Cody makes. The emergency call. You shouldn't be out there without cell service. Regardless."

She frowned at him as he crossed to her. "I'll have my radio when I'm on duty."

"I'm talking when you're off duty, babe. It's a drive from here to there."

She wrinkled her nose and finished with her hair. "I do not like *babe*."

"Sweetheart, honey, darlin'." He tugged the tight braid. "Red."

Her mouth curved. "Red's okay."

And it was that, her standing there in a rumpled T-shirt, her hair smoothly braided and her smile still sleepy that did it, completely and irrevocably. "I love you, Felicity." He hadn't meant to say it out loud, or if he had, he hadn't thought it through. Things were different for her. He'd been halfway in love with her for something like two years, and she'd been mooning over his twin brother, no matter the reasons. "You should take some time with that. I've had longer to think about it."

She stared up at him as if she'd frozen when he'd said those words. She blinked once but, other than that, didn't move. But he knew she was thinking, taking it in, in that rational way of hers. "B-but l-love doesn't really have to do with thinking," she said thoughtfully, eyebrows knitting together. "Accepting it does, I guess, but love is there, either way."

"I don't know."

"You wouldn't have *chosen* to love me, Gage."

"Why not? You're beautiful and sweet and smart, and kind of a badass, if you haven't noticed."

She nearly grinned at that. "You're all of those things, too, you know." She inhaled deeply, keeping her gaze steady on his. Her hands curled around his forearms, and he was almost certain she was about to let him down gently.

"I love you, too," she said, instead. "Maybe I need to think some about what to do with that, but I feel it, either way."

He had to clear his throat to speak. "Well, same page then, Red."

She nodded, still staring up at him. "You know, when I got that first summer internship at the National Park Service, I didn't let myself really dream about someday getting the full-time position here at home. When I finally got it, I told myself I'd believe that my dreams could come true if I worked really hard."

"I think you ended up with the wrong twin," he half joked.

She shook her head. "No. Brady was a nice enough placeholder, but I didn't want *him*. I wanted someone kind and good who understood me and made me feel like… this. That was never him, not really. But it's been you."

"Well. Hell."

She grinned up at him, brushed a kiss over his mouth. "Come on, I'll make you some breakfast before I go."

He slid his arms around her waist, pulling her close, nuzzling into her hair. "I have some different ideas."

She leaned into him for a second, then gave him a little push. "I'm hungry." She laughed, sounding a bit bewildered, as if she couldn't quite believe this was all happening. "But maybe after."

Chapter Eighteen

It took a few days to work out, especially without any of the Wyatt boys being tipped off. They wouldn't let her do this thing, and she had to do it.

It required a secrecy she wasn't very good at, and then waiting for her own day off to align with when she could accomplish the task.

Getting back to work had been good. It kept her mind busy, and though she struggled to forget everything that had happened at her cabin or on the trails, it was better to struggle than to avoid.

Routines were good. Having a plan was better.

Now she was going to enact it. She felt sick and nervous leading up to it but it had to be done. When it was over, maybe she would tell Gage, even if it made him mad.

She couldn't tell him before. He'd stop her, and she would not be stopped on this.

Luckily, Gage was back at work, though he was relegated to desk duty until he had his checkup next week. He'd grumbled about it all morning. Felicity had let him grumble, made him breakfast, then sent him on his way.

It was a bit like... Well, she didn't like to think about it too deeply, but waking up with him, whether at his apartment or her cabin, felt a bit like living together.

She shook her head as she got out of her car. Thoughts for another time. Today wasn't about Gage or how good she felt there. It was about closing the book on the unfinished chapter that still weighed on her, even if Gage allowed her to take a considerable amount of that weight off at any given time.

She tried not to think too hard about Gage as she pulled into the jail parking lot. He would hate this. He wouldn't understand it, and he was going to be so ticked off when he found out.

He had no one to blame but himself, though. He'd been the one to tell her she didn't have to be happy just because everyone expected her to be. He'd been the one to help her find the courage to do this.

He'd hate that even more.

Now she was here, and she was ready. She'd close the door on this, if she could, and then her life wouldn't feel like it was in an awful limbo.

Felicity stepped into the jail, followed the instructions to be a visitor, and then was taken into a room with plexiglass partitions. She took a seat and waited. She breathed through her nerves and focused on portraying a calm, unflappable exterior.

It didn't matter if she was a riot of nerves inside. If Ace didn't see it, it wouldn't matter at all.

It didn't take long for Ace to be escorted to the other side of the glass. He was handcuffed and in a prison uniform. He looked haggard and pale, his face more hollow than lean in that dangerous predator type of way. He wasn't having the best recovery from his gunshot wound here in jail.

Good.

When their gazes met, he smiled just like he had back

at her cabin, as if he had all the control and power in the world.

She wouldn't let that rattle her. She had the power now. She kept her expression neutral and her posture as relaxed as she could muster. "Hello, Ace."

"Felicity Harrison. This *is* a surprise. My would-be murderer wants to speak to me. I could hardly resist my curiosity."

"You mean the opportunity to try to mess with my mind?"

Ace's smile didn't dim. If anything it deepened so that he looked normal. Like a kind man happy to see someone. Not even a prisoner happy to have a visitor to talk to, but like a man at a family Christmas dinner.

The fact it could look real was far more chilling than him calling her his would-be murderer.

"Care to take a guess as to why I'm here?" she asked. She'd practiced this. Perfected what she would say, how she would broach the topic. Being too direct would give him a kind of ammunition. She didn't know what Ace could still do to her, especially with his impending move to a federal facility, but she wouldn't take any chances.

"So many reasons. But I note you're alone, which means not one of my sons, and probably not one of your little Knights, knows you're here. They wouldn't let you do this alone."

"I'm not afraid of doing anything alone." It wasn't totally true. She'd told Cecilia. Just in case something happened, though she couldn't think of anything that would. Still, she'd realized that someone needed to know, and Cecilia was the only one who'd be true to her word not to tell anyone unless she needed to.

Ace didn't need to know that. Let him think she was

alone. Let him know she could handle it. "I shot you without anyone's help."

"Good. That's good." Ace leaned back and chuckled. "I like you, Felicity. I do." His gaze sharpened. "You don't like that, though. Gage wouldn't be too keen on me liking you, would he?"

Her blood ran cold, but she kept her mouth curved and forced a little laugh out herself. "Yeah, he's that gullible. He'd drop me because *you* said you liked me. And I'm that pathetic, I came here to talk to you about your son."

"Fancy yourself a strong woman now?" Ace's smile got a sharp quality that no one would be fooled into thinking was kind. "You shot me, Felicity. But I'm still here."

"Yeah. Looking a little rough around the edges, though." Felicity leaned forward, trying for his fake kind smile. "Not sure how federal prison is going to agree with you, but I can't wait to find out."

"I can't wait to drag you into a long, painful trial. You and Gage. It'll be a real joy. To taint your lives for years. To always be the dark cloud over your future. To twist and bend the law to my will until I'm walking free again. And when I am—"

It sent a cold shudder through her, but she kept her expression neutral and shoulders relaxed. "The law can be tricky, it's true, and it fails a lot of people."

"When I'm free—"

"But we won't let it fail you. Trust me on that."

Ace yawned, gave an exaggerated stretch. He pushed away from the table in front of him. "Well, if that's all."

She knew she shouldn't blurt it out, but he was standing up. She should let him go. Come back another time. Play his little game, because if she didn't, he'd end up playing her.

But she had to know. She had to.

"My father didn't know about the dead woman."

Ace stood there, smiling like he'd just been crowned the King of England.

Felicity had to swallow at the bile rising in her throat. She'd lost. Already. She should give in and leave.

But she had to know. Mind games or not, she had to know.

Ace sat back down and leaned forward. He clasped his hands together on the little table in front of him and pretended to look thoughtful. "Did you two end up having a little chat?"

She refused to answer.

"Was it tearful? Did your heart just swell right up, being reunited with your daddy?"

She couldn't affect nonchalance, but she could keep her mouth shut, and she did, even if she looked at him with a black fury coating her insides.

"The state never should have taken you away. Is that what you'd like to think? He was misunderstood. It was just the once. He really, truly loves you deep down underneath all his problems."

It stung because once upon a time that *had* been her fantasy. That there'd been a mistake. That her memories were made up. The way Ace said it made it seem so possible.

But she remembered now. That hike in the Badlands, hiding from her father, it had reminded her of a truth she'd known and hadn't wanted.

She knew what her father was.

She just had to know for sure what he'd done. "He said you forced him to help you. He didn't know about the murder. He didn't know what I was talking about."

Ace sat back into his chair, lounged really, rangy and feral even with the sick pallor of his skin.

She'd shot this man and he still held the cards.

"So, you've come in search of the truth," Ace said thoughtfully. "Without my son."

"It's my truth." He wouldn't use it against her. She wouldn't let him.

"He won't see it that way. You and I both know that. Nothing is yours once you're involved with a Wyatt. They fancy themselves better than me, but they're the same. Their name means everything. Their vengeance is all that matters. Every woman they've ever brought into the circle gets swept right up into the Wyatt drama—don't they? Liza and Nina, your *sisters*, banished because of your boyfriend's brothers."

It wasn't true, but he voiced it so reasonably. Because he believed it. In his warped brain, that was true, and love and duty had nothing to do with it.

Because he had no love, and no duty other than his own evil. It would be sad if he wasn't such a monster.

"My father came to visit you here," Felicity said, keeping her voice bland and steady. She would get to the bottom of things, no matter Ace's tangents. "Before you two showed up at my cabin to enact your little failure. You have a connection."

Ace inclined his head. "He did come. He did indeed. Came to visit. We had a good chat about some things. Then, as fate would have it, Michael was the one who helped me out when the tornado, my divine intervention, set me free. Michael has been a good friend."

"If the tornado was divine intervention, what was that bullet I put in you?" she asked, and didn't try to smile or laugh. She let the disgust—and her win over him— show all over her face.

Ace smiled. "The divine requires payment. Suffering. I didn't become what I am until I had been abandoned, until I suffered and nearly died. This is only my second coming, Felicity. I hope you're prepared."

She shook her head. He struck fear in her and she hadn't come here to be brainwashed. To be made afraid. She'd come here for answers, and that had been stupid. Ace would never give her real answers. Which made her more tired than afraid.

"You know what? Never mind." She had started to get up, when Ace spoke. Quickly and hurriedly as if, for once, desperate.

"Two possibilities, right, Felicity? One, your father was the bumbling idiot he portrayed himself to be. I used his weakness and stupidity to get to you. He didn't murder his own daughter. It was all me and I framed you both, or at least the people who work for me did. It's a nice story. I know it's one you'd like to believe. But I think you know... I think you know there's another story. Another truth."

She should walk away. He was lying. He had to be lying.

"Once upon a time a man came to visit me. I owed him a favor, from a long time ago. Your father wasn't so much *in* the Sons as he was an associate, one who'd saved me from a particularly bad run-in once. I knew your mother."

She made a sound. Couldn't help it. She knew nothing about her mother, except that she had died. But Ace, this monster, had known her.

"I knew your mother very well."

She almost retched right there.

"But I digress. Your father, excuse me, this *man*, came to see me in jail a few weeks ago. He'd been holding out asking for the favor returned until he really needed it. Apparently, he'd accidentally, or so he said, killed his daughter. He needed an alibi. A sure thing so it never came back to him—murder would certainly put him in jail for the rest of his life. He wanted me to use my Sons influence to make sure that didn't happen."

Felicity absorbed his words. She didn't want the second story to be true, and maybe it was a lie. Ace was nothing if not a liar.

But it made more sense. Unfortunately, the dead body in this scenario, and her connection to Felicity and Michael, made the most sense out of anything.

"Well, I left him to die," Felicity said, knowing her voice wasn't as strong as it had been. "So I suppose it doesn't matter."

"Nightmares never die, little girl. I'm living proof of that. Your father played the fool well, but he was no fool. The truth is, I don't know the truth. I know I didn't kill that girl. Whether she was your sister or not, I don't know. Michael and my resources collaborated to try and make it look like you did it, sure, but you deserved a slap back after getting involved in Wyatt business. As for the murder itself." He held up his hands. "All I know is it didn't have a thing to do with me. So, I guess you'll have to have a conversation with him."

Ace grinned when Felicity said nothing. "Oh, I forgot. He's missing. Very convenient."

"He's dead," Felicity said flatly. She believed that. She did.

Or had. Until talking to Ace.

"That'd be easy, wouldn't it?"

Felicity knew those words would haunt her, and that was her cue to leave. Maybe she didn't have answers, but she'd gotten what she'd come for.

Her father was no hapless pawn of Ace's. But he was dead. Had to be.

GAGE CHUGGED THE bottle of water he'd pulled out of his pack. He wouldn't admit to Brady his head was pounding and that he wished they'd quit two miles ago. Not when he'd been the one to insist on another two miles.

The search for Michael Harrison was fruitless. Worst of it was, he hadn't told Felicity that's what he'd planned on doing today. He didn't want her getting her hopes up. He'd made a good choice there. This was utterly useless.

"Need a break?" Brady asked mildly.

"Nah. We can head back. Rest up. Try again tomorrow."

"I have to sleep sometime. Some of us aren't on desk duty. And you're not coming out here alone. Not until that doctor clears you."

Gage wouldn't be stupid on this, though it was tempting. "I'll see if Tuck or Cody can come with me."

"Be sure that you do. That is, if you make it through the hike back."

"He's got to be out here somewhere," Gage said, using his sleeve to wipe the sweat off his forehead. "Even if he's dead...he didn't just evaporate."

"You've got the winds, animals, caves. Plenty of people disappear without a trace in plenty of places. Especially if they're dead."

"You've always been Mr. Positivity."

"Reality isn't often very positive. You know that, Gage."

Gage followed Brady's path back, scanning the area around them. Not a hint of Michael Harrison where Felicity had left him—or in the miles around where she'd left him, and the worst part was Brady was exactly right.

There were a lot of ways to disappear—dead or alive.

Gage just wanted to give Felicity some piece of closure. It ate at him that he might not ever be able to and that it would weigh on her. Forever.

Gage sighed. Life sucked sometimes. He'd accepted that a long time ago. It was harder to accept for the people you loved, he was coming to find. Growing up, there'd been nothing to do about Ace. Even now there was only so much to be done. He was who he was and his sons were what they were. There was no option of shielding or protecting his brothers—that ship had sailed probably before Gage and Brady had been born.

But finding Michael for Felicity felt doable, and the fact he couldn't do it might drive him crazy.

He could tell when he and Brady got into cell range because both their phones started sounding notifications like crazy.

"That can't be good," Brady said grimly.

Gage pulled his phone out. Ten texts. Five missed calls. Three voice mails. "No. Not good." He opened the texts, read them. Listened to his messages, all variations of the same theme: call me.

What he couldn't figure out was why they were all from Cecilia. She was a tribal police officer on the rez, and spent way more time there than out at the ranch. Of all the Knight girls, Gage had the least to do with her on a personal level, though sometimes their lives intersected on a professional one.

Maybe it was that. Maybe it was something to do with one of her cases on the rez. Relief coursed through him at the solid explanation. "I'll call her, assuming all your messages are from Cecilia."

"Yeah."

He hit Call Back and Cecilia picked up before the first ring had finished sounding. "Gage."

"Hey, Cecilia, what's up?"

"Don't be mad." She sounded breathless and worried, which was the antithesis of Cecilia's usual demeanor—which was either cool as a cucumber or hotheaded as all get-out. Cecilia had no in-between.

His nerves were humming. "Gee, that's a good way to ensure that I'm going to be really, really mad."

"Felicity's missing."

Gage went cold, despite the oppressive heat of the day. "What?"

"She went to visit Ace. I—"

He gripped the phone so hard it was a wonder it didn't crumble. "She did *what*?"

"I can't get it out if you don't listen to me. She went to visit him in jail. That all went fine. But after? She was supposed to call and check in. She didn't. I can't get ahold of her. I already called Tuck, and Jamison for that matter. We've checked in with the jail, and they're working to figure out what happened between leaving the jail and…not coming home. We're handling it, but I knew you'd want to know."

"You're handling it?" He wanted to rage and punch something, but all he could do was grip the phone. "It's hardly handled if she's missing."

"Gage."

"You knew about this. You knew and—"

"I don't have time for you to berate me. She needed to do this," Cecilia snapped. "Alone. And she knew I was the only one who wouldn't—"

"Keep her safe?" Gage replied.

There was an intake of breath and the call ended. Gage swore, but he didn't stop moving. They still had a good quarter of a mile before they got to Brady's truck.

"Well, I heard all that," Brady said grimly, following after Gage. "Felicity's probably back at her cabin. Upset.

Visits with Ace are upsetting. She forgot to check in. Took a shower, maybe."

Gage kept walking at the breakneck pace he'd set for himself. "She wouldn't. She just wouldn't." If she told someone, she'd be sure to say she was all right.

Why did she tell Cecilia?

"We should check," Brady insisted.

He had no patience for his brother's calm reason. "No time."

"Don't you think we should be sure before we go anywhere with guns blazing?"

Gage wanted to whirl on his brother and pound some sense into him, but there was no time. Instead, he broke into a jog, no matter how it made his head ache or his stomach roil. "What happened to Nina and Cody after their visit to Ace? They about got themselves killed, but they had each other. She's alone. And she put a bullet in Ace, which means he won't rest…"

Gage swore again. He hadn't fully grasped how much of a target Felicity had made of herself.

All because of him.

He reached the truck and held out his hands for the keys.

Brady had jogged after him, but he stopped resolutely out of reach. "I think I should drive."

"Don't fight me on this."

Brady hesitated, then handed him the keys. "Where are we going?"

"The jail."

Brady winced. "I was afraid of that." But he got in the truck and didn't lodge one complaint when Gage drove like a bat out of hell. Luckily, they'd already been out in Pennington County rather than back at the ranch, where it would take way longer to get to the jail.

Gage parked haphazardly, taking up two spots. He saw Brady eyeing the bad parking job. Gage tossed him the keys. "Here. Fix it. I want to do this alone."

"What exactly?"

"I'll kill him this time. No qualm."

Brady put his hand on Gage's shoulder. "In the jail? Gage. Take a minute. You have to think before you act. Going in there with murder on the brain is a recipe for a whole new disaster we most certainly don't have time for."

Gage shrugged off Brady's hand. "I'll think once we know where she is."

"We know she isn't *here*."

But Ace had to know where she was. What had happened. Why the hell had she thought to do this on her own? Why had Cecilia *let* her?

She should have told him, and he couldn't deal with the hurt of that when she was God knew where. Gage strode forward, about to wrench open the front door of the jail entrance, badge at the ready, but Tucker stepped out of the door first.

He came up short, looked from Gage to Brady. "Well. You got here fast."

Gage only growled.

Tucker held up his hands. "Listen, we've got a few leads. Her car is still in the lot, so wherever she went, it was with someone else."

"How is Ace doing this?" Brady asked, too much bafflement and not enough fury.

Gage wanted to whirl on him, rage at someone, but it was only the impotent terror building inside of him. He couldn't let it win because it was clouding all rational thought.

"He's not," Tucker said grimly. "At least, it seems really unlikely. The security footage seems to point to a van. No windows. No plates. We've got an APB out."

"And that's not Ace because?"

"Because…" Tucker sighed. "We went over the past few days of security footage, and that van was here every day for the past four, only during visiting hours. No one ever got out. The only time the van moved before the end of visiting hours was today. It moves after Felicity enters the jail. We caught a quick glimpse of the driver. It's not… It's not a clear shot, and there's room for interpretation, but I'm about sixty percent sure the driver is Michael Harrison."

Chapter Nineteen

Felicity had spent the first ten minutes trapped in the back of a van berating herself for her stupidity. She'd been so shaken when she'd walked out of the jail that she'd turned to the sound of her name rather than run from it.

She'd been pushed into the back of the vehicle before she'd had a chance to get her footing. Before she'd had a chance to fight or run or scream—the doors had closed on her.

She was an utterly worthless fool.

The back of the van was completely black. She'd spent most of the drive feeling around, trying to find a handle or some way to get the door open. She could tell the car was going fast because every time it turned she'd tumble around like loose change.

If she could find a door, and open it, she would jump out regardless. Even if he were driving 100 miles per hour. Anything was better than being at her father's mercy.

He was alive. Alive and well from the looks of it. He certainly hadn't been trapped or lost in the Badlands for the past few days.

The van came to an abrupt stop and she pitched forward, painfully banging her elbow and hip against who knew what.

She didn't let the jarring pain stop her from hurrying back to her feet, crouched and ready. He'd have to open the doors, and he hadn't tied her up or hurt her. Maybe he'd taken her somewhere terrible. Maybe he had a gun.

But she wouldn't go down like she had in that parking lot. Stupid and off guard. No. Absolutely not.

She didn't let herself think about how he'd survived or why he'd come for her. It didn't matter.

She'd fight him no matter what.

He'd taken her purse, and that stung, because she'd been dumb enough to put Cody's little button in there. When Cody had given it to her, he'd told her to wear it on her person. She had, every day, but she hadn't wanted questions about it when she'd been searched at the jail, so she'd put it in her purse before heading inside.

Everything that was happening was because of stupid choices she'd made out of arrogance or ignorance or something. Desperation? Why couldn't she have left it all alone? For her own stupid, pointless conscience.

That line of thought did nothing to help her. She wouldn't let it be the end of her life. She had to be smart. She had to fight her way out of this.

Beating herself up could—and *would*—come later.

The van was still stopped, so she remained crouched in a fighting position. But when the doors opened, the light was blinding and she winced away from it out of instinct.

Nothing happened as she adjusted to the light. She clenched her fists and blinked as her father came into focus.

He stood outside the van looking grim. "Never could leave well enough alone. You should have let it go, Felicity. Gone back to your life. But you just had to keep poking."

She stayed back in the van, fists clenched as she got

used to the light pouring in. "You're the one who dragged me into this. You killed her, and you had me framed."

He sighed. "Ace going to blame it all on me? Typical. But he's in jail and I'm not."

"You killed her," Felicity repeated. She would get his confirmation—if she had been stupid enough to be caught here, she would get his confirmation.

"Yeah, I did. But she had it coming. Did you believe me, Felicity? I ain't killed no one. Oh, I'm so hurt. Don't leave me here to die." He scoffed, not even pleased with himself. Just disgusted. "I'll give you credit for leaving me there to die, but you should have finished off the job if you really wanted me dead."

It dawned on her how much he'd fooled her. Not just about the murder, but about everything. "You weren't hurt."

"Man, you're dumb. Come on out now." He gestured her forward.

The fact he expected her to listen to his directive made it seem like he, in fact, was the dumb one. She wasn't about to scuttle out there to die just because he told her to.

She stayed where she was, crouched and ready.

"Going to make this harder on yourself." He groaned like an inconvenienced teenager. "Fine. But I warn you, I like a struggle. You won't."

"You'll have to drag me out of here, kicking and screaming," she replied, ready to do whatever it took. He would physically overpower her, no doubt, but she wouldn't make it easy.

He shrugged. "No problem there." He leaned forward, his big body and long arms giving him the reach he needed. She kicked, scratched and bit, but it was no use. He got ahold of her arm and dragged her out. If she landed any blows, he didn't so much as grunt. He jerked her arm so hard and violently she wasn't altogether sure her arm was still in the socket.

Pain radiated through her and for a moment she was too bowled over by it to fight. He dropped her onto the ground, a patch of gravel in front of a run-down trailer.

She tried to breathe through the pain, tried to stand. She managed to get to her knees. He stood over her and reached a hand back, as if he expected her to cower and take the blow.

No. She wasn't a little girl anymore.

She used everything she had to push forward and crash into his knees. Apparently, it was enough of a surprise to knock him backward, and he tripped over the edge of the gravel, sprawling onto his back with a grunt.

She stumbled on top of him. He immediately fought her off, trying to pin her to the ground. He was bigger, but she was faster. She was slithering away when he caught her by the ankle and dragged her back across the hard, painful gravel.

She kicked out, tried to shake off his grasp. He kept pulling her toward the trailer and she knew she couldn't wind up inside. She watched his legs move, timed them and then managed to kick her heel out to strike his ankle. He tripped and lost his grip on her.

She jumped up, knowing she could outrun him. She had to. But before she'd made it three strides, he grabbed her by the shirt.

She'd never grappled with anyone before, let alone someone nearly twice her size, but she didn't let that stop her. She knew the important thing was getting in as many blows as possible. So she punched and kicked and kneed, while his breath wheezed out.

She gave him a nasty blow to the nose, which had blood spurting out. Triumph whirred through her, but it was only a second before his meaty fist connected with the side of her face, sending her sprawling.

Her vision blurred, and her mind seemed to echo in on itself.

Get to your feet. Get to your feet. She could feel her mind telling her to do it, but her limbs took forever to cooperate.

She struggled to her feet again—and she would keep doing so. No matter how many times he knocked her down or got in her way—she would fight.

Fight!

Dizzy and bleeding, pain radiating through her, she stood there ready to fight him off again. There was nowhere to run behind her. It was all rock wall and trailer. But there had to be a way to get past him.

Except Michael didn't come after her again. He leaned into the passenger side of the van and came back out with a gun.

"See, if you didn't fight me, Felicity, you would have avoided this. I didn't want to kill you. Well, not with a gun. It's hard enough getting away with one murder—two would be pushing it." He laughed a little. "But now you're hurt. And you've got my DNA on you, so no wandering in the Badlands till you die for you."

She was woozy and out of it, but she knew one thing for sure. "I'd never have died in the Badlands."

"I'd have made sure of it," he replied, turning the gun on her.

He'd shoot her. No matter what. She could run, but there was nowhere to go that a bullet wouldn't find her. So she wouldn't run. At least not away.

Instead, she ran toward him. If he killed her, at least she'd gone down fighting for her life. At least she'd tried.

She rammed into him just as the shot went off. She

didn't feel the piercing pain of a bullet, but the blast of sound next to her ear made it feel as though her head had exploded. She pressed her hands to her ears, trying to somehow ease the horrible sound and pressure.

It was a heck of a lot better than being shot, but the pain was still a shock to her system. Such a shock she couldn't think past the fact she couldn't seem to hear. Everything was a buzz. She looked around, trying to understand...

Fear gripped her, and in that fear, he won.

He wrenched her arms behind her back. She could feel him tying something around her wrists. The blow must have knocked out more than just her hearing, because it didn't occur to her to fight him off.

She knelt there in the gravel, rocks digging into her knees, hands being tied behind her back and just... prayed.

GAGE TAMPED DOWN the panic. He'd had a lifetime of doing that. Danger had been the story of his first eleven years, and if he was able to survive that, to survive that cave with Ace, he could do it.

His profession had given him the skills to disassociate. To focus on one step at a time to get someone to safety.

He could find Felicity. He would.

He had to.

There had been different sightings of the van, giving different possible directions. Tuck had asked a few deputies to go check Michael's last known place of residence, though no one expected him to be there.

And he wasn't.

Gage had wanted to go, but he knew himself well enough to know his temper wasn't suited for searching.

Not for clues. He wanted to be searching for *her*. But he needed a lead, a damn plan.

"We could head back to the Badlands, where she left him," Gage offered to Brady as they drove down a highway someone had claimed to have seen the van driving on. "It's what Ace would do."

"He isn't Ace," Brady replied. "Did you look at his record?"

Gage shook his head. He hadn't given a thought to Michael Harrison other than finding his body so Felicity could rest easily. Quite frankly, when he hadn't been searching for Michael, he'd been headfirst lost in Felicity and what having a normal life with a woman he loved felt like.

"Threats. Assault. Battery. Over and over again. Dude can't control his temper, and thanks to lawyers and judges, never stays behind bars for very long. Which I know isn't exactly a comfort, but I don't think he's enacting the kind of poetic justice Ace is always after. This is just vengeance."

"Why? Felicity didn't do anything to him," Gage returned resolutely. Because if it was just vengeance, she might already be gone. At least with Ace you always knew you had a chance to save someone while he showboated his anointed routine.

"Felicity left him to die and, from what Cecilia said, confronted Ace about his role in that woman's murder." Brady's calm faltered. "He did it. I think Michael killed that poor girl. Not Ace."

"And Ace is innocent?" Gage asked incredulously.

"No. But I think Ace got involved for different reasons, and I think once we've got Felicity back, you'll be able to think the same thing."

"Getting Felicity back is all I care about." Who cared

about the reasons. Who cared about anything except her safety.

He looked out at the highway, analyzing every rare vehicle that passed him by. This was going to drive him slowly insane. Not that he could stand anything that wasn't finding her. If this was all he could do... Well, maybe it'd help him come up with something else.

"You sure you want me to ride shotgun on this?" Brady asked, squinting out the passenger seat window.

Gage blinked at his brother—his twin. "Why wouldn't it be you?"

Brady shrugged. "Because you're mad at me for being calm."

"Any of you would be calm," Gage returned, and though disgust laced his tone, he was glad someone could be. Without Brady and Tucker's calm, he would have already done a hundred stupid things.

"Dev wouldn't be calm," Brady offered.

"I don't need Dev making my worst impulses even worse," Gage muttered, frustrated with the conversation. "I need you, Brady. Ticked off at your calm or not, I need it."

"You got it."

Gage blew out a breath. It didn't ease his fear, but it calmed some of the ragged edges. They were the Wyatt twins. They had a whole army of Wyatts looking for her.

They'd find her. Who knew. Maybe she'd already saved herself. She could face down Ace, surely she could take down Michael.

Gage's phone rang and he answered it tersely.

"Don't get too excited just yet," Cody's voice said without preamble. "But I think I've got a track on her." Gage hadn't heard from Cody this whole time. Gage had figured it was because he was all the way in Bonesteel and not law enforcement in any licensed capacity.

But Cody knew tech and computers.

"Explain," Gage snapped.

"I didn't want to say anything until I was sure it would work. But the button I gave her… Even though she didn't hit it, I'm tracking her. At least the button. If it's on her, I can tell you where she is."

"Then do it." He tossed the phone at Brady, then followed Brady's instructions as to where to drive.

It was a good twenty miles from the jail. Gage didn't let his stomach curdle at the thought of how long she'd been gone, and how little of it would have been in transport.

He focused on action, on reining in his temper. Felicity was in danger. True, mortal danger. He couldn't let his temper be the thing that killed her. "We can't go in guns blazing."

He felt Brady's surprise more than saw it.

"He has her," Gage said, keeping that tight control on his rage, because fear and rage were too dangerous a combination. "We can't risk her. We'll stop here. Go the rest of the way on foot."

Brady nodded. "Stick together until we have our target, then split up if she's not immediately visible."

Since that was exactly what Gage had been thinking, he slowed the truck to a stop. "Ideally, backup is here before we have to engage, but I can't make promises on stopping if she's hurt. I need you not to get in my way. She's too important to me. I need you to understand that."

Brady didn't nod at that. He didn't even agree. But he didn't argue. "Be smart. For both of you—not just her."

Gage flashed a smile he didn't feel. He couldn't promise his brother he wouldn't lay down his life for Felicity. He wouldn't be able to live with himself if he didn't. "We'll see."

Wordlessly they silenced their phones, unholstered their weapons and slid out of the truck. The location of the button was one mile due north. Gage had parked the truck outside a cluster of trees. He and Brady moved forward—two men, one unit, one purpose.

The trailer came into view slowly. It was settled in among thick trees, a rock wall at its back.

Hell of a spot to hide out—but also a hell of a spot to get trapped. Not many ways to escape. The van was parked on a patch of gravel and the back doors were wide open, as was the passenger side door.

It was eerily quiet.

Brady nodded to the right, and Gage gave assent, peeling away to head to the left. If Michael and Felicity were still here, they were in the trailer.

He didn't let himself consider what might have happened if they weren't here.

The windows were covered on the inside with thick curtains, on the outside with dust and grime and a collection of dead bugs.

There was no way to see inside. No way to tell if they were in there. Gage moved slowly, quietly, gun trained on the trailer. He skirted the side of the trailer, looking and listening for any sign of people.

As he came to the back, Brady appeared from the other side. There was a narrow yard, if one could call it that, between the trailer and the steep rock face. If he and Brady could block both sides, there'd be no way for Michael to escape.

If he was in there. If they could get him out here instead of him running out the front and to the van.

Gage studied the back of the trailer. It was the same

situation. The few windows there were covered. The door didn't have any kind of window in it. And everything was quiet.

If they weren't in there, they were somewhere on foot. Unless Michael had another vehicle at his disposal.

Based on this setup, Gage doubted it. They had to be in there. The quiet threatened his ability to stay calm. There was nothing good about quiet—too many awful possibilities.

He wouldn't let himself think about any of them. He crept forward, Brady moving to flank him. Both had their guns drawn and ready for anything.

When shouting from the inside started, Gage gave Brady a look. Brady nodded. Gage eased the storm door open, wincing at the squeak and hoping the shouts covered the sound.

He had one chance. One chance to get in there quick and clean and without putting Felicity at more risk.

He counted to three in his head, then kicked as hard as he could, the door splintering open.

Inside things were dim and dingy, and a metallic smell clung to the air. Felicity was on her knees in the corner. Clearly, her hands were tied behind her. She looked up at him like he was a ghost, but Gage had his eyes on the gun in Michael's hand.

"What is it with you Wyatts?" Michael gave a bit of a shrug, and Gage had been in enough situations to know what that shrug meant. He wasn't going to fight his way out. He was giving up.

But not before he killed everyone he could.

So, Gage pulled the trigger. It was the only thing to do—the only way to save Felicity—he had no doubt about that. Blood bloomed on Michael's dirty T-shirt and he jerked back, crashing into the wall. But his face went hard and he got off his own shot before falling to the ground, the gun clattering out of his grip.

The shot didn't hit Gage, but he heard a crash behind him. "Brady." He whirled.

Brady had fallen, but he was struggling back to his feet, swearing a blue streak as he held his shoulder.

He glared up at Gage. "Get her out of here, damn it."

Brady had been shot. Fresh rage swept through Gage, but if Brady was on his feet it couldn't be all that bad, and they had to get Felicity out. Get all of them out. He rushed forward, putting his arms around Felicity.

"Come on, sweetheart. Can you stand up?"

She struggled to get to her feet, even with his help. Gage had to work hard to tamp down the impotent fury raging through him.

"I'll untie you when we're outside. Come on, sweetheart. Red, let's move outside."

She didn't move except to shake her head. "I can't hear," she shouted, making him wince as her mouth was close to his ear.

Michael's gunshot must have gone off close to her ears. He bit back a curse and nodded. "Okay. Okay. That's okay. It'll wear off." He tugged her toward the door, giving one look at Michael, who'd gone still.

Good riddance.

Chapter Twenty

By the time the doctors were done with her, she could hear a little bit. If the room was quiet and someone was close enough, speaking slowly. Her ears still rang, and the ibuprofen they'd given her helped her headache but didn't eradicate it completely.

She much preferred thinking about all that than the fact her father was dead, and worse—she'd be dead if it wasn't for Gage.

And Brady, who was currently in the ER having his gunshot patched up.

All because she'd been stupid. She sighed. She kept trying to work up enough blame and guilt to think this was all her fault, but she couldn't muster it. If she went back, she'd do the same. Maybe put up a bit more of a fight in the jail parking lot, but she still would have gone to see Ace, without telling any of the Wyatts.

Would that have changed anything?

It might have changed everything.

But she'd done what she'd done, and she couldn't really hate the result. Except Brady being shot.

She wanted to go home. She wanted Gage. Most of her life when tragedy had struck, she'd wanted to be alone, to deal in peace and without having to worry if she looked weak or stupid or whatever.

But Gage had showed her that it didn't really matter how you looked, especially when the other person understood. He'd understand the complicated feelings at her father being dead.

She wasn't so sure he'd understand her decision not to tell him she was visiting Ace, but she didn't know how to deal with that, so she just kept pressing forward.

She walked through the hospital, the buzz still in her ears, but she could hear some things. She could understand people if they were close enough and talked directly to her.

The doctors had said the hearing loss would likely wear off, but she had to come back in a week to be checked out again. It had been a relief to know her hearing wasn't irreversibly damaged, but she would have accepted that. Accepted anything over being dead.

She found Gage exactly where she knew he would be, in the waiting room of the ER. She wasn't sure she could accept it if he was angry enough at her to want to end things.

She swallowed. He looked desolate. Pale and lost. But when his gaze moved to her entering the waiting room, he tried to hide that away.

"How's Brady?" she asked.

He spoke in low tones, looking down at his hands.

When he was done, she tapped his arm and then her ear. "Sorry, I didn't catch all that." She slid into the seat next to him.

He shook his head and forced a pathetic smile. "That's okay. He's okay. You're okay." He touched her cheek and slid his palm over her hair. "It's all okay."

She put an arm around his shoulders. "Then why do you look so miserable?"

He shook his head and looked down at his hands for

a while, until she tipped his chin toward her so he had to look at her.

"It should have been me," he said simply.

"Why?"

"He wouldn't have been there if it wasn't for me."

"And you wouldn't have been there if it wasn't for me." He gave her a look and opened his mouth to argue, but she shook her head. "You can't play it only the way you like. Either we blame the people who are actually responsible, or you have to blame me."

"Why didn't you tell me?"

It was hurt that chased across his face before he shook his head again and tried to turn away, but she kept a firm grip on his chin. "I should have," she said, hoping her voice sounded as strong as she wanted it to. "I knew you wouldn't like it, so I didn't tell you. I wanted to handle it on my own, thought I hàd to. Thought you wouldn't let me. But I should have told you. I shouldn't have been... If I was determined to do it, I shouldn't be afraid to tell people. I can't be afraid to disappoint people. If you had been mad at me, I would have dealt with it. I should have told you. Things would be different if I had."

"Well, hell, Felicity, you make it real hard to hold on to a mad."

"You weren't mad. You were hurt." He tried to turn away again, but she wasn't done. "You saved my life. You really did. He was going to kill me. The only reason it took so long was he was trying to find a way to make sure it couldn't be connected back to him. It wouldn't have lasted much longer. He was losing his patience."

He blew out a breath like she'd physically hurt him. "Well, guess we're even, Red."

She swallowed at the lump in her throat. "I'm sorry Ace isn't dead."

"I'm not." He brushed a hand over her hair. "I wouldn't want that on your conscience." He pulled her in, so she leaned on his shoulder.

She wasn't sure it would have weighed all that heavy, certainly not any heavier than him being alive to wreak havoc.

"So, you're not…" Felicity didn't know how to put it. They hadn't been dating in any traditional sense. It had been a relationship, of course, but the words of how to describe anything failed her. Still, she had to be sure. "We're okay?"

It was his turn to take her chin, tip her face up and make her look him in the eye. He brushed his mouth against hers. "You and me, Red? We'll always be okay. One way or another."

She wouldn't cry at that, though she wanted to. So, she looked away. "Where is everyone?"

"Brady told me not to call anyone. Said he was fine and—"

Felicity made a noise of outrage. "What! They're going to hear it through your cop grapevines? I don't think so. If you don't call them, I will."

"You can't hear well enough to make a phone call."

"We'll see about that." She made a move to grab her phone, then realized her purse was still somewhere in her father's van. Dead father. She shuddered. It was necessary, but that didn't mean she'd have the images from today out of her head anytime soon.

Gage handed her his. "Here you go, tough girl."

She took it primly, then wrote a text because Gage was right—trying to talk to anyone on the phone would be difficult.

When she handed it back to him, he was just staring at her. So serious. Everything inside of her jittered with nerves.

"I love you. It would have killed me, just killed me, if he'd hurt you. And I can't promise you that Ace will never come after you again. Worse, I think if we're together, that'll make it more... He'll take it as a challenge to hurt us. All the ways he can. I don't know how to live with that."

She reached out and pressed her palm to his cheek. She'd known he was a good man, but she thought he didn't have that core of nobleness that Jamison and Brady had, which was often more annoying than impressive. Like this was. "You'll have to find a way, because I love you, too, and I'm not going to be shaken off that easy. Ace can try to hurt us."

"Feli—"

"No. You don't have a choice. Quite literally. I won't live my life afraid of Ace. Neither will you. If he tries to hurt us again, we'll fight again. Together. So, just shut up."

He managed a chuckle. "All right. Sounds good."

"Good." She let out a breath and leaned against him. "You're probably going to have to marry me, too, but we can talk about that later."

She felt him stiffen underneath her, but it made her smile. It'd give him something to be anxious about besides his brother and trying to protect her, so that was good.

A nurse came in and smiled kindly. "Gage. You can go back and see your brother now." Felicity stood, too. "I'm afraid you'll have to stay out here, ma'am."

Gage gave her arm a squeeze. "By the way I'm telling him it's your fault when everyone shows up."

"That's just fine."

Since he still looked haunted, she reached up on her toes and brushed her mouth against his. "It's over, and it's okay." She was ready to believe it.

BRADY WAS LAID out in a bed. He was pale, but at least he looked pissed. It took energy to be pissed.

"Hey. How's it going?" Gage asked lamely, hanging by the door rather than stepping farther inside.

"You know, I'm a trained paramedic. I know a thing or two about medicine. You think any of these doctors or nurses will listen to me?" Brady grumbled.

"So, it's true. Medical professionals really are the worst patients."

Brady grunted as he eyed Gage. "I'm not going to shout all the way over there to have a conversation with you, and you can leave the guilt right there. I'm fine."

"You won't be able to work for weeks."

Brady pulled a face, but then he lifted his uninjured arm. "It happens. It's what we risk every day we work, isn't it?"

"It wasn't work. You didn't have to be there."

"Where else would I be?" Brady shook his head. "Reverse it, Gage. Where would you have been?"

Much as he didn't want to admit it, he would have been right behind Brady. Always.

"I don't think you realize what you did," Brady said, once Gage got closer to the hospital bed.

"Let you get shot?"

"Gage. You stepped in front of me. We both saw what Michael was going to do. We've both been there before. The only reason I couldn't get off a shot, too, was because you'd stepped in front of me, blocked me. Damn stupid. But that's what you did. The only reason I got shot was because…well, bad luck really. Your shot got off first and his aim was off."

"I don't—"

"Maybe it's not how you remember it, because you were focused on Felicity, but that's what you did. I'm not going to argue about it. I'm tired and my shoulder hurts and they keep wanting to pump me full of medicine I don't want. So, if you can't get over it, get out."

Get over it, maybe not. But he could set it aside.

"It isn't like you to play martyr," Brady said with no small amount of disgust.

"I'm not—"

"And since it's me, why don't you just say what you're really all wound up about."

Because it was Brady, it was hard to pretend he wasn't right on the money. "I guess I know what she felt like after she left Michael to die. I thought I did. I did, in a way, but not like this. I know I did the right thing."

"There's not a doubt in my mind he would have killed her."

"Mine, either. Or hers. But, Brady, if this was all Michael, those charges don't get used against Ace."

"Ace tried to kill you. Himself, not through some two-bit lackey. You can testify to that. Even if we can't get him on murder, he'll go to a higher security prison for attempted murder."

"If he doesn't, Felicity is in even more danger."

"Then I guess you're pretty lucky to have each other's backs, huh?"

Gage didn't know if he'd go so far as *lucky,* but it was certainly a blessing to have…this. His brothers, his family. Everyone would rally around and protect. It was what they did.

"We know how this goes, I think. He took a swing at

Jamison, then Cody. It doesn't work, then he moves to the next. If he finds a way to go after one of us again, it's probably not going to be Felicity."

Gage looked at the bandage on Brady's shoulder. They left it unsaid, but it was pretty clear that if Ace found a way to manipulate the system again, Brady would be the next target. He was weakened.

"He said he had a list. A list and I'd messed it up. I wasn't supposed to be next. Which means, we could—"

Brady shook his head. "I'm not here to out-manipulate Ace. If we ever beat him, really beat him, it won't be using his own tactics."

Gage looked down at his hands. "Growing up, Ace told me I was smart, and could take his place, so I did a lot to prove I wasn't and couldn't. He told you you were stupid and weak, so you did a lot to prove you weren't." Gage had never believed he was his father, though sometimes he'd been afraid he could have inherited his impulses. But he fought them and that was all that mattered. He'd never considered that his father might have stamped him in different ways. "Did he shape us?"

"Are we running the Sons? Come on, Gage. If he shaped us, if he left a mark on us, it only got us here. We help people. You saved Felicity. Whatever he did, didn't work. We're the good guys."

Gage looked up at his brother, pale but alive and irritable. He smiled a little. "Felicity saved me first."

Brady chuckled, then winced. "Your ego can take the hit."

Gage studied his twin. "Thank you," he said, letting the words have the weight they deserved. Brady opened his mouth, and Gage had no doubt it was to argue. He shook his head. "You were there. It means something. Thank you."

"Fine. You're welcome. Now leave me alone."

Gage nodded, headed back to the door. He stopped there, knowing exactly what Brady needed. "Oh, by the way, Felicity notified the cavalry, so expect some visitors."

Brady swore and Gage laughed. It felt good to laugh, though it died when he reached the waiting room and Cecilia was standing there with Felicity.

She was still wearing her tribal police uniform. When she saw him, she squared her shoulders and lifted her chin, like she was ready for a fight.

"I came to—" she made a face like she was forced to swallow something bitter "—apologize."

"Don't."

Cecilia frowned, looking at Felicity. "That's what she said, too."

Gage smiled at Felicity. It was good to be on the same page, to understand without discussing. He turned back to Cecilia. "If you thought she'd be in danger, if either of you thought that, I know it would have been different. We all know if she *hadn't* told you, and you hadn't told us right away things weren't right, everything would be different." He swallowed at the horror that tried to get through, but it hadn't happened. "We can't change anything. We just have to… Look, this takes away the charges against Ace. And…"

Felicity slipped her hand into his. "It just means we have to look out for each other. Together. And we agree no more trying to do things on our own. Not when it comes to Ace."

Cecilia didn't say anything to that.

"You want to go in and see him?" Gage asked, nodding back toward the door he'd just come out of.

"Uh. Well. I mean, I guess," Cecilia replied, looking uncharacteristically unsure.

"I'm going to take this one home. She needs some rest."

Cecilia nodded. "You both do."

Gage gave Felicity's hand a squeeze and they headed for the exit. Felicity looked back at Cecilia, who was straightening her shoulders again, all soldier ready to go into battle.

"What?" Gage asked.

"I don't know." She tilted her face toward him and smiled. "Just...should be interesting."

"What should be interesting?"

She laughed as they walked out of the hospital, into daylight and freedom and hope. "You'll see."

Epilogue

Trials weren't fun, even when you won. It had been grueling days of testimony—including Felicity's own and Gage's. On the stand she'd had to relive shooting Ace, and she wasn't particularly thrilled about it.

Especially with what else was twisting inside of her, uncertain and scary and huge.

But it was over now, Ace guilty of too many charges to count and being moved to a higher security prison much farther away.

It was relief, even if it wasn't full closure. They walked out of the courthouse, a group of four Wyatt boys and three Knight foster girls who'd survived Ace's influence. Out into a sunny day that felt completely right.

Gage's hand slid over hers. Her stomach jittered with new nerves, because now that the trial was over she couldn't ignore her suspicions. And she could hardly not tell him.

Still, she smiled easily and exchanged hugs and goodbyes with her sisters. They shared something now, and even without that, Felicity had come to understand some things about growing up the way they had that made it easy to forgive Liza and Nina their choices to leave. And embrace their decisions to come back.

Gage said his goodbyes and gave Brady a gentle hug.

He'd had a setback with his gunshot wound, an infection, that had left him on desk duty for way longer than any Wyatt should have to endure.

Still, she liked to think the trial's outcome had taken a bit of a weight off his irritation.

She and Gage went to Gage's truck and slid in. He would drive her home, and spend the night in her cabin, but he'd be gone before she woke up—to get back to Valiant County and his job.

Her stomach jittered more. Things would have to be different. She hadn't figured out a way that would make them both happy.

"Nothing quite like testifying together, right?"

She forced a smile. "Better than doing it alone, I think."

"You think right," Gage said, patting her knee as he pulled out onto the highway.

Gage chattered the whole way home, and though Felicity tried to keep up, she was caught in her own loop of thoughts and worries and what she had to do.

Gage pulled to a stop in front of her cabin and she quickly slid out, afraid if they dawdled she'd blurt it out.

It needed more finesse, and she should be sure.

But Gage was right behind her, his arm around her waist as she walked up to the door. "All right. What's up, Red? Something's freaking you out, and it's not the trial. Tucker himself is going to oversee the jail transport. Ace won't—"

"I think I'm pregnant." She closed her eyes as the words fell out. Flopped there in between them as they stood awkwardly on her front stoop.

He didn't say anything. Didn't move. And she just stood there with her eyes squeezed shut, not having a clue what to do.

She'd tried to plan it out, tried to know what else to say and how to handle his reaction, but she always reached this point and then shut down. She could only wait, eyes closed and panic keeping her frozen.

"I guess it's a good thing I applied for the opening at Rapid City."

Her eyes flew open. "What?"

"Rapid City is hiring. I was tired of being that far, and you could hardly leave your dream job."

"But you work with your brothers, and now..."

"And now, God willing, I'll get the position, and we'll be in the same county and...and..." He inhaled sharply. "You sure?"

"No." She shook her head a little too emphatically. "I bought a test, but I didn't want to take it until the trial was over. I should have taken it first. I just had to tell you."

"Well, hell, go take it," he said, all but pushing her toward the door.

She nodded. Her keys shook in her hands, but she finally opened door and went into the bathroom to take the test. She went through the motions, set the timer on her phone and then let Gage into the bathroom.

"We have to wait three minutes."

"Okay." He swallowed, looking down at her, but the concern and worry in his expression slowly changed into something else. Then he pressed his mouth to hers in a gentle, calming kiss. "I love you, Felicity."

"I know, but before we know for sure, I don't want you to feel like... Duke isn't going to hold a shotgun on you. I mean, he might, but you don't have to marry—"

"I applied for that job for a reason, Felicity. Yeah, to be closer, but because I wanted to start getting things situated for the future. And maybe I was waiting for a little kick in the butt—but here it is. I was getting there before this."

"This is faster."

"Yeah. But I think we can do it." He lifted her hand and pressed a kiss to it. "I *know* we can do it. And so do you."

The timer on her phone went off and they both jumped.

"Okay." She *did* know they could do it, but it helped to hear. Helped to be steadied by someone else. She took a deep breath and looked at the test sitting there.

"Translate for me," Gage said, his voice a bit strangled. "What does two lines mean?"

"Pregnant," Felicity said, staring at the results window, where there were two lines clear as day.

"Pregnant," he repeated. Then he laughed and lifted her clear up off the floor, still laughing. Happy.

"You're happy," she murmured, because he was a constant marvel. She knew they were good together, knew he'd want to do the right thing, but she wasn't sure he'd jump right to happy.

"Yeah, hell of a thing, but yeah." He put her back down on her own feet. "Are you happy?"

Since her throat was clogged with tears, she could only nod and rest her forehead on his chest. *Happy* didn't seem a big enough word. But there was reality, too.

"He might get out some day. That trial wasn't the end. God knows he'll appeal. Ace touching our lives isn't over."

"Maybe not," Gage agreed.

It was scary, especially with this new life growing inside of her, but he was holding her. They were in this together. She lifted her head and looked up at him. "But we'll have even more to fight for, right?" She put her hand over her stomach. It was impossible to believe something was there—a life. Impossible to fully grasp, and yet true.

And right. So right.

"We have everything to fight for," Gage agreed, sliding his own hand over hers. "And we already have, so we know we can again." He pulled her close, tucked her hair behind her ears. "So, you going to marry me? Before the baby, just in case Duke gets any ideas about making me disappear."

She tried to say yes, but her throat was too tight with tears. And hope. And joy. So, she nodded, and he kissed her until she thought her knees might dissolve.

"It's going to be a good life," he said, a promise and a vow.

"Yeah, yeah, it is."

* * * * *

COMING SOON!

We really hope you enjoyed reading this book.
If you're looking for more romance, be sure to
head to the shops when new books are
available on

Thursday 14th May

To see which titles are coming soon, please visit

millsandboon.co.uk/nextmonth

LET'S TALK

Romance

For exclusive extracts, competitions
and special offers, find us online:

MILLS & BOON

THE HEART OF ROMANCE

A ROMANCE FOR EVERY KIND OF READER

MODERN

Prepare to be swept off your feet by sophisticated, sexy and seductive heroes, in some of the world's most glamourous and romantic locations, where power and passion collide.
8 stories per month.

HISTORICAL

Escape with historical heroes from time gone by. Whether your passion is for wicked Regency Rakes, muscled Vikings or rugged Highlanders, awaken the romance of the past.
6 stories per month.

MEDICAL

Set your pulse racing with dedicated, delectable doctors in the high-pressure world of medicine, where emotions run high and passion, comfort and love are the best medicine.
6 stories per month.

True Love

Celebrate true love with tender stories of heartfelt romance, from the rush of falling in love to the joy a new baby can bring, and a focus on the emotional heart of a relationship.
8 stories per month.

Desire

Indulge in secrets and scandal, intense drama and plenty of sizzling hot action with powerful and passionate heroes who have it all: wealth, status, good looks…everything but the right woman.
6 stories per month.

HEROES

Experience all the excitement of a gripping thriller, with an intense romance at its heart. Resourceful, true-to-life women and strong, fearless men face danger and desire - a killer combination!
8 stories per month.

DARE

Sensual love stories featuring smart, sassy heroines you'd want as a best friend, and compelling intense heroes who are worthy of them.
4 stories per month.

To see which titles are coming soon, please visit

millsandboon.co.uk/nextmonth

t might just be true love...

MILLS & BOON

HISTORICAL

Awaken the romance of the past

Escape with historical heroes from time gone by. Whether your passion is for wicked Regency Rakes, muscled Viking warriors or rugged Highlanders, indulge your fantasies and awaken the romance of the past.

MILLS & BOON
MEDICAL
Pulse-Racing Passion

Set your pulse racing with dedicated, delectable doctors in the high-pressure world of medicine, where emotions run high and passion, comfort and love are the best medicine.

JOIN THE
MILLS & BOON
BOOKCLUB

* **FREE** delivery direct to your door

* **EXCLUSIVE** offers every month

* **EXCITING** rewards programme

50% OFF
YOUR FIRST
PARCEL

Join today at
Millsandboon.co.uk/Bookclub